Du Rose Sons

The Hana Du Rose Mysteries

K T BOWES

Would you like to be part of it?

I'm a believer in 'try before you buy.'
There's nothing worse than forking out your hard earned cash
on a doozy and regretting it.
I don't want stinky reviews. I want you to love my work and feel
like you got value for money.
If you'd like 4 free eBooks. you can get them by joining my
mailing list at ktbowes.com
They'll arrive in your inbox.
I will take care of your email address and won't be sharing it or
spamming you.
You can unsubscribe at any time. I promise not to send Rohan
Andreyev after you...maybe.

Acknowledgement

I dedicate this novel to all the women out there with sons they
will never understand.
May the sorority of mothers guard and sustain us all.

Chapter 1

Nothing rivalled the sight of breaking glass; a crashing, glittering parade of beautiful prisms; each one lethally charged with death. The transparent panes of the French doors were aged, placed into the wooden frames by hands long since dead by the time the rugged, red brick passed through their mottled surface. The clay missile fractured the wooden struts and caused two of the panes to hang like a torn curtain. The third shattered spectacularly, showering the room's single occupant with spiteful shards of glass.

"What was that?" The first ear-splitting sound was followed by a deafening second as the hotel's elderly housekeeper burst into the family room, her eyes wide and frightened and her ample breasts wobbling under her work shirt. "I was next door. What was that crash?"

The dark skinned *Māori* approached the woman on the sofa, who sat with her hands over her head as though pinned to the cushions. The housekeeper halted at the sight of the speckling of glass littered in the curly auburn hair and blood on the shaking hands. "Oh my goodness, oh no! Get Mr Logan," she cried to a waitress who appeared at the heavy door and propped it open with her foot. "Tell him the missus is hurt!"

The face and the foot disappeared. "Hana?" The housekeeper, *ngā hāwini,* touched the redhead, disturbing the glass which tinkled down onto the sofa cushions and pinged off the wooden rimu floor. "Did you see who did it?"

Auburn hair bounced and the glittering glass shone like diamond dust, beautiful and deadly. "No, it happened too fast."

The redhead put her right hand up to her face and winced as she contacted a series of tiny open wounds, bleeding steadily and dripping stains onto her white blouse. The elderly book on her knee fell to the floor with a clunk - yet another damaging moment in its long suffering existence. The cover fell over the pages of guilty secrets, hiding them from view.

Another face appeared at the door. "Sal says she's radioed Mr Logan. He's on his way. Shall we bring the vacuum cleaner to get up the small bits of glass? Or do you want us to call the cops again?"

The housekeeper pursed her brown lips and gave the matter much thought. "Wait for the boss to get here. He'll decide. Find me a comb. There's glass in the missus' hair. You should bring me the first aid kit from the kitchen too; she's bleeding."

"Look, Leslie, I'm fine really. Let's just clear it all up. There's no need to bother Logan." Hana attempted to stand and glass cascaded down like a snow storm. Some of the substantial pieces hit the floor with a tinkle.

The waitress arrived in the doorway with a comb and handed it over to her superior, who took it without thanks. Hana protested futilely as Leslie bustled around her, raking savagely through the coils and ringlets with a small black comb. "Whose comb is it?" Hana protested. "That's gross!"

"Stop your complaining," the old woman tutted as numerous tiny shards pierced her fingers in her efforts. Finally she stood back and admired her handiwork. "I think it's all out," she announced, her brow creased in concentration and annoyance. "But we'll need to get your clothes off. Best do it here and we'll clear up in one go, otherwise youse might track the glass all through the house and then my *moko* will cut her bare feet."

Hana sighed and bit her pretty lip as she considered her daughter. At barely eighteen months old, Phoenix Du Rose refused to wear shoes and toddled around the hotel corridors with barefoot enthusiasm. "Fine!" Hana groaned. "But I'm only doing this for Phoe!" Her cheeks pinked with embarrassment as she stripped down to her bra and knickers in the middle of the family room, aware of the hotel full of people nearby.

Leslie slapped Hana's bottom with a flat palm and chuckled. "Youse still a gorgeous girlie for your years. No wonder that boy can't keep his hands off you. My Alfie would love me to look like that."

Hana turned and screwed up her face. "That's just weird," she said. "You can't say things like that about my father-in-law." Knitted brows communicated Hana's distaste and Leslie gave a belly laugh, her ample bosom wobbling with glee.

"Youse way too serious, girlie. Now, stop shifting yer feet or there'll be more cuts to mop up."

By the time her husband arrived, the slender redhead was wrapped in a large black tablecloth from the dining room, mopping at painful cuts on her cheek and hands with a scratchy corner of the starched fabric. "Geez, Hana!" Logan said in dismay.

"Don't come in!" Hana turned towards her husband, releasing one porcelain toned hand from the tablecloth to ward him off. "There's glass everywhere. You'll walk it out into the hall."

Logan Du Rose shifted awkwardly in the doorway, the heels of his cowboy boots grinding the glass shards which had spread that far. His olive skinned face betrayed agony at not being able to reach his wife and Hana sensed him reading the distress in her face. She was coping just fine until she saw him, but fought the urge to cry as relief flooded over her. Logan's six foot four inch frame tensed as he made his decision. "Sod it!" he exclaimed and strode over to his slender wife, bending at the knees as he scooped her up into his arms, tablecloth and all. "Take her socks off," he ordered the housekeeper, who gently peeled them off

Hana's delicate toes. Glass tinkled everywhere and Hana giggled as Leslie patted gently at her bare feet.

"Where's Phoe?" Logan asked and the housekeeper replied in *Māori*. Hana caught the word *kai* and realised her child was eating without her.

"You should have told me. I didn't know she'd woken up."

Leslie smiled. "Little *moko* is fine. Thank the good Lord you didn't push her pram down here to choose your book. She would have been hurt." Leslie formed the sign of the cross on her breast with great reverence.

"I was only going to be a minute." Guilt flooded through Hana, compounded by maternalism. She left the baby with Leslie in the family dining room, next to the hotel's enormous industrial kitchen. The wall clock told her it was over half an hour ago. Hana bit her lip, tears prickling behind her eyes. She hadn't been choosing a book, but trying to find somewhere safe to read the old brown journal in peace. One minute she was engrossed in the crabbed handwriting and the next, woken by glass showering her face. Hana rubbed the back of her hand across her eye and felt the sting as small particles ground in the cuts. She hissed under her breath.

"Shower," Logan spun on his heels and crunched across the floor with determined steps. He shouldered the fire door open and turned back to Leslie. "Leave the glass and lock the door. Get the cops again. My daughter could have been in here too."

"My book!" Hana held her hand out, green eyes widening in her face. "I should probably read it after all this trouble."

Leslie placed the worn journal into her palm, eyeing the tattered fabric cover with fleeting curiosity.

The shower in Logan's childhood room took a while to warm up as the cold spring water surged through the pipes to the heating element. The hotel was full and the guests had used much of the copious supply earlier, not to mention the post-breakfast washing up in the kitchen. Logan balanced Hana one-armed on his hip in the ensuite, his biceps bulging through his shirt while he ran water over his hand and nodded once, satisfied. He flicked the handle and the water ceased so he could lower his wife and her shroud into the cubicle. Hana kept her arms wrapped tightly round his neck, resisting as Logan tried to release her onto her feet. She nuzzled at the skin under his jaw. "Mmnn, you smell of horse."

Logan laughed, a deep, gorgeous sound that reminded Hana of the mountains and she sighed, noticing the tiny fragments of glass on his shirt. "You're covered now!" She smiled with mischief in her eyes, putting her feet down and hauling her husband into the shower. "You have to get undressed in here too."

Logan narrowed his grey eyes and gave his wife a sultry look. "I was actually in the middle of something important."

"Drenching horses isn't as important as me." Hana bit her lip, tears of shock threatening again in her pretence at bravado. Logan saw and took his cowboy boots off in the wet shower tray, rubbing the soles on his jeans to release the clinging shards. Then he threw them out of the cubicle and closed the glass door, trapping his body close to Hana's.

"Drenching's important if you're the horse."

He peeled the tablecloth gently away from Hana's body and let it drop, running his fingers over her cold shoulders and up underneath the fiery coils of hair at the back of her neck. Hana shuddered with relief as he bent to kiss her, tasting the remnants of chewing gum on his lips and allowing herself to feel safe.

****

"You saw and heard nothing, Mrs Du Rose? You didn't hear anyone run up to the doors and throw the brick, or see movement through the corner of your eye? You were sitting side-on to the doors, you said, which is why the cuts are all on the right side of your body?"

Hana sighed audibly. She felt under interrogation. The South Auckland policemen were battle weary, suspicious of everyone and everything and she began to think they didn't believe her. "I sat down with the book and got distracted. I think I nodded off," she began, interrupted instantly by the jaded blond cop.

"You nodded off! But the call came at just after ten o'clock this morning."

Hana glanced fearfully across at Leslie, whom Logan drafted in to sit with his wife during her statement taking. His head stockman had called him with another problem and he left with an apology, nominating the housekeeper as his replacement. The wise old lady's eyes bore knowingly into Hana's and she quailed and heard herself gulp. "I didn't sleep too well last night," she ventured, watching Leslie out of the corner of her eye. "I think I'm probably still out of sync after our trip home from Europe. With all the worry about what's been happening around the property lately, it's affected my sleep patterns."

Hana picked at a knot on the massive wooden dining table, which generations of Du Roses had eaten over, argued over and smacked the snot out of each other over. It had probably seen its fair share of the other kind of passion too and Hana put her cut hands back underneath the table. She heard the clank of metal pans in the kitchen next door. Phoenix sat in her high chair, still eating and learning to make an art form out of it. Her father's grey eyes fixed on her mother's face and twinkled as she beamed, displaying her tiny, pearly teeth. The little girl waved her third piece of Marmite splattered toast at her mother and giggled. Hana focussed on the brown streaks on the child's lips and face and felt bile rising up into her gullet, accompanied by the familiar surge in her stomach. *Phoenix's teeth look like marbled stalagmites.* Hana kept her breathing shallow and smiled back at her daughter, whilst deliberately distracting herself with the sound of cars crunching in the gravel at the front of the hotel as guests came and went. The policeman's eyes were on her and she blanched. "Sorry, was there another question?"

Hana glanced across at Leslie, finding the older woman studying her, much as a butterfly collector inspects his pinned bugs. Leslie's once black hair was white at the front, receding into grey towards the tight bun which she restrained her long tresses in. Her olive skin had wrinkled over time and her body spread into an A-line shape like a Christmas tree. But her hazel eyes held all the sparkle of youth, revived through her recent marriage to Logan's elderly father, Alfred. Hana smirked at the memory of Logan's disgusted face when the old folk's coupling was mentioned. She wiped it quickly off when Leslie narrowed her eyes and jerked her head towards the policeman. "Sorry, what did you say?" Hana struggled to recover and turned her body towards the policeman's growing annoyance.

"I asked if you thought whoever threw the brick, knew you were in the room."

Marmite. Brown, streaky Marmite.

"I honestly don't know."

Bored with her late snack, Phoenix entertained herself making finger pictures on the surface of the high chair. Hana's senses went on red alert as the scent of the awful brown stuff invaded her nostrils and Leslie watched with curiosity, as Hana's face went from white to pink and back to white again.

Hana just made it to the dustbin in the corner, ripping the lid off and sticking her face into the massive black bin bag inside. The remnants of the stockmen's breakfast; bacon, eggs and fried bread, stared back at her and finished the last of her resolve. She threw up spectacularly - mimicked by her daughter who copied the noise - and watched by two policemen and her mother-in-law.

Chapter 2

"It's fine now, I often puke when I'm stressed." Hana continued to slot Phoenix into the car seat, ignoring the scent of Marmite still on her breath. It was surprisingly easier than pretending Leslie wasn't standing over her, watching her every move. "Does Logan know you're 'stressed' enough to vomit in front of two cops?"

"We're all *stressed*, Leslie. Someone's damaging our property and trying to cause us expense and misery and it's working!" Hana's patience diminished as another wave of nausea threatened. "I just need to go home and put Phoe to bed. I'll be ok."

"Stay here," Leslie urged. "Logan's room is always free and you've got clothes there. I've told the girls to put your other clothes in a bin bag and they've managed to get all the glass out of the shower. I'll look after my *mokopuna* and you can rest for a little while. Seeing as you're not sleeping so good..." The old lady narrowed her eyes at Hana, keen to play along with the charade for now.

Hana felt tears brimming again, joining with the sickness to make her utterly miserable. She raised her eyes up to the clear blue, winter sky to stop the leakage and found Leslie's strong brown arm around her shoulders. Sniffing, Hana placed the keys into Leslie's outstretched palm and went to the passenger side, climbing into the high utility vehicle and struggling to close the door. By the time Leslie had launched her elderly body into the driver's seat, Hana's cheeks were already wet.

"Mum, mum, mum," came Phoenix's tired voice as the engine started and her eyes closed as if by magic.

Leslie spun the big vehicle round with skill, pointing it towards the sweeping drive but hanging a precarious left onto a small road that wound up through the colourful New Zealand bush. Despite the winter, hues of natural green dominated the native growth which seemed unperturbed by the cold temperatures. The road was sound, tar covered and metalled with the familiar grey chips. Logan had made sure that access from the house deep in the bush would be easy.

"Christian conference." Leslie's gentle voice cut across Hana's rambling thoughts. Her hazel eyes locked onto Hana's deep green ones with a knowing look. "Last night's guests. They used the ball room for a Christian conference. They were nice people. None of them would have aimed a brick at a glass door with someone sat right behind it. Hell, they wouldn't have known where to find a brick!"

"We know it wasn't them." Hana's comment had an edge of exhaustion to it, causing Leslie to raise her eyebrows in concern.

"Promise me it's not your heart again?" the old lady begged, referring to the massive heart attack Hana had suffered almost a year ago. The vehicle swerved as Leslie looked pointedly at Hana and took her eyes off the road too long.

"Careful!" Hana grew annoyed. "It's not my heart, at least, *it wasn't!*" She bit her lip and looked out of the window at the passing bush, the weight of the world pressing down on her shoulders.

Leslie drove up the mountain road in silence and Hana used the welcome relief to try and process her own thoughts. But ten minutes was not long enough to even get beyond planning that night's dinner and they arrived at the metal farm gate far too quickly. Leslie hauled her body out of the ute to open the gate and then drove the vehicle through, leaving it open behind them.

Hana's home was new and stylishly constructed. Logan had designed it in his head throughout his childhood and commissioned the build after their wedding. It was completed whilst the couple travelled in Europe on a belated honeymoon and Hana returned to New Zealand and moved in, enjoying the newness of the house amidst its ancient surroundings. Leslie rolled the truck under the covered porch adjoining the hardwood front doors and Hana hopped out and walked back along the drive to close the gate. She lingered for a moment by the old kauri tree which stood guard over the land, studying the list of Du Rose names inscribed in its elderly bark.

From this angle the house looked stunning. Long and low, it occupied a third of a green paddock covered in lush, sweet grass. Logan intended to landscape it into gardens but since they had been home, work on the hotel and farm, in addition to the merging of their property with his half-brother's, had demanded all his time. Hana quite liked it as it was, natural and unspoiled by human hands. Behind the house, a railed metal fence prevented their baby daughter falling over the sheer cliff which faced west, the wide expanse of the Tasman Sea and Port Waikato below. Hana closed her eyes and remembered her first visit here. Logan had carried an entire picnic in his saddle blanket and shyly showed her this land, left to him by his paternal grandmother. In her will, she told him to 'build a house' and he had. But the physical structure was only a representation of the strong family and subsequent legacy that he struggled to birth, from the ruins of the Du Rose name.

The roof of the house was constructed from dark brown concrete tile which muffled the sound of the driving rain that often came at night. Dark brick and tinted windows protected the interior from the baking sun, although Hana had missed this year's New Zealand summer, swapping it for an English winter.

Inside, the house was full of wide open spaces and skylights which allowed plenty of light in. Hana loved it.

In the noisy bushland outside the gate, an old tui bird cackled and trilled high up in the branches of the kauri. Hana shielded her eyes with her hand and stared up through the canopy, blinded by sunlight as the winter clouds parted and dazzling rays peeked through. Hana's eyes watered and she stepped back involuntarily, staggering over a tree root. Strong hands gripped her upper arms and through her sun-induced-tears, Hana saw Leslie's hazy silhouette.

"Careful girl!" she exclaimed, supporting Hana's slight frame as the younger woman mopped at her eyes with the sleeve of her sweater. "Please tell me what's wrong?" The old lady's voice sounded agonised as she shook Hana slightly, her fingers digging into the delicate flesh and feeling bone.

Hana exhaled heavily. "I'm pregnant!"

Leslie's mouth dropped, giving her the appearance of a gaping trout and she let go of Hana abruptly. "Pregnant, again?"

Anger filled Hana's throat as her long-buried redheaded temper flared unexpectedly at her mother-in-law's reaction. "Yes, again! Pregnant at forty-seven. Don't you think I know how disgusting everyone will find it? I'm a grandmother and I'm expecting a baby. It's hideous, I'm *hideous!*"

Hana put both hands over her face and felt hot tears course down her cheeks. *How could I say that? Is that really what I think?* Guilt compounded her misery and she redirected her anger at herself. She had made it sound as though she didn't want her baby, when in reality it was fear that consumed her. Hana had known for weeks what was wrong. Visiting her grown up son in Hamilton on her return from overseas, she called in on her old doctor on the off chance, hoping to find medication for the niggling stomach upset that didn't seem to want to go away. "I think I caught something when we were in Paris," she said, blissfully ignorant.

"You certainly did!" he laughed, holding up the vibrant yellow urine sample and waving the tell-tale stick at her.

Leslie's arms were comfortingly strong as she wrapped them around Hana and the younger woman sighed and leaned into her. "Don't you ever say that about yourself!" Leslie chided. "You're beautiful and if I hear you call yourself hideous again, I will beat your ass all the way down that driveway to the bottom of the mountain and back up again!" The old lady sounded fierce and Hana didn't doubt she meant every word. "Logan must be thrilled!" she said, adding another hefty squeeze. "No wonder he was so tender with youse this morning, carrying you up the stairs and all..." Her voice tailed off at the look on Hana's face.

"Don't start! I keep meaning to tell him and then something else happens. Why do you think I came down to the hotel this morning? He left so early and I thought I might catch him at morning tea and then the window broke."

"He doesn't know?" Leslie looked and sounded appalled. "Well you better get a move on girlie. He ain't gonna be too happy when you've got a belly out here and..." Her jaw dropped again as she seized Hana's over large sweater hem in both hands and pulled upwards, ignoring the hands that tried to slap hers. "Oh good Lord! You do have a belly out here! How pregnant are you girl?"

"Mind your own business!" Hana's retort was sharp as she wrenched the material out of Leslie's hands and hauled it back over her protruding stomach. Her stretching skin felt taut and paper thin under her shaking fingers.

"How does your husband not notice a belly like that? Him what's all doey eyed over you."

"Well you didn't notice when I had to strip off to my underwear." Hana stuck her nose in the air triumphantly.

"I was more worried about all the glass over you, girlie. I weren't checking you out. But your husband can't keep his eyes off you. I dunno how he's missed that one right under his *kanekane*."

"I distract him," Hana admitted, the coyness of her face disappearing back under the mask of rage as Leslie chuckled wickedly.

"Obviously!"

Hana squared her shoulders and tried to regain her composure, strutting back up her driveway at speed. She could hear her mother-in-law wheezing as her blancmange body struggled to keep up. Back at the car, Hana rounded on her, "I'll put Phoe to bed and then you can take the truck back down to the hotel. I'll text Logan and ask him to bring it back up later on."

"You ain't getting rid of me that fast, young lady. Not unless you want me to get on the radio and send your husband straight up here. I'll put my *moko* to bed and you put the jug on. I'm gonna need a strong coffee in front of me for the details of this one!"

Phoenix's dark curls bobbed on her head as she lay sprawled over Leslie's shoulder. The septuagenarian's buttocks wobbled from side to side on her meaty legs as she negotiated the wide hallway down to the little girl's room. Hana stood in the kitchen on the other side of the house and watched the aqua water moving around in the distant seascape. There wasn't an ounce of blood between Leslie and Phoenix and yet the woman had adopted her as her own grandchild from the start, fiercely coveting time with the baby. Logan's own mother had died the night before Phoenix made her traumatic entrance into the world, birthed under the old kauri tree at the top of the drive, early but determined to thrive. Miriam Du Rose had walked into a house fire deliberately, intending to die with her lover, Reuben Du Rose, Logan's birth father. Her death was a terrible shock, not least to her husband of almost fifty years, Alfred, but also to Logan, who had no idea that his uncle was his father.

Leslie humphed as she came into the enormous room and bustled over to the kettle. "You didn't even fill it up," she chuntered at Hana but the other woman remained lost in her own thoughts.

"Sorry."

Leslie fiddled around with the kettle and found some mugs, preparing the drinks wordlessly, perhaps understanding that Hana was miles away with her problems. Plonking the steaming drinks down on the centre island, she seized Hana's arm and forced her to sit down on one of the fancy bar stools lined up underneath the counter. Hana sat obediently but pushed the coffee mug away from her, pulling a face. Leslie smirked. "So obviously, you must be just inside the first trimester, seeing as you threw up at the house and can't drink coffee," Leslie looked pleased with her deductions. "How come you're showing so big though?"

Hana pulled a face and ran her hand over her eyes. Leslie sipped her drink and Hana could almost hear her brain calculating. "So when did you fall pregnant then? When you got home?"

Hana shook her head. "No. It happened in Paris. I know when it was."

Leslie's aged face appeared even more wrinkled as she screwed it up to concentrate. "But you were in Paris in April and it's almost the end of July. That can't be right. You're not...three months gone, are you?"

"Worse," Hana let out a huge sigh. "I'm getting on for four and I still haven't told my husband."

Leslie's eyes bugged in her head and then she tried to disguise her misgivings, "Aw honey, what's the worst he can say?"

Chapter 3

Calving began early and Logan arrived home late, falling into bed after a shower. Hana traced a lazy finger down his damp skin and he enclosed her hand in his before his breathing deepened and he slid into an exhausted sleep. Unable to settle, Hana got up and went to the kitchen, making hot milk for herself and getting her treasured book out of the change bag housing Phoenix's things.

Its hard backed, fabric cover was brown and aged and the pages inside were yellowed and speckled with mildew. Hana stroked the diary, one of many, written by Logan's paternal grandmother - the original Phoenix Du Rose. A box of objects the previous summer had been dropped off by the *marae* elder, left with his family for safekeeping by the old lady, only months before her unexpected death. He had held onto them for more than forty years, waiting for the right moment. "*Keep them,*" she told the *kaumatua*, "*keep them until the mountain is joined and only then, pass them onto my mokopuna, Logan.*"

The later diaries made hard reading, detailing the argument between her two sons, Alfred and Reuben. The older brother stole Reuben's sweetheart after a spat between the soul-mates and Reuben had been devastated. Miriam had produced three children for Alfred, but her youngest belonged to Reuben. Phoenix had divided the mountain, giving a smaller share to the disgraced son who was widowed with young children of his own, condemning them to scratch a living away from the homestead. She bitterly regretted her actions, missing her favoured son dreadfully, but couldn't reverse her decision. So she put her energies into Logan, showering him with everything that Reuben should have had, instructing him in *Māori* lore, *tikanga and kawa* and instilling in him a bond with the land which would never be broken. And then she died, unexpectedly and much too early. Logan was there with her on the site of the house he now slept in, unable to prevent her death, sitting with her until it was past dark and knowing in his five year old head - she wouldn't wake up.

While Alfred's lack of business sense on one side of the mountain ruined a thriving family business, Reuben's keen mind and skilled accounting went to waste, decimating his land without the will to make it into anything special. After his death in the fire, accumulated debt made his sons unable to keep the property and when Nev, the oldest of Reuben's offspring offered it to Logan, he had taken it, keeping his half-brother on as manager. The land had joined and before the ink was even dry on the documents, the *kaumatua* had come and offloaded his burden in the shape of six extremely large and ratty cardboard boxes.

This diary was dated April 1968 and spoke of a time when Phoenix Du Rose was queen of all she surveyed. Despite the fabled *Du Rose curse* that had killed her husband, she built her farm into the biggest employer in the area. The locals bitched about the family in the township, but were happy to take her cash to pay their bills.

As the hot milk went to war with Hana's indigestion, she donned a pair of white cotton gloves and began to read. Will, the museum curator at the hotel would be cross with her if he had seen Hana in the family room, touching the elderly artifact without gloves. Hana cringed as she opened the diary and glass tinkled down onto the worktop. The spine made a horrid cracking sound as Hana tapped it lightly to make the rest fall out. "Sorry, Will," she whispered, leafing through to find her place and losing herself in Phoenix's memories.

The next page decried the behaviour of Reuben's late wife. Reuben and Alfred had married sisters from the wider *whānau*, continuing the mess of interbreeding and bad genetics.

'Antoinette is a ridiculous girl. Does she think we are all such fools that we don't know what she's been doing? Her father is perfectly well. I saw him in Ngaruawahia last week at the marae, yet Reuben tells me his wife is away taking care of her dying father. Miriam knows nothing of his 'illness' and yet, she would be the first to know. She went strangely quiet when I asked her about her sister's return.

The blond drover is gone, so at least their affair is at an end. Reuben hit him so hard, his head left a notch in the doorframe. It set the disease off in Reuben's fingers and will be a while before he is able to use his left hand. Foolish boy. It was lucky he didn't kill him but the man left soon after, JD said. It wouldn't surprise me if they had killed him and buried the body.'

Hana's jaw went slack and then she closed it again. Nothing about the Du Roses would surprise her. She smoothed her glove over the black ink. "Who's JD, Phoenix?" she asked the dead writer. *JD* had been mentioned numerous times before. "Who is your mysterious man?" It was clear from her writing that he was a trusted confidante of Phoenix Du Rose. The diary went on to detail herd and dairy prices and things that didn't interest Hana in the slightest. The family had introduced the Charolaise cattle and ventured into raising beef at the beginning of the 70's. The creamy white beasts roamed the mountainsides, prime purebred after forty years of careful breeding. They were shaggy coated and muscular, many of the females sold internationally as breeding dams.

What Hana really loved about reading the diaries, was the history of the family into which her daughter had been born, adding a context to the sprawling land and lives lived on it over almost two centuries. Phoenix Du Rose was a hard woman, mainly through necessity but also genetics. At her *rangatira* father's death, a brooch disappeared from his coffin, thought to have been stolen by her wayward, drunkard husband, Henri. When Henri died a few months later of his haemophilia, legends of the Du Rose Curse were born, involving tales of divine retribution for the theft of the *tapu* object. But Phoenix was the thief, keeping the brooch hidden from the questing hands of her sister. The diary had revealed her guilty sixty year secret - but sadly not the brooch.

Hana yawned and covered her mouth, her well-bred English manners winning through even though nobody else saw. The hair prickled at the back of her neck like a ghostly hand stroking her and Hana swung round on her stool, feeling as though she was being watched. The house was so far from the hotel and even further from the township, she and Logan never closed the curtains, not even in their bedroom. The prickling feeling persisted and she got off her stool and went to the window. Blackness stared back at her, but it unnerved Hana enough to drop the blinds over the sink and pull the drapes across the ranch slider. She shivered, wondering whether to wake Logan, but he was exhausted and would be up before light if calving had started already.

Turning back to the diary, Hana immersed herself in a tale which went back more than forty years. There were more herd prices, physical logs of profits as though Phoenix had used the diary as an account book and then came an interesting entry.

'Reuben won't talk to me about it. He has allowed his unfaithful wife to just come home as though nothing happened. Women from the Ngapuhi tribe at the sale yards yesterday told me where she's been; hiding up north until delivered of her pakeha spawn. It's not that she's borne a white-man's child that has made me angry, but she is married to my son! They say the child is so white haired she cannot possibly be Reuben's. He angers me with his indifference. I don't understand.'

"But you will." Hana stroked the pages sadly. Reuben's affair with Miriam had stretched decades. It was a wonder poor Alfred had managed to father any children at all with his own wife and a miracle that Logan was the only one belonging to his brother. Hana pondered the identity of the white haired child or where she was now. A dawning realisation began in her breast, curdling the milk in her stomach and reviving the mild morning sickness she had mistaken as a bug. Hana took the book over to the sink, knowing she was going to retch but not wanting to stop reading.

Nothing. The pages rambled on about local people, the staple gossip of the township documented by an intelligent and literate woman, whose skill with the pen had increased visibly over the years from illiterate to gifted. Jack, the deaf stable manager had taught Phoenix to read and write - or so the rumours said. The earliest writings had been almost unintelligible and fraught with error.

Hana turned the pages, doing her best not to damage them. The gloves frustrated her and she removed them, hoping Will wouldn't somehow know she had handled the artifact with her bare hands. Towards the end of the book and into 1970 came two revelations, bisected by more numbers and accounts. Hana had been dreading the first, but expected at some point to come across the second. It was about Logan. In historical time, Logan's conception had eclipsed the first disaster but for Hana, the first was far more damaging now, in real time.

'Antoinette's bastard has arrived. My father would be turning in the urupa. The northern tribe cannot control her. She is demon possessed. She has hair the colour of morning frost and Reuben has allowed her to stay! My son is a fool and I have told him so. I cannot look at the child. She vexes Reuben's boys to distraction and is artful and wicked, even though she is only five years old. She has ruin in her soul.'

Hana began to skim read, not finding what she wanted, frustration burning as her fingers turned the pages.

'I could kill him! I knew he was being untrue. Miriam has the makings of a pregnancy she has been at pains to hide and Alfred

has been gone for months. Reuben looked like a whipped dog since Antoinette's death and I had thought it was grief, in addition to being left to care for the demon child. It is guilt. My sons have outdone themselves this time. Why must they carry this tragedy forward? Miriam's child is Reuben's and I feel a fool. Only last month, I convinced Alfred to return home and save his marriage. He is due this week, once he has finished up working for my sister's family. This disaster will carry forward through the generations and we will be damned.'

Hana skimmed. This was old news and not what she was looking for. And then she found it.

'23rd March 1971

It is my own fault. I should have anticipated this with us all residing in one house. Miriam's boy child is the image of his father and to my shame, I favour him above the others. The woman has been low in spirits since the birth, which is little wonder with what is happening around her. She is tearful and I fear for her mind. There was a fight today when Alfred walked in and discovered his brother cradling the baby. He attacked him even though Reuben was holding the child. The mother was bereft. Reuben has agreed to leave the property and take his family with him. We have no choice and we rode up to the high point to work it out. I am devastated.'

Hana raised her eyebrows in interest. Legend told that Phoenix Du Rose threw her son off the property and divided the mountain - but it wasn't true. This was the proof. But the written words hadn't finished with their final punch.

'Reuben's boys are becoming out of control and it would be best to remove them from the rest of the whānau. Kane, in particular is showing signs of derangement. That girl has been the undoing of my son's legacy; she is unhinged and her demons are spreading. He feels he can exercise better control over them away from an audience. Reuben will leave tomorrow with Kane and Neville and set up a makeshift camp on the eastern side of the mountain and return for the girl. Until then, Miriam is left to look after her sister's bastard. Reuben wishes to adopt her but that is one thing I

will not allow. She will never be a Du Rose. Caroline Marsh she will remain, until long after I am dead and in the urupa.'

Hana dropped the book onto the draining board as sickness enveloped her and she retched into the stainless steel sink without control.

Chapter 4

It wasn't just the fact that Logan almost married Caroline, which affected Hana so badly, or the woman's destructive influence on their early relationship. It was that Alfred and Miriam had knowingly almost allowed the disaster to happen. *Reuben too.* It was painful for Logan that Reuben and Caroline conspired to rip him off; organising a wedding that would never happen and using alleged debt from it to secure the flat piece of land on the mountaintop. Forty years of buried grief had made Reuben ruthless and dangerous in his desperation for contact with his son. But it destroyed everything, forcing Logan into legal action and financial ruin for his birth father. Probably all Reuben ever wanted was a face-to-face conversation, a traditional *hui* in which he would undoubtedly reveal his ace of spades. It was the one time Logan Du Rose had done things by the book and it had taken everyone by surprise.

Hana ran water into her hand and sipped it, hoping the sickness had finally abated, her hot milk long gone down the plug hole and into the septic tank underneath the driveway. And then she remembered something far worse and the retching began again. A recalled conversation with Leslie returned to her. *"I see that that Marsh girl finally got her hooks into a Du Rose! You'd think that poroheahea Kane would 'ave more sense. She's been poison to them boys their whole life and now he's stuck with her. She'll be thrilled. Hankered after that name as long as she's 'ad breath. Wahine kairau!"* Leslie spat on the ground with force, realising too late that she'd gobbed on the kitchen floor.

Guilt seized Hana and she pushed her face further into the sink. "I pushed them together," she moaned, her voice echoing against the metal. "It's my fault! But I knew he loved her." The nausea was Hana's punishment and she stayed there, trying not to think of gorgeous blond Caroline dangling the Du Rose men, including Logan, like a spider toying with flies in her copious web. Them and many others.

"Oh God, please forgive me," Hana pleaded out loud, laying her sweaty forehead on her arms. Her breaths came heavy and hard won as she pushed the aged diary away from her, no longer caring that it was out in the open air and decaying by the second. It had morphed from a treasured thing to a cursed.

The obvious fact remained that in finally securing the Du Rose name, Caroline Marsh had unwittingly married her half-brother. Hana felt ill. She knew sleep would never come now. Her cell phone was charging in the enormous lounge and she turned the light on, feeling that same creeping sense of being watched. Drawing all the curtains around the room she grabbed her phone and sent a hurried text to the museum curator. '*Massive problem with this last diary. I think we need to destroy it! Talk tomorrow.*'

Will was in his late sixties and had been the archivist for the large *marae* in Ngaruawahia, which was the seat of the royal *kīngitanga*. Diabetes robbed him of his legs from above the knees and Hana engaged his services to restore the contents of Phoenix Du Rose's treasures the previous year. When Logan approved her hair brained scheme to display the family heirlooms in an on-site museum, to her surprise he employed the disabled man to set it up. Will moved from Hamilton to the hotel while Hana and Logan were in Europe and occupied a room in one of the motel suites on the property. Logan employed Will's son as his carer, helping him practically in his quest for normality. It was a blessing for the family following the man's redundancy at the Hamilton sawmill. Will's son was an enormous *Māori* man, terrifying to look at with his *ta moko* tattoos covering his face, but gentle as a puppy and tender with his father. Logan also gave him work as a groundsman.

Hana huddled down on her knees next to the wood burner, trying to settle her stomach and draw comfort from the heat. It was two thirty in the morning so Will wouldn't text back until he started work and the fire was almost spent. She shivered, dropping her phone in surprise as it rang in her hand. Hana wasn't even given the chance to greet the caller.

"You destroy an artifact in my care, woman and I'll whoop your pretty ass all the way back up that mountain you live on!"

"Why are you up?" Hana felt the sickness of anticipation return to her guts.

"Because some damn woman started textin' me!"

"Oh, sorry."

"Na, me an' me boy've been watching the rugby. I'm likin' this Sky TV thing. Ain't never been able to watch them international games before. This'n was All Blacks versus Springbok. They's eatin' dirt now them green an' yellas. That'll teach 'em."

Hana toyed with the idea of politely asking the score but she knew Will wouldn't tell her. She had never managed to fool him yet and this was not the exception.

"So, what's your problem, bro? And don't bother askin' bout the rugby cos I know you don't care. What you wantin' to destroy?" His voice sounded hoarse down the phone line. He'd probably been shouting at the TV. He had been known to get so excited that he pitched himself out of his wheelchair.

"It's this damn diary of Phoenix's," Hana tiptoed over and closed the lounge double doors, a ridiculous effort as Logan and her baby were miles away at the other end of the house. "She's said the most awful things about family members. If this gets out it'll cause a whole heap of trouble for a lot of people."

"History's like that the world over, girlie. It's the nature of the thing. Your husband employs me to take care of the truth and that's what I'm gonna do."

"I've got two choices here," Hana tried to be firm with him. "Either I destroy it and nobody is the wiser, or I rip out the offending pages..."

"Rip out!" Will's shout echoed in Hana's ear and she had to hold the phone away and wait for the sound to finish pinging around her ear drum. "Don't you bloody dare!"

"You don't *understand*. Someone's married their half-brother without realising. Oh dear God," a terrible thought occurred to Hana and she sent up a further plea to the God of Heaven. "If they have children, it could be a disaster! Besides which, they've broken the law. Oh this is awful," she flapped. "We have to destroy it."

"You return that bloody book to me in one piece tomorrow or I quit! You hear me, madam? I'll be inspecting every damn page and if I find anything missin', I'm done here."

Hana gulped and nodded, hearing a hiss of exasperation as Will couldn't see her. "I feel sick," she said, to no-one in particular and he humphed loudly.

"You will if you touch that diary!"

"Ok, ok, we'll talk tomorrow." Exhaustion settled on Hana like a shroud.

"Fine," Will said with an edge of grumpiness. "Come to the museum and we'll talk. But remember what I said, girlie. Touch it and we're done!"

Will rang off, leaving Hana feeling no better than she had before. "I should have just burned it," she said to the dying embers. "He wouldn't have noticed." But she knew he would. He was an incredible archivist and catalogued everything that passed through his hands. He would have missed it eventually and no amount of blagging would have gotten Hana out of trouble then.

Hana hid the tattered diary full of its damaging secrets in her underwear drawer. Some wicked part of her nature acknowledged the innate glee that wrecking Caroline's new life would bring, but a bigger part urged the need for self-preservation. Whilst Caroline was busy in Christchurch with her new husband, hopefully not producing incestuous two-headed babies, she wasn't pestering Logan or trying to destroy Hana's marriage. Hana crawled into the massive four poster bed with her husband, edging across towards his warmth and touching various parts of his satisfyingly hot skin to see if he reacted. He grunted and shifted in bed, until she risked it and put her freezing cold feet on his bare legs. "Geez, woman!" he complained, wakened with a start. "Have you been outside?"

"No, I can't sleep."

"Well I was managing just fine, but now that I'm disturbed..." Logan put his warm hands up under Hana's nightshirt and she giggled, her cares and worries temporarily pushed into the background, as her husband set about restoring her body temperature to a little above normal.

Chapter 5

H ana's dream was peculiar, involving a ringing cell phone and some kind of lost cat. It was persistent, intruding on her slumber without mercy, stopping and then starting again for what seemed like hours. She gave up searching for the cat and allowed herself to be pulled from sleep, not surprised to discover the cat was unreal, but astounded to find the ringing phone was. "Yes."

Her greeting was abrupt and there was a pause at the other end. Then he let rip, "Where's that diary? I've been waiting for you for hours. Get yourself down here now and let me see it. You'll be the death of me, girlie."

Hana yawned and looked gormlessly at the clock in the right-hand corner of the phone's screen, taking it away from her ear to do so. She could still hear Will shouting, "Do you 'ear me?"

"I was up all night, I wasn't..."

"I'm not interested in what you were doing with your evening." Will sounded beyond agitated. "I saw your man earlier and I've got a fair idea from the smile on his face. Get your pretty ass down 'ere and quick!"

Hana flopped back on the comfy pillows. It was half past ten in the morning. Logan had put her mobile phone on his pillow next to her, along with a carefully written note in his perfectly scripted left-handed writing.

'Leslie's got Phoe. You looked so peaceful and our girl was up so I thought I'd leave you. Jack fetched us so the ute up top with you. Come down when you feel like it. Thirty calves in two days, not bad. Only lost two so far.'

Hana rubbed her eyes, finding them crusty and horrid with sleep. Getting out of bed to get a shower she checked her bedside table. The diary was still buried in the top drawer, snuggled between a pair of sexy red knickers and a friendly old, greying pair that were actually her favourite. She kind of hoped it would have been spirited away in the night somehow, like an answer to prayer. Deliberately delaying her fate, Hana wasted time cleaning the kitchen sink she had spent half an hour barfing into earlier. Then she locked up, started the ute and drove down to the hotel, the diary bouncing carelessly on the passenger seat.

Will waited for her in the museum. His wheelchair faced the door and his arms were folded across his chest, his face set in a practiced snarl. He held his hand out for the diary straight away. "You look like crap," he said after he had pulled on a pair of cotton gloves and checked the spine for evidence of ripped pages.

"Thanks," Hana said sarcastically. "I told you I was sick."

"Not on this, I hope?" He shook the diary at her and inspected the pages all over again. Hana sighed and huffed like a sulky teenager. Will moved his spectacles down his nose and eyed her with amusement. "What's with you at the moment?"

Hana hurled herself into one of the elderly chairs along the wall of the museum. Her shoulders slumped and she ran a hand over her tired eyes. "Lots of stuff. I'm fine." She indicated the diary with a stabbing finger. "That's not helping! You have no idea how defamatory it is. I want to get rid of it. If you won't burn it, then at least find somewhere to hide it, where it can't hurt anyone it relates to."

Will wheeled himself over to Hana and put a comforting arm around her shoulders. They spent the next hour discussing the diary and the implications, should its damaging contents ever become widely known.

"Have you ever stood inside and watched the rain pour down a window?" Will asked. Hana nodded. "A life is like that, see. It runs down fast, finding a way through obstacles, joinin' with others or runnin' alone. It leaves the bottom and is gone. The sun dries the window and there's nothin' to see anymore, except a faint trail. That's what people come seekin'; that faint trail. We don't have the right to wipe it out as though it never happened."

Will placed his large, arthritic fingers over Hana's pale, delicate ones, gripping them gently. A high blush of shame worked its way steadily into her cheeks. Will moved so that his brown eyes were close to Hana's, forcing her to look at him. "Honey, we're the guardians of the past, not the judges. And besides, *e hara i te mea, he kotahi tangata nāna i whakaara i tō pō*."

"What does that mean?" Hana asked, irritated by the old man's lapse into his native tongue. Will smiled sadly and drew his gnarled hand across his mouth. "Listen up good girlie, it means this: It was not one man alone who was awake in the dark times." At Hana's still obvious confusion he explained, "Never take one viewpoint for history; it's dangerous. There's always more than one way of seeing the past." He waved the tattered diary under Hana's nose. A small section of the fabric spine fell off and fluttered into his lap. Hana contemplated pointing it out, wanting the old man to know she hadn't done it - he had. But her motivation was childish and she kept quiet. "I can restrict this for seventy years, or until everyone involved is dead. I'll seal it and lodge it somewhere, but I ain't destroying it, my love. It's not how you safeguard history and youse know that."

Will bobbed his head as he touched Hana's arm lightly. His hair was thinning on his brown head and he had lost weight since moving up to the hotel. Getting to work for him involved great physical activity, wheeling himself down the road and up the ramp into the museum entrance. It had forced him to get busy and his zest for life was visibly increased. His wrinkled hands reminded Hana of her father's, thousands of miles away in England. She missed him and the sensation bit with unexpected force, stealing the colour from her cheeks as she remembered the tearful goodbye at Heathrow Airport. Her fingers strayed involuntarily to her stomach, wondering if her child would ever meet his Scots grandfather and when she looked up, Will's eyes watched her with a knowing expression.

A slight smile played on his dark lips and Hana's face impeached him, begging him not to ask. The elderly man respected her plea and didn't refer to his opportunist's knowledge. "You promise you'll lock it up *safe?* Nobody will see it." Hana stood up feeling strangely light headed.

"I promise," Will assured her. "As long as youse remember one thing, little one. We all comes to a point where we crave the route home to us roots. Don't matter how old we get, life has a beginnin' and an end and them's what can't see the whole story feels permanently lost. One day, maybe long after I'm gone, you might have to hand this book over to them's what comes lookin' because it's a witness statement of their life. It's their route map home. As long as youse never lose sight of that, youse gonna know when that time is."

Hana stumbled from the museum feeling stressed and ill. She roamed the hotel searching for her daughter and husband. Logan came to his own conclusions concerning his failed wedding to Caroline Marsh, believing the whole thing to be a sham. Hana now knew for sure that he'd been played by a ruthless Reuben Du Rose, but perhaps so had Caroline. The other woman had genuinely loved Logan in her own sick, controlling way. She possibly had no clue that Reuben would stop the marriage somehow. For whatever else Reuben was guilty of, the diaries made it clear; he would abide by his mother's wishes, until time immemorial.

As Hana searched the family areas for her lover and child, Miriam Du Rose's words clanged forcefully in her mind, spoken on Hana's wedding night when they were alone together in the kitchen. "Keep him away from *her*. Promise me?"

Logan and Caroline. Not just lovers, but cousins.

Chapter 6

Hana didn't find Logan or Phoenix in the busy hotel and her travels took her down to the stable yard behind the main building. The deaf stable manager, Jack supervised the farrier as he tried to trim the feet of one of the nastiest brood mares. Rawhiti, the stable lad, attempted to occupy her as she fought to take lumps out of the farrier's bent backside. Jack was in his nineties, bent over and wizened by age but he missed nothing. Hana closed the gate after her and walked towards them, feeling an odd sensation as her child kicked out at her bladder. *Please stop*, she implored the child in her belly. *I need to tell your daddy about you before you start doing somersaults and making it any more obvious!*

The thought of confessing to Logan and his subsequent anger at her subterfuge was enough to make Hana come over all hot and bothered despite the chill in the air. She flapped at her face and hung back, not wanting to disturb the men at their unpredictable work. Jack had a good hold on the huge white mare in his care. Nothing would ever get past him. But Rawhiti was not so sure of himself. A young man in his twenties, he loved horses and sought Jack's vast ninety year experience with an insatiable hunger, but he struggled with the deaf-man's communication style and so missed the significant and hastily grunted warning.

Rawhiti's temperamental brood mare decided she'd had enough of being messed around with. The expensive Appaloosa reared up on her back legs and aimed a well-placed kick at Rawhiti's upturned face with a neatly trimmed front hoof. He ducked and the lead rope ran painfully through his fingers, removing skin with each rutted edge that passed through. The farrier went sprawling face first on the cobbled surface and the mare was loose. Stamping and snorting, her eyes wide in fury and her nostrils splayed open like velvet blow holes, she made a beeline for Hana and the closed gate.

The pregnant woman stood frozen in place as the tonnage of horseflesh bore down on her, the mare hardly breaking stride as she transitioned into a smooth canter. Terrified, Hana closed her eyes and held her breath, powerless against the oncoming collision and the surety that she would come off worse. The clatter of hooves came closer across the wide yard, seeming to double in intensity and noise. It was a snapshot in time, just seconds of her life, but Hana had no time to react. The sound of skidding hooves on the slippery surface was followed by a breath of warm air and then the sense of a huge, sweating body close to Hana's face. She smelled paddock grass and hay, horseflesh and...Sacha.

Her eyes snapped open to find Logan's mare in front of her. Sacha was side on, her ears bent so far back into her head that she could have been born without any. She snaked her neck viciously at the Appaloosa and snorted quick, angry threats. The Appaloosa backed away, her moment spoiled and allowed herself to be caught by the embarrassed Rawhiti. Hana lay her forehead against Sacha's neck and let out a moan of relief. "Thank you, Sacha!" She pushed her face into the dappled furry coat and tried to catch her breath. Her legs seemed wobbly and pathetic.

The mare turned a kinder face on her master's loved one and snuffed at her hand affectionately. Hana put her shaking fingers up to the mare's withers and seized a reassuring chunk of mane in her fingers, steadying herself against the surge of shock that claimed her body as adrenaline fought for exit.

"Are you all right, Mrs Du Rose?" Rawhiti's voice sounded shaken as he called from the other side of the mare. Hana nodded, realising he couldn't see her.

"Just give me a minute," she answered. "I'm just a bit shaken."

She felt Sacha's body shudder and pulled her face away from the comforting fur, seeing the mare snake her neck angrily at Rawhiti's approach, baring her teeth and threatening. "Stop it now, Sacha," she said with a waver in her voice. "I'm really fine." Hana moved to the mare's head and stroked her forelock lovingly, kissing her on the pure white, regal forehead. Sacha rubbed her poll against Hana's shoulder and snuffed in her ear, snorting when Hana giggled. Hana placed her hand on the horse's halter and led her back to the farrier, who dusted the front of his leather apron with quick movements.

"No way!" he commented, throwing his tools into his bag and making a clanging din in his haste. "Now I know why you lot do your own smithying. Your stock's out of control!" He rushed from the stable yard still wearing his leather tool belt and hopped over the gate to the hotel without opening it.

Jack looked at Rawhiti and Hana caught sight of a flicker of victory in his smirk.

"I'm so sorry, Miss," the younger man began and Hana shook her head in confusion.

"Why is it your fault?"

"I met that guy in the township and he said he could do a reduced rate on the shoeing. I thought we could give him a go. Jack's..." He turned his face away to stop the old man lip-reading. "Jack's looking a bit infirm sometimes and I know he finds it hard to bend for long with his back. That guy was going to teach me how to trim properly."

"Why didn't you just ask Jack?" Hana asked, perplexed.

Rawhiti shrugged and it contained all Hana needed to know. The men weren't getting on. Jack turned and walked away, his shoulders hunched in irritation. He hadn't needed to read the young man's lips to understand what he had just said.

"Get Logan to teach you," Hana said quietly. "He can show you how to shoe as well." Then she set off quickly after the old man, following him into the messy office in the far stable.

Jack pulled a half-full bottle of whiskey from the top drawer of an old green filing cabinet, waving it in Hana's direction as he set two dirty mugs down on the paper saturated desk. She shook her head and signed clearly twice, *'not for me,'* but he ignored her and poured her one anyway. He took a long slug of the nectar and smacked his lips loudly before signing words about the young upstart in the stable yard, which Hana pretended not to understand.

"He's just young," she mouthed, urging him to have patience. The old man sighed and shook his head, while Hana sat and pretended to drink the whiskey. Even the taste of it against the rim of the mug made nausea rear its ugly head. Jack eyed her with amusement until, to Hana's horror he pointed directly at her stomach.

'How long?' he signed.

Hana's heart sank and she rolled her eyes, laying the whiskey laden mug on the paperwork with trembling fingers. She shrugged and put a finger to her lips, imploring him with her eyes to say nothing. He made a zipping motion with his finger and thumb and beamed at her. She gave him a grateful thumbs up, but still looked immensely discomfited.

Hunting around in the desk-mess, Jack retrieved a stained refill pad and pen. He scribbled something on it and then pushed it across towards Hana. She noticed his large fingers bore no signs of blood or graze and it occurred to her that he had deliberately sent Sacha to head off the other mare.

'What's wrong?' the words on the page asked in cursive, old-fashioned script.

'Just stuff,' she replied. *'Mainly Du Rose family stuff.'*

He read it and cocked his head on one side like an eagle, the tufty hair growing from his useless ears making the effect more real.

'What family stuff?'

Jack's family had been with the Du Roses for centuries. He was in his early nineties although nobody was entirely sure of his age. Jack taught Phoenix Du Rose to read and write English, although Hana often wondered how they managed without the spoken word. There was no doubt he had kept an extremely watchful eye over the young Logan Du Rose and showed him everything about horses he could possibly teach, much to the jealousy of the other Du Rose children. He and Logan communicated in an odd way, few words or signs; just a knowing borne of hours spent together.

Still weighed down by the knowledge contained in the diary, Hana wrote a question on the paper. With hindsight, it was foolish and she never should have done it. But often the best lessons are learned from mighty mistakes.

'What happened to Caroline Marsh's father? The blond drover.'

Jack's tanned face paled to a sickening hue. His countenance became hard and angry, his brown eyes flashing in his head with a fury that Hana had never seen in him. Her brow knitted and she remained fixed in place in the uncomfortable chair. Jack leaned over and snatched the pen violently from her hand. He wrote so hard on the pad that the sharp point of the pen went through several pages. Then he flung the pad back so hard, it missed the edge of the desk and landed at Hana's feet. She picked it up gingerly, a tremor reigniting in her fingers.

'Stay out of things you don't understand.'

Hana dropped the pad onto the desk as though it was contaminated. She stood up to leave, eyeing the old man with trepidation and jumping as he lurched across the desk and seized the incriminating pad. To her horror he threw the whole thing onto the fireplace, pen as well. With a hiss and a roar, the objects were devoured by the orange guards flickering in their lair. Hana backed out of the office with her heart beating a tattoo in her chest.

She hurried back to the house with the words of the diaries running uncontrollably around her brain. *The blond drover hadn't just disappeared. Phoenix was right. They killed him. The Du Roses killed him.*

Chapter 7

"**G**et your own house in order, girlie!" Will had said, calling the words as Hana high-tailed it out of the museum door. *He was right. She had problems of her own right now.*

Hana finally located Leslie in her upstairs apartment, teaching Phoenix *Māori* words and drawing pictures for her on a scrap of paper with ancient crayons. "She's quick!" the old lady beamed at Hana. "She might be just a babe, but she knows what's what, my *moko*."

Phoenix appeared to be pushing the crayons around the paper, producing random squiggles and lines, but obviously Leslie saw some hidden meaning in it all. "*Te ngeru*," Phoenix said with confidence, jabbing at the paper with her stubby brown crayon. She did a funny victory dance on feet which were clad in blue woolly tights and then she settled again. She stood on her chair, her elbows on the dining table and carried on colouring.

"That's a beautiful cat, *moko*," Leslie said, smiling warmly at the child.

Hana tried not to feel left out. Often Logan would speak to his daughter in the old language and she would jabber happily back. Hana knew she could try harder to learn but something stopped her, some intrinsic self-alienation that she couldn't seem to get past. "I'm going to tell Logan tonight," Hana interrupted, placing the English words between them like a wall. Her symbolism was wasted. Leslie smiled and looked relieved.

"Well, thank the good Lord for that," she commented. "It's been real hard to keep your secret this last day or so. I'm glad youse gonna get it out in the open. He'll be thrilled with you. He loves his family."

Hana nodded. "I thought I'd cook him a special dinner, something he really likes and dress up nicely and then just come out with it."

"Good on ya!" Leslie concluded cheerfully.

Hana helped herself to some large, prime cuts of steak from the hotel freezer under Leslie's watchful eye. "That's it, girl. Soften him up with his own produce...no, get a bigger cut than that! You want him full of *kai* and then he won't have the energy to get mad!"

Leslie seemed to be finding the whole thing hugely hilarious. Hana, in contrast, was nervous and afraid. It wasn't that she didn't want to tell Logan about the baby but she was afraid of the whole process of pregnancy. The pacemaker beneath her left collarbone reminded her she was no longer youthful, or particularly healthy and Phoenix's birth had been sudden, early and unexpectedly traumatic. Bodie and Izzie had been born in a white, sanitised hospital in mid-Wales, but the *Māori* baby had come into the world outside, surrounded by native bush into the bosom of her ancestors.

"I don't know if I can do this again," Hana's voice sounded sad in the depths of the freezer and Leslie's arm snaked around her shoulders. The old lady carried Phoenix, who joined in for a cuddle and they stood clasped together, growing quickly chilly.

"*Pēpe*," Phoenix said into the silence and Hana smiled. Leslie didn't, biting her lip and giving Hana a warning look.

"What does that mean?" Hana asked, sensing the awful exclusion again.

"*Baby*," Leslie answered. "You need to get that husband told, before this'un does it for youse."

Hana sat up on the mountain as dusk claimed the land early, bowing to the winter shroud with respect. Logan had promised to be home for seven o'clock and everything was ready. His steak rested in the oven covered in the juices of a marinade his mother showed Hana how to make. Miriam had promised her the recipe but died that night without imparting the precious family knowledge. Hana had done all the chopping and fetching of herbs under Miriam's tutelage. She made a decent attempt at producing the same, convinced as she spent the afternoon peering in the fridge, that there was still some secret ingredient her mother-in-law had sneakily added. Hana's marinade had a greenish hue, when Miriam's had definitely been brown. Roasted pumpkin and kumara sat keeping hot and a bowl of mashed potatoes nestled close by.

Hana's dress looked glued to her body and showed her four-month pregnancy as it blossomed under her ribs. She felt more rotund than she had with Phoenix and the dress insisted on riding up over her belly in awkward ridges. When seven o'clock turned into eight, then nine and Hana's texts were unreturned, she used the wireless intercom to rouse Leslie. "Sorry darlin', he's delayed," the old lady's voice crackled through the phone. She sounded tired and heavy.

"Sorry, did I wake you?" Hana's voice bore its own natural droop of disappointment as the steak hardened off to a leathery strip and the vegetables sat in their cold dressing on the kitchen counter.

"No, love. Not at all. He's just dealin' with somethin'. He'll be home soon."

"Dinner's ruined," Hana sighed, yanking the dress back down over her knees for the millionth time.

"He won't care," Leslie reassured her, "but Hana...maybe keep your news for another night."

"What? Why?" Hana's frayed nerves went on red alert. "What's going on down there?"

"Talk to Logan." Leslie's voice sounded ominous and Hana spent the next two hours alternately worrying and dozing off. When she heard Logan's heavy tread on the hall floorboards she got up from the sofa and went to greet him.

"I made dinner," she said, rubbing her eyes and forgetting she had makeup on. Mascara spread along the bridge of her nose. Her hair had fallen out of its clip, sprawling across her shoulders in a riot of untidiness and her dress had rucked itself up like a set of tyres over her stomach.

Logan stood where she intercepted him, watching her with an unreadable expression. His jaw worked furiously and he was shrouded in a forbidding silence that made the air around him crackle. Fear blossomed in Hana's chest and she instinctively touched the space on her collarbone where the pacemaker lay just underneath the skin, sensing the rhythm of her heartbeat change with the prolonged atmosphere. "I'm not hungry." Logan's statement came out so forcefully, his face displayed surprise at his own vehemence.

"Oh." Hana felt mortified, biting her trembling bottom lip in confusion at her husband's attitude. Her raw, painful emotions were barely concealed within her chest, her eyelashes flickering nervously, fingers hovering at the throat of her dress. The stalemate continued until Logan broke it, smashing the atmosphere with a nonchalant shrug and turning on his heel. To Hana's dismay he left without explanation, striding purposefully down to the master bedroom and closing the door behind him.

Logan's wife stood poleaxed in the cavernous hall. A large pot plant near the front door swayed in a hidden draught and the rimu grandfather clock which had belonged to his grandmother, continued its relentless slow tick-tock as the pendulum danced to the beat of an endless drum. Hana's feelings came in waves, tossing her from desperation to anger in seconds and then pitching her back again. "What the hell did *I* do?" Hana's words echoed back to her in the empty space.

The lovingly prepared dinner made a sorry sight in the fridge, untouched. The roast vegetables congealed on the bottom of the dish and the plastic wrap made them look like something in a mortuary as condensation bubbled along their surface in the cold atmosphere. Hana cried a little as she carefully placed the dried out steak on a dinner plate and stowed its wrapped shape in the top of the fridge. During the cooking process, her marinade had browned to match Miriam's perfect, legendary recipe.

The spectacular dining room seemed sad and depressed without its expected occupants. The long, wooden table still wore its candles and special platters that hardly ever got used. Hana couldn't face disrobing it and blew out the tea lights, padding down to her bedroom with trepidation. She hadn't felt this emotionally low since her pregnancy with Phoenix.

Logan's shower had been quick and purposeful and he was in the process of climbing into bed in his boxer shorts. The long, ugly scars on his torso looked raised and angry in the lamp light, agitated by the hot water and his face wore a veiled look through which nothing could penetrate.

"Did I do something wrong?" Hana stood next to his side of the bed, twisting the bottom of her dress in agonised movements.

"Just leave it," Logan's voice held warning as he lay his damp head on the pillow and stares at a fixed point on the ceiling.

"No, you can tell me. If I've messed up or caused a problem, I don't mind if you say. Then I can put it right."

The awful fear burgeoned in her heart that perhaps someone had blabbed about her pregnancy and he was angry at being the last to know. But then Leslie had said not to tell him tonight - so it had to be something else. "So, can you tell me?" Hana pushed and Logan exploded.

"Why does everything always have to come down to *you?*" he snapped. "Why do you assume that my business has anything to do with *you?*"

Logan had referred to her as his *business partner* often. Didn't that mean she *was* involved? Hana stood bemused on the rug, the toes of one stockinged foot resting awkwardly on the other like a schoolgirl about to be growled at by the principal. Logan's eyes bore cruelly into her soul as he pulled a face filled with agitation. "Either come to bed or sod off, Hana. It's been a really hard day and I'm knackered!"

Hana jumped as though struck. She backed away from the stranger in her bed, jabbing her elbow on the door handle as she struggled to turn without taking her eyes off him. Her heart felt crushed and it was painful to breathe. A familiar voice began in her head, reassuring her, *this isn't happening, this isn't happening.*

The lounge fire exuded a leftover warmth and Hana worked with shaking fingers to restore its blaze, placing more logs in the wood burner and stoking it until finally, they caught light. Their glow was deceptively cheery and contrasted with Hana's devastation. A few short hours ago her life had been orderly and controlled, jogging along nicely with the odd curl thrown in for good measure. Now it felt as though one of Logan's purebred Charolaise herds had stampeded their white bodies through her house and wreaked havoc. Hana didn't know how to start fixing it, because she didn't know what was wrong. Perhaps Logan was right and she did make things all about her. In which case, that made her extremely self-centred and shallow. Hana accepted the mantle of blame and rebuked herself for crimes both terrifying and unknown.

The thought of climbing into bed with her husband's rigid back facing her was an unpleasant one. Hana resigned herself to the four seater sofa and snuggled down with a blanket. The television played quietly to itself for most of the night as she dozed fitfully, waking and sleeping in equal measure. The comforting sound of a horse moved around outside, grazing vigorously near the windows at that end of the house. Hana recognised Sacha's contented sigh and relaxed. Logan sometimes rode her home and allowed her to feast on the un-landscaped garden. The presence of the white beast offered a sense of alliance in the chill of the early hours.

Hana woke surprisingly late, feeling the rays from a watery sunshine filtering through the blinds. The sofa was extremely comfy within its stated purpose, but as a bed, it was poor. Hana resembled an old woman as she shuffled through to her bedroom to use the toilet. The room was empty and the bed neatly made. Logan had already gone. Hana felt ready tears pricking at the edges of her eyelids and fought them. Last night had taken her by surprise, drawing a characteristic defence reaction from her, borne from years of living with Vikram Johal. He had married her out of duty, not love and their marriage had reflected that throughout. Hana had never felt good enough to be his wife, ever grateful that he didn't leave her pregnant and alone, but it hadn't been what he wanted. His affair had lasted a full year before death robbed him of a planned escape from the drudgery of marriage to Hana. She had been blissfully unaware. Visiting the day after Vik's funeral, his mistress had informed Hana of their plan and it broke her. She knew then she wasn't - and had never been, *good enough.* "I promised myself I wouldn't put up with this again," she chided her reflection in the ensuite mirror. "So now it's time to make good on that promise. You're better than this, girl!"

Hana splashed with her daughter in the wide corner bath, putting the jets on and enjoying the freedom of their nakedness in the bubbles. After a late breakfast, Hana readied herself and the child for a visit to the hotel at the bottom of the mountain, determined to find out what had happened to detonate her life into smithereens. If Logan wasn't going to tell her, then Leslie would have to.

"Gone!" Phoenix stated, in a matter of fact tone.

Hana stood under the front porch holding her daughter's hand and staring at the empty space where she had parked the black truck the night before.

"Poop," the child added, pointing to a large horse dump in the middle of the space where the car was meant to be.

"Stay there!" Hana ordered her daughter, plonking Phoenix on the ornate bench outside the front door and walking out onto the crushed grass. She looked around the huge garden. Sacha's downy head poked up from around the water tank and she moved gracefully towards Hana, eager to see if the woman had anything nice in her pocket.

Hana gave a heavy sigh and looked back at the little girl, swinging her legs casually on the bench. "Daddy took the car."

"Horsey!" Phoenix cried in excitement as Sacha's regal head came into view next. "Horsey for me!" Phoenix clambered down from the bench by rolling onto her stomach and approached Sacha, fully aware of the kind of respect demanded by these creatures. Sacha obligingly dropped her head so that Phoenix could stroke her forelock. "Ride horsey," she said, as though there was no difficulty with the swap.

"I'm four months pregnant and you're not two yet," Hana sighed. "And even though Dad's saddle is probably in the garage, I can't lift it, let alone get it on her." Hana drew her cell phone from her pocket. "Maybe Nonie will come get us."

"No, horsey!" Phoenix insisted, pouting and knitting her brows at her mother.

"Absolutely not," Hana replied.

Her cell phone had no signal and Hana messed around, persuading Phoenix to come back inside. The house phone, nothing more than an intercom with the hotel, gave a prolonged busy signal. Logan had allowed a national phone company to put a cell phone mast on the top of the mountain nearest theirs, but there had been nothing but problems with it ever since. It failed more than it worked, unable to cope with the extreme weather conditions. Hana rested her forearms on the kitchen counter and lay her head on them, trying to stem the frustration that built in her. She needed to get down to the hotel. "I can't get hold of Nonie, Phoe," Hana spoke into the empty kitchen. The thought of explaining her evening to Leslie sent an ashamed shiver down Hana's spine.

"Oopsie!" The clatter brought Hana out of her despair as her daughter chased a white riding hat around the smooth surface of the hall floor. She managed to wedge it onto her head and held up her chin for Hana to close the fastener. Phoenix had been five weeks old the first time her father lifted her up onto the white mare and Hana had found it hard to keep silent. Only the fact that Logan grieved for his mother and birth father had stilled her tongue but after that, she insisted the child wear a helmet. It was pointless banning the hazardous activity in a family full of ranchers. Alfred had chuckled, "Logan rode bareback at three years old and mustered cattle at five."

Insistence on the helmet proved a masterstroke as it only recently began to fit, although Hana knew Logan must have disobeyed her and put the baby up on numerous occasions without her knowledge. Walking down the mountain would take more than an hour, especially pushing the pram. Willing to risk it, Hana then discovered the pram was in the back of the truck Logan had taken. It seemed she was left with no choice.

Sacha was gentle and considerate as Hana fixed the halter around her face and hoisted the child up onto her withers. Poor Hana had to discard all the usual paraphernalia that she carried, taking only her purse, door key and useless cell phone, futilely protecting her skull with Miriam's old Jillaroo hat. Phoenix held tightly to a clump of mane, looking like a professional jockey. Growing up around large stock animals, she knew not to scream or behave unpredictably. "Come up, mama," she said with encouragement as Hana heaved herself onto the mare's back, using the top rail of the wooden fence as a mounting block. The ridge of Sacha's bony spine felt uncomfortable between Hana's legs and she wriggled around, trying to get a more solid seat.

Hana aimed for the road using the halter rope one handed to guide the mare, but Sacha didn't want to walk on the metal and set off towards the bush. Hana had massive misgivings until she relaxed, telling herself that Sacha was perfectly able to find the quickest way home. Bred in the mountains, she had traversed every inch of them. They emerged in the paddock above the hotel in less than half an hour. The mare picked a steady downhill slope, winding her way carefully through the mountain and arriving without mishap. Rawhiti was checking on the pregnant brood mares close to the stables and came to open the gate, just as Hana wondered how on earth she was going to stay mounted, hold onto the baby and undo the metal catch.

"Jack was just about to come up," he said, looking confused as he surveyed the incongruous scene. "Logan said he left her up at the house and there was something wrong with her. He asked Jack to go and take a look. She was acting real vicious and turned her backside on him. Mind you, that's nothing unusual for her, is it?" He smirked and then stepped back as Sacha flattened her ears to her head and snaked her neck spitefully in his direction. The dark eye nearest Hana was closed in anticipation and the woman fancied that the horse was smiling.

"There's nothing wrong with her." Hana's tone was sharp and Rawhiti closed the stable yard gate and kept silent. Sacha plodded obediently over to the kauri table, once beautiful but now a mounting block and allowed Hana to deposit herself on the top of it without grace. Her legs ached and constant contact with the knobbly spine had made her want to pee. Phoenix had surprisingly fallen asleep and grumbled as she was lifted off the horse and handed to Rawhiti. "Sacha needs her breakfast," Hana said, putting authority into her voice to stem the threatening meltdown. "We need to get her feed ready."

Phoenix kept her hat on as Hana read the ingredients for Sacha's feed out loud, off the blackboard in the feed room and helped the child carry the bucket back to the horse. Rawhiti had tied her up in the yard and dodged the threat of a kick as he tried to groom the sweat out of her girth area. The riding hat was a bit too big and Phoenix kept pushing the peak out of her eyes as she fed the unpredictable mare by hand. Sacha munched happily, careful with her teeth on the tiny fingers. "I'll do it, Rawhiti." Hana took the curry comb from the reluctant groom's hand and brushed the furry stomach and flanks in brisk, capable movements.

A tension descended on the stable yard with frightening speed, dousing all sense of safety and comfort. It was so sudden that it caused Hana to look up. Rawhiti looked awkwardly towards the stable office, where Jack leaned heavily against the doorframe shaking his wizened old head. Confused, Hana thought at first it was aimed at her, until she heard Phoenix say, "Daddy."

Hana's head whipped around, her eyes meeting the steel grey of Logan's. He looked at Sacha and then at his wife, betrayal oozing out of every fibre of his being. His gaze took in Phoenix, constantly pushing the riding hat out of her eyes and carrying her head at an upturned angle and it was obvious he knew he had missed out on a big moment in his daughter's development. Hana opened her mouth to speak, possibly to apologise but then closed it again. Logan was not alone.

"Logan darling, I had no idea you owned all this." The blonde woman hung from his arm, one slender hand threaded through his elbow while the other stroked his muscular bicep. Hana gaped at the obscenity, the stupid thought flashing across her brain, *Logan hates to be touched*. But obviously not by this woman. The blonde hair looked perfectly coiffed and piled on top of an elegantly shaped head in a beautiful knot, allowing for tendrils to curve around an attractive, sensual face. A decent covering of makeup was neatly applied to disguise her forty plus years but the woman was charismatic and pretty, getting away with it effortlessly. She was taller than Hana and had an easy grace which made the other woman feel frumpy and awkward.

"Logan and I knew each other in London," the woman simpered with a smile that revealed perfect teeth. "It's so good to be back together." To Hana's horror, the woman lifted herself up on the toes of her high heeled shoes and planted a kiss, intended for Logan's cheek. He was so tall that it ended up near his jawline but left Hana in no doubt as to the nature of their former relationship. Worse, it had evidently been rekindled.

Hana heard her own sharp intake of breath at the same time as Logan squatted down and beckoned to his daughter. Confused by the presence of the stranger and more so by her proximity to Phoenix's daddy, she refused to come, pushing her hat back on her head and hiding behind Hana's legs in apparent shyness. It was so unlike her that Hana finally woke up. The stable yard was eerily silent and Hana felt the eyes of the yard workers drilling into the back of her head. Maternal instinct screamed at her to remove Phoenix from the horrid situation and Hana reacted, quickly handing the comb back to Rawhiti and hoisting her daughter onto her hip. She nodded curtly to the woman, ignored her unfaithful husband and turned on her heel, leaving the stable yard at a steady pace.

"Is that your horse then?" the woman's English accent cut through the silence. "How quaint that you use them as transport here."

Hana gritted her teeth and headed for the mudroom, managing to hold herself together until she got there.

Chapter 8

Phoenix was difficult, refusing to take off the riding hat but unable to see properly to walk upstairs in it either. Hana ended up carrying her up the back spiral staircase to the middle floor and then up the next level to Alfred and Leslie's apartment over the west wing of the house.

"What have we here?" Alfred said with a good-natured smile as Phoenix make a drunk looking beeline towards him and Hana stood at the top of the stairs and detonated. "Leslie!" he shouted in panic, as Hana put both hands over her eyes and heard her own sobs dragging themselves from her chest in sickening, ragged breaths.

Strong arms surrounded her body as Leslie's heavy but surprisingly nimble footsteps reached her and she heard the woman say, "Bastard," as she buried Hana's wet face in her ample bosom and confirmed her very worst fears.

Hana cried pathetically until there was nothing left except a ringing in her ears and a bone weary exhaustion. Alfred occupied Phoenix in the lounge while Leslie comforted her mother in the large master bedroom overlooking the boundary fence from its high vantage point. "Oh God," Hana wept, "what's wrong with me? Not *again*."

"Hush child," Leslie's anger was open and filled with violence. "Don't say that. You don't deserve none of this!"

When Hana reached a point of utter numbness and even the waterfall of tears had finished, Leslie went to make her a cup of tea. Hana laid on her side on the wide bed, watching the bush through the long French windows which in summer, led onto a tiny balcony. Hana wondered absently if this was Miriam's bed, or if Alfred and Leslie had bought another, preferring to start again rather than lay on an adulteress' mattress. *What did it matter? They were in their seventies. Perhaps it was no longer important.*

It wasn't Leslie who brought the drink, but Alfred. He laid it on the bedside table but to Hana's surprise, he didn't leave. He set his rangy frame down gently on the bed next to Hana's prone body and stroked her hair with gnarled, work-worn hands. "Leslie told me," he said without preamble. "Apparently she turned up last night looking for him. They had dinner in the restaurant and talked until late. Then he came back to see her this morning."

"He ate in the restaurant?" Hana sat up and turned towards her father-in-law. She heard Leslie sigh from the doorway.

"I wasn't gonna tell her that part," she chastised her husband. "She cooked for the good-for-nothing..." She tutted instead of adding the colourful swearword on the tip of her tongue. "I don't know what that stupid man's playing at, risking everything for some English gold-digger who turns up like that. He needs a good slap!" Leslie looked pointedly at Alfred.

Hana rubbed at her puffy, swollen eyes. She had been here before and the taste felt bitter on her tongue. "So, she's staying here then?" Both adults were silent and Hana looked from one to the other. "Where is she staying?"

Leslie looked away and it was Alfred who answered her, "Downstairs. In his old room."

Hana felt bile rise up into her throat and wasn't sure she could prevent its escape. Logan had installed the woman in the room they used when they stayed over at the hotel. She was sleeping in their bed, in full view of the hotel staff, possibly even with him. She worried at her thumb nail and tried to take it all in. It had all happened so fast that she struggled to process the differences between yesterday and today. "Where's Phoe?" She remembered her daughter with a fresh injection of guilt.

"She's fallen asleep on the hearth rug," Leslie reassured her.

"She saw the woman all over Logan." A tear trickled down Hana's cheek and dived onto the bedspread, surprising her as she thought they were all gone. "She was hanging off him and...kissing him and it freaked Phoe out." Hana struggled for composure and felt a wave of gratitude at Leslie's obvious fury on her behalf.

The old lady pursed her lips so hard that they disappeared and her jaw worked frantically through the skin of her cheeks. The woman's brown eyes flashed with latent danger. "Why don't you and the *mokopuna* stay here with us?" she offered.

Hana was shocked by the sarcastic laugh that escaped from her body. "What and have to see them coming out of our bedroom together and going down for breakfast hand in hand? No thanks. I don't know where I'm going but I am *not* staying here."

"You're not leaving!" Logan's voice was harsh and raised, making everyone in the room jump. He stood in the doorway flexing his fingers angrily and his grey eyes flashed hard as granite.

Hana felt the fight return in a welcome wave and she turned her face determinedly away from her husband.

"You're going nowhere," Logan said again, irritated by the silence. He took two long strides into the room, his body rigid. Hana sensed an incredible calm descend on her and was grateful for the peace that accompanied it. She said nothing, keeping her gaze fixed on the track that Miriam had worn along the side of the property - the old boundary. They always thought it was the stock, tramping a well-worn track to higher grazing, but for forty years it had been Logan's unfaithful mother, wearing a path to her brother-in-law's bed. Hana smiled a serene, Madonna-like smile and felt her soul link with Alfred's, the husband who had been second-best. *Like me. Only I've been second-best twice*, Hana thought, refusing to allow depression to gather any more of her soul into its black bosom.

"Get out!" Leslie broke the silence first, issuing her order with authority and *mana*.

Logan sneered at her. "This is my house. You forget yourself, woman!"

Hana felt the bed shake as Alfred rose from it. He was wiry and spare, a tall strong man stripped bare by life and circumstance. He raised his bent body to its full, impressive height and stared his wife's bastard eye to eye. "If you want it," he waved his arm to take in the long wing, the rooms bisected by dividing walls that didn't reach the apex roof and the old-fashioned, worn out decor. "Take it. We can be gone by tomorrow."

Logan took a step forward. "I don't want that. I don't want you to go...Dad. I don't want anyone to go." He looked imploringly at Hana but it was Alfred who spoke and his words cut the younger man like a kitchen blade.

"Don't call me *Dad*, please. You're no son of mine. I tried so hard with you, Logan. I wanted you to understand what faithfulness was, *whakapono*. Despite it all, I tried to do right by you and your mother. She ground my face in the dirt anyway and now I see you following in her slutty footsteps. You're nothing to me now. You're no better than her or your father. They'll rot in hell for what they did and now...well, you're bound there too it seems. Take it all, Logan Du Rose. Take it all. I hope it makes you happy, because it never did me. Now get out of my home, while I can still call it that. We can be out as soon as you want."

"No," Logan flailed, "you don't understand! None of you do." He tried to reach Hana in an act of desperation and she saw fear behind the bravado as he faced the loss of absolutely everything he held dear. But she was surprisingly well protected, not just by the ample body of Leslie but by Alfred too.

"Get out!" Alfred said and his tone held an ancient authority. The *mana* his mother believed he didn't have, rose out of him and shrouded him in influence and superiority.

Logan shook his head and tried again to reach for his stricken wife. Alfred's punch when it came was practiced and well-timed. Reuben Du Rose taught his son guitar, masquerading as a guitar teacher to get near him, but Hana realised that Alfred was his boxing master. It was a boxer's hit and Logan staggered back in shock. Alfred rubbed the arthritic fingers of his right hand and flexed them gingerly. Then he looked up at the shocked man in front of him, already rubbing at his bruised eye. "I said, get out!"

"She had a child and I didn't know. I've got a son!" Logan's words sounded agonised, torn from the depths of him.

Hana felt a curious tension build in her forehead, a stress headache spreading out across her face. Her chest tightened and her breath came in short rasps. Hana fought to fill her lungs, wondering if her heart struggled to beat. She tensed, waiting for the pacemaker to kick in and administer the promised electric shock. She dreaded it daily. They told her it wasn't so bad, like a punch to the chest - *not* as bad as dying anyway.

Her feet found the floorboards through her socks as time seemed to halt for her. The world spun horribly and she kept her right hand clutched to her left collarbone to protect her from the inevitable shock. Logan's anguished face danced around her in a fast circle, too fast to be real and Hana saw the bedside table come up to meet her face at a terrific speed. Then nothing. She saw nothing, heard nothing and felt nothing. *Except her child.* She sensed the tiny being keenly in a linking of souls. It was as though in this strange, surreal world there were just the two of them together. It moved sluggishly in her belly and she felt it, understanding as the blood pumped too quickly through the umbilical cord that it struggled, just like her.

Chapter 9

"**I**s she gonna to be ok?"

Hana recognised Logan's scared voice and wanted to call out to him that she was fine. Then she remembered - he didn't love her anymore and her head silenced her seeking, hopeful, foolish heart. Hana lay on the squashy bed in mute silence. She heard Phoenix asking Leslie for a biscuit with an impassioned "*Peees Nonie, choc-choc one,*" and felt cool hands on her forehead. Thinking it was Logan, she pushed them away.

"Back in the land of the living, Mrs Du Rose?"

The voice belonged to the local doctor. He practised in the Rangiriri township and Hana took Phoenix to see him once with a strange rash that turned out to be an allergy to tinned tuna fish. Hana said nothing, turning her face away from his striking Samoan features and watching dusk settle on the native bush. *Where had the day gone?* "Has your pregnancy been checked out by a doctor?" the kind man asked, sitting his rounded bottom down on the bed next to Hana. She nodded but the effort to speak evaded her. "Your blood pressure spiked this afternoon. That's really dangerous for you and your baby. It's getting back to normal now, but I'm not happy with you.

It's important you avoid stress for a while if you can, otherwise you'll end up in hospital."

Hana sighed, comforted by the numbness that whispered it would take care of her. She believed in God and hoped it was him. Her first words were croaky and rattled from her chest as Hana grasped the doctor's hands in one of hers. "How can I get away from him?" she asked, looking nervously at Logan's dark shape in the doorway. "Can you help me?"

The doctor widened his hazel eyes in alarm and Hana realised it wasn't just him and her. They were all there, Alfred over by the window and Leslie nearby, clutching Hana's daughter. The doctor rose in an awkward, jerky movement, feeling outnumbered in the Du Rose household. "Er...do you feel in danger, Mrs Du Rose?"

Hana nodded slowly, realising she did. Perhaps not physically, but definitely emotionally. She clung to sanity by her fingertips as an old archenemy threatened again. *Rejection*. She closed her eyes and tried to sort out the curious feeling of need that assailed her spirit. *Isobel*. She wanted her grown-up daughter. "Can you get in touch with my daughter?" Hana asked the doctor, her speech slow and laboured. He looked across at Phoenix and knitted his brow, perhaps thinking she was delirious. "She lives in Invercargill. I need to go and see her." Hana heard the pleading in her voice and it made her want to cry with pity for herself. *Pathetic*.

Relief lit the doctor's face as a bead of sweat slithered down his cheek. "You can't travel to Invercargill, not in this state," he said, putting more surety in his voice than he obviously felt. "You won't get a certificate to travel on the airline and you'll put yourself and your baby at terrible risk."

"I'll look after her," Leslie volunteered. "We'll be moving out of here soon, but until then, I'll take responsibility for her."

Hana stole a look at her husband. She expected to see victory but instead witnessed heartbreak. She closed her eyes, feeling nothing for him and glad for the absence of the extreme pain that was only a breath away. It would come, but thankfully not now. The doctor with wooden lips that turned it into a grimace and looked around him, desperate to leave the awful atmosphere. Hana hadn't finished. "Doctor?"

The man stopped and turned back towards her, dreading whatever it was this woman had the power to unleash. He looked expectant. *And terrified.* "My husband's having an affair with an old girlfriend who turned up yesterday. If I should die unexpectedly, please could you make sure everyone knows I was disposed of? The Du Roses do that, you know. They dispose of their problems and bury them."

The doctor's eyes were as wide as tennis balls in his head and he left quickly after that. Hana saw Logan's jaw drop and it made her want to laugh. He looked stupid.

"Want to come with daddy?" Logan held his arms out to Phoenix and Hana's heart clenched in fear. The denial was on her lips but before it could escape, her daughter did it for her.

"No! Stayin' mummy." The little girl sounded petulant and stubborn and Hana knew deep down it was dreadful to use a child as a weapon. Is *this* what would have happened if Vik had lived? Had she been spared his access visits with Bodie and Izzie and the agonised child-swap in various lay-bys around the Waikato, so that neither of them had to trespass on the other's new life?

Hana tried to regulate her breathing, thinking as much of her new child as her daughter. She knew she should try and reason with Phoenix. After all, the little girl had two parents and surely this would get easier in time. But the energy to argue evaded her. Logan put his arms by his sides and left the room, taking the angry storm of emotion with him.

"You gave us such a scare!" Now the drama was over, Leslie collapsed in tears, needing Alfred to console her. Phoenix curled up on the bed next to Hana and poked her thumb into her mouth, providing a childlike security. She still wore the white riding hat and it dug painfully into Hana's upper arm, but she enjoyed the scent of her daughter, wondering how soon Logan would draw the battle lines for custody of her. He could afford the best solicitors and make Hana appear insane.

She tried to block the thoughts from her mind, aware they only fuelled the stress Doctor Seuli told her to avoid. She ran her hand gently over the growing mound under her ribcage and felt a reassuring kick from inside her stomach wall. The baby was happier now. "That wasn't exactly how I wanted him to find out." Hana couldn't bear to say her husband's name. Leslie shook her head and patted Hana's shoulder.

"Don't think about him now. You've got us."

Hana stayed in the spare room of the upstairs apartment for a few days recovering. Leslie minded Phoenix for her, getting someone else to cover her shifts in the hotel. Alfred disappeared for a few days and when he returned, he and Leslie did a lot of whispering in the kitchen. Hana stayed upstairs, watching out of the long windows towards the boundary fence, feeling again Alfred's anguish over the years he had watched his unfaithful wife make the journey to her lover. "I always knew how that felt." Hana ran her finger down the condensation, leaving a watery trail. "I just never wanted to feel it again."

Hana was driven from the apartment out of desperation, needing to grab a handy change of clothes. She watched her husband's new *wahine* walk around the topiary garden from upstairs and figured she was safe. The code for Logan's bedroom hadn't changed in years and Hana pressed the worn keypad, the numbers long since rubbed away. She turned the handle and found herself in a haze of hairspray and perfume which cloyed and blocked the back of her throat. The contents of a beauty parlour were aligned along the dressing table and the bed was rumpled and unmade. "I bet the maids don't come in here," she commented into the empty room and then remembering why she was there, hurried across to the tall dresser in the corner. The clothes that should have been there were gone. Hana's spare jeans and sweaters had been replaced by silky lingerie and thong underwear with as much substance as dental floss.

"Damn it!" Hana cast around, wondering where her stuff could have been put. Another woman's clothing covered every space which had been Hana's and the woman's heart constricted even tighter. On a whim she opened Logan's drawer, finding his clothes neatly where he left them last time they stayed over. It was pointless being in the room and Hana rubbed her stomach as angst attacked her fragile nerves. Tears rose to the surface at how easily her presence had been expunged and Hana strode over to the door, intending to leave and crawl back up to her attic bedroom.

"What are you doing in *my* room?" The woman's voice was like acid, dripping easily from bright pink lips and her eyes were threatening and unhinged.

"What have you done with my clothes?" Hana asked, aware of the sadness in her voice and the way the other woman's eyes lit up with glee as she tasted victory.

"In the bin." A perfectly manicured hand pointed in the direction of the dustbin and then Hana saw the hem of a denim pants leg poking out. Anger making her body shake, she walked over, spotting a pretty floral top nestled amongst oozing teabags.

"Why would you do that?" she bit, turning in time to see the woman's smirk.

"I figured you wouldn't need them, seeing as I'm sleeping in here with Logan and you're not. I don't like the idea of sharing drawer space with his ex. It's too...gauche."

"I'm not his ex, I'm his wife!"

The woman smiled openly. "That's not what he said last night when he slept here with me. In fact, *he* put your stuff in the bin."

Hana's face paled horribly and she felt the familiar pounding of her pulse coursing through her stomach and smashing against the placenta. Her child deserved better than this dreadful scene. Without a word she left the room, abandoning her ruined clothes in the dustbin. She managed to get to the top of the attic stairs before she broke down, trying hard not to cry loudly and give the woman a few metres below, the satisfaction of knowing she had broken her.

For another day Hana hid, unable to face the thought of emerging at the bottom of the apartment steps and running into Logan's new girlfriend on the landing. Hana convinced herself she was protecting her unborn baby, but knew inwardly that she protected herself. Logan came numerous times to see her, but each time, Leslie sent him away. "Youse don't come near her!" she threatened him. Hana covered her ears so as not to hear his raised reply.

"Have a bath, *kōtiro*," Alfred suggested that evening. "Me and the auld woman's takin' *moko* down for some dinner. Youse enjoy some peace. Leslie has some bath crap somewhere in the cupboard. Use that and freshen yourself up."

They left, taking an eager Phoenix with them, on a promise of chocolate cake. Isolation crowded in on Hana as soon as the bottom door closed. "You look a right mess," she told herself, prodding at the swollen skin around her eyes in the mirror. "No wonder he prefers English Barbie. You're a pregnant blob of tears and snot!"

Hana filled the tin bath tub with bubbles and hot water and soaked until the feeling returned to her bones. It made her rally and find her strength and she sighed and ducked her head fully underneath the water. When she emerged, something unpleasant fell away from her soul and the fog cleared. "You need to go home, Hana," she told herself. "Whether that's to pack up or dig in, it's up to you. But you can't hide here any longer."

Hana sauntered through the apartment wrapped loosely in a fluffy lilac towel. Her washed red hair was piled on her head with another towel and she resembled a turbaned princess. She hummed to herself, a melody from Phoenix's favourite cartoon and she sensed a lightness in her spirit and a renewing of confidence. "God help me," she whispered to herself. "I know you're with me in this, but do you think you could maybe lessen the pain somehow?"

God smiled indulgently and refused.

"So this is your little eyrie, is it? High above the world like the crazy wife in the tower." Her lilting voice made bile rise into Hana's throat and she coughed on it, almost dropping her towel in confusion. The other woman waved a manicured hand at her as Hana grappled with the soft fabric to hide her modesty. "Oh goodness! Don't mind me. I've seen far worse in old peoples' homes, darling. Don't feel you have to hide your wrinkles and faults from me."

Hana took a deep breath and fought the urge to commit murder. There were little more than five years between them and Hana felt every single one stick into her heart. *Thou shalt not kill, thou shalt not kill…except in very special circumstances…no, thou shalt not kill.*

"You're surprisingly fat for your build, aren't you?" The woman waded in with the insults. "Have you tried the gym?"

"I'm…not."

"Oh it's fine, darling. It doesn't matter what shape you are anymore. I have no idea what Logan ever saw in you, but that's what I'm here to let you know. You and he are done. As soon as the divorce is through, we'll be married. I'm prepared to accept Logan's daughter as my own. It'll be good for our son to have a sibling after all these years. It's been hard for Ryan, poor sweetheart. We'll be seeing a solicitor soon and I thought it was only courtesy to warn you. Logan wasn't bothered. He thought the legal documentation would be clear enough, but I'm of the gentler variety. It's only fair really."

Hana's breathing came in short gasps and she remained silent, not through any force of will but because it took all her energy to work her lungs. "Divorce?" she managed.

"Yes, darling. Don't take it hard though. It was fairly inevitable under the circumstances. I'm sure Logan will make sure you're all right financially and perhaps you can see Phoebe a few times a month? I think Logan will work those details out with the legal people."

"Phoebe?" Hana repeated, as though the woman spoke a different language altogether.

"Yes darling. Remember? Your daughter. Goodness! You do have it bad. Is it alcohol or drugs? Or both?"

"Get out!" Hana managed with effort. "Just get out."

"Goodbye darling. All the best." The woman clattered over the floorboards towards the stairs and clumped down them one by one.

With a valiant degree of self-control, Hana succeeded in not rushing after her and giving her an almighty push. But then her wrath found Logan in its sights and by the time Phoenix returned with her grandparents, bearing a bowl of custard and some interesting looking pie for her mother, Hana resembled the crazy lady in the tower in all respects. "I didn't hear her coming," Hana sobbed. "I hate Logan. I hate him."

Despite Leslie's best efforts, she made no sense of Hana's ramblings and whispered fearfully to Alfred in bed hours later, "I think she's going mad like Miriam."

"Can you take me up to the house?" Hana asked Leslie after four days of seclusion. "I need some things."

"If you're sure," the old woman replied.

They drove up in silence with Phoenix singing softly in the back seat of Alfred's old Land Rover.

"Do you think she's been up here...with him?" Hana asked as they pulled up in the driveway.

"No, I don't."

"How do you know?" Hana turned her wide green eyes on Leslie and watched her carefully for the truth.

"Because I've been keepin' an eye on 'em," she said. "I don't think it's what we first thought. They went up to the airport yesterday to get the boy and when they got back, Logan looked fed up of her. He's been working real hard to stay out of her way and at night, he comes back here to sleep. *Alone.* She can't get up here without a ride. She don't drive. She arrived at the hotel in one of them shuttle things from the airport."

"Does the boy look like him?" Hana asked distracted. She winced at Leslie's answer.

"He's definitely a Du Rose, my love. I'm sorry."

Hana lay her head back against the headrest and tried to run her hands through her hair, her fingers snagging in the red curls. "I don't know what to do," she sighed. "I think I want to stay up here because then I don't have to run into his fancy woman. But *then* I have to share a house with *him* and I don't want that either. I can go to Bodie's place but I don't think I can cope with explaining it all. Bodie will just love this. I can hear him now telling me how he warned me what a loose cannon Logan was and how he could have told me how it would all end. What is it about me, Leslie? How can I get things so wrong?"

Leslie stroked a tendril of hair out of Hana's face, her eyes sending love into the poor woman's tortured soul. "I don't think he's slept with her. *Sylvia*, she calls herself. I think she wants him to but I don't think he has. I judged him and now I've taken a step back, I feel sure it was all one-sided."

Hana shrugged. "I don't know if I care anymore. When I reach for the place in my heart that Logan used to occupy, it's empty. It's like a jewellery box that's been raided, all the precious things taken away and just the crap left hanging over the sides waiting for someone to throw it out. I cooked him a special dinner and got dressed up like a fool to tell him about the baby, only to have him treat me like dirt when he got home. Then he humiliated me in the stable yard. How could he let me find out about her with everyone watching?"

Hana ran a shaking hand over her face. She'd been down this road far too often. It led to nowhere but a shredded glass path with barbed wire handrails.

"Let's get you settled, then you might know what you wanna do." Leslie's face was full of compassion and Hana was grateful for her presence.

Hana decided to lay claim to the master bedroom. She wasn't going to be able to keep her blood pressure down if her night on the sofa was anything to go by. She and Leslie spent the afternoon moving Logan's things out and the busyness of the activity stemmed the pain at what Hana was actually doing. They took the drawers through one by one and then Leslie carried the cupboards. The little family had moved into the house three months ago, returning from Europe and greeting their new life with enthusiasm and hope. The two spare bedrooms remained empty of furniture and Hana put Logan in the room furthest from hers. She told herself she didn't care if he had to sleep on the floor, but inwardly worried she was simply driving him further into the other woman's arms. "The bedroom door's got a lock on it," she told Leslie, "so I'll be safe. But I don't want Phoenix out there on her own. I want to move the cot in with me."

"I think you're taking things a bit far," the old lady chided her. "He's not going to hurt you or my *moko*. He wouldn't!"

Hana shrugged and insisted. The wooden cot was purpose built so that the sides could be taken off and allow it to convert into a small single bed. It was too heavy and Leslie couldn't lift it on her own. She went into the hallway with her cell phone and made a call. Hana realised her phone was probably in one of the carrier bags Leslie had bought up from the hotel. The battery would be flat for sure by now and she didn't know if the phone mast had been fixed. Staying at the house and unable to summon help suddenly seemed like a foolish idea.

Twenty minutes later there was a knock at the front door and Leslie dropped her pillowcase and waddled off to open it. "That'll be Flick," she called over her shoulder.

"Pardon?" Hana carried on changing the sheets on the king size four poster bed, resisting the disgusting urge to sniff them for evidence of the blonde woman's perfume. When she turned abruptly at a noise in the doorway, Robert Dressler leaned against the wooden frame watching her. He had removed his boots, revealing a hole in his sock and his jeans were covered in some kind of engine oil. His mousy fringe hung in his eyes, his rampant beard shaved back to designer stubble. His blue eyes studied Hana as she fiddled with the edge of the duvet, trying to fit the awkward poppers together to close it. His pink lips curled back in a half smile and he winked at Hana lazily.

"Don't look at me like that, Bobby," she warned the man, resisting the urge to cry under his kindness. Hana heard him sniff and couldn't help herself, glancing in his direction only to find him stood at her elbow. His hands were coarse and rough as he snagged the duvet cover and tugged it free from her fingers. Then he took her in his arms and bent his tall body around her, shielding her from the world for just a moment.

"You don't need my pity," he whispered into her hair, "you're better than that."

Hana cried softly into the tough fabric of his shirt, not understanding anymore why tears appeared without warning. Bobby held her and Hana felt his love flowing into her bones. Once, it was his mission to harm her and he had been good at it, wreaking an awful kind of havoc into her life without caring. His penance now was to love her from a distance and watch her trying to make a life with her husband. That was his self-imposed punishment. Hana sighed, no longer having the energy to take responsibility for another's suffering. "Just say the word and I'll drop the bastard over a cliff," he muttered into her curls, kissing the side of her head.

Hana laughed and he swore, "I'm not soddin' joking."

For some reason it seemed inappropriately funny and Hana struggled to hold in her mirth. It felt good to laugh. Gently she extracted herself from his grasp, not wanting to unfairly lead him on. The man was besotted and stayed at the farm because of her. A fugitive, he was in hiding from the cops but that was old news. Hana's policeman-son had told his mother Flick was of little interest nowadays, his warrant a long way down on the list of police priorities. They were overworked and underpaid. If he got picked up, it would be pure bad luck.

Hana sat down on the bed and looked around her. The room looked oddly strange with only one bedside cabinet and tallboy. It seemed unbalanced; like her marriage. Leslie clattered away down the hall, sliding the drawers back into place in Logan's new room. Bobby sat his backside down on the expensive sheets after running a hand over the seat of his jeans to ensure they were clean. "Not too bad," he said, inspecting his hand. Hana smiled at him.

"You set out to kill me and yet you're the only person who's made me smile in days. *Twice.*"

"It's my sparkling personality. Besides, I'm done making you cry."

The moment felt intense and Hana felt his gaze fixed on her, wanting more than she was able to give. Hana bit her lip. "Please would you be able to help Leslie carry Phoe's stuff in here...before..."

"Before he gets home?" Bobby finished the sentence for her, reaching across and taking her fingers in his. His hands were warm and infused Hana with a sense of comfort and well-being. She tasted danger in the back of her throat. "Why did you come back up here?" his voice was low and husky.

"I have nowhere else to go." Hana's admission invoked a stab of pain. "I have high blood pressure in a high risk pregnancy. I'm not allowed to fly to see Izzie, Bodie will enjoy my misery far too much and I don't have the energy to run around looking for alternatives right now."

"Fair enough." He caressed her fingers softly. Then he let go as the sound of Leslie clumping down the hallway reached their ears. "Just tell me where you want stuff."

Sweating and swearing, Leslie and Bobby hefted the heavy wooden cot down the hallway and got it stuck in the bedroom door. Hana laughed at them until she cried and almost peed her pants. It was too wide for the bend just before the master bedroom and couldn't be turned on its side owing to the rails. They were forced to back down the hallway with Phoenix sat in the cot like an Indian princess committing suttee. Leslie kicked it as they put it back where they started. Phoenix scaled the cot sides like a monkey, rendering them pointless.

"Tama taught her to do that," Hana sighed. "Idiot boy."

"Want me to take it apart?" Bobby asked and Hana wondered whether he meant with a screw driver or his fists. The latter looked probable.

"No, thanks. She can just sleep with me," Hana said, feeling apologetic. "Look, we'll be fine. You both go back now."

Darkness shrouded them as Leslie hugged Hana on the front porch. Bobby chased his cowboy boots around the floor for a moment and then pressed his lips to Hana's forehead with revealing tenderness. Leslie's face was comical as it registered shock and then understanding. Hana knew where the old woman's brain ran with it, but was too exhausted to reassure her.

They left Hana to her torturous thoughts and went their respective ways with hearts separately laden with misgiving.

"Hana?" Logan's voice sounded hopeful as he came into the kitchen and found her sat in the light from the open microwave, picking at the crust on a frozen steak pie. It seemed like a good idea but her appetite left her as soon as it emerged from the microwave, wrinkled and sweaty instead of crusty and lush. "Hana, can we talk? Please?" Logan sounded desperate and Hana battled with a sense of victory, that somehow things hadn't all gone his way.

"No," she replied. "I don't want to speak to you. Stay away from me." She made the mistake of looking at him, seeing his inner agony and feeling it attack her resolve. It made her harder than she needed to be. "Just think of me as a...flatmate really. We just share airspace until I'm well enough to get the hell out of here. Then we can talk through a solicitor."

Logan looked at her in confusion. "But I've done nothing wrong. I haven't been unfaithful, I haven't..."

"Well you certainly looked it! Strutting around your property with Cosmopolitan Barbie on your arm, snogging your face off at every opportunity. Am I meant to be ok with that or something? I mean, she's in the bedroom we usually use so what am I supposed to think?"

"You're not leaving me and you are definitely not taking Phoe!" Logan's voice had an edge of steel and Hana cringed visibly.

"You can't stop me."

Logan's voice was cold and hard, "I can and I will. If you hate me that much and feel you really have to go, then go." Hana turned to look at him, sensing the rising threat. "But once you set foot off this property, you forfeit all rights to our daughter for good. You will never see her again."

Hana felt sickness rise into her gullet and the baby pushed awkwardly into her back. Fear and dread snaked wicked fingers over her heart at the thought of losing her daughter. Tama's mother, Aroha, was never permitted back to claim her son and it destroyed her life. *And his.* Tama didn't understand how going against the Du Roses, had been impossible for the teenage girl two decades ago.

Hana scraped the wasted pie angrily into the dustbin and clanged her crockery into the dishwasher with shaking fingers. Opening the fridge to retrieve milk for a cup of tea she spotted the dinner she made for Logan a lifetime ago, to celebrate their new baby. The few small bites of pie continued to curdle in her guts and rage added itself to the gnawing ache in her stomach. "Oh, guess what?" she started, seizing hold of the platters and thumping them onto the centre island. She stripped off the plastic wrap, seeing how the beautifully cooked food had crinkled at the edges in the days since. "Here's that gorgeous meal I cooked you to celebrate our new child. I wish you'd seen it, it was perfect. Look," she held up the steak, dripping marinade onto the counter. "Miriam's special recipe from out of my head. Just for you. She would be so proud of you, Logan. Such a credit to her aren't you? An adulterer like your mother and a bully like your *real* father. I bet they're counting down the days until you join them. *In Hell!*"

In anger Hana flung the steak at her husband, feeling a sense of satisfaction as he put his arm up to prevent the accurate shot from hitting him in the face. The marinade smeared down his sleeve and the steak fell to the floor with a *splat*.

"Don't forget to eat your veggies," Hana said in a sing-song voice and threw the platter at him. It was a skilled underarm shot that flew like a slow Frisbee. Logan managed to catch the plate with his excellent reactions but the veggies stayed airborne, flying off the fairground ride and smashing into his body. Orange pumpkin and red kumara mixed with yellow grease and slipped down his shirt, landing unceremoniously on the tiled floor. Hana wanted to add the perfectly beaten mashed potato to the casserole on her husband but resisted. He looked like a pressure cooker about to blow a valve.

"I'd probably throw that shirt away," Hana said, injecting an eerie calm into her voice. "You shouldn't find that too hard to do. You're better at throwing things away than I ever gave you credit for."

She left the room with catwalk precision and dignity, denying Logan his retort and leaving him with a mess that would offend his neat-freak tendency enough to allow her to get to sleep. But not everything was destined to go Hana's way. She had put Phoenix to bed in the four poster in the master bedroom but once down there, Hana was alarmed to find her gone. The little girl had climbed out and taken herself back to where she felt she belonged, scaling the cot sides and putting herself to bed.

Denied her final victory, Hana was unable to shut and lock the bedroom door like she planned. Instead she was forced to leave it ajar in case Phoenix needed her. She lay down on the familiar mattress, relieved at the scent of freshly laundered sheets. She heard Logan come and stand outside the door, seeing his outline in the light from the hallway. He stood there for a long while and eventually Hana fell asleep, too tired to cry or even think straight.

Chapter 10

Hana always hated arguing with Logan. He was stubborn and resolute once he made his mind up and it was like disputing with a power pole. It drove Hana into displaying unreasonably childish behaviour out of sheer frustration and that in turn, made her angry with herself. His words came back to her in the darkness, *"Once you set foot off this property, you forfeit all rights to our daughter for good. You will never see her again."*

It was the sense of futility washing over her as she lay in the elegant four poster bed alone, that disturbed the woman's sleep. It carried her into dreams in which she was powerless to change any of the terrifying circumstances embodied in the mortifying illusions. Believing her daughter was lost without trace in a strangely familiar English seaside town, the poor woman sat up in bed, her heart pounding like a jack-hammer in her breast. Her nightdress stuck uncomfortably to Hana's body, the sweat cooling as she pulled the fabric away from her clammy skin. Her hair was damp and twisted through her clothes and once freed from inside the collar, it hung lankly down her back to the waist.

Pushing back the restrictive duvet, Hana climbed out of bed feeling the chill air on her bare feet and legs. Logan's side of the bed was cold and empty and his absence exacerbated the brick lodged in her chest. Hana wondered if he was on the sofa or down at the hotel with his other woman. A sob caught in Hana's throat as the hopelessness of her situation hit home again. Already on the verge of tears it was the catalyst to send her plunging over the edge into despair and she shuffled around the end of the bed in the darkness, seeking the comfort of the ensuite and copious amounts of toilet paper.

The overhead light was harsh and revealed to Hana a sad, tired face peering back at her in the mirror. She used the toilet and then sat on the closed seat trying not to look at her reflection, avoiding the obvious wrinkles in her pale skin or the puffy eyes from where she had spent the last three nights crying herself to sleep. Hana slumped on the hard plastic seat and rubbed her eyes, feeling the pummelling of little feet under the skin of her blossoming bump. She blew her nose on a wad of tissue, trying to contain the miserable howl that threatened to escape from deep inside her breast and wake up the mountain. Hana's insides felt empty, the emotions of her awful dream resonating in real life and her own powerlessness creating monsters in her imagination.

It felt as though Hana sat in the ensuite and cried for hours. She was exhausted and drained by the time the tears abated enough for her to move her aching body off its ungainly perch. Her legs tingled from inactivity and her baby did somersaults like a professional kick boxer, objecting violently to the constricted position. Hana's breath hitched in her lungs and she was light headed, her blood pressure dangerously spiked from her angst. With sobs still occasionally escaping with involuntary shudders, Hana padded down the long hallway to the kitchen in search of a cup of hot tea to calm her down and help with the evasive good night's sleep.

The darkness through the glass of the front door looked black and forbidding, reminding Hana of her isolation and enhancing her sense of despair. She pottered around filling the kettle and fetching her favourite mug, trying not to clank and disturb Logan *if he was even there*. The frequent convulsing of her recovering lungs caused her to spill the milk, the spasm coming at the wrong moment and Hana sighed in frustration. She turned to reach for the dishcloth, working by the light of the halogen spotlight over the hob and jumped in fright as she found Logan standing quietly behind her, leaning his boxer short clad backside on the centre island.

Their eyes locked and another redundant sob hitched in Hana's chest, making her appear like a small, vulnerable child that has cried itself into a tizz. "Hana," Logan's voice was soft, caressing and addictive, washing over his wife's psyche like a balm. Frozen on the spot, her body betrayed her with another shuddering breath and Logan risked a step towards her.

Hana smelled the aftermath of his shower in the large family bathroom down the hall, the masculine scent filling her nostrils with pleasant memories. The black tattoo on his upper arm cast a dark shadow over his skin, twisting and turning as it wound his genealogy over his flesh, Hana's own name acting as the italic border at the bottom of his bicep. Soft, downy skin called to her, tantalising her with the knowledge of how it felt under her fingers and Hana sensed the baby still, as a familiar feeling pushed down from her navel. Loving Logan Du Rose was like riding on a swing far too high with her eyes closed, sick-making and exhilarating. "I hate you!" Her voice sounded childish and petulant.

Logan took another step towards her, manipulating and winning her over like he did the fillies in the arena, where he free lunged them before bending them to his will. "No you don't." His breath caressed Hana's cheek as he dipped his head and kissed her neck. His fingers slipped underneath the shirt and slid gently up her flesh, coaxing and controlling. In that moment, Hana knew it wasn't a cup of tea which would soothe her aching soul. Logan's fingers were gentle and full of promise as they travelled slowly across her rounded belly and Hana tensed as they moved into the waistband of her embarrassingly tatty, comfort underwear. Logan was skilled and persuasive and

Hana's resolve fell like a line of dominoes, cascading into her finely balanced good sense and self-respect and knocking them all to the ground. As Logan lay on top of her in the huge bed, his grey eyes locked on hers with a frightening intensity, Hana knew it was a big mistake. She tried to use thoughts of the blonde Englishwoman and her thieving lips on Logan's cheek, to still her increasing sense of passion but it was futile. Her body shuddered under her husband's touch and there wasn't a thing she could do about it.

Logan was gone by the time Hana woke up, but at least his side of the bed looked as though it had been slept in for once. She snaked a foot tentatively across the mattress, feeling a slight warmth which told her he hadn't been gone long and Hana sought comfort from their temporary nearness. The skylights at the end of the room either side of the apex ceiling channelled a dull, grey wintry light, adding to Hana's sadness. She was tempted to pull the swags of cloth around the four poster bed and spend the day hiding, but couldn't be bothered to move and get cold outside of the covers.

The buttons on her nightie gaped from bottom to top, testament to her husband's reluctance to talk at all, but he had demonstrated he still loved her without words. Hana's fingers were clumsy as she fixed the shirt closed, pushing away the spectre of Sylvia with her perfectly straight blonde hair and her amazing figure. Hana knew Logan had left early to check on the calving and relieve the overnight workers, but still the fear persisted that he had gone for an early morning tryst with the mother of his love-child. By the time the final button was slipped into its slot in the fabric, Hana's unease had returned and she realised with a sickening sadness that nothing had changed. The other woman and her offspring still challenged everything in Hana's life, bringing a frightening precariousness to tinge and shape her fate. Logan had left his wife up on the mountain again, a prisoner until she complied with his wishes and succumbed to his authority. He would not let her run to safety and clear her head, not with his tiny daughter in tow. *Not again.*

"Mama," the voice came from the end of the bed. She sat up to greet the small, perplexed face at her side.

"Hey baby," Hana held out her arms and Phoenix used the duvet to clamber awkwardly into the bed and under the covers, her delicately framed body freezing cold. "How did you get out of your cot?"

"I climbin' out. Tama done it."

"Oh yes. I must remember to thank him next time he's home." The sarcasm was wasted on the child who adored the muscular twenty year old male with a passion. At eighteen, the boy had been a loose cannon, directionless and without focus, quitting school after a torrid affair with a female staff member. His relationship with his uncle's new wife had turned from hate to love as Hana recognised the need for boundaries and continuity in him and offered him security. Michael's illegitimate son had bound himself to Logan and Hana, allowing them to parent him and stepping into adulthood with the intention of making them proud. Until he got with Phoenix and then he was a delightful idiot. "I wonder how he's going to take all this," Hana said out loud. "He'll think he's a jinx. Every parent figure he aligns himself to, seems to bust up their marriage and cut him loose. Poor kid."

"Porky," Phoenix sighed around her thumb.

"That's not actually what I said, but it doesn't matter." Hana snuggled her daughter tightly into her, feeling her chilled little body thaw out. As she ran her hands down the child's pyjamas she made contact with the bulging nappy, in a fragile state of disrepair. Phoenix put her legs over Hana's thighs, resting her feet on her mother's flesh. They were like blocks of ice. "What have you been doing?" Hana asked into the mop of black curls.

"Playin'. Daddy's gone work wiv baby calfies aye?"

Hana nodded but daren't trust herself to speak. *She fervently hoped so.* She smoothed the soft hair back from her daughter's face and kissed the downy forehead. Phoenix giggled. "What?" Hana asked, curious.

"Pardon!"

Hana laughed, "No, I mean *what* are you laughing at?"

Phoenix sniggered again. "That boy. Kickin' me."

Hana smiled with wonderment at the insight of her little girl. She might be right. Hana sensed she carried this child so differently to Phoenix. He hadn't made her half as sick as her girls but was far more energetic. Her mind went back in time to her first pregnancy. A terrified eighteen year old, Hana was oblivious to her condition until the pregnancy was well into its second trimester; like this time. Pathetic, lacklustre spotting fooled her into counting false periods and she quailed as she remembered having to tell her Indian boyfriend the distressing news.

Vik wore a turban that day and a vibrant robe having returned on the train from a Sikh gathering in London. He looked strange standing in the scruffy bedsit in all his finery, like a sparkling diamond on a landfill. Hana shook with fear, her puppy fat appearing suddenly obvious to the dense teens, destroying their combined worlds in its increasing girth. Vik was livid and then subdued, his visit to the affluent family of his betrothed paling into insignificance against the weight of Hana's revelation. His family subsequently extracted him from the contract with much wailing and gnashing of teeth. Somehow, it ended up as Hana's fault as the years progressed, as though she had gotten pregnant with Bodie all by herself.

"More bruvvers," Phoenix sighed and popped her thumb in her mouth. Her toes twinkled icily on Hana's thigh.

"Sorry," Hana yawned. Bodie was a policeman, stormy and unpredictable like his father. He regarded Phoenix in a hair-ruffling kind of way. At twenty-eight, her presence embarrassed him. Phoenix held more affection for his six year old son, Jas, who spent hours trying to teach her the skills most valuable to him; kick boxing and commando crawling. Phoenix learned patiently and without guile, eager to please her good-natured nephew, roughhousing and tussling with him as though she was more than nineteen months old. She never cried when he accidentally hurt her and put up with his bone crunching hugs of apology. She recently administered a decent poke in the eye and a bloody nose, earning her a promotion in his imaginary army, to major, first class.

"You hungry?" Hana asked, hoping that the bulging, urine filled nappy would hold a minute longer while she enjoyed the proximity of her daughter.

"Yep," Phoenix answered, but didn't bounce up or wriggle, happy to stay cuddling.

A knock on the bedroom door made Hana's heart skip, wondering if Logan had returned to talk to her. *Why would he knock on his own bedroom door, idiot?* By the time Leslie's face appeared next to the furthest wooden post of the bed, another disappointment had been filed in the misery folder of Hana's mind.

"Logan sent me up." The old woman smiled down on mother and daughter with fondness, auburn hair mixing with black on the pillow. Hana looked away, hiding her anger poorly. So, she was still a prisoner of her husband's insecurities and archaic world view.

"Get in, Nonie," Phoenix swung her arm behind her and patted the bed without breaking bodily contact with her warm mother.

"How about I make you some breakfast?" Leslie changed the subject, seeing the stiffness of Hana's body. "It'll be all right, Hana," she said softly, "they're only on holiday. She'll be gone soon."

"Will she?" Hana responded, the bile from her heart spilling out of her mouth. "I think she's in for the long haul personally. It will be me who goes first."

"Your husband dunt want that," Leslie began, her placation drowned out by Hana cutting across the rest of her sentence.

"He can't stop me!"

"Well, he can today actually." Leslie looked guilty. "He's taken the truck and says you have to stay up here and rest.

"So, I'm confined to barracks, am I? So he can have his cake and eat it. Stupid, dumb wife!"

"Dupid, stumb rife," Phoenix repeated, speaking awkwardly around her thumb and Hana knew she needed to be quiet. "Cake for Phoe?"

Leslie held her arms out to the child and Hana's heart quailed as even her daughter abandoned her, in exchange for a clean nappy and some toast, even if she mistakenly believed it would be cake.

"Leslie, yesterday you were on my side, helping me move all Logan's stuff out of here. How come today you're doing his dirty work?"

Leslie shifted her feet awkwardly and Hana watched Phoenix give a little shudder as she did another lazy wee in the already bursting nappy. She looked across at her mother and gave her a sly smile.

"Alfie went up north to his father's *whānau*. We was gonna move there when Mr Fancypants threw us out. But then he came to see Alfie yesterday and they talked. My Alfie says Logan Du Rose is a broken man. He wants us to stick around here for a bit."

"And that includes being my jailer," Hana retorted. "Well, thanks so much for that!"

Leslie took a step towards the bed and Hana's cross body. "Don't you accuse me of back-stabbing my girl! Last night you're all determined that the marriage is over and this morning, you lie there in that bed spouting your rights with bloody great hickeys all over your neck! Ain't me what's the hypocrite, girlie. Take a look in the mirror."

Hana went for a hot shower, mortified at the awful love bites Logan had given her. Thankfully most of them decorated her right collar bone but one had been carefully placed on the delicate flesh behind her ear. "You are such a pushover!" Hana grumbled to her reflection, getting only a heightened blush to her cheekbones as she dwelt on the activities of the night. Perhaps it wouldn't have been so bad if it had only been the once.

Hana dressed in a scruffy grey sweatshirt and some tracksuit pants. There didn't seem much point caring about her appearance, so she opted for comfort instead. Leslie put her head round the bedroom door just as Hana hauled the top over her full breasts and struggled with the hood, which turned inside out. Leslie dealt with Hana as though she was a child, righting the hood and helping it slide down over her bump. She rested her wrinkled, work-worn hands over the rounded stomach. "What are you and him doing to each other?" Her voice sounded gentle and reassuring. "You need each other right now."

"Logan doesn't need me, I'm just his baby factory."

Leslie looked astounded. "He never said that!"

Hana looked down at the ground. He hadn't said that at all. But he may as well have. He said she could leave but not take Phoenix. He couldn't have been much clearer. Leslie visibly considered comforting Hana, but the woman was prickly as a hedgehog and she thought better of it, carefully withdrawing her hands.

"I'm lookin' after Nev's wee boy this morning. Logan said I could fetch Phoe and take her down to play with him. He gets bored with just me and Alfie, but he likes her."

Hana's eyebrows drew together as she frowned. "You can't take her. I don't want to be up here on my own."

"You come then," Leslie offered. "A change of scenery will do you good. Everyone's been asking after you."

Hana hesitated, but then the image of Sylvia's carefully made-up face misted into view, looking down her nose at a flustered Hana with her messy curls and raggedy old clothes. "No," she replied rudely, shaking her head. "Logan said I have to stay here, so I'll stay here." Hana managed to greet her dressed daughter with a smile. Leslie had fed and changed her so all that remained for Hana to do, was fit her into her little coat and settle her into the car seat in the back of the Land Rover.

"I hate you!" Hana railed against her husband's cunning as the vehicle disappeared from view. The only vehicle left in the garage was his motorbike and he knew Hana wouldn't try to escape on that. She was trapped. As the truck left the property, Hana raised her hand sadly in the air, her heart broken by the sight of her daughter obliviously waving to her with a wet thumb. Turning back to the luxurious but empty house, Hana found herself in tears again.

The sight of a cigarette butt lying next to the front door brought her up sharp. Rules about smoking on the entire property were harsh and strictly enforced and as the nearest supplier was a decent drive away, many of the stockmen had either never started smoking or just given up. Hana stared at the offending item feeling perplexed. "That's weird." Not wanting Phoenix to pick it up, she fetched a piece of kitchen roll and used it to put the butt in the plant pot by the front door. Her shoes were dirty and she promised herself that she would go in and get rid of it later. The discovery was unsettling as it meant that a stranger had been to the house, possibly during her sojourn with Leslie and Alfred.

The deck ran around the full circumference of the house and Hana traversed it, her footsteps echoing on the dry wood. Hana counted ten cigarette ends littered around the property and an area by the lounge, where someone had stood for a long while, leaving a flattened area of scrubby grass. Sacha's footsteps had cut deeply across the small disturbed patch, proving that the visitor had come before Hana's failed attempt at dinner with her husband. Hana worried at the edge of her thumbnail and felt uneasy. She recalled the sensation of being watched and her skin prickled uncomfortably on the back of her neck. Odd things had been happening for a while around the hotel, but recent acts of vandalism centred on her and Logan. The window smashed in Hana's face was preceded by myriad other things, too many to name. But the day before the window incident, the house mysteriously ran dry of water. Logan discovered an outside tap left on just a little, draining the water tank over a series of days. It was easily fixed and Phoenix got the blame.

"She might have fiddled around when she played outside on her tricycle. Maybe watch her next time," Logan concluded.

"I was watching her!" Hana argued. "What do you think I was doing?"

"Fine then, Hana! But there's no other explanation unless..."

"Unless what?"

"Nothing. It's ok." Logan spent an hour fitting locks to the taps, switched the water source to draw from a nearby stream and eventually torrential rain replenished the water tank, but it was irritating and time consuming during a really busy period on the farm.

"But I was with her all the time," Hana had protested, yet there seemed no other explanation. Things had gone missing or got broken, with Logan eager to blame it on the wind blowing things away or smashing plant pots. Hana wondered now. Maybe they were targets for deliberate mischief. She shivered despite the sunshine and walked quickly back to the front of the house.

As she slammed the front door deliberately hard, a fat envelope caught the breeze and flew off the hall table, too heavy to flutter. It plopped onto the wooden floor with a thud. Hana picked it up, recognising her son's scrawled handwriting on the front. It hadn't been opened, which surprised her. Maybe Logan wasn't quite taking things to the extreme just yet.

"Most prisoners usually have their mail screened," Hana spoke into the empty house. "It must be my lucky day." She sneered, gulping as the hall mirror reflected her ghoulish expression back at her. Logan knew Bodie's writing and teased him about his spelling. He wouldn't be bothered about a letter from her son reaching Hana.

She turned the envelope over in her hands and stared at her cell phone. No signal. *What would she have said anyway?* "Hey Bo, you were right all along about Logan. He's moved his mistress and love-child into the hotel and won't let me leave unless I agree to give him full custody of Phoenix." She said the words out loud and stifled a sob with her hand as she heard them spoken. Bodie would either think she was insane, or crow about having tried hard to warn her when she ignored him, *which she had.*

The package was sellotaped up, the back fold of the envelope barely containing the bulging contents. Inside were four white envelopes, bent and ragged as though they had knocked around for some time. The words *Waikato District Health Board* were emblazoned on each of them. A hastily scribbled note in Amy's handwriting declared,

'Sorry for the delay, Hana. Bo kept saying he'd forward these on to you but I just found them in his work trousers. Jas is fine but missing you and Hope is cutting teeth so is permanently miserable. We haven't heard from you for a while, so hope all is well? Love Amy.'

Hana fondled the note in trembling fingers. It felt like a lifeline. Amy hoped that everything was ok, but it wasn't, was it? She bit her lip and moved on to the curled and folded letters. She had missed three scan appointments. *Great!* That's what she got for lying to the doctors and pretending she still lived at Culver's Cottage. One of the letters contained a snotty note from an admin, warning Hana that if she failed to attend this next scan date, she would not be offered another and would have to go back to her GP and start again. Hana raked the letter for a date and time, her eyes widening as she found them in bold down near the bottom. It was today, at midday.

In the garage, she eyed her only remaining mode of transport. The huge Ninja motorcycle seemed to cringe at her inexperienced touch, probably remembering she had only ever been on the back of it for a handful of terrifying pillion rides. Even then, she leant the wrong way on a bend and almost pulled Logan off. Hana fingered the handlebars and wondered if it would matter if she stayed in first gear for an hour and a half, or at least until she worked out how to change it. Logan had bought her a new helmet the previous year and she fitted it onto her head, struggling to poke her fingers through the visor hole to bend her ears back up again. Trying to cock her leg over the seat, she noticed she still wore her slippers and went over to the shoe cupboard to find her trainers. The helmet was heavy and overbalanced her as she fought with her laces and she stunned herself nutting the cupboard. Her belly seemed to get in the way of everything, as though the child was in league with its father. Frustrated, Hana laid on her back on the concrete floor and pushed her laces into the top of her shoes, unable to do them up.

Another go at getting on the bike would have been humorous in other circumstances, but Hana grew hotter and more frustrated by the minute. Her legs were too short and she couldn't touch the ground with both feet at the same time. She would be fine on the motorway but might have to get off and push it through Hamilton as she would be unable to put her feet down at traffic lights. Gingerly turning the ignition key, Hana felt the bike give a low throaty roar and surge slightly but it didn't move forward. She inspected the marks on the handle, wondering if bikes had a neutral gear and then realised it was still on its stand. *Did Logan start it on the stand or off?*

The whole thing descended into ridiculousness as Hana couldn't work out how to get the bike off its stand. It didn't look complicated, but pushing and huffing had no effect and she was forced to tramp through the house in her trainers to go to the toilet again. Back in the garage she regarded the machine haughtily. "I'm wasting time!" She stamped her foot. The bike remained loyally rigid to its master, like everything else in the Du Rose domain. With a show of temper, Hana stood behind it and kicked the back wheel, releasing her pent up aggression. The bike gave a click and groan before rolling forward, the stand pinging up neatly into its undercarriage as it propelled itself forward into a pile of packing boxes. There was a sickening crunch as the heavy machine crushed the contents of the brown containers and buried itself nose first into a shelving unit. Guilt stricken, Hana turned the key to 'off' and left it lying on its side in the mess it had made, locking the front door quickly behind her as she bolted down the mountain on foot.

Chapter 11

"**B**obby, I need your help."

The blond man turned at the uncharacteristic use of his first name. He was in the process of fixing a metal plate onto the old tractor in the workshop near the stables. "Hey Miss," he said and eyed the redhead with wary anticipation. Hana stood slightly to his right, wringing her hands together and panicking. She breathed hard from the hour and a quarter walk down the steep driveway and her thighs and calf muscles complained from the exertion.

"I don't have anyone else I can ask," she began and Flick moved out of his crouch position next to the machine and stood up, rubbing the backs of his knees. Seeing the state of Hana, his face softened and he took a step towards her. "What have you been doing? You look like crap!"

"Just walking. It's a long way down and...Logan won't let me have the car anymore. In case I..." Hana couldn't finish the sentence. "I have to stay here now. *Forever*." She glanced nervously back at the hotel. "Please help me?"

Flick came forward wiping his oily hands on a dirty blue rag. He looked rugged but far healthier than he had almost two years ago. Hana noticed that his stubble had become streaked with grey, disguising a face he said was still on the 'wanted' list and his hair was longer, obscuring much of the top half of his face. He flicked his fringe out of the way of striking blue eyes, filled with compassion and poorly disguised love. "What do you need?"

The man held Hana's gaze, his heart wide open for her to see and she gulped, realising the unfairness of her request. *Of course he would do anything for me. He spends his whole existence trying to pay me back for the wrong he did.* Somewhere along the line, Hana's easy forgiveness of Flick had muddied the waters and produced a mutual admiration. Only his had turned to the most painful kind of love. Hana saw it in his face again, the same as last night; the agony of self-denial and felt crushed for him.

Reaching out, she touched his arm, sensing him react as though she had shot an electrical current through him. "I'm sorry. I had no right to ask. You've already done more than enough for me." Defeated, she turned away.

"No." Hana felt his hand on her arm, gentle but firm as he prevented her leaving, as though even this slight contact was better than nothing. "Please. Let me help you. I told you last night that I was here for you. I meant it. "

Desperate, Hana conceded, "I need a vehicle."

It felt wrong driving away from the hotel knowing Phoenix was still there. It created a sickness in the pit of Hana's stomach that was so vile, she feared she might throw up. Tama's mother, Aroha left Kane Du Rose when her son was only a year old, unable to bear her partner's violence against her any longer. Kane couldn't have cared less about the baby boy, knowing his birth father was from the wrong side of the stricken family but Reuben Du Rose, having already lost Logan to his own brother, would not let Tama go when Aroha plucked up the courage to return for him. It was a mess of epic proportions, which resulted in Tama receiving the most miserable childhood imaginable and Aroha being denied her son permanently. The damage between Aroha and Tama had never been repaired, despite her recent relationship with Michael, his real father and their subsequent new daughter.

"I can't do it, I can't leave Phoe," Hana leaned her head against the side window and closed her eyes. "Stop the car!"

'Once you set foot off this property, you forfeit all rights to our daughter for good. You will never see her again.'

"Too late." Flick cleared the front gates and the old red Jeep laboured up the driveway and headed for the mountain pass. "I've nicked this thing from Jack, so I'm already in for a kicking. It might as well be for something worth doing."

"But I've left my baby," Hana wept, screwing her face up and wiping her eyes on the back of her hand. The phrase *out of the frying pan and into the fire* sprung to mind. "What if Logan won't let me back in? What if he sends me away like Reuben did to Aroha?"

Flick drove one handed, reaching across with his left to seize Hana's flailing fingers. His hands were warm and comforting and she stopped her thrashing. "This is totally different, Hana. You're not thinking straight. You're not a prisoner and Logan won't stop you going back onto the property. He just doesn't want you to leave him and doesn't know how else to stop you. Can't you see that? He loves you but he's reasoned in that stubborn head of his that if he's going to lose you, he's not losing his daughter as well."

"If you love someone, you're supposed to let them go," Hana sniffed. "Not trap them."

"Not in this family, love," Flick laughed. "Reuben let Logan's mother go and look where that got him. Watching his own son brought up over the fence by his brother his whole life and never able to talk to him, or pick him up when he fell down or teach him stuff. Logan doesn't want that for your wee girl. He'll never let another man bring up his kids." Flick squeezed her hand and then put both of his back on the steering wheel to make the turn out of the driveway and onto the main road. "But you must have known that when you married him."

"I didn't know what a mess this stupid family was," Hana sulked and Flick glanced sideways and smiled at her.

"You'll be fine," he said. "You've got enough spirit to see you out. Besides, if you really want out of here, I'll get you out. You and the wee girl as well. I'll make sure he never finds you."

Hana began to calm down as they left the mountain and its occupants behind her, but the emotional umbilical cord stretched between her and Phoenix like a gossamer thread and she ached for her daughter. Bobby's words brought some comfort though. She didn't doubt that secretly, he was a single-handed match for the Du Roses. She tried to distract herself by talking to him. The man was uncommunicative to everyone else on the property, preferring to keep to himself but with Hana, he talked openly. "Yeah I miss my boys. Little shits both of them though."

"Do you wish you could see them?" Hana asked, wondering if it felt as painful for him, as her absence from Phoenix did.

"Course," he answered. "But I'm meant to stay up at the ranch and not come to town, so that's that really. It's no good telling them where I am because trouble will follow them up there and I'll end up arrested, knowing them pair. Both of them have big, skyting mouths between them. And then if they tell the missus, well, she still thinks I owe her big time from the divorce so she'll follow me there an' all and there won't be any peace for anybody. So no, it's best they think I'm dead, or on the run. But I think about my two boys every single day and wish them well." Flick became silent, processing his thoughts some more privately.

"I'm sorry," Hana sighed eventually. "I feel partly to blame that you have to spend your life hidden away."

Flick placed his hand back over hers, knowing if Logan saw him, he would lose more than just his fingers for touching Hana. "No, it was my mess. My boy hid the land deeds under your car and I had to get them back. But I didn't have to hurt you to do it and I certainly didn't have to enjoy it as much as I did. I'm sorry for all the times I scared you and that other time, when I nearly broke your wrist."

"I'm sorry for trying to stab you with the carving knife and for whacking you round the head with the rolling pin."

Flick touched the spot on his temple where the blow had landed over two years ago under very different circumstances and took a peek at Hana out of the corner of his eye. She was smirking. "You're not feckin' sorry at all, are you?" he growled.

"A bit," she replied, "but you did deserve it. You terrified me, Bobby. I was so upset when Logan took you up to the hotel to hide out. I felt like he was being disloyal. Yet you've become one of the people I trust most in the world. It's funny how things work out, isn't it?"

The look Flick bestowed on the beautiful redhead was one of adoration and worship and Hana felt cruel playing with his emotions. It began to dawn on her quite how much he liked her and against her better judgement, she sensed the shiver of a thrill entering her bones. It felt good to be desired.

An hour and a half later they managed to find a parking space in the multi-storey car park at the Waikato Hospital in Hamilton. Flick nosed the Jeep into its slot almost burying its bonnet into the concrete surround. "Tax has run out," he explained as Hana looked at him curiously.

"We're supposed to be inconspicuous!" she complained. "I thought you would have taken something roadworthy so we didn't get pulled over! Geez Bobby. Do you want to get caught and locked up or something?"

The look he gave her was withering and Hana ended up apologising. "I'm sorry. Look, you stay here and I'll go to my appointment. I'll be back as soon as I can. It's just a scan and hopefully they'll be running on time. We could be out of here in an hour. What are you *doing?*"

Flick bounced down from the drivers' side, placing his Jackaroo hat firmly on his head. He resembled something from the Wild West.

"You're not coming in, surely," Hana said, looking horrified.

"May as well be hung for a sheep as a lamb," he said smiling. "And don't call me, *Shirley.*"

Hana arrived at the reception flustered, trailing a man in cowboy boots and Jackaroo hat who wandered in with his hands in his dirty jeans pockets.

"Ah, Mrs Du Rose," the receptionist said with a grimace and two other hospital personnel also turned and raised their eyebrows. "We've finally managed to summon you."

Hana looked apologetic. "Sorry, I haven't been at home much. I only found out about the appointment this morning."

"You've missed three others." The receptionist sounded hostile. "Those appointments could have been taken by other women."

"I'm sorry."

Chastened, Hana was given a number and went to sit down in a row of blue plastic chairs all joined together.

"What do you mean, you haven't been at home?" Flick asked in a loud whisper as he plonked himself down unceremoniously next to her. Hana caught the faint whiff of horse poo, probably from his boots.

"My home down here, which is now Bodie's home. I want to have my baby in the Waikato, not in Auckland. Stupid boy hasn't been passing on the letters. Amy forwarded this one on to me and Logan brought it up last night. Thank goodness he didn't open it. It had 'hospital' emblazoned all over it." Hana pressed her lips to Flick's ear to whisper and he winced when her breath tickled his skin.

"Er, about Logan," he started to say, visibly dismayed when Hana raised her hand in warning.

"I don't want to hear about Logan right now. I need to be calm for the scan and I already need a pee real bad. I need to think nice thoughts." Hana exhaled slowly and deliberately and tried to slow her heart rate. She stopped her mind from straying towards contentious things and imagined standing on the porch at Culver's Cottage, looking out over the Waikato River on a hot sunny day. The problem was, in her mind, Logan kept coming up behind her and wrapping his strong arms around her waist. She sighed in exasperation as the imaginary

Logan moved her long hair out of the way and kissed her neck seductively. All happy thoughts seemed to include him nowadays. *Life could be so unfair.*

"Mrs Du Rose," the radiographer called Hana's name and she started abruptly from her day dream. The pretend Logan had progressed beyond her neck and Hana realised that she missed him with a tangible ache, deep in her gut. Blaming the pregnancy hormones, she walked quickly after the uniformed woman, fanning herself rapidly with a leaflet about sexually transmitted diseases that she'd grabbed off the chair next to her. "What about your husband?" The woman stopped and Hana almost ran up the back of her, alarmed when the lady beckoned to Flick with manic enthusiasm. He looked around him awkwardly, before pointing at his own chest and then following at a discreet distance.

At the doorway to a darkened room without windows, Flick halted and shook his head. "I'll wait here," he said grimacing. "I'm just the driver."

The radiographer closed the door in embarrassment, sitting on her swivel chair and fiddling around with a keyboard after pulling a curtain across the door. Then she asked Hana to raise her sweatshirt above her bra and slotted blue paper towels around her clothing to prevent the lubricant staining them. Hana's tracksuit pants rolled down over her belly obligingly. The radiographer looked at Hana's stomach and then at her notes. "Is this your first scan?" she asked.

Hana nodded, hearing excuses tumble from her lips. "I've been out of town staying with relatives. The pregnancy sort of...got away from me before I realised it. I just need to know that everything's all right and then I'll be fine."

"The notes from your doctor say you should be about nineteen weeks pregnant, is that right?"

Hana nodded lamely. "My husband and I went travelling. We ended up in Paris and..." Hana flapped her hand at her unborn infant in explanation, feeling stupider by the second.

"Well, just by looking at you, I'd say you're more like twenty-three weeks, at least."

"No, definitely not." Hana looked and sounded certain, blushing hotly at the thought of the passionate night in Paris and the missed contraceptive pill which caused all this.

The gel for the probe was cold and made Hana uncomfortable, but not as much as its gliding action across her bladder. That was positively excruciating. The radiographer took measurements and scanned around, letting out an annoyed hiss when a loud knock came at the door. She looked sternly at Hana. "I take it your husband's changed his mind?"

"He's not my husband," Hana said, biting her lip at how wrong that sounded. She gripped the leaflet and fanned her face again as the woman went behind the curtain and opened the door. Noticing suddenly what she was using to cool herself with, the leaflet screaming, *Herpes - Early Detection and Treatment,* Hana looked horrified and searched for somewhere to hide it. She managed to throw it behind her head overarm and it hit the wall and made a shushing sound as it slipped down behind a trolley. She had just got her hands back down by her sides when the whispering at the door stopped and the woman returned, with Logan behind her.

"This man says *he's* your husband." She turned angrily to the imposing Du Rose male at her shoulder, "I asked *you* to wait outside!"

"Sorry I'm late," he said with conviction, "I'm here now." He strode confidently across the small space and planted his neat derriere on the chair next to Hana. He caught his wife's eye once but any warning there was tinged with amusement. Hana wanted to slap him. *And then you want to kiss him.*

Feeling betrayed, Hana gritted her teeth and thought murderous thoughts about Flick. Then again, if Logan found out some other way, Flick was probably sitting at the bottom of a flight of stairs with a black eye by now. The radiographer ran through some more checks and then turned the screen towards the baby's parents. The 3D image was spectacular. Hana gasped at the sight of the little person in front of her. She felt as though she could almost reach out and touch her child.

"Do you want to know the sex of your baby?" The woman fiddled with more keys. Logan opened his mouth and Hana knew he was going to say, *no* and devilment rose up in her from somewhere painfully raw.

"I already know thanks," she said, enjoying her husband's discomfort.

"I guess it is quite obvious," the radiographer chortled and Hana laughed too, more at the confusion on Logan's face as he peered hopelessly at the screen. The baby began to wriggle and the picture distorted. He would never be able to see now. Logan sat back and stared at Hana, his grey eyes leaking acid glares. She didn't care. For once she felt powerful and in control and it was releasing. *My body, my baby.*

It was cold in the toilets and Hana's stomach felt sticky and miserable after the scan. She wiped away lumps of gel with a wad of toilet roll and stopped to apply lip gloss and ruffle her hair a little. She expected Logan was at the reception desk buying pictures of his son and sniggered at the secret she hugged to herself. Lunchtime was past and Hana's stomach gurgled hopefully, but the thought of facing Logan outside was enough to stem her appetite. She wondered if she could call security or make a scene to get him to go away. *But then how would she ever see Phoenix again?*

Hana poked her head out of the toilet door finding Logan leaned against the wall right outside. He seemed calm and unruffled but Hana still eyed him warily. To her surprise, he handed the packet of photos and DVDs to her. She took them gingerly, having assumed he would keep them for himself. Their fingers touched and she felt their chemistry arc between them, all the tantalising emotions that made up who they were together. Logan's pupils dilated for an instant and Hana saw that he felt it too. Like a spooked deer, she wanted to run.

Logan took her arm with gentle fingers. "I don't want to fight you. I'm hungry. Let's find somewhere to eat."

Hana looked around the reception. "Where's Bobby?"

"Gone. And you should have known better than to make him come here."

"Did you hit him?"

"No!" It was enough of a reprimand to silence Hana. She hoped her friend wasn't in trouble now.

Logan sensed her unease as they found the Jeep in the car park. "I sent him home in our ute. No sense him being pulled over for this heap. In case you're wondering, you dropped the letter from the hospital in the yard. Jack found it and got Rawhiti to call me. I knew the only person you'd ask would be Flick." He sounded so sad when he said it, as though he seriously expected Hana to have invited *him*.

She felt an odd trickling feeling down the inside of her chest as though her heart cried cool tears for her husband's loss of *mana*. She couldn't think of words to justify herself, knowing inwardly that if she had asked, Logan would have been thrilled to take her to their baby's first scan. In the honest recesses of her soul, Hana knew she had turned it into an intrigue purely to hurt him. It had worked.

They left the hospital grounds in silence and Logan drove to a local hotel with a restaurant. He didn't touch Hana at all as they walked inside and she felt self-conscious in her pregnancy-hiding clothes and the lack of contact with her husband burned keenly. She was quiet as they ordered, uncommunicative throughout the meal and unable to eat the soup she had chosen. She picked at the bread roll but her appetite abandoned her.

"You look knackered."

Hana looked up to see that Logan's fork half way to his mouth. He didn't look like he had done much better than her and his plate was littered with the graveyard remains of food, which had only been picked at. He went over to pay the bill and Hana waited patiently, not looking forward to the long journey back to the hotel, undoubtedly conducted in silence. She sat in her seat and closed her eyes for a moment, startled when warm fingers slid into hers. "Come on. Let's go." Logan's voice was gentle and the grey eyes that looked down on her contained only kindness. His face was momentarily the husband she knew and loved and Hana sniffed as ready tears invaded her eyes. Logan smiled wistfully at her and pulled on her arm, willing her to stand and Hana obeyed, hauling herself up on unsteady feet.

But Logan didn't take her to the car.

"I don't want to stay in a motel room with you!" Hana was being childish and nasty and she knew it, quailing inside with guilt. "I want my daughter!" The sob was up and out before she could control it and Logan strode over to her. He took her in his arms and held her tightly against him. Hana cried, loudly and without any shred of dignity, crying for her relationship, her marriage and the husband who had been snatched away with a simple knock on the door, claimed as part of another family that did not involve her. "I feel so alone," she wailed between sobs. "I don't want to be on my own."

"Hana please..." Logan's arms were strong and comforting but something inside Hana couldn't bring down the solid walls she had spent the last days building. An image of Sylvia's lips on her husband's cheek pushed into the moment and Hana shoved at Logan's chest, driving him away with her fists.

"Get off me! Don't touch me!" Her green eyes flashed with danger and hurt and she rubbed her hands down her body as though wiping off something distasteful. "How dare you touch me when your hands have been all over *her*." Hana's voice broke, "I loved your hands, I loved every scar and mark and now they're just filthy to me." Hana behaved as someone whose flesh crawls with the thought of something insanitary against their skin and Logan's reaction was one of horror. For the first time in their entire union, his guard collapsed to rubble on the ground. His grey eyes glistened with real fear, all humour and bravado gone. It had all gone too far and Hana saw him unravel in front of her. Usually he would humour her, show his strength and cajole or bully her. He would seduce her, using his body to keep her on his side and Hana saw his tactics stripped away from him. He was the fourteen-year-old boy on the train again, sat before her with his guileless grey eyes and his raw, unshielded heart.

"Hana, I..."

"No!" She backed away as he approached, viewing him with raw open hatred. "It's all over. We're over. You can't have two women, Logan. This isn't tribal law and it's not ok. Have her Logan. Enjoy the delectable Sylvia for as long as you live. Make the most of your shiny new son, but you know what?" Hana's voice became a hiss, the dangerous sound of a woman scorned. Her hands strayed to her rounded stomach, an involuntary contact with her unborn child. "You will never see this baby. *Never*. Not as long as I have breath in my body. His name will be McIntyre and I will poison him against everything the Du Roses stand for. I'll rear him to hate the sound of your name. And as for Phoenix. Fine! You try and keep her if that's your game. But watch out, Logan. Be very careful with your threats because I have money of my own and I'll fight you through every court in the land for my daughter. I don't care how big your lawyers are or how strong your case. I am *not* Aroha and I will never walk away from my child. I'll waste it all on fighting you and I will love every second of making you pay. Do your worst, you poor excuse for a man, because I will break you without a single moment of regret."

Hana's tears had dried and courage and determination flowed through her veins like mercury, hot, damaging and chemical, spreading her fire to the four corners of the room. Sweat dripped down her neck underneath her hair and she felt hot and sticky with the flash of temper born from defeat and resignation. The old Hana was back, the Hana whom Vik had crushed underfoot; with his laughter and ridicule of the redheaded fight in her. She was the Hana who sat on a London tube train and understood her life would never be the same again, her strong, Celtic persona dripping down her yellow dress as tears. Twenty-eight years later came a long-awaited revival and nobility flared like her daughter's namesake. Hana MacIntyre rose from the ashes of her life as an ethereal, radiant thing and she had never looked more beautiful.

Hana's eyes flashed and her face set hard. She held the trump card and she knew it. Not only did she have his unborn son, she had enough collateral to start a war that Logan Du Rose would never forget. Sylvia could have Logan, but as his wife, Hana was entitled to half of everything else.

Logan slumped onto the bed, his shoulders bowed with defeat and Hana pressed the final knife into his chest and twisted the handle. "By the way, *Mr* Du Rose, when you settle your debt to me - and you will settle - I intend to sell my half of your miserable legacy to the developers. So just make sure Sylvia knows she'll be sharing her new Barbie house with a housing estate, won't you?"

Hana's smile was ghoulish and dreadful. A voice inside her head screamed at her, *stop this! This isn't you!* She ignored it. Logan had pressed down so hard on Hana's soul that he had found the bottom, littered with shards of glass and nasty, splintered thorns. He had cut himself, but with it, he had destroyed her.

Logan Du Rose withered visibly before his wife as she burned slowly in an ecstasy of victory. She stood in front of him, her hair messed up and curled around her face, her eyes glittering like huge emeralds in their sockets. She glowed with radiance but he couldn't look at her.

With a, "Pfft," of pure irritation, Hana turned sporting an ugly a sneer and walked into the bathroom, closing the door behind her. "So this is what happens when someone stands up to the Du Roses, is it?" she muttered quietly to herself, adrenalin from the fight making her feel shaken and unsteady on her feet. Her child stayed ominously still in her womb, coping with the increased blood pressure slamming his mother's blood against the fine, inner workings of his safe place. Hana leaned over the sink for a while, trying to find her equilibrium, glad Logan hadn't followed her into the small, windowless room. She couldn't trust herself not to injure him as days of misery escaped her in violence and bile. Her heart rate slowed and she slumped down onto the toilet seat, wondering which of her threats had rocked her husband the most. Was it the thought of losing his land; having it stripped away in an acrimonious divorce settlement? Or was it the loss of his son and the potential damage Hana could do to any relationship between the child and his father. *Would I do that?* Hana's conscience sought validation and with bitterness and regret, Hana knew she would. For Phoenix. She had to get her daughter back.

With a surge of misery, Hana recognised she could bury her husband with the things she knew about his business dealings. She had seen and overheard enough to set Bodie on overtime for the rest of his life and make sure Logan had nothing at the end of it. *But would she? Could she?* "Perhaps I've been complicit too long," she said sadly to her reflection in the glass of the shower cubicle.

The slam of the motel room door shook the cubicle momentarily and Hana knew her husband had left. She sighed and a sense of abandonment washed over her, threatening to take her into a ready pit of misery and self-pity. "No!" she told herself, patting her ashen cheeks to get the blood flowing. "I won't be going there again, thank you!" She leaned in and turned the nozzle on the shower, running the water until it was hot enough to make her skin red and unattractively mottled. Then she stripped off her dowdy clothes and soaped herself, washing off the stench of another marriage filled with betrayal; until she felt at least partly clean.

Chapter 12

Hana checked her wallet and made sure she still had Logan's credit card. It sat in its usual pocket, nestled behind her other cards, rarely used. "I'll have to pay for the room somehow," she told herself as she used the motel's assortment of face creams to make herself feel more presentable. Then she did something she had never done in her life; she called room service.

Hana snuggled up in the motel robe while her clothes drip dried over the heated towel rail. The washing powder which the motel owner brought up, smelled heavily of chemical scents pretending to be floral but she didn't care. She had washed and scrubbed her clothing in the sink until her hands were red. Hana had no intention of going back to the hotel for now and quelled the ache in her heart for her daughter. She *would* get her; she just didn't know how yet. Hana peered at the screen of her cell phone, watching Flick's number summoned to the screen from her contacts list. She observed as it sit there like an unspoken question and then with shaking fingers, she sent it away again, back to rest amongst the other people she couldn't call for help either. The stockman could definitely get Phoenix for her; he had promised. But it would be harrowing for the child and risky for him. Hana knew he would do anything for her, just for a smile of acknowledgement or a chance to be in her presence. It was the one reason she couldn't ask anything more of him.

Hana tipped her phone back onto the plush sheets and watched it sit there, pink and vibrant against the white linen. Her brain worked overtime. Hana chewed her thumbnail trying to second guess her husband. Strategising gave her confidence and distracted her from the Phoenix-sized hole in her heart. Logan would be back home by now and welcomed into the bosom of the lovely Sylvia. He would batten down the hatches and cover off every rescue plan Hana could come up with. Everyone would be loyal to him and Flick would get himself killed. Her mental image of Logan smiled sweetly from his constructed body, handsome and dangerous as he closed off another access gate to Phoenix. Hana buried her face in the pillows and concentrated on her breathing, one hand over the pacemaker for protection against her complaining body. Her unborn son remained silent and still.

The sandwich which the waitress from the restaurant brought to the door, sat on the dressing table uneaten. It seemed like a good idea at the time. Watercress poured out of it like a green waterfall and bile rose into Hana's gullet as soon as she bit into it. "Maybe not then," she said to the empty room and left it there, the cheese melting underneath the heat pump and the bread hardening to concrete. Hana curled up on the bed with the DVD she had requested. She watched *Dirty Dancing-*, speaking out all the words like a mime, crying in all the usual places and feeling sad and empty at the end. "Nobody puts Baby in a corner," she said in a gruff imitation of Patrick Swayze's masculine voice and started the movie right back at the beginning.

Hana nodded off during the third re-run, sinking into the soft pillows as sleep claimed her, her frazzled brain working hard to repair the damage done during her temper tantrum. The click of the motel door shocked her awake as gasping, she clawed her way to the surface, clutching a pillow to her breast. Her heart pounded like a jackhammer, the curse of the abruptly woken.

Logan closed the door behind him and pulled out the stool from under the dressing table. He lowered his body down onto it as though it hurt him to move. Hana's assumptions about her strong husband had turned him into a monster in her head and so caught completely unawares, she pushed her bottom up the bed and eyed him like a rabid dog.

Logan ran his hand over his eyes and placed both palms carefully on his thighs with extraordinary precision. He splayed his long fingers over his jeans like a fan and then closed them again. Blood adorned the front of his shirt in lengthy tracks and short spatters and Hana traced the source to his bleeding nose. *You don't care*, she reminded herself, blocking out maternalism and compassion with a force of will. Either he had gotten into a fight, or stress had caused the little blood vessels in his nose to burst and his haemophilia had cashed in on the opportunity to further Hana's cause.

When Logan's grey eyes rested on Hana's, she was shocked enough at their appearance to betray the flicker of concern she tried so hard to shut down. They were pale and lacklustre, his pupils tiny dots in exhausted irises and dark shadows had stamped their mark underneath. Logan held his hands out, palm upwards in defeat. "You win," he said, resignation dripping from every syllable. "Take whatever you want. Have half the land. Take Phoe, but in return, I want one thing." Logan's eyelashes flared around pain filled orbs that resembled a tortured, Pacific Ocean. He waited until he saw Hana's tiny nod of acceptance, although she was wary of that one condition. "Please let me still see my kids?" The last was a plea and Logan barely got it all out. He gulped with a rush of emotion and to her alarm, Hana saw a single tear drip vertically down from her husband's eyes. It touched nothing on the way. It plopped onto the dark carpet and became invisible. Then it was joined by another and another.

Victory was hollow for Hana. Her chest felt tight as though a tug of war was in play for her heart, pulled by two strong teams clutching a metal wire. It ached inside her, worse than the pain of the heart attack which had rendered her temporarily dead last year.

"Please don't poison my kids against me," Logan begged and his voice was laden with grief and thickened by his tears. "Not that, Hana. I have to trust you not to do *that*." He pinched the bridge of his nose between his finger and thumb and Hana felt brittle inside.

Many times she had wished Logan would let go and show her who he really was. He hid under a facade of the strong, silent alpha male, able to bend the world to his iron will. She had been trampled underfoot often by his pig-headedness and backbone of steel. But she never foresaw this.

Logan's body convulsed as he failed to hold himself together. His bearing dropped and his elbows sank to his thighs, as everything he had worked for slipped through his fingers like sand. The weight of his legacy bore down on him and failure ebbed from every pore. Hana climbed to the end of the bed and sat facing him, their knees almost touching. She laid her hand gently on his thigh, alarmed when he jumped as though she hit a reflex. "I won't," she whispered. "I promise I won't do that."

Logan's shoulders heaved and shook as sobs rocked his body with relief. Hana's promise withdrew the blade from his heart and removed the overt threat from above his head. Hana knew what she'd done and its outworking sickened her. She had used her husband's fractured childhood against him, turning the mirror of mind games and deceit on him again; but the victims this time would have been his children. *I wouldn't have followed through*, Hana promised herself, but the thought of Sylvia's pouting lips and silky tongue on Logan's body, said different. *Children are not weapons*. Shame bent Hana like a bow and her own mental agony roiled within her stomach, bringing sickness as far as her throat.

Blood dripped onto the carpet from Logan's tears but it was dilute and faint. He ran his nose across his sleeve, leaving a pink streak in the material and he fixed his grey eyes on Hana's face. "Thank you," he said and with absolute sincerity. It broke her heart like nothing else ever had and tears coursed down her cheeks from her own empty well, until she had no idea where they came from.

Any woman who has ever watched a strong man break his heart knows the consequences. It ruins something in both of them which can never be recovered, laying them bare in ways previously unknown. Logan didn't know what to do with himself, writhing in his own skin as an unwilling participant in its destruction. Hana felt powerless, knowing she had caused this catastrophe with her barbed words, but acknowledging in the deeper recesses of her mind; *she was not sorry.*

Logan couldn't bear to be touched at first, thrashing out years of grief and anguish in weeping and writhing but once he calmed, he accepted Hana's embrace like a drowning man. She stood next to him and he cried tears and blood into her motel robe, his arms fixed around her as though she were driftwood in a hungry sea. She cried with him and for him, her tears dropping onto the top of his head, shedding some of them for herself. Time had shifted once more and history clicked. Nothing could return to what it was.

"Do you want me to leave?" Logan's voice sounded muffled and Hana heard the hitch in his chest.

"No," the mother in her responded, feeling responsible for her husband now she had reduced him to this. Logan seemed ashamed of his weakness, refusing to get eye contact with her once the crying ceased and he went to the bathroom on shaking legs, to blow his nose and splash cold water on his face. When he came back to the room, he didn't seem to know what to do, loitering by the bathroom door awkwardly as though nervous about an audience with royalty. Hana sat on the end of the bed, twirling the cord from her robe between her fingers. "We should probably sort some things out," she said quietly. She sought Logan's eyes but failed. "I don't have the energy to argue anymore."

Logan nodded. Hana thought he would resume his seat on the stool in front of her but he didn't. To her surprise he sat behind her on the bed, forcing her to turn and sit next to him. She peered at him sideways and he turned away, not wanting her to look at him in his weakened state. His chest hitched painfully with sporadic jerks that rocked the bed. Hana's heart ached and she squashed it back behind the battle lines. "What would you like to sort?" he asked, his voice cowed and broken.

"I'm not really sure," Hana's statement emerged as a sad exhale. "My last husband just had an affair, planned to leave me and died. I've never had to break up a marriage before, not with anyone living anyway." It was a pathetic attempt at humour and caused an ache in her stomach that she wasn't prepared for. "How does anyone sort this kind of thing out?"

Logan shook his head. "I don't know." Their eyes met and he smiled wistfully. "What a bloody mess."

Hana nodded in agreement. The words stuck in her throat but she needed to know. "Will you marry Sylvia, once I'm out of the way?" Somehow his answer would invalidate their marriage and allow her to go back to hating him but instead, Logan looked ashen.

"Hana, I don't want Sylvia! I haven't touched her. She hooked me in because of the boy, but I don't fancy her. She's made a play for me, but I haven't broken my wedding vows and I never would. If we're done, then *I'm* done. There's nobody else for me, you know that. I've told you a million times." Logan punctuated his sentence with an almighty sniff and wiped his nose on his saturated sleeve.

Hana stared at him and refused to look away. "That's not what your girlfriend's saying. Besides, many men have used that line." Her voice sounded brittle, "I've often wondered, if I had just asked Vik outright, '*Are you having an affair?*' would he have denied it to my face. There's a whole list of lying, cheating men who have said exactly that, Logan. What makes you think I'll believe you?"

"Because I've never lied to you." His grey eyes flashed with injustice and tears had made his dark lashes glisten, black and long like a girl's. At his reply, Hana snorted and looked away in disbelief. Logan reached across and took her balled fist into his hand. His temperature was hotter than hers; the after effect of his distress and it felt like putting her hand into a flame. "I've *never* lied to you, Hana. I've omitted to tell you the truth and I've opted not to tell you some things at all. But when you've asked me straight, I've always told you the truth."

"It's the same thing!" Hana's face displayed outright disdain in an ugly sneer and Logan recoiled at the aggression in the emerald, flashing eyes. He closed his eyes in acknowledgment of how much hurt his subterfuge had caused.

He shook his head. "It's not quite the same thing," he answered, but he kept hold of her hand. They sat for a while as seconds stretched into minutes. Hana felt her heartbeat aligning with Logan's at the contact with his skin and it was soporific. She felt exhausted and shifted her body weight, aiming to release the leg she sat on from underneath her. Logan put both hands over hers, increasing the temperature and making her feel overheated and sweaty. "Ask me," he said and she looked at him with irritation.

"What? Let go of my hand."

"After you ask me. If I'm lying, I promise I'll let go."

"No," Hana said, dragging her fingers out of his. "I'm no good at detecting liars, Logan. Doesn't my stupid, gullible life tell you that much?" She walked to the head of the bed and sat back down in her nest of pillows. The bed felt uncomfortably cold, her former nest ruined.

"Please ask me anyway?" Logan begged and it seemed so pitiful. He wiped his nose on his sleeve again and looked hopeful; a small boy desperate for approval.

"Fine!" Hana responded crossly. "But you could lie your head off and I wouldn't know. *I'm stupid*. Haven't you worked that out yet?" She pulled the duvet over her legs and lay her head back against the pillows with a sigh. "*Have you slept with gorgeous, sylphlike Sylvia, with her perfect hair and never-ending legs?*" Hana's tone was mocking and childish and Logan's face so earnest and open, she felt a prickle of shame in her chest. She stared doggedly at a greasy mark on the ceiling, fixating on it with all her attention. "There! That's what you wanted, wasn't it?"

"Please look at me, Hana?" Logan's hushed voice implored her, but she shook her head.

"No. I'd rather you said nothing at all, than lied to my face. I don't want the last fibre of respect I have for you to die, like the rest of what I felt." Hana put her hands over her ears and closed her eyes, telling herself that it didn't matter what he said.

Logan moved up the bed and put his hand around Hana's jaw. He pulled her face down to look at him and his was still open and broken, his grey eyes wide pools of misery which sparkled like the lahar at the top of Mount Ruapehu. He pulled her hands away from her ears and made her listen. "I have *not* had sex with Sylvia." The baseness of his words cut into Hana and she winced visibly and tried to pull her head away from her husband's fathomless eyes. He bit his lip, not done yet. "She's tried to get me into bed lots of times, especially when you and I argued and you stayed with...Alfred." He gulped at not being able to call the old man, *Dad* and instead of cloaking the hurt, Logan allowed Hana to see exactly what the rejection did to him. "She kissed me and we fell out. I take my marriage vows seriously, Hana. I promised you on our wedding day I would never cheat on you and I *haven't*. And I *won't*."

"It won't be my problem anymore." Hana's voice was a whisper and her heart rolled another tear out of the corner of her eye, smashing it on the side of Logan's hand.

"Hana, Hana, Hana," he breathed and gathered her into his arms like a giant, fluffy ball of dressing gown, crushing her body against his. "I love you, so much." He sniffed and she heard him weeping again, washing him clean from the inside. Tear ducts which had only ever watered because of a sharp wind or a foreign object, shed a waterfall of hurt in a single night.

Logan curled up on the bed with Hana in his arms and they fell asleep, two severed, pulsing halves of the same smashed heart.

Chapter 13

Hana woke with a crick in her neck. The lights in the motel room were on and the television flickered freakily on the menu screen. Patrick Swayze and Jennifer Grey swirled around the screen in a dance without a finale and the music repeated over and over, waiting for an audience that wouldn't now come. A wall clock declared that it was two in the morning.

Hana remained still for a moment, tasting salt in her mouth from her incessant tears earlier and her eyes felt sore and swollen. There was a hard bar across the centre of her back and its presence forced her to shift away from its pressure. Hana pushed herself up to a sitting position, meeting resistance.

The bar was Logan's arm and he didn't want to let her go. Her face remained pressed into his shirt, her nose squashed upwards like a piglet. The ache in Hana's heart returned and she remembered the torturous dissolution of a marriage she thought she would be in until death.

It was obvious Logan had hardly slept. Hana's sleep memory recalled the sensation of his kisses on her temple and the way he smoothed her hair back from her forehead. When he wouldn't let her past, she circumnavigated him, sliding off the other side of the bed and shutting herself in the bathroom. His face as she left the room looked more defeated than she had ever seen him and the sight of his resignation was more than Hana could bear. She leaned her head on her arms over the sink in the bathroom, and shut her eyes to the sight of her wedding ring, stark against the white porcelain. Despondent, she used the motel's toothpaste and the brush in the plastic wrapper, feeling her clothes on the rail with shaking fingers and finding them still damp. "For goodness sake!" she complained at the injustice of her life.

Hana moved the clothes around a bit, folding them differently and rearranging them so that other areas got a chance to touch the heat. She showered and returned to the bedroom wearing two of the motel's towels.

Logan was no longer on the bed. Standing by the dressing table, he fiddled with the car keys in his hand. His eyes were dull and his face impassive. He had regained control somewhere in the lonely hours of the night while Hana slept. His face was that of a man who had accepted his fate. Logan ran his hands through his hair and bit his lip. "I'll set off now," he said and tried to smile with kindness at his wife. His jaw worked to stop his face trembling. "I'll sort out your stuff for you so you don't have to come back..." His weak composure failed him and his voice broke. Logan raised a shaking hand to his face. "Let me know where you'll be and I'll get someone to...I'll make sure that..." he couldn't finish his sentence. This wasn't the Logan Du Rose whom Hana knew. It was as though his *mana* had been trampled underfoot, emptied out and cruelly smashed. He looked crushed; like...Alfred.

"Oh, Logan," Hana sighed out the word and put her hand over her mouth. Again her wedding band flashed with accusation in the harsh, overhead lighting.

"It'll be ok," he said, trying desperately to sound strong for her, but he spoke words he didn't believe. He looked like a man who would never be ok again.

Hana heard the awful noise that seemed to be ripped from her soul. If she truly believed she had no emotion left, then she was sorely mistaken. It gripped her in a relentless battle for her sanity and great heaves left her body. She bit into the fabric of the robe, trying to muffle the sound and failing. A fleeting, rational thought made her feel sorry for the other motel guests nearby, but it was shut down before she could distract herself further. She didn't care. Hana knew she sounded like a heart broken four year old and couldn't seem to stop. She felt grateful for the strong arms that held her and let her cry, smoothing back her sweaty hair and rubbing her back.

"I'm sorry, I'm so sorry," Logan said, over and over, pressing his cheek to hers and letting her tears run down his face and onto his shirt.

The well in Hana's heart dried up without warning, just as she suspected it would feed the spring of her tears forever. Her face felt scratchy and horrid, her eyes so puffy she could hardly see and she fell silent abruptly. *This is what all cried out feels like.* Through her bunged up nose she caught Logan's musky scent, grass, sunshine and mountain air. She wanted to bottle the essence of him for the long, lonely nights ahead and experienced an urge to be closer to him.

It didn't seem enough to be nuzzled into his jacket; Hana needed to feel his soft olive skin under her palms. She knelt up on the bed they had sunk onto, pushing Logan's jacket off his shoulders without explanation. She attacked his shirt buttons, hearing the material rip underneath those that wouldn't obey her frantic fingers. Closing her eyes, she smelled the heat coming off him and sighed with contentment, pressing her face close to his neck and remembering him as though she had somehow forgotten. Hana felt Logan's fingers run underneath her robe, fluttering and sensuous against the small of her back and she placed her lips against his, revelling in the warmth of them and the strong masculinity of his body. *Pregnancy hormones,* was the last rational thought she had. *I'm going to regret this.*

They had never loved like that before. Logan was so different, it filled Hana with an insatiable need for him. He was raw and unguarded and she wanted to savour everything about him, understanding that the portcullis would shut down on her soon and probably take her fingers off in its mechanism. There was no facade, no strong macho Logan, forced to hide who he really was. Their lovemaking was intense, refreshing and completely vulnerable. Logan always made Hana feel desirable, but this time she saw herself as powerful.

The flaws in their marriage had been exposed and in that painful process, both recognised the blight on their relationship. They had dropped into roles that neither wanted. Logan made all the decisions and Hana acceded, doing as she was told and playing the *good wife*, just as Vik had taught her. It jarred awkwardly, as Hana tried to wear an outfit she had long since outgrown. She wasn't that woman anymore.

"What do you want from me?" she whispered to Logan as their bodies lay tangled together, sweating and tired.

"Nothing," he replied, his lips near her ear. "I never asked for anything."

Hana pulled herself up onto her elbow and searched his face, raking the darkness with her eyes. "But I gave you everything!" She felt shocked and indignant when she heard the sound of Logan's hair rustling on the pillow and sensed him shake his head.

"No, you didn't. Neither of us did. We only gave each other what we felt they could be trusted with."

Hana lay her head down on her husband's shoulder, thinking about his words.

"Hana," Logan's voice came out of the darkness, husky and low. "Are you frightened of me?"

She sighed heavily, wanting to deny it. "A bit. Yes." She felt his breath on her cheek as he faced her.

"Why?" he asked.

"You're scary," she replied, sounding like a petulant child. "Sometimes you feel more like a father figure or a boss, than my husband. You're so stern when I tell you things and I feel like I have to always ask your permission."

"Is that why you didn't tell me about the baby?" His voice was laden with sadness and Hana nodded.

"Partly. A bit of it was embarrassment that I'd got caught again. I feel too old to be having babies. But I also didn't know how you'd react. Last time you just rode off in a temper and I didn't understand what I'd done wrong. That's why I cooked the meal and tried to smooth the way. I kept wanting to tell you, but the words just wouldn't come out so I made it impossible for myself not to follow through and tell you properly. The meal meant I couldn't back out. Then Sylvia turned up and it all went wrong."

Logan shifted and rested his hand on Hana's bare hip. A lightning bolt of desire shot through her stomach as his light touch caressed her vulnerable skin. "I'm sorry," he said, his breath warm on her cheek. "I suppose I became this austere husband because I wanted to keep hold of you. I thought I could do that by making all the decisions and keeping you safe. I wanted you to see that I was strong and capable and didn't have any weakness in me. I saw Vik that day on the train and he looked like an idiot, sat there wiping at this negligible cut on his eyebrow and ignoring the fact that his pregnant girlfriend cried an ocean in the seat next to him. I thought he was a dick and I never wanted to appear like that with you. I was afraid you would...leave me." Logan's voice stilled, emotion catching in his throat in acknowledgement of his failure.

Hana snuffed into his chest, finally understanding. "But I fell in love with you because of who I saw up on the mountain that day, when we rode to your special place. You were so gorgeous and vulnerable, pulling that huge picnic out of the saddle blanket. Then on the way back down, you saw the development and the access road and a shutter came down over your soul. It made me doubt you even back then. I felt like just hitching a lift back to Hamilton and ignoring you for the rest of my life. I hate it when you do that. You become unreachable and then I feel like I'm in a marriage all by myself. *That's* what reminds me of Vik."

Logan resumed his gentle stroking motion, his strong fingers moving back and forth over her hip bone. It was ticklish and sensuous at the same time. Logan inhaled a deep breath in Hana's hair and kissed the top of her head. "Hana, it's important to me that you believe me about Sylvia. Do you?"

"I don't really have a choice, do I?" she replied, a hard edge creeping into her voice. "*She* told me that you *were* sleeping with her and spent countless nights in her bed. She can't prove that you did and you can't prove that you didn't. I'm not about to start questioning her about your various body parts or shortcomings, just to see if she's lying. I don't have the energy and I really don't want that conversation."

"So where does that leave...us?"

Hana sighed. "Well, ironically, part of what knocked me sick was the thought of making love to you when you'd been with *her*. I couldn't seem to cope with the thought of it. But we've inadvertently done it a few times now and I haven't thrown up. I don't know, Loge. I really don't know. I feel so vulnerable and strange, like we're balancing on a knife edge and any small upset could throw us one way or the other. I don't know what to do about anything. I don't even think I can make a reasonable decision about where I'm going tomorrow - that's if my clothes ever dry! I think I just need to sleep and do what I want when it comes to it. Whatever happens, I need to be with my daughter tomorrow, wherever that is."

"Ok," Logan sighed and his heart sounded heavy. It was unresolved; his fate still hung in the balance and Hana knew she held all the aces. He had retaken possession of her body, but her mind may still reject him. Hana closed her eyes and breathed in her husband's smell, trying to imagine a life without it. It would be dreadful. She kissed the downy hair on his chest, pressing it between her lips and tugging gently as she contemplated life alone again. Logan sighed again and sought her chin with his fingers, pulling her face up so he could place his lips gently over hers. He parted her lips and probed with his tongue, seeking out hers for one last dance. His fingers strayed to Hana's buttock and down the back of her thigh, pulling her into his muscular body with a slow but gentle tug.

"Logan," Hana whispered into the darkness and felt his body still. "I wish it had always been like this."

"What do you mean?" he asked, confusion in his voice.

"You. Like this," she replied. "Without the hard shell. Talking about feelings and listening to me. I don't feel so lonely." She heard him tut and his lips pressed against hers again, picking up where he left off. He held her tightly and moved over her body, keeping contact with her at every point. Hana felt the sensation of warm water slide down her neck and plop onto the pillow behind her, but when she felt for its tracks, it was gone. Logan sniffed and resumed his kiss but Hana felt the tell-tale tears in her hair, as she loved her husband for what felt like the very first time.

Chapter 14

"**I**'m still knackered," Hana yawned, her face against her husband's naked chest. She fingered the dusting of hair lightly under her fingers and felt him pull her harder into him. Their eyes locked and he smiled at her, the temporary contentment in his expression backed by fear. "Do I look like I spent all last night crying?" Hana asked, sounding like a vulnerable child and Logan laughed, a deep, comforting sound low in his chest.

"You asked me that on our wedding day." He pushed a coil of red hair out of Hana's eyes. She sighed and snuggled in deeper.

"I should have guessed it didn't bode well." Her body shook against his with the force of his chuckle.

"I didn't know what to say then and I sure as hell don't know what to say now," he whispered. "Back then, I handed you a handkerchief and told you that you looked fine."

"Was it a lie?" The question hung between them.

Logan shook his head, "No. You always look *better* than fine to me. You looked amazing at eighteen, pregnant, with your dress too tight and snot and tears running down your face. I held onto that image for twenty-six years and adored you. Anything else is an improvement. It's *aroha*, Hana. Love."

They lay still for a while, Hana dozing at the soporific sensation of Logan's long fingers stroking her shoulder. She jumped as he spoke, "Hana, why wouldn't you let me know what sex the baby was?"

She inhaled deeply and tried to move, but his arm muscles flexed and he prevented her from balking him. They had come too far for him to allow everything to slip back down the dismal tunnel of relationship doom. Hana shrugged, reluctant to dig up yesterday's hurts, still not sure what today held for her.

"Hana, nothing's changed, babe. I still love you, Phoe and this baby." Logan's fingers moved over the sensitive skin of Hana's stomach and she shivered. The child shifted under his father's hand. "Whatever Ryan is or isn't to me, it doesn't change any of that. I need you to believe me."

"Is that his name? Ryan?"

Logan nodded. "Yeah."

Hana pressed her lips together. "You've already got a son now. A full-grown heir. I didn't want my little boy to begin life in competition, like you did."

"Geez Hana, you have no idea how left-field this all came from." Logan sounded confused and desperate. "I don't know how to handle it or how to *be*. I drove home that night wondering how the hell I was going to tell you and then you'd made this gorgeous meal and I felt like a complete git!"

"You behaved like one."

Logan stroked under Hana's right eye with his thumb, pulling her naked body harder into his. "I'll never stop feeling guilty for that, no matter how long I live. You didn't deserve it." He silenced his wife with a smouldering kiss. "I was pretty floored to see my wife riding our daughter down the mountain on my mare though," he smirked. "I thought there was something wrong with Sacha when I tried to mount up. She turned her backside on me and when I finally managed to get the saddle on her, she bucked me off. I'm surprised you didn't hear me swearing!"

"She was an angel for us. I wanted to come and talk to you, to try and understand what had happened, but you took the truck. Then when I saw you, you were..." Hana put her hand over her mouth to stem the painful memory.

"I'm sorry," her husband whispered again. "Look, having Ryan around won't make me love our son any less. He's a bit sullen but I think he'll come right. It must be hard being sixteen and dragged half way round the world to meet your father for the first time." Logan sighed. "I think that's what got to me most - this sense of blame. I hate that I grew up not knowing who my father was and then this kid ended up with the same fate. It made me feel sick to my stomach. I won't let him being at the hotel affect us."

"*He's* not the problem!" Hana interrupted, her tone sharp and unyielding. "Him I can deal with. He'll be just like any other grasping, desperate teenage boy looking for validation. It's *her* I can't deal with. *Logan darling.*" Hana mimicked Sylvia's annoying voice. "There's no place for me because she's taken it. It's not your *supposed son* that's ruining our relationship, it's his mother and what's more, she's doing it on purpose."

"What's she been doing?" Logan sounded disbelieving and Hana shook her head and tried to push him away.

"Just open your eyes, man! Ask Leslie, ask anyone. I feel like the mad wife kept up in the tower while the mistress rules the castle. In fact, she said that exact sentence when she walked up to see me in Leslie's apartment unannounced. Apparently, we're getting a divorce and there's nothing I can do about it. You might both let me see Phoe occasionally - if the mental asylum deems me fit. You wonder why I've cracked up, sat at home wondering how you're going, rekindling your love affair. I'm over it, Logan. I'm not doing this anymore!"

Logan swore and reached out for his wife, his eyes blending rage with agony in their grey depths. Hana pushed his hands away and escaped the bed, stalking her slender body angrily over to the ensuite and locking herself in. As the hot water ran over her rounded belly like a waterfall, she looked down at it in dismay. She could no longer see her feet. *When did that happen?* Hana slid her fingers thoughtfully across the brown line which had grown darker over the last week, running from her breastbone past her navel to somewhere she could no longer see. *Paris.*

Hana needn't have bothered locking the bathroom door. A misspent youth ensured very few locks kept Logan Du Rose out. Hana heard the door click behind him and jumped in fright as the shower cubicle opened and water droplets cascaded out onto the tiled floor. Logan's naked body was cold as it pressed up against hers, but that wasn't the only reason Hana shivered. He brought his face down so his lips almost touched hers and rested his forehead against her fringe. Through the gushing water he whispered, "I regret many things in my life. But the biggest is not having noticed what was happening under my nose. I'll sort it, Hana, I promise. Nobody will ever take your place, not in my heart and certainly not in my house. Please trust me and give me a chance to make it right? *Please don't leave me, Hana?*"

Hana moved her head just slightly and the water slapped and pounded in her ears as her wet lips found Logan's. She slipped her tongue gently between his teeth and flicked at his, nestling there waiting. She heard and felt his sigh escape. A dawning realisation blossomed in Hana's chest like an opening flower. She'd been doing this all wrong, backing off and giving Sylvia room instead of playing her at her own dirty game. Something about the other woman jarred strangely in her psyche, but Hana knew deep down that the truth would eventually come out. *It always does.* She settled into the task of satiating her pregnancy hormones and some of her own and let Logan along for the ride, confident that nothing Sylvia had to offer could rival this.

Chapter 15

"Twelve hundred bucks!" Logan hauled the Jeep's sorry ass all the way back up State Highway 1 to the hotel. "Why would Jack let the road tax run that far out? He's going to bloody pay me back!"

"At least he had a Warrant of Fitness for it," Hana sighed, "otherwise you would have paid for that as well."

"I needn't have damn well bothered anyway. I haven't seen a cop car all the way home!"

Hana's smile died on her lips at the sight of the hotel nestled at the bottom of the valley. If it wasn't for Phoenix, she didn't care if she never came back here again. It felt ruined somehow. Logan reached across and took Hana's stiff fingers into his, pulling her hand onto his thigh. She saw in his eyes that he sensed her reluctance to return. "Logan," her voice sounded plaintive and she resented the weakness she heard escaping from her soul, "why did you put my clothes in the bin?"

"What?" Logan glanced across at her tracksuit pants. They were still a little damp when she put them on in the motel room and Hana had entertained him as she hopped around complaining.

"I need you to tell me the truth," Hana persisted, pushing through her husband's confusion. "My clothes were in the dustbin in our...*her* room. I went to fetch some stuff and they were in the bin. She said you put them there when you were there with her...well, *there* with her, if you get my meaning. Apparently it was symbolic - you threw me away too." Hana chewed her lip with anxiety.

Logan flung the Jeep round the turning circle in front of the hotel entrance and left it there with its wheels askew, the engine cooling with a series of clicks and the odd worrying hiss. "Do you honestly think I would do that?" The aggression was back in his voice and Hana refused to feel intimidated by the flash fire of Logan's emotions.

"It was my jeans and the lovely top you bought me in Italy, the floral one." Hana's fingers writhed in her lap. "I just need to know. I can't do this..." she waved a flailing arm at the huge building to her left which stared down at her, sapping her strength and syringing her resolve out through the soles of her feet.

Logan tipped the keys onto the driver's seat and kicked the front tyre as he slammed the door. Hana's shoulders slumped as she realised the foolishness of her question. Twice she almost asked him at the motel, but was too afraid of wrecking their fragile equilibrium. The door next to her was yanked open, creaking and grinding horribly on its ancient hinge. Logan squatted down in the gap. His fingers sought the ready tears on Hana's cheeks, his eyes dark and forbidding.

"I can't go in there unless I know the truth," Hana persisted, turning Logan's answer into a grail that needed to be won before she could proceed. "This is pointless," she sighed. "It's all too hard." It was futile wallpapering over the cracks in their marriage. It would render it as false and empty as her relationship with Vik, which would have detonated spectacularly in her face had he not died before tearing down his family with his own hands. Logan's fingers pressed along her jawbone, turning her to face him, his hand insistent against her resistance.

"Look at me, Hana. Besides the fact it was a designer shirt and cost a fortune, why the hell would I do something like that? I'd be more likely to smuggle it away and keep it because it was something of yours, than throw it in the bin. The situation between us has been killing me and I would do anything to keep you here, even threatening that you'd never see Phoe again if you left. That was desperation, not hatred."

Hana swallowed, finding her throat dry. "Please just get Phoe and take me home. I don't want to go inside there. I want to go home."

"Soon," Logan said, standing up and straightening out his jeans. "Come in for a while and then I promise, we'll go. I just need to make a phone call."

With a body that oozed reluctance, Hana climbed from the car, feeling the gravel through the soles of her trainers. Logan's fingers were warm as he took her hand in his. "Hana, do you trust me?" he asked, his face serious as his grey eyes searched her green ones. Hana shook her head and his face broke into a smile. "Well, at least there's no change there then."

She smirked as he led her up the wide concrete steps into the hotel lobby.

The receptionist gave a happy wave at Hana from behind her desk in the far corner and she returned the greeting with a smile that went quickly sour, as Sylvia rose from one of the comfy sofas over near the roaring fire. "Loge, darling. I've been looking for you," she simpered, walking over to Hana's husband and striking a pose intended to be seductive. "Where did you go?"

Logan held tightly onto his wife's hand but Sylvia placed her body carefully in front of Hana's, eclipsing her completely from view and making the mother fear for her unborn child against Sylvia's sharp elbows. Hana tried to release her grasp on his iron fingers, but Logan would have none of it. Misery and depression washed over her like a rock fall smashing everything in its path, but Logan's eyes were opened. *He saw what was under his nose.* "Excuse us," he used the back of his other hand to move Sylvia out of the way and bring Hana forward between them. Without a backward glance he put a muscular arm protectively around his wife's shoulders and led her away down the long corridor to the family dining room. The delicate blonde woman tottered behind on her heels, struggling to keep up and mewing Logan's name all the way to the heavy fire door. She struggled to open it after it closed, pushing against it until she burst into the room, finding Logan sharing some private joke with his wife and kissing her tenderly on the lips, his hand nestled on her rib cage very close to her breast.

Sylvia's face betrayed a woman for whom things were no longer going to plan. She blustered a little and tried to move closer to Logan again. "Darling, I would really appreciate some help with something in *our* room." She glanced at Hana, who tried not to rise to the bait even though the woman's mischief rattled her volatile blood pressure through the roof. Hana took quiet, deep breaths and gazed unseeing through the window. Sylvia ran her fingers up Logan's shirt in a physical show of defiance to Hana, who was paralysed with her husband's arms around her.

Just as she could stand the ridiculous tug of war no longer and knew she would have to bow out gracefully, Logan spoke, "I'm booking us a little trip to Auckland in a few days. We can *all* go." His steely voice made Hana freeze, her body rigidifying in his arms. The thought of being trapped in a moving vehicle with Sylvia and her offspring was like purgatory.

"*All* of us?" Sylvia tossed her blonde hair and looked put out. Hana knew she would spend the evening trying to work out how to get rid of her competitor and Hana shivered as her blood ran cold. Smiling with blue eyes filled with hate, Sylvia left the room, clattering down the corridor loudly in her upset.

Hana rounded on Logan. "Is this your idea of..."

His lips pressed firmly to hers, silenced her question. He bit her bottom lip and moved around to her neck before whispering, "I promised I'd take care of it."

"You better had!" Hana retorted nastily. "Otherwise I might be tempted to take out a hit on her. Someone once told me it was biblical."

Before Logan could answer, a raucous knocking came from the lower portion of the heavy dining room door. He strode over and opened it, finding Phoenix on the other side. She was dressed in a strange, ancient looking pinafore dress and had two odd bobbles in her dark hair, which made her look like an alien. Pleased to see her daddy she launched herself into the air and showered his face with wet kisses. "Dada," she breathed between each kiss. Leslie wasn't far behind, huffing and puffing through the doorway and leaning on the jamb for a moment to catch her breath. Her brown eyes took in Hana's rumpled appearance with concern and her expression was questioning as she looked at the younger woman. Hana smiled, conveying nothing and Leslie looked unsatisfied. But Hana knew she daren't pry, not with Logan in the room. Whilst he valued her running of the hotel, they clashed horribly on personal issues and he hated her meddling in his affairs. Leslie wouldn't risk it and so Hana was safe for the moment.

"My *moko's* been doing drawing with her granddaddy," the old lady announced with pride, dropping an enormous sheaf of papers onto the dining table.

"Horseys for you," Phoenix told Logan, tilting her face so she could peer directly into his eyes, grey on grey. "And for Mummy."

"Granddaddy Alfie does a good horsey, don't he, *moko?*" Leslie commented, urgently trying to catch Hana's eye with Logan's temporary distraction. Phoenix nodded enthusiastically at Leslie and listened when her step-grandmother asked her, "Why don't you take mama up to see him in the flat? He'd love that now, wouldn't he?"

Phoenix smiled and wiggled to get down, keen to take her mother up to the highest point in the house to see the old man. He was calm and quiet unlike most of the other people in the hotel. He was rarely too busy to make time for a little girl and they sat in front of the long window facing north and he told her stories about the old days. "Come, mama." Phoenix held her tiny hand out to Hana, the thumb still wet from sucking. "I got Liza's on, look." She patted the elderly pinafore and Hana smiled, understanding. The heirloom dress would be ancient if it belonged to Logan's half-sister, probably a hand-me-down from even further back. It looked like it should be in the museum, not being abused by biscuit crumbs and streaks of crayon.

Phoenix didn't want to be carried, happy to waddle along holding her mother's hand. But half way down the corridor she halted abruptly, her hand going to her mouth and her eyes troubled. "Oh. No."

Hana stopped and looked down at her daughter, curious.

"Fuffy, back ner." Phoenix's cheeks grew pink and tears sprang into her pretty eyes.

"Let's get him then," Hana said patiently, referring to the fluffy horse Tama had bought the child when she was only a few weeks old. They turned and made the journey back to the kitchen past the ballroom and the smaller guest dining room. Voices could be heard through the dining room door despite its robustness and Hana cringed. Phoenix looked up at her mother and to Hana's surprise, put her finger up to her lips. Hana wondered where she'd picked up that little gem but didn't need to ponder on it too long. Leslie missed very little and was obviously passing the skill down to Phoenix.

Inside the room, Logan and his step-mother argued. It was a common occurrence, and Hana hovered outside nervously. "That conniving bitch is running up one hell of a hotel bill with no intention of paying it. She just keeps telling the staff to speak to you."

"Well now you've spoken to me," Logan's voice sounded low and angry as he narrowly managed to keep his patience.

"What do I put her expenses down to then?" Leslie became irate and Hana felt a stab of guilt as her mother-in-law poked the scorpion on her behalf.

"I've told you, I'll deal with it! For God's sake, leave it woman!"

"Don't you blaspheme at me, Logan Du Rose. You're not too old to go over my knee for a whack!"

Hana put her hand over her mouth to hide the giggle which threatened to escape. *I'd pay good money to see that!* Phoenix beamed at the hidden joke, a co-conspirator. But then Leslie took it too far, even for her. "You're as bad as the other weak men in this family. There's one upstairs that let a woman shame him and raised another man's son as his own and the other one in his grave, who yearned his whole life for his boy and allowed women to rule his life. He raised his wife's bastard and watched you grow up from a distance. Youse are weak, the whole bloody lot of ya. Youse let that English madam walk in here and rule Hana's roost like she belongs. And anyone with a pair of eyes can see that boy's not your blood. I know who his pa is and it ain't you. Youse are nuthin' but a big disappointment to me, Logan Du Rose. I thought you was different, but you ain't!"

Oh crap! Hana needed to intervene. She hauled Phoenix off the floor and onto her hip, pushing open the door and staring wide eyed at the furious occupants of the room. Logan balled and unclenched his fists, his jaw gritted and his face a mask of fury. Leslie, red faced and sweating, was more livid than Hana had ever seen her. Hana's voice impeached them both, "Guys, please. Stop this."

"I'll stop," Leslie interjected. "I quit. Run your own damn hotel, run it into the ground for all I care. I'm too old for this *whānau's* rubbish. I'm done!" She breezed past Hana as fast as her chunky legs could take her, letting the door slam on its closer as she huffed up the corridor, still muttering to herself about *ungrateful men.*

Logan swallowed and visibly wrestled with himself, fighting to calm down. Phoenix wide eyed, absorbed the atmosphere and frightened, snuggled into Hana's shoulder. Spotting Fluffy, dropped on the floor behind the door, Hana bent down awkwardly and managed to snag one of his soft hooves between thumb and finger, her heart hammering in her chest. Her husband's body was tense and rigid, oozing naked fury and resentment. Hana hesitated, wanting to touch him and show solidarity, but too afraid. The atmosphere was fraught with warning and the towering, muscular male ticked like a bomb about to detonate.

"Naughty Syva!" Phoenix's admonition ripped into the air like a spark and Logan looked straight at his daughter with irises the colour of storm water. "Naughty Syva spoil everfin'. Daddy an' Nonie sad now. Cos of Syva!"

From out of the mouths of babes! Hana couldn't look at Logan. She hoped he didn't think she bore any responsibility for coaching the child with hate speech. It wasn't her style.

At just the wrong moment, a teenage boy slouched through from the kitchen, clutching the remnants of a pie in his hand. He hit the wall of silence and seemed to bounce off it, looking startled. He was tall and dark, of slender build, not yet properly filling the promised adult body. Good looking, he eyed the scene before him, the angry adults and the wall of tension. Pie crumbs tumbled from between his fingers and littered the smart wooden floor. Hana was filled with sadness at the realisation that Leslie wouldn't be the one to shout about it anymore. "Dad?"

Ryan's single word cut into the room like a knife, powerful enough to split the fizzing atoms. Logan jumped as if bitten and Hana gritted her teeth, but Phoenix reacted badly enough for both parents to see Leslie's bile come straight out of her rosebud lips. "No!" she shouted. "*My* daddy. Mine!"

She threw her favoured toy at Ryan's head and proved a capable shot as it bounced off his face and Fluffy's flailing hooves slapped the pie out of his hand. Instead of feeling happy with her incredible bowling arm, Phoenix became apoplectic, dropping forward towards her horse with her arms outstretched and almost overbalancing her mother. "Fuffy!" she wailed.

Hana paled as the wiggling child accidentally kicked her stomach and she almost dropped the girl. Logan moved quickly, hoisting Phoenix easily onto his hip. He fixed his grey eyes on her identical ones and gave her a look which silenced her mid-wail. Phoenix's bottom lip shot out and seemed to cover her whole mouth, wobbling with emotion as her eyes filled with tears and the short breaths began. Her outburst was so uncharacteristic that it took both parents by surprise and possibly even the child herself, as she created monsters in her head and then struggled with their rampage through her safe world. Logan retrieved the pie encrusted toy from the stunned boy's feet and returned it.

Phoenix leaned towards Hana as Logan came level in his bid to exit the tension filled room with the distraught child. The little girl touched her mother's face with her hand. "Sowwy mama," she said and remorse caused the grey eyes to leak prolifically.

"I'm ok, baby."

"I'll go and make that phone call. I won't be long." Logan nodded to a shocked Ryan and opened the heavy door one-handed with ease.

Hana waited until Logan removed his daughter, before sinking into a dining chair and rubbing the space where the rugby player in her belly had executed a full somersault with pike and wedged his feet over her hip bone. It felt excruciating.

"What did I do?"

Hana had forgotten about the sullen sixteen year old male who still occupied the same air space. Unexpectedly he looked less sulky and more concerned. "There's a dustpan and brush in the cupboard in the corner of the kitchen." Hana rubbed at the side of her stomach, trying to persuade the foot to move somewhere more accommodating. "You need to clean up that mess. Maybe if you use a plate next time?"

He disappeared and Hana didn't expect to see him again. She was surprised when he cleared up the dropped pie and crumbs and plonked himself down next to her at the table. "I shouldn't have called him Dad, should I?" The teen's body slumped like a rag doll and Hana noticed acne on the side of his face underneath the furry dusting of teenage beard. "He's so cool. I want him to be my dad."

"He is pretty awesome," Hana winced at another distracting jab in her abdomen and then with her usual English politeness, she held out her hand to the boy. "I'm Hana, Logan's wife."

He took her hand gently, his eyes confused. "I'm Ryan. My mother said you weren't around."

Hana smiled wryly. "I'm very much *around*. That little girl is my daughter...Logan's daughter. She's finding all this quite difficult at the moment."

"Yeah, it's all a bit weird, really."

"Why don't you tell me about yourself?" Hana suggested. "If you're going to be sticking around for a while, we might as well try and get to know each other."

Ryan's grey eyes turned on her and his expression reverted back to the spiteful, grasping nature it had temporarily dropped. For a second, he reminded Hana of Tama a few years ago, before she and Logan made him part of their family unit and parented him. It was the same look which screamed out for love and acceptance, shrouded in a veil of wounding and hatred. It woke Hana up and forced her to look more carefully at the young man in front of her. "Mum said you weren't around," he repeated. "She wants Logan for herself."

"I know, Ryan. But it's not going to happen. You need to learn to live with that otherwise you'll never be welcome here."

Ryan was surprisingly frank once they bridged the first obstacle. With quiet determination, Hana made it clear she was going nowhere and he calmed down. They chatted about England and Hana's recent visit, trying to forge some kind of understanding through shared experience of their homeland. "Why were you back there?" Ryan asked, picking sub-consciously at a spot on his chin.

"I went to see my father and his wife," Hana replied. "I hadn't seen him for twenty-six years when he turned up in Hamilton last year. We lost touch and I thought he'd died. Now we're trying to make up for lost time. He's been quite sick." Hana steered her emotional thoughts away from Robert's tearful goodbye at the airport and changed the subject. "So, apparently your mum lost touch with Logan when he moved to a different area of the UK. Did she ever marry? Did someone step up and be a father to you?"

"I've never had a dad," Ryan scoffed. "I've spent my life in care!"

Hana tried not to reveal her shock. In her sixteen years working in an all-boys' school, she learned when to stay silent. It was best not to react or ask leading questions. She smiled with encouragement through gentle green eyes and focussed on his obvious physical needs. "You didn't get to eat the pie. How about I make you a sandwich before the dinner rush?" Ryan looked at her with confusion and then nodded slowly in agreement. Hana hauled herself upright feeling every bit her age and nudged the boy's shoulder gently. "Come on. You can choose what you want and I'll make it."

Chapter 16

Hana buttered the bread and Ryan placed chicken between the pieces and added copious amounts of ketchup. "I don't need all that," he commented, misunderstanding Hana's task.

"Oh, I know. I'm making something for Logan and Phoe. We didn't get lunch and she's probably hungry after her meltdown."

Ryan collected the buttery slabs and dutifully laid strips of meat between the layers. He seemed to take more care over theirs. Hana cut them up neatly and placed them onto plates, covering them with film and suspecting she might have to hunt down her husband and baby. The teenager stood with his back to the kitchen worktop, carefully eating his sandwiches over a dinner plate. He looked vulnerable when he was eating and Hana felt the iceberg in her heart towards him drop a few melting chunks. She cleaned up the mess they made, spraying the surface with cleaner and placing the knife into the dishwasher. Leslie would usually shout if she came down for service and found a mess in her spotless kitchen, not like the days of Miriam Du Rose.

Logan's mother allowed family to sit around the table in the middle, covered in horsehair or mud, depending on what they'd been working on. She served the family breakfast or dinner with the industrial kitchen in full swing and the poor girls from the township falling over themselves, as they tried to service the busy hotel dining room. If Leslie's short-lived reign was truly over, Hana wondered what would happen for dinner tonight. "Just don't look at *me*." She spoke aloud without realising as she dumped the dishcloth into the laundry sack in the corner. When she looked up, Ryan had stopped eating.

"What?"

"It's pardon, not *what*. And I was talking to myself, wondering what they were going to do tonight. The housekeeper just quit."

"Because of us?" The boy was astute. Hana shook her head.

"Definitely not you personally, unless she's seen you ransacking the chiller. But even then, she was more likely to give you a bash round the ear. Your mother's gotten on her nerves, but it's other things too I'm sure."

"Yeah, she hates Mum. They had a row yesterday. Mum told her she could do the job with her eyes closed."

"Your mum said that to Leslie?"

"Yep." Ryan filled his mouth with sandwich but at least put his hand over it this time when he spoke. "Don't give her the job though. She can't really."

"Oh, ok."

Ryan's face had relaxed completely and Hana felt dismay bite at her heart. He was pure Du Rose, there was no mistaking it. They all had the same facial features and those grey eyes were a genetic mutation carried forward as a gift from the randy Frenchman, who bought the huge tract of land from the *Māori* chief a hundred and eighty years ago and then bedded his daughter.

Hana sighed and rubbed her hand over her aching lower back. Her stomach protruded eagerly through the fabric of her sweatshirt. Ryan pointed a greasy finger at it and struggled to swallow a mouthful. "Mum dunt know about that," his gaze fixed on Hana's belly almost hungrily and she cringed. "You should play it. It's your trump card. The legitimate heir to the throne."

"What?"

"Pardon," Ryan corrected her with a cheeky grin. Hana busied herself pulling the sweater straight to hide the bump. "She's only after the money. She dint know he 'ad this much though. She thought he was a student."

Hana's face paled horribly. The stray crust of bread she'd forced down whilst cutting them off Phoenix's sandwich, rose up into her gullet. Her eyes strayed to the hand holding the diminishing sandwich and she exhaled in a whoosh at the confirmation. Hana took deep breaths to stem the sickness and leaned against the counter to support herself as her head cleared.

"You're not havin' it are you?" Ryan looked fearful. "Shall I get that shouty old woman?"

Hana shook her head, trying to cover the emotions coursing through her harried brain. *It all makes sense now.*

Hana surveyed the young man in front of her with less fear. He was a child struggling to find his way in life, as much Sylvia's pawn as Hana and Logan. It was quite pitiful. "Why were you in care?" she asked. "I'm assuming you mean Social Services? Children's homes and foster care?"

Ryan sighed, accidentally spraying chicken crumbs everywhere. "She was an unfit mother. Kept leaving me alone and stuff to go out working. Mainly escort work, which is how she met Logan, I think. She liked him a lot and saw him loads, reckons she even stopped charging him. But then he just upped and left. She thought she'd struck lucky getting pregnant but when she found out and tried to find him, he'd gone. Instead of being carted off over here with her Prince Charming, she was left with a kid and worse off than before. She got married to this real old bloke when I was twelve but he didn't like me so I stayed in foster homes. The old guy died last year and left her his house.

She sold it and used the money to come here to find my dad. She says I have to make him like me otherwise we're stuffed."

Hana worked hard to keep her face neutral, vindication singing loudly in her heart. She hadn't imagined any of Sylvia's divisiveness, even though everyone had done a great job of making her seem paranoid. Sylvia had a game plan, but so far only played the hand which Hana could see.

"I like cooking." Ryan finished his food and placed the plate into the dishwasher with extraordinary care. "I did it at school for two years. I want to be a chef."

To Hana's surprise he washed his hands in the sink specifically for that purpose, not running them under the tap by the draining board as she carelessly did. She wouldn't have dared do it if Leslie was there. Ryan used a paper towel and balled it up, shooting it expertly into the waste paper bin next to him.

"Well then Ryan," Hana turned her acquired Du Rose charm onto her new family member, determined to ruin Sylvia's game, but have some fun first. "How about we get you ready for tonight's service and you can show us what you're made of. I think they're a man down and so when everyone else steps up, there'll be a vacancy at the bottom."

"Yeah, I don't mind washing up," he said, surprising Hana with his willingness.

"No, not washing up. We have a man who comes from the township to do that. He's...special." Hana used the kindest term she could think of to describe Benaiah's Down Syndrome. She hoped one day others would give her little granddaughter, Elizabeth, the same courtesy.

"Handicapped then?" Ryan asked perceptively and Hana nodded. "Cool, no worries. My best friend back home's got Tourette's. He once shouted '*shit*' really loud in McDonald's and we thought he was just doing what he always did, but then this kid slipped over in it..."

Chapter 17

"We're booked in for a DNA test on Friday." Logan sounded tired as he laid his daughter in her cot. Phoenix pulled her fluffy horse up to her nose and inserted her thumb.

"You don't need me for that." Hana stroked a stray dark curl from her daughter's brow and pulled the blankets higher over her shoulder.

Outside the bedroom, Logan reached for his wife and pulled her tired body into his. "We're in this together. It's my mess and I'll sort it out but I want you there. No more secrets, Hana." He kissed the end of her nose. "Besides, I never want to be left alone with her again, thanks. She's like a bloody octopus."

"Why don't you and Ryan go together?" Hana asked, seeking avoidance altogether.

"Because it's more accurate if the mother's there," Logan replied. "Don't you remember third form biology?"

"No," Hana tried to pull away from him, aggression leaking into her blood. "I don't want to sit in the back with my daughter and watch Sylvia putting her hands all over you, thanks. It's sick-making and I don't feel up to it."

"I'm borrowing Nev's seven-seater and I'm sticking her in the back. You or Ryan can ride shotgun." Hana sighed and her body went limp with exhaustion. She didn't have the energy to fight. Logan's strong body took her weight and he rocked her like he did their daughter. "I'm doing my best here, Hana. Please help me out."

"It's just...weird!" she protested. "Your current wife and daughter coming along to a DNA test to confirm whether Ryan is your love child with some plastic tart from England, who thinks she's going to move in and play happy families..."

"Shhh," Logan soothed. He laid his chin on the top of Hana's head. "Let's just get through it and face life one day at a time, ok? I can't undo the past any more than you can. I wish...I wish it hadn't happened and I've no idea how it did but I have to get on with it now."

"Maybe you need the biology lesson if you can't remember how it happened," Hana said with sarcasm.

"I don't mean that," Logan said. "I had two relationships in England and neither of them were with her. Both petered out because I was a crap boyfriend and couldn't seem to commit or get my head in the game properly. Maybe I was too busy riding the tube, looking for someone else..." Logan sighed and Hana sensed the weight in his heart. He had searched for her endlessly and without result because she was no longer in England. By some strange twist of fate, she was in the one place he would never think to look; his precious homeland. Logan continued, "I remember Sylvia's face and having a drink together with other people at some point. But I must have got well-hammered on the booze because I sure as hell don't remember her...in any other way."

"Great. Ryan must be so thrilled with that little piece of news," Hana sighed heavily. "Please can we stop talking about Sylvia now? It makes my stomach heave."

"Ok," Logan kissed the top of her head. "I'm just trying to be completely open and honest with you."

"I know, but it's actually a bit too much at the moment. I'm not used to it and all this talk of your previous sexual partners isn't helping our save-the-marriage-spirit. It makes me want to run away and hide."

"Do you want to save our marriage, Hana?" Logan asked, leaning back to see his wife's face properly. His grey eyes were intense and glittered with hope.

Hana looked up at her husband. He towered over her like a massive presence, full of bearing and authority and it was frightening to know she had the power to strike him down with one word. He was her strong rock with a hidden fissure right down the centre, fragile and flawed in its tainted excellence. He completed so much of her that without him, she no longer knew who *Hana* was. She shook her head as she started her sentence and saw him already diminish before her. "I don't think I know how to live without you," she said and Logan's face moved through a range of raw emotions as he struggled to process the confusing *yes*.

He held her tightly in a body that shook with reaction. He resembled a foal using his brand new, wobbly legs for the first time as Logan Du Rose allowed himself to grasp hold of the relief that smothered his senses. "I promise it'll be different," he said with a quiver in his voice.

"Logan," Hana whispered as she snuggled into his armpit in the huge bed. She felt him stir next to her and the arm around her back pulled her in tighter. "You told me that you'd never been so drunk you didn't know what you were doing. Was that a lie?"

"No," he replied without the customary irritation. "I've never lied to you. I said it because I believed it. I really thought I never had."

Logan stuck close to his wife in their big bed, keeping one large palm on her skin at all times. It was as though he still expected her to disappear in a puff of fairy dust and leave him alone and bereft. Whenever Hana woke up, the heat from his body radiated across towards her and even when she moved away, Logan quickly disturbed and followed after. Without meaning to, he contributed to a poor night's sleep for his exhausted, pregnant wife. He had offered to sleep in the spare bedroom with his dumped belongings, but she refused in their spirit of reconciliation.

In the early hours and wakeful, Hana turned over on her side, shielding her stomach from his strong bent knees and studied her husband's face. He looked peaceful with the moonlight dappling on his face through a chink in the curtains. Logan was handsome, dangerous and beautiful, his long dark lashes resting like silken wings on his cheeks, shrouding piercing eyes that possessed far too much understanding sometimes. He was everything Hana had ever desired in a husband, courageous, sensuous and loyal. She always knew a frightening turbulence lay beneath the muscular chest, but until yesterday, never comprehended how deeply or rapidly those waters moved, containing the power to sweep everything away. Logan Du Rose was an enigma and Hana would never completely fathom his ways. But she broke him, callously and deliberately and she owed it to him to help glue the shattered pieces back together.

"I'm sorry God," she whispered into the half-light. "I pray that you and my husband forgive me for the things I said. I'll never poison his children against him. I love him. I won't let history repeat itself, not through him and definitely not through them."

Hana stroked her husband's stubbled cheek and saw his eyes snap instantly open. His pupils regulated themselves quickly against the growing light and his fingers gripped her waist in possessiveness and fear. "It's ok," she whispered into his confusion and shifted her body so she could put her arm around his neck and pull his cheek onto her breast. It was a shameful realisation that in their years together, Hana regularly sought physical comfort from him, but rarely offered it. She pulled his head fully onto her chest so his hair tickled her nose and wrapped both arms firmly around Logan's neck. It was an act of open maternalism and Logan accepted it, resting his head half on her bare shoulder and half on her breast. Hana sensed him relax and allow himself to be temporarily cossetted, like a horse that permits the saddle for only as long as it chooses to be compliant. But it was new and exciting and Hana felt a wave of power.

As he awoke fully, Logan's hand strayed from Hana's waist to the smooth, rounded skin of her belly and he sought comfort from his sleepy son, who kicked him in response. He snuffed out a hollow laugh into her skin and then moved his head so their eyes met. "Stay with me, Hana," he said, half command, half plea and she nodded, a slow action full of surety.

"I will," she answered.

Logan's fingers moved over her hip and down her thigh, his long hand spanning the width of her leg. His thumb strayed and she sighed and bit her lip, looking at him with accusation. He smiled back in answer and kissed her with his full lips, pausing only to promise, "I love you. I won't let you down."

"You'd better not," Hana replied, the threat no longer veiled but out and in the open. Logan's eyes glittered with the addictive lure of danger and Hana saw the moth in him dance with abandon around the candle flame. Logan came alive again, out of the harness and back in control, his *mana* restored. Only this time, he knew what it took to break him and wisdom and bitter experience would stop him pushing his wife to that point again. He pulled her half onto his body, her rounded stomach in the way.

"I love you, Hana Du Rose," he said, his eyes sultry and full of promise. He ran both hands up the back of her neck and into her hair and Hana closed her eyes and gave in to his kiss.

Chapter 18

Hana couldn't sleep as the child in her belly kicked and turned like a Judo professional. Indigestion plagued her and she went to the living room with her gloves and another of Phoenix's diaries. The revelation about Kane and Caroline's parentage had been dreadful and Will had confiscated that book, only allowing Hana another tome if she promised not to destroy that one either. "Just cos youse don't like what's in it, don't mean youse can bugger it up!" he shouted at her.

"But I wanted them in order," Hana grumbled. "It's too hard reading them out of chronology. You're mean!"

"Take it or leave it," Will warned and Hana had grabbed the proffered manuscript and beat a hasty retreat.

Hana settled down on the cream leather couch and pulled her cotton gloves over her fingers. She sat for a moment and then got up again to pull the curtains closed against prying eyes. The feeling of being watched seemed constant and Logan had laughed at her earlier when she wanted to close their bedroom curtains. "What's the point?" he said. "There's nobody for miles."

Hana shrugged and pulled the expensive swags of material together, overlapping them in the middle. She sat back down on the sofa and reached for the diary, turning to a date which preceded Logan's birth, way back in the summer of 1967.

'It is not over. They came looking for the blond drover. His brothers travelled down from Auckland in search of him. They will not leave it. JD has dealt with them but the rumours have begun in the township. I am at a loss to fix this. Damn that foolish woman and her fancies. He tells me it is done with but I am not certain. I asked JD how he dealt with it but he wouldn't tell me. It would not have been pleasant and I am fearful.'

Hana sighed and laid the book down on her knee. "Who's JD?" she asked out loud and the silence offered nothing back. Hana curled up on the sofa and thought. She had a memory of Logan saying someone else owned part of the property and felt sure that the mysterious *JD* had cropped up then. That would suggest he was still alive. She didn't want to raise the question with Logan again, afraid that if he probed her for the reason behind her enquiry, she would blurt out the information about Caroline and Kane before she could stop herself. It burned like a hot knife in her chest and made her want to find the damning diary and destroy it once and for all. But it would make no difference because she *knew*. The awful secret was already out there and it was only a matter of time before it burst into the open like a catastrophe.

"Why are you telling me all this?" she asked the ghost of Phoenix Du Rose, hidden within the fragile pages. Hana's white gloved fingers stroked the ink and she felt wretched. "You couldn't have picked a worse secret keeper," she said to the diary. "I'm almost scared to read any more." But she had to. Hana read on, cringing with the next entry.

'The police came today. They were white men, aggressive and overbearing. JD became animated and I feared that they would carry him off. One of them disrespected me. He spat on the whenua at my feet and JD was sent into a fury. I thought he would hit the constable and then where would I be? He is the only protector I have left. Thank Atua for my Reuben. He was quick to smooth things over. He has no idea about the absence of the blond

drover and was convincing with the constabulary men. He thinks the man ran away after their fight. He fought with his father afterwards in an angry exchange although it was one sided.'

"Whoa," Hana sat up straight in shock. "Back up there a minute Phoenix. What did you just say?" Hana read it again. "So the cops came looking for the blond man and this 'JD' sent them packing. So how come in the same sentence, Phoenix says that she had no protector but then Reuben has a fight with his *father*. That doesn't work. Henri died when Reuben was a child and this diary is dated years later when Reuben was an adult. Unless...oh no." The dawning realisation made Hana feel tight in her chest. She pressed her right hand onto the pacemaker, checking it was still there. "Oh no." Rational thought drained away from her as she struggled to process the woman's words. Henri Du Rose was *not* Reuben's father. "So who is?"

If the man was not a Du Rose then neither was Reuben and that meant nor was..."Oh, please no. I can't take any more of this." Hana closed the diary with a careless snap. If Logan wasn't a Du Rose it would kill him. Hana felt the weight of ages settle on her head and hated Phoenix Du Rose for her betrayal. Now she not only knew her daughter's forebears were murderers, disposing of the blond drover because of his indiscretion, but also that Phoenix herself had birthed a child out of marriage. Hana's body felt heavy and sick and she put her head between her knees to get rid of the lightheaded feeling. She groaned and covered her head with her arms.

Logan found her like that. "Hana, what's wrong?" He sounded panicked and anxious.

"I just don't feel good." Hana pulled a cushion towards her to cover the object of her misery, lying impassively on the sofa next to her.

"What can I do?" Logan sounded so frightened she felt her heart weighed down by guilt, only adding to her burden.

"I just need to go to bed," Hana wailed. "I need you to hold me."

Logan picked his wife up in one fluid motion and Hana watched with horror as the cushion moved, exposing the ruined leather cover of the diary. She lay her head against her husband's shoulder and closed her eyes, praying that the cursed thing would just disappear in the night. If Logan found it, he would be irreparably broken. It could undo everything he knew to be truth. "Oh God," Hana cried into Logan's bare shoulder and he stopped in their bedroom doorway.

"Hana, I'm getting the doctor. You're scaring me."

"No, please. I'm sorry." She kicked her legs in protest. "I'm just tired. Please, I want to go to bed and be held."

Logan laid Hana on his side of the bed and she scooted over so he could get in next to her. "Sweetheart, what's wrong?" he asked and she shook her head in the darkness, her hair swishing on his pillow. Logan brushed her fringe back from her forehead and kissed the soft freckled skin, pulling her into his broad strong chest so that her nose tickled with the hairs and made her want to sneeze. "Whatever it is," he breathed into her ear, "it will be ok."

Hana pulled herself in even closer, wrapping her thighs over Logan's legs so that there was nothing between them. *Nothing was ever going to be the same again. Never.* "Hold me," she begged him, deceit and treachery scoring her heart into ribbons.

"Was it a dream?" Logan asked and Hana shook her head against his chest.

"No," she replied truthfully. "It was a nightmare."

Hana woke up the next morning, the sickness and sense of distress still thick within her throat as soon as she opened her eyes and remembered. Her face was pushed into her husband's brown chest and her nose pressed upwards like a pixie's. They had jointly occupied the tiniest space in the huge bed, tangled together like fishing line. Hana stirred first and Logan's arms tightened round her in sleep, his heavy bicep weighty against her temple. Hana ran her fingers down his back, making him squirm and wake up to her kisses. "You all good now?" he asked her with concern in his grey eyes and Hana nodded and faked a smile.

"Yes thanks. Your cuddles fixed it."

Logan kissed the top of her head and snuggled her in. He held her quietly for a long time. Against her better judgement, Hana fingered the detonate switch and sought clarification from the only person on hand who might know the answer. "Loge, what do you know about a blond drover?" She ran her fingers lightly over her husband's taut stomach muscles as she played with fire and cursed her own curiosity. He shuddered and grasped her fingers to stop the tickle spreading.

"Flick?"

The answer surprised her. "No, not him. Years ago. Before you were born. There was a blond drover that apparently had an affair with your Aunt Antoinette and then disappeared."

"I don't know anything about him. Where did you get that from?"

Hana guarded her secret carefully, choosing her words. "Just some stuff I read. It doesn't matter."

"Ok," Logan turned on his side, his eyes crinkled at the edges. His beard growth scratched Hana's cheek and she squeaked and pulled away from him. "You had me worried last night," he ran his finger down her face and smoothed it behind her neck and into her hair. He kissed her forehead. "I woke up and you were gone. I..." he ran his tongue over his lips. "I thought...maybe..."

"No, Logan," Hana silenced his words with a kiss. "I had indigestion and went to sit in the living room. I should have just got some milk. *I wish I had*," she sighed with conviction. "If I'm going to leave you, you'll know. I'll be loud and shouty and there won't be any doubt about it."

"You snuck out before," he said accusingly, sounding like a child.

"I went to a hospital appointment and you left me no choice," Hana replied, with warning in her tone. "I thought we were good now. Aren't we?"

Logan nodded. "I can't bear the thought of not coming home to you. My life would be as empty as it was before. My family's all I've got. At least now I know where I've come from and with you and Phoe and our baby boy, I know where I'm going. It's all that matters to me."

Hana pressed her lips over Logan's, desperate to stop him talking. Tears welled up behind her eyes and caused a pressure across the bridge of her nose. "Sshh," she told him. "I'm not going anywhere. Not now I've got this hunk who knows how to show his feelings. It's actually quite a turn on."

Logan laughed and looked embarrassed, but his eyes showed a wariness that warned Hana. He knew something was wrong and suspicion leaked out of every pore of his body. She slipped her index finger into the waistband of his shorts and sought the curve of his hip, running her fingers lightly over it. "How long before you have to be at work?" she whispered and injected mischief into her green eyes.

Logan smirked, instantly distracted. "I'm the boss," he said huskily. "I don't have to go in at all."

Chapter 19

Hana slapped the diary onto the workroom table, the bang it made resounding throughout the museum. "I can't do this anymore," she postured with her hands on her hips, her stomach poking incongruously through her sweatshirt.

"Don't do that!" Will's wheelchair squeaked on the polished floor as he wheeled himself towards her. "You'll crack the bloody binding."

"I *want* to put it on the fire!" Hana stated, her cheeks flushed and her red hair floating round her face like a halo.

"What now?" Will reached for the book and cradled it in his hands like delicate china. Hana looked around the empty workroom and lowered her voice to a frenzied squeak.

"It says, Logan's not a Du Rose!" she raged. "It says that Phoenix had an affair with a mystery man. *He* was Reuben's father and not Henri Du Rose. The whole damn family is a farce. I've had enough! I can't cope with this mess. I don't *need* the extra upset. Every time I open one of her diaries, I learn something even more dreadful than the last hideous revelation. I've had enough. Just seal them, hide them - I really don't care. But I suggest you keep them away from me or I won't be held responsible for my actions."

"Sit!" Will dragged a chair behind Hana's legs and glared at her. She sank into it, wringing her hands together and staring hungrily at the diary. Phoenix Du Rose called to her from the pages and Hana turned her face away. The problem was that she desperately wanted to open it and find out more. It had successfully sucked her into its intrigue and mystery and it took every ounce of her willpower to resist.

"Hana," Leslie's voice clanged in the silence of the museum and Hana jumped guiltily, shooting a look of terror at Will. Satisfied she was listening, Leslie continued. "Me an' Alfie's taking Phoe to the zoo. We've got Nev's wee one an' all. That ok with you?"

Hana's brow knitted in anxiety and Will's face softened. "Er...I'm not sure." Hana rose to a standing position, still wringing her hands. "How long will you be?"

"Just a couple of hours, *tuhi māreikura*. Is something the matter? She just wanna come and see the elephants. But it's ok if youse not happy with it."

"She's fine," Will interjected. "Go. Have a good time. Leave the missus with me." He reached up and gripped Hana's writhing fingers in his claw like hand. Relieved, Leslie withdrew her head and closed the door.

"What a mess!" Hana sank back down into the chair and covered her face with her hands. "I'm not the right person to be doing this. I can't cope with the information. It's all too damaging. I now know that Logan's half-brother has married his own half-sister without realising. And Logan is only half a Du Rose and not a whole one. It will kill him. And I've never been able to keep a secret, it's my worst thing. I can't cook and I can't keep secrets. What am I going to do, Will?"

The old man wheeled his chair next to her and to Hana's surprise, fixed his arms firmly around her shoulders. "Hush, hush," he crooned. "Sometimes the burdens are too big to carry alone. History can be a wicked master for a delicate soul. Let me deal with this and you concentrate on that wee *pēpe* of youse." He kissed Hana's tear-stained cheek and his bristles scratched at her delicate skin. He smelled of coffee and the medical tape on the stumps of his legs. Hana sniffed and rested her chin on his shoulder and felt grateful for his support.

"What shall we do?" she whispered.

"You will clean the photographs as I direct you," he replied softly. "And I'll deal with the matriarch's memories. I'll seek the truth and when I find it, I'll decide whether or not you need to know."

"But what do I do with the stuff already in my head?" Hana asked, a stray tear rolling down her cheek.

"You file it away in a safe place and make sure you control it and don't let it control you. It changes nothing, unless you let it."

Hana sniffed and nodded, doubtful she would be able to file it away like the old custodian said. "It burns," Hana sighed, touching the spot just above the rise of her belly and Will covered her hand with his.

"I know my darling," his voice was soothing. "I know. Some things can't be un-known, can they? But you're improving your heritage here and now. Youse and your old man, you're makin' a good foundation for your little ones. You've a solid marriage and a legacy that's gonna be different."

Hana sighed and rolled her eyes. "You have no idea," she began and Will raised his hand.

"I knows more than you think, my girl. Youse doin' good and don't you forget it. This ain't an easy family to graft into and that man of yours is closed and dark-hearted. It's gonna just take time but youse doing ok." He patted Hana's back like she was a child and let her rest her forehead on his shoulder. Hana was comforted. She reached her wrangling hands around the old man's neck and hugged him tightly, turning her face sideways and closing her eyes. He hushed her and soothed her.

They didn't hear the door open quietly or the blond man poke his head in. "Sorry," Flick stammered. "I didn't know you were here Han...Miss."

Hana sat up quickly and sniffed. "Come in Bobby. I'm just being emotional and silly."

The drover shuffled forward but kept his body turned sideways, seeming awkward and wrong-footed. "There's a delivery arrived. Some big glass cabinets. Want me to get the guys to bring them in?" He directed his question at Will, ignoring Hana and she assumed he was embarrassed by her tears. She found a tissue in her sweatshirt pocket and dabbed her eyes with it.

"Yeah sure," Will answered gruffly, palming the offensive diary easily into his hands. Hana watched the action with accusation. He wasn't wearing gloves, but she wasn't about to point that out to him. He lay the manuscript on his useless legs and wheeled himself over to the safe. "Fetch 'em in, son."

Flick left the room quickly without looking at Hana and a sense of alarm went through her. She stepped towards the door to go after him but Will stopped her. "Leave it!" he said sharply and Hana turned to face him, confusion on her pretty face.

"Pardon?"

"Just leave things alone, will ya?" he said, sounding irritated. "You bring half your problems down on youse own head, girl."

Hana was stung and stood against the wall while three of Logan's strapping men brought the heavy cabinets into the museum and set them up at Will's direction. Flick hung around in the doorway, ignoring Hana and she stared at him feeling perplexed. It had to be because of the hospital appointment a few days previously. Perhaps Logan had bawled him out for interfering. Hana hated the atmosphere between them but did as she was told for once and respected Will's advice.

"Back to work!" Flick barked at his men and they jumped to attention and re-joined him. Each click of the heels from his work boots cut into Hana like a guilty knife, as she heard her friend walk past reception and towards the front doors.

"Hana!" Will spoke sharply to her and she jumped. "Let's get these photos out of their frames. You'll need some sturdy gloves. They've got sharp, rusty nails holding the back onto the surround."

Will kept Hana busy for two hours. She didn't see him put the diary in the safe but her painstaking work helped to numb the crawling sensation of needing to know absolutely everything. Will had promised he would find out the truth and she trusted him. Hana sent a prayer heavenward to her God, asking him to help the old man solve the mystery and make his difficult decision. He would either put her out of her misery; *or not.* Either way, she would have to live with the result.

Breaking for lunch and finding herself not hungry, Hana wandered outside into the crisp, cold air and walked around, filling her lungs and exercising her cramped body. The small cuts on her hands smarted in the air, the victorious nails having punctured the gloves and her skin. Miriam's rose garden failed to provide its usual brand of welcome peace and Hana ventured to the stables, hoping to see Logan.

Jack used a wide broom to sweep hay and muck into a loose pile in the centre of the yard. He waved to her, but continued his task and Hana's brow furrowed. Without Phoenix, she felt strangely naked. Hana peered into each of the loose boxes and found them disappointingly empty. She wandered to the equipment shed and rested her backside against the familiar green quad bike. "I still hate you," she said ungraciously to it. "So don't get any ideas!" Twice the bike had caused her harm, once when Michael had stopped sharply in it and Hana's heavily pregnant body had hurtled into the foot well and the second time, it had broken down at the worst possible moment. Hana had given birth underneath the old kauri tree which now nestled at the edge of her driveway. The bike had abandoned her to a terrible few hours of agony and fear. With a sense of devilment, she twisted the wing mirror to face skyward, feeling instantly guilty. David Allen, Logan's resident mechanic had gone back to England after lovingly restoring the old vehicle. He wasn't due back until the end of the year.

A deafening clang made Hana jump out of her skin and the air was rent with the sound of vociferous cursing. Hana turned as Flick's ash-blond head appeared from a tractor parked inside the shed. He hurled something metal to the ground. "Sodding thing!" he kicked the heavily treaded tyre and then picked up the spanner he'd thrown onto the concrete floor. Hesitating for only a moment, Hana picked her way through the haphazardly parked machinery until she reached the drover.

"What did it do?" she asked and he started and jumped away from her.

"You can't be here," he said with violence and Hana looked at him in amazement.

"Is it about the hospital visit?" She tried to placate him, realising the futility of her efforts as he turned his back on her and moved away.

"No!"

Hana wrenched on his elbow, overbalancing the tall man and he stumbled and banged into her, causing her to groan loudly as he accidentally elbowed her in the ribs.

"Geez, Hana, I'm sorry. I'm sorry. Are you ok?" The man's eyes were instantly filled with remorse and concern. Hana rubbed at her ribs and glared at him.

"What's with you? What on earth have I done to deserve this...?" Her words died on her lips as she caught sight of his face. "What happened?"

Flick's right eye was swollen almost shut and the small bit of eyeball that Hana saw, was reddened and bloodshot. Her ribs forgotten, she reached up and pulled his cheek towards her. "Tell me, what happened?" she insisted.

Flick's fingers closed over hers. "Leave it, Hana. Please just forget you saw."

"No. I need to take you to the hospital. Can you see out of it or do you think you've damaged your eye?" she fussed.

"I can see fine, when I get it opened," Flick said, gently stroking Hana's fingers. "Please, don't worry about me."

"How did you do it?" Hana was unyielding. "You were fine the other day…" The thought occurred to her like a black, nauseating wave, washing over her head and restricting her airways. "Did Logan do this?" she whispered. She looked crushed, her face crumpling in sadness, quickly replaced by anger. "If you tell me Logan did it, I'll kill him!"

"Logan didn't do it," Flick said. "Please Hana. Just leave it."

Hana reached up again to the engorged eye, her beautiful face concerned and loving. "Bobby, tell me the truth."

"I can't." Flick leaned in close to Hana. He blindly reached his arms around her neck and pulled her in close to him. His body shook and Hana was rocked with fear. Betrayal coursed through her veins with growing cynicism. She thought Logan was changing and becoming softer. *Was he such a good actor?* Hana didn't think so.

"Did he do this at the hospital, when he found you outside the room? Bobby…" Hana's voice broke with sadness.

"No, no. Shush," Flick placed his finger over her lips. "You weren't meant to see. You need to go now. *Please.*"

"Don't be ridiculous!" Hana was indignant and the man took a step back.

"You're going to make this worse for me if you don't go now!"

Hana shook her head. Something was badly wrong. A sense of evil unexpectedly pervaded the air, which became thick with a choking awfulness. Flick went dead still after dropping his arms to his sides and he took a step back from Hana. His voice became detached and he over-pronounced his words. "You need to leave me alone, Miss. I have to get on with my work now."

"What…pardon?" Hana felt totally lost in this bizarre charade.

"I need to get on now. I hope you find whatever it is you're looking for." Flick turned his back on her, striding from the shed and out of the stable yard altogether. Hana stared after him, mystified. Her eyes were drawn to the centre of the stable yard, her pupils shrinking back against the strong light outside. Jack and Logan stood in the court yard discussing something.

Hana's husband gesticulated for the old man's benefit and Jack nodded with understanding, even though he hardly paid attention, his eyes flicking towards his employer and back into the darkened shed. Hana wondered if he was still mad about their spat. It seemed like such a long time ago. The disappearance of the blond drover had rattled him dreadfully. It sat on Hana's chest like a lead weight, more disturbing because nobody else cared - or had ever cared.

"Logan said whatever was in the box would cause trouble," she sighed out quietly to the tractor and quad bike as they surrounded her, a silent audience. "He was right. He just can't know *how* right."

Jack looked terrifying as he watched Hana across the yard. His elderly bent shape had been forced out of its comfort zone as the man hauled himself up to his full height. He must once have been over six feet tall and his eyes bore into Hana across the distance, staring clear over Logan's shoulder. She sighed and ran her hands over her face. *No wonder Rawhiti was scared of him.*

Flick had run from someone and Hana directed her anger at Logan's strong back. *How could he?* Not yet ready to face her treacherous husband, Hana tried to sneak out of the shed. Her foot banged against an old bucket, discarded in the detritus on the floor and the scraping it made attracted Logan's attention. His grey eyes joined the stable manager's as Hana emerged shakily from the shed. *Perhaps he hit Bobby before he changed,* she reasoned with herself. But the bruising around Flick's eye looked more recent than that and her heart sank. "Hey babe," Logan's eyes narrowed and he seemed frighteningly perceptive. "What are you doing in there?"

A lie came instantly to mind and was out before Hana could stop herself, her conscience pricking her dreadfully. "I took a break from the museum and came looking for you." It was sort of the truth.

"You look a bit pale. Do you want to go to...?" Logan almost said *my room*, but stopped himself in time. His face clouded at the thought of his unwanted house guest.

"No thanks!" Hana's response was sharp. She would never sleep in that room again, the perfume of the delectable Sylvia staining its peace for her forever. Defensiveness made her daring. "I was just talking to Bobby." She looked at Jack, slowing her speech for his benefit. Logan looked confused for a moment and then recognition dawned.

"Why don't you just call him Flick, like everyone else?"

"Because his name is *Bobby*." Hana felt defiant and a little voice inside her head screamed, *are you trying to get him killed?*

Jack still studied Hana as her body language gave off obvious distress signals and he screwed his face up in confusion. He couldn't hear the shrill voice of Sylvia as she clattered through the hotel gate in heels which were highly inappropriate. Logan's shoulders slumped and the tension in the yard hiked up a notch. "Logan, darling. I've been looking for you." She made a loud clip clopping beeline for her quarry and Logan stepped back physically as she lurched for his arm. Comprehension dawned on Jack's wrinkled face. He turned his rage on her instead and the air around Hana seemed to clear. Jack made angry guttural sounds and pointed down at the woman's feet in disapproval, as she danced around his pile of muck. Sylvia was clearly revolted by the elderly man and wrinkled her pretty nose in disgust at his sounds and gestures. She lurched for Logan's arm again and Hana saw his muscles clench in distaste. She felt tired and old and the sensation washed over her. The ugly disappointment at her husband surfaced again, overwhelming in its force, like a body blow.

Hana exited the shed and walked away, her shoulders rounded in defeat. *Why am I even bothering? Hana, you're a fool*, she sighed to herself. *Nothing's changed.* Logan had battered a friend just for helping her and Sylvia hadn't cooled her ardour in the slightest. Hana took a circuitous route back to the museum, ignoring Logan's shout to her to wait.

"Hana!" he caught her up at the mudroom door and she stopped, head bowed with her hand still on the handle. "Sorry about her," he apologised. "I th...thought she would have got the hint by now. She'll l...leave after the DNA test. Even if Ryan's my son, she can't stay. I was hoping you'd st...stick around and see her off." Logan's occasional nervous stammer had never annoyed Hana, but at that moment it was just another beacon of his weakness and her redheaded temper flared. She was momentarily relieved at the tiny flash of power it offered.

"What, like your guard dog? You seem to be making a big enough mess all by yourself," she said with pointed sarcasm. "And if you want her gone, *you* get rid of her!" Hana left him stood by the door, closing it in his face. She saw him turn away and punch his fist into the door of the tack room, his teeth gritted in fury.

Her feet dragged as she went back to the museum. But she couldn't settle and after she broke the glass on an old photograph and stabbed herself with more nails, Will wheeled himself over to her and put his hand on her shoulder. "I'm hearin' a lot of cursing going on from over here," he said with a knowing smile and Hana's face crumpled.

"I can't be who they want me to be," Hana whined. "I just want my nice, boring, easy life; back when the biggest worry I had was how I could fill my evenings. A glass of wine, a job I liked and the odd good novel. It's not much to ask, is it?"

"But you were lonely," Will said perceptively. "I can see it in your face."

"Was not!" Hana bit and he laughed.

"Sometimes the route out of somewhere isn't what we think, is it?"

Hana shook her head. "I miss my church and my friends. I feel isolated here and there's this bad feeling that hangs around my head all the time; a cloud of misery trying to suck me into its horrid black pit. It feels like what used to settle on Miriam and I don't want to be depressed. But there's so much going on all the time, all this conflict."

"Finish for today," Will said softly and patted Hana's hand with his wizened paw. "Go for a walk. Your baby will be home from her trip soon with tales to tell you. Get your game face on for her."

Chapter 20

Hana wandered outside in the cold, fresh air and sat in Miriam's rose garden. The quiet place held many memories for her. She had made peace with Tama here after months of hatred and antagonism and she had laboured with Phoenix here in secret. The flowers were Logan's mother's, chosen and tended by her, but after more than a year, there was nothing else left of her here. Will's capable son cared for the roses and cut the grass and it was sad that a life spent dedicated to cultivating the special place had left little trace behind, apart from the choice of blooms. Miriam was gone and the world spun unconcerned.

Hana sat on the bench and closed her eyes, pulling her sweatshirt closer around her cold body. She tuned into her surroundings, trying to touch God with her mind. The bush noises were peaceful and comforting, the call of native birds and the stamp of horses. The occasional lowing of distant cattle numbed Hana's shattered nerves and gave her peace. Perhaps God was in that small sense of solitude and concord.

Hana heard a car pull onto the gravel and let it fit into the sounds of the hotel, separating it from the bush noises. In her busy mind she divided the sounds into natural and manmade, occupying herself and preventing the constant agonising and rehashing of unkind words and actions. Two strong arms snaked around either side of Hana's neck and joined in the middle of her chest. Hair tickled the back of her neck and a heavy head rested on her shoulders. "Hi, Ma. You miss me?"

"Of course I missed you." Hana kissed the strong brown forearm and a rush of gratitude caused a waver in her voice, "But did you miss me?"

"Always." Tama's face was bristly as he planted a kiss on her cheek. He came around the front of the bench and sat down next to her, fixing his long arm around her shoulder. Hana cuddled into the young man and closed her eyes. "Why are you sad?" Tama asked, resting his cheek on her head.

"How do you know I am?" Hana asked with a sigh.

"I can just tell," Tama replied, sounding wise for his twenty years. "And Toby texted me and told me to get my ass home because it had all turned to shit."

"Oh. Lovely. So my emotional and mental state is what the stockmen talk about over morning tea is it?" It came out with more sarcasm than Hana intended. It was wasted on her adopted son.

"Sure is. It's headline stuff. What is the gorgeous Mrs Du Rose wearing today? Will it be jeans and a sunhat and nothing else, or will it be a flower print dress with matching shoes?"

Hana shook her head. Tama oozed Du Rose ego and confidence through every pore. She adored him. She laid her head against his arm and wished all her problems could breeze out as easily as this upbeat young man had breezed in. "Why are you back?" she tried to keep suspicion out of her voice but Tama knew her too well.

"No, I haven't been fired or chucked out. I'm doing good actually. I passed my first lot of exams and I've even been allowed to play with real fires." He became serious. "Na, it's mid-course break and I wanted to spend some time with you and Loge and catch up with Lucy in Hamilton. I wanted to see if it was ok to invite her here. She's got a few days leave and then I can see you all at once."

"Of course it's ok," Hana said immediately. Then she remembered all Logan's gear piled in the spare bedroom and cringed.

"Ok, so are you gonna tell me what the story is, or do I have to tickle it out of you?" Tama asked, releasing Hana's shoulders. He leaned forward with his forearms on his knees and looked back at her. His dark hair was shorter than usual and tidy, but his grey eyes peered sideways at her, narrowed and insistent; just like always.

"Just ask Toby," Hana said rudely and Tama smirked, lifting one side of his mouth like Logan did.

"Tickle it is then." He sat up abruptly and Hana shrieked as Tama's sharp fingers dug into her ribs and forced their way into her armpits.

"Stop, stop," she begged, pushing at his hands and failing miserably. The fireman easily overpowered her until she was a blithering wreck, unable to control even her own dribble which leaked unattractively between her lips and onto the floor. "I give in!" she cried.

"Too slow," Tama lowered his probing fingers to her waist where he knew she was most sensitive. He tried to squeeze and then stopped unexpectedly. His hands strayed to Hana's rounded abdomen and he lifted his head and looked her straight in the eyes. "Geez, Ma. Have you been at the pies or what?"

Hana's body went from rigid and afraid of his reaction, to indignant and offended. "You just called me fat! You shouldn't do that to a woman, don't you know that?" She was huffy and cross but enraged when Tama pulled her sweatshirt apart like an eager peep show punter and tried to lift her tee shirt. It felt obscene in the public garden.

"I wanna see!" he insisted and Hana slapped his fingers.

"Do you really?" she asked him, pushing his hands away. "What do you think that will look like, just as Logan walks around the corner? Or even better, your mate Toby. Wouldn't that be a story for smoko break? Did you hear the latest...?"

"Ok, ok." Tama released Hana but turned sideways on the bench. "So how about you tell me what's going on?"

"Nothing," Hana sulked and he laughed at her, just like he always did. It was infuriating. Tama reached for her hands clasped firmly in her lap and Hana jumped.

"I won't tickle you," Tama said softly. "But I do know what a pregnancy looks like, Ma. Why didn't you tell me?"

Hana inhaled, slowly and deeply. But when she exhaled, a hideous, pent-up sob escaped. She clapped her hand over it but it was followed by fifteen minutes of crying on the shoulder of a young man who felt more like blood to her, than her own son.

Tama held her and occasionally kissed Hana on the side of her sweaty temple. Her hair was frizzled and stuck to her face and she knew her eyes must resemble something stolen from a frog. Whenever she thought she might have got a hold of herself, more emotion would take her by surprise. Tama's shirt was soaked and stuck to his chest but his hands were gentle, rubbing her back and stroking her hair. Hana told him everything and when she finally sat up, looking a mess, she felt exhausted but strangely better.

"So what's this kid look like?" Tama asked her. "Do you think he's Logan's?"

"I don't know." Devastation washed over Hana. "He's definitely a Du Rose. Everything about him screams of you lot apparently. He's actually not the problem. It's his mother who makes my life an absolute misery. She's out to get Logan back and I feel like I just pale into insignificance next to her perfect make-up and expensive hairdo. It's like Troll meets Barbie."

"That's your problem, not hers," Tama said sagely and Hana stared at him, hurt. "Well it is," he justified himself. "If you let people put you down and make you feel nothing, then that's your fault. It's not Logan's and it probably isn't hers."

Hana sulked, knitting her brows and folding her arms. Tama laughed. "Oh, crikey. Phoenix does that. Now I know where she's learned it."

Hana slapped his thigh and hurt her hand. "Have you been working out or something? Your legs are like tree trunks."

"I have to. I need to carry heavy equipment and people, sometimes both at the same time. They didn't pick me because I had spindly arms and legs and couldn't carry more than two sheets of paper at any one time, did they?"

"You're still mouthy," Hana said crossly and Tama shrugged.

"Ah well. Not everything can change at once," he concluded. "So, have you asked Logan about hitting Flick?"

"What's the point?" Hana asked. "What can I do to change it even if I know? Logan will somehow justify it and Bobby won't tell me the truth anyway. I'll end up the loser, just like I always do."

"So Flick didn't admit Logan did it?"

"Of course he didn't!" Hana grew crosser, raising her voice in irritation. "Logan's his employer. What would he have to gain by telling me that my husband hit him for helping me get to a hospital scan? Nobody else cared that he was keeping me prisoner and holding my daughter to ransom to keep me here?"

Tama raised his eyebrows at the drama in the tale. "Flick would have quite a lot to gain actually." He turned towards Hana and moved in closer to her. "Look, all the other lads respect you, right? You're Mrs Du Rose and that gives you an entitlement. But they respect you even more because of who you are. You've changed Logan, you've seen off Caroline and they all know that you've thumped Kane and Michael Du Rose for having a go at Logan. Gossip goes round this place like a...virus."

"You were going to say 'bushfire' weren't you?" Hana looked cute as she peeked up at Tama from under her eyelashes and he smiled sadly.

"Yeah, I was. But in view of Poppa Reuben's house burning down, I figured it probably wasn't appropriate."

Hana nodded and Tama continued, "But everyone knows you can ride Sacha and she's only ever let Logan before. And you gave birth to a baby in the bush all by yourself. You've got *mana* and they all know it."

"This is all very...nice." Hana wiped her nose on her sleeve. "But where are you going with it?"

"Flick's different. He doesn't just respect you, Ma, he's *in love* with you. He hangs on your every word, he'll do anything to get to see you and it's really obvious. It's gonna get him into real trouble. He's got his head in the clouds if he thinks you'd run off with some blond drover, when you've got Logan."

Hana's head whipped round. "What?"

"Yeah, I know. Maybe you didn't realise, but he's got it bad. Logan must be aware of it and you know what he's like..."

"No, what did you call him?"

"Flick?"

"No, you called him the *blond drover*. Why?"

Tama pulled a face and shook his head. "He's blond, Ma. I don't know who started it but last time I was home, the other guys referred to him as that."

"David Allen's blond. Do they call him that?"

"No. You're missing the point, Ma."

"Which is?" Hana grew frustrated.

"Which is, that I would give him a slap if he was in love with my wife and not doing an awful lot to hide the fact!"

"Oh." Hana inhaled and ran her hands over her eyes. Most of her mascara was on Tama's shirt and she knew she looked like a panda.

"So don't be so hard on him, Ma. You're smarter than this."

Hana nodded. "I just hate violence."

"Fine then. I'll just ask him to leave. That will solve the problem."

Hana's face creased in dismay. She rounded on the young man. "But he has nowhere to go. The cops would pick him up straight away and lock him up for all that stuff a few years ago. That would be cruel!"

"They would lock him up for menacing you, Ma. He stalked and harassed you for a year. You went into hiding and he terrified you. Don't you forget *that!*"

Hana hung her head and sighed. Confusion tormented her as she tried to blend the old Flick, with the Bobby she knew now.

"Do you have feelings for him?" Tama asked softly and Hana cringed.

"I knew I could rely on him when I needed help. But I don't love him, no. I love his company and how he makes me feel around him." She thought about Bobby offering to get her and Phoenix out if she ever needed it. His support made her feel strong and safe against Logan's irrational and unbending might. She shook her head, knowing she had abused the man's affections and guilt stormed into her heart and took up residence.

"Ma, listen to me. Logan's never hit someone who wasn't asking for it. And he and Flick have come to blows before and they're pretty evenly matched. Logan could throw him out in a heartbeat but he hasn't. Maybe Flick just needed the line drawing for him. It's over now. That's how it works out here. Leave him alone and worry about your own problems. You're having another baby, your marriage has got more holes in it than a Swiss cheese and there's a woman getting her claws into your husband. So why are you worrying about some blond drover who's got ideas about the boss' wife. Come on, Ma. Get a grip."

Hana looked sideways at the gorgeous, dark haired young man next to her. She scooted close to him and put her arms around his neck, wondering when he had grown from the troublesome, randy teenager into this wise adult. She kissed him on the cheek and sat back down. "You're right," she conceded.

"Tama!" the screech was shrill and urgent. He and Hana whipped round to see Phoenix struggling against Leslie's grasp. The old lady held onto the toddler with an iron grip and the child showed her status as Logan's daughter, refusing to be contained.

"Wait!" Leslie told her firmly and Alfred scooped the child up and carried her towards the bench. He hated the rose garden and stopped just outside the arched entryway, memories of his dead wife creating hard edges to his face.

"Somebody wants to see her favourite person," he chortled and attempted to smile at Hana. The expression failed to reach his eyes and she smiled back, resisting the urge to run to him and embrace his twisted body in solidarity. Phoenix's legs were running before her feet hit the ground and by the time her body contacted Tama's legs, she was in tears, overcome with emotions too big to deal with. It made Hana want to cry again, the simplicity of the little girl's love for the Du Rose male, as she fixed her spindly arms around his neck and drooped down his chest, holding on as though she would never let go. It was always like this when he arrived and much, much worse when he left.

"Hey Wiri," Tama said kindly to Nev's boy as he marched across the gravel. Tama ruffled the four-year-olds hair under his large hand as the boy smiled up at him and put both arms round one of Tama's thighs.

"You ok?" Alfred said to Hana and she nodded. He eyed her puffy face doubtfully and grimaced. His own wife's foibles were enough for him to deal with. "Oh," he turned. "The missus said please can you take the kids to the kitchen for some food. She's going to change her shoes. They been killin' her feet all day, stupid pointy things. Then come up to the flat for a visit. Yeah?"

Hana smiled and nodded. "Thanks for taking Phoe. I bet she loved it."

Alfred nodded, stuffed his gnarled hands into his pockets and strode away.

"Oh, damn!" Tama looked at Hana. "I need to talk to him about something. Will you be ok on your own for a bit?"

"Yeah," Hana nodded and with difficulty, peeled her daughter from the young man's neck. "Come on, baby. How about we go and make some special food for Tama in the kitchen?"

It took some persuasion but finally Phoenix let go, only satisfied when Hana put a sandwich on the table between her plate and Wiremu's for Tama, which she guarded with her life. Hana settled the children on cushions on the dining chairs. They looked cute, reaching up for their food with only their eyes peeking over the table. She grabbed ready-made sandwiches from the chiller and bags of potato chips. When she returned to the dining table, Logan stood in the corner of the room, shooting searching looks at his wife through brooding eyes. Not wanting to reopen her wounds, Hana went back to the empty kitchen and found some custard which she heated for the little ones, leaving her husband to sulk and watch over them in her absence.

Chapter 21

"Oh no! Oh no! Mummy! Daddy's beedins," Phoenix cried out as blood dripped in a relentless torrent from Logan's nose. The little girl continued picking the filling out of her sandwich, while Neville's son watched wide-eyed and nervous. Logan sat on a dining chair and leaned forward. It was pointless trying to stop the flow so he concentrated on containing it in one place on the wooden floor. Hana abandoned the children's steaming bowls of custard in the kitchen and appeared with a towel, hastily snatched from the counter and a roll of industrial catering paper. Hana folded the towel carefully and pressed it with gentle fingers underneath her husband's nose. Then she tore off a length of the blue roll and laid it on the floor over the red puddle. Instantly it grabbed the blood like a sponge, saturated in seconds.

Logan swore as the flow continued over the towel and dripped onto Hana's wrist as she mopped at the puddle. Hana wiped at the spatter, smearing more than she removed. "Sorry," Logan put his fingers over the mark on her skin and tried to rub the red stain away. He held the towel one-handed, his grey eyes watching Hana intently over the fold. His fingers moved to hers and he covered Hana's hand, holding it firmly and not letting go. It made it impossible for her to stand up again.

"Logan, let go," she said quietly and his grip tightened. "Logan!" she repeated, aware of the children behind her at the table.

"Daddy!" Phoenix called and Logan's eyes flicked upwards to his daughter. He rolled his eyes. "Daddy, do dis!" she squeaked and Wiremu next to her let out a peal of laughter.

"No, Phoe," Logan shook his head and the blood sprayed as he coughed. Hana rested on her knees and twisted her body to look at her daughter. Phoenix beamed up at her parents, having demonstrated her helpful suggestion. Two bread crusts dangled from her nostrils and Wiremu laughed until the tears ran from his eyes.

"Do dis, Daddy," Phoenix said again and shook her head to make her unusual wadding shake. She grinned at the four year old next to her, who looked in pain with his extreme mirth. His laughter was like the tinkle of bells and Phoenix revelled in his attention.

"Phoe, take it out!" Hana said firmly and the little girl pulled both crusts out with a pop. "Logan let go!" Hana tugged at her hand as Phoenix looked in confusion at the one and a half crusts in her fingers.

"Oh, no!" she wailed and held her trophies in the air.

Logan released his wife's hand and watched as Hana attempted to prise the bread from her daughter's left nostril. "Don't do that again!" Hana told her. She ventured near enough to her husband to snatch up a length of the blue roll and held it under her daughter's nose. "Blow!" she told the child. There was the sound of snorting as Phoenix expelled the bread from her nose. Her face was completely hidden in the giant tissue and Wiremu creased in half with a groan of pain as his stomach complained at his belly laughter.

"Look," Phoenix said with childish bemusement. "Crumbs comed out my nose. Look Wiri, I maked a sammich in my nose 'oles."

Wiremu laughed so hard that he fell off the dining chair onto the floor and then threw his lunch up on the wooden boards. Phoenix popped out of her tissue and looked to her right, perplexed at her companion's disappearance. "Where Wiri gone?" she demanded.

Into the scene of domestic bliss walked Sylvia, her high platform heels tapping on the boards. Hana rolled her eyes and shook her head in irritation as the woman sneered at the child on the floor bawking up his food. "Oh dear," she said condescendingly and then spotted Logan bleeding into the towel. "Oh my!" she shrieked and looked accusingly at Hana. "What did you do to him?" She hurried over to Hana's husband and leaned over him. "Poor baby," she crooned and patted him on the top of his head as though he were the four year old and not Wiremu. Hana sighed and rubbed the boy on his back as he finished being sick.

"Never mind," she said kindly, reaching for the blue roll again. Hana wiped Wiri's face and helped him blow his nose, ignoring the woman currently fawning over her husband. But her heart twisted in her chest and made her want to scream. *I can't do this,* her brain lectured her, further damaging her commitment to her marriage vows and making her want to run.

Hana seated the now subdued little boy back on his seat and pulled a drink of water towards him. She cleaned the sick off the floor with the roll and dumped the pile of mess in the dustbin in the corner. "That better?" she asked and he nodded.

"Luff you, Mama," Phoenix said generously and patted Hana's bottom with a crumby hand.

"I luff you too," Wiremu said, his words echoing into his glass.

"Does your daddy do beedins too?" Phoenix asked him chattily and he shook his head, slopping water down his shirt.

"Oops. Nope. Daddy don't do that. But Uncle Kane does it."

The children seemed unconcerned that a grown man steadily haemorrhaged in the corner. Hana's brow furrowed at Wiri's offhand revelation that Logan's half-brother was a haemophiliac. She felt a flicker of guilt.

"You made 'im bleed once, dint ya, Hana?" Wiremu reminded her helpfully.

"Yes," Hana replied. "It was very wrong of me and I'm sorry."

"You slapped 'is face and kicked 'is leg. He said you was hot and he'd like to..."

"You should be ashamed of yourself!" Sylvia launched her bile in Hana's direction, misreading the situation completely. "I've a good mind to call the cops!"

"Oh, shut your face!" Hana told her, irritation growing in her breast. "I keep hoping you've left, but here you are again."

"I'm not going anywhere," Sylvia simpered. "I still have feelings for Logan and I know he loves me. Why can't you just accept it?"

"Just get off me," Logan said from inside the towel, getting to his feet and towering over the woman. Sylvia took a step back as blood cascaded down from Logan's nose and splattered onto the floor again. Hana sighed at the mess on the polished floorboards, which seemed to mirror the devastation in her marriage. "What do I have to do or say to make you understand, *I'm not interested?*" Logan raised his voice and the children fell silent. Phoenix looked instantly sad. In an action of solidarity, the big hearted boy next to her reached across and held her hand tightly. Their grey eyes locked and the child squeezed his cousin's greasy hand. Hana had a moment of unease as she remembered Logan and Caroline's relationship, fostered in the same way. She dismissed the unwelcome thought. Wiremu was *definitely* no Caroline. He was sweet and generous like Nev and adored Phoenix. Sensing the children's distress, reflecting what came off Logan in waves, Hana moved towards her husband, heartened by the look of gratitude he shot her.

"Excuse me," Hana said forcefully and pulled the towel from her irritated husband's face. Blood dripped up her arms and onto her sweatshirt sleeves. "It doesn't matter," she told Logan softly as he tried to keep his hand under his nose. "Let's get your tee shirt off."

Logan let Hana pull it up from the waist and wrestle it off over his head. Apart from a couple of spots, she managed to salvage it. "I don't know why you insist on white shirts," she chastised him, her voice kind. Hana held the soaked and bloody towel back up to his face. "I'll nip next door and get you another."

"No like lady," Phoenix whispered to Wiremu, her brow furrowed. He nodded knowingly and put his slender arm around Phoe's shoulders, cuddling her close in what looked like an unfortunate headlock. Phoenix didn't complain, used to Jas' attempts to 'army train' her.

Hana returned with another towel, already grubby from her bloody fingerprints and admired her husband's gorgeous physique as she walked across the wide dining room. Logan's muscle definition was borne of hard work on the farm and weight training in the garage at home. He was fit and thick veins stood out along his muscular torso and arms, accentuated by his olive skinned complexion. A thick line of dark hair weaved its way into his jeans along a taut stomach and a gold St Christopher dangled enticingly between his pectoral muscles.

Sylvia ogled shamelessly and Hana felt like slapping her. Logan had turned away from the children and faced the window, his left side towards the women. He moved at the sound of Hana's footsteps and carefully lowered the soaked towel. "It's slowing," he said with relief and smiled wistfully at his wife. Hana saw the uncertainty in his eyes as he sought to make everything right, failing dismally with the presence of the *other woman*. Sylvia's existence blighted everything without trying. Hana handed him the towel and Logan lifted his right hand to take it, still holding the dirty one in his other hand. Sylvia gasped audibly as his action revealed the long, ugly scar which ran from under his armpit down his side before disappearing into his jeans and ending on his right hip. It was ridged like a watershed in his skin, the wickedness of his half-brothers exposed in all its hideousness. Sylvia clapped her hand over her mouth and Hana felt horrified at her overtly awful reaction.

The pit-pat of little feet on the floorboards heralded Hana's daughter bearing a packet of baby wipes. "Here go," she said sweetly and stood on tippy-toes to hand them over. On her way back to her seat she shoved at the drawer in a large wooden dresser, closing it roughly.

"Thoughtful girl, thank you," Hana smiled at her daughter and watched anxiously as she scaled the chair on her way back up, grunting as she fought the pretty dress that hindered her progress. "Here," Hana extracted a wipe for Logan, moving to block Sylvia's view of his nakedness. He fumbled with it and his face was shrouded and dark. When he looked at Hana she knew he had seen Sylvia's reaction to his scarred body and was upset. Hana's expression softened at her husband's self-consciousness, a muscle twitching in his cheek. She used another wipe to clean blood from around his face and chin. When he stumbled slightly, lightheaded from the blood loss, she kept hold of his forearm until he was safely seated.

Logan leaned forward and squeezed the bridge of his nose between his fingers. He looked crushed. "Oh, Loge," Hana whispered and pulled his head into her, holding him tightly despite the turmoil in her heart. Logan reached around with both arms and clung to his wife, turning his face sideways and closing his eyes against the rough zipper of her sweatshirt. "Poor boy." Hana kissed his soft, dark curls and laid her head against the top of his.

"Ahhh," Phoenix said. When Hana peeked at her, she grinned like a maniac and had managed to fit the offensive bread crust over her top lip like a moustache, gluing it on with snot. Hana sighed and heard the sound of feet moving behind her, reminding her that Sylvia was still in the room. Her heart sank.

"How do you feel now, Loge?" Hana asked her husband, stroking his hair back from his forehead. "Do you want me to drive you to the hospital?"

"I'll go with him," Sylvia's voice squeaked from behind Hana. "You stay with the children. He'll be better off with me."

Hana's body twitched involuntarily and her back grew rigid. Logan raised his head. "I don't need the hospital. I'm just going to lie down."

"Ok, I'll help you up to *our* room," Sylvia simpered and the heaviness settled back on Hana's head as the familiar mantra started up again. *I can't do this anymore. I can't win this fight.*

"No thanks," Logan's tone was cool, his authority restored. He passed the wipe across the underside of his nose one more time, seeing only a pink streak for his trouble. Satisfied, he rose to his feet and stood up straight, dwarfing both women. "We'll go to Mike's room. Come on kids, let's go upstairs." He wadded up his various blood-soaked tissues, wipes and the towels and slung them in the rubbish bin on top of the blue roll.

"Plates, Daddy," Phoenix said, pointing to the mess on the table.

"Leave it," her father said firmly. "The paid staff can do it or I'll get it later." Logan hoisted Phoenix onto his hip and put his arm around his wife's waist, drawing her into his scarred side. "Come on Wiri," he said to the little boy, who popped off his seat and immediately latched onto Hana's other hand.

"But you need peace and quiet," Sylvia piped up, tugging at the hairy forearm locked around Hana's waist. "You'd be much better without all these..." the woman wafted her arm, encompassing Logan's wife, daughter and nephew.

Logan stopped, spun on his heel and fixed his stern grey eyes on Sylvia. "I'd like you to leave my hotel," he said with determination. "I apologise for what you think I did or didn't do, but I'm not going to leave Hana for you and I'm not going to abandon my family. There's nothing between us and never will be."

"But what about our trip to Auckland together?" she cried, desperation mingling with disappointment and adding a snarl to her voice.

"You can stay for that on Friday and then I want you gone. Ryan can stay long-term if he wants," Logan said. "But I've had enough of your games. *This* is my family." Logan's head jerk took in his girls. "I've waited too long to be happy and you don't get to ruin it. You've got until the weekend to find somewhere else to go. Then I want you out. One of the boys will drive you into the city and I don't want to hear from you again. Thanks for everything you did for Ryan and I'll try to make it up to him. But I don't need you, to do that."

Logan's hand was strong in the small of Hana's back as he pushed her towards the door. She felt a sudden release of pressure in her chest, which caught her by surprise, realising in the hallway that she'd held her breath for far too long. It gratified Hana to hear her husband state that he felt nothing for Sylvia. But more than that, Hana knew from the other woman's reaction to Logan's scars, she had *never* seen Logan's naked body before.

Chapter 22

"Sit down and I'll take your shoes off." Hana pushed Logan into a sitting position on Michael's old bed and he kept his arms tightly around her waist, his face pressed into her stomach. Phoenix tried to clamber onto the bed from the other side and Hana rolled her eyes as Wiremu boosted her capably up and then bounced up after her.

"No," the small boy said firmly as she bounced on her knees. "Uncle's not well so you have to be good."

"I good," Phoenix said, poked her thumb into her mouth and settled down on the pillow. Wiremu inspected his bare feet for dust and muck and then satisfied, laid down next to her on his back and stared up at the ceiling. Hana smothered a smirk at their unintentional portrayal of the archetypal old married couple.

"If you let me go, I'll make you a sugary drink." Hana soothed her husband and stroked his silky hair. "It helps with the blood loss." She absentmindedly wound one of his dark curls around her middle finger and watched it uncoil itself and dive back onto his head.

"Not letting you go," Logan muttered, sounding like a little boy.

"Well you need to. You have to lie down and I need to get you a drink to help you recover."

Logan held her tighter and the child in her stomach did a somersault and kicked Logan in the face. Hana winced and squeezed her eyes shut in discomfort and Logan put his head back and looked at her. "Sorry," he said, the apology ruined by the wonder in his voice. "Wow. Babies are so amazing." He ran his fingers softly over Hana's stomach, feeling the definite contours of a foot protruding just below her navel. "Does that hurt?"

"Yes. Of course it hurts," she replied impatiently.

Phoenix snuffled on the bed and rubbed her nose, her eyes squeezed tightly shut. Wiremu didn't move his gaze from the ceiling but reached out and patted her on the head. "Sshh," he breathed and ruffled her hair. Phoenix snuggled in close to his boy body and he popped his own thumb into his mouth and closed his eyes. Logan followed the direction of Hana's contemplation and his brow knitted at the two small children curled up together on the other side of the huge bed.

"I think the zoo with Alfred and Leslie tired them out," Hana said. Logan's head whipped back to face her.

"We just need to be a bit careful with them though," he said and he looked genuinely concerned.

Hana was immediately irritated, hushing her voice to avoid waking them up but hissing at her husband. "They're four and not yet two. What do you think they're likely to get up to, Logan?"

"Fine," he replied. "But it's not funny. It's how this whole mess started. I don't want him growing up and laying claim to my daughter. We're breaking that pattern right now."

"At least she'd know what she was getting into," Hana mused thoughtfully and Logan narrowed his eyes at her. He pulled her down to sit on his knee. "I get that it's hard marrying into the Du Roses. But we'll cross that bridge when we come to it."

"Fine," Hana lay her head on Logan's shoulder. "But can we not be suspicious of babies please?"

"Deal." Logan held her in his strong arms and kissed Hana's neck through her hair. "Hey, how many times have I told you how beautiful you are today?" he asked, his voice muffled.

"None," she sulked. "And you owe me all those days when we were fighting. You didn't tell me then, even though you promised at our wedding that not a single day would go by when you didn't."

"That's true," Logan whispered. "I might just combine all the days and do one big show and tell." He worked his fingers under the side of Hana's tee shirt and touched the soft skin under her ribs.

Hana shivered. "There's children present and I'm still cross with you."

"Pity," he sighed. "Later then."

Chapter 23

Hana peered at the photograph, knitting her brow in concentration at what she saw in the digital screen of her phone. They lay on the bed and chatted, the imposing Du Rose men. Logan was half-propped against the pillows, his feet crossed at the ankles and his toes still touching the footboard. Tama lay next to him, his head bowed so that his uncles could talk over the top of him, Wiremu cuddled up on his chest. The young man held his mobile phone over the top of Wiri's head and watched something on YouTube. His body leaned in towards Ryan and their heads almost touched. They were both about to laugh at something. Nev perched beside Ryan, not relaxed or stretched out but half-sitting with one long leg reaching the floor. His face was turned towards Logan. Nev's features were frozen in a frown and Logan's enquiring; a snapshot in time. They had been discussing something to do with the Charolaise herd. They were all alike, identical peas in a pod. Their uniform was the wavy dark hair and piercing grey eyes. Hana saw just by looking that they were brothers and nephews. Ryan's head was slightly turned away from the camera lens but the likeness was overpowering.

Hana zoomed in and examined something. "I would never have got away with taking a photo like that," she said to her daughter. "How did they not notice what you were doing?"

Phoenix looked up from her task. She unwound a toilet roll with delicate fingers and settled it gently into a cardboard box for her toy horse to sleep in. It was wasteful, but she had asked so nicely and it seemed essential for her game. "Photo," Phoenix repeated in her silky voice, busy making her fake straw comfy for Fluffy. She patted it into the corners already aware of how hard it was for a horse to rise from a lying position. Her olive face creased in concentration as she made sure that her companion wouldn't get cast and die in the night because he couldn't get up again in the smooth bedding. She had forgotten about the quick snaps she took on her mother's phone and Hana cheerfully deleted the close up of Logan's sock and the one the little girl had clambered over Nev to capture; Wiri's nostrils.

"How can a baby work an iPhone?" Hana mused. "I didn't even know how to turn the camera on."

"Camera on!" Suddenly Phoenix was interested.

"No," Hana said with a decisive edge. "Mummy's camera."

"Mama's camera." Phoenix held her tiny hand out hopefully. Hana shook her head.

"Another time maybe. Come on, Fluffy needs some tea before bed. He looks hungry."

Phoenix felt torn. Hana saw her working through the dilemma in her mind and then decide that her horse's needs were paramount. "Pees carry 'im?" she asked her mother, pointing to the box. She looked anxious.

Phoenix sat at the centre island on a bar stool and Fluffy balanced on the one next to her. His furry face poked over the edge of the box, his head at a jaunty angle as it rested on the smooth surface of the work top. A raw carrot sat on a plate in front of him untouched. Hana finished her dinner, reheated shepherd's pie and moved her plate gently to the side so she could drink her cup of tea. Phoenix spooned the mince and mash into her mouth eagerly. She beamed at Hana with the mixture in her mouth and teeth and Hana smiled and gently suggested she closed her mouth until she had swallowed. "Fuffy eat cawot," Phoenix told her toy and patted his forehead gently.

Hana slid her phone out of her pocket and peeked at the photo again under the counter. She nagged Logan for reading his emails during mealtimes and felt like a hypocrite. A glance at Phoenix found her nibbling at the carrot. The chance photograph was both revealing and damning. It was a beautiful snap of a family scene and would look amazing as a record of the Du Rose poster boys. Hana would get a copy to Will for the archives. Its unforced naturalness was appealing, but it also caused her heart to clench in pain. It was obvious who Ryan's father was. The likeness was unmistakable.

"Where Daddy?" Phoenix asked and Hana slipped her phone back into her pocket.

"He's sorting something out with Uncle Nev," she replied. "Something important."

"Daddy no more beeds?" the little girl asked, compassion in her eyes. She put her fingers up to her button nose and winced. "Dat sore."

Hana smiled. "All gone. Daddy's all better now." She wished it were true.

"All better now," Phoe repeated and beamed happily, her little world faithfully restored. She pointed a delicate finger at her friend, "Fuffy like cawot. Phoe like cawot."

"I think Fluffy's full up now. How about you help him out?" Hana suggested and the child gave her a coy look, reaching for the bright orange vegetable without breaking eye contact with her mother. Once it was in her hand she leaned into the horse's face. "I helpin'," she whispered and took loud, crunchy bites.

Hana bathed Phoenix, a happy, splashy affair which proved the necessity of the wet room design which Logan had insisted on. The excess water ran towards a dip in the tiled floor and exited though a plug hole in the corner of the room. Hana shut the door afterwards and left the room to dry itself without her frantic intervention with towels and effort. She was determined to enjoy time with her daughter, remembering how Isobel's appearance had robbed Bodie of her time, attention and smiles for far too long. "Maybe that's what's wrong with him," she mused as Phoenix popped her head through the neck of her pyjama top. "He feels hard done by."

"Dum by," Phoenix repeated.

The darkness imposed upon the floor length windows as Hana read Phoenix a story. The little bears in the picture book were finally put to bed by their frantic bear mother and tucked up for the night. The moral of the story was 'do as you're told' but Phoenix wouldn't realise that for a few years yet. "Cow," the little girl said and turned Fluffy's face to see what she was looking at. Hana shook her head.

"No cows, babe. Just bears."

"Cow," Phoenix insisted and popped her thumb from her mouth and pointed with it. "Cow."

Hana followed the direction of the wet thumb and gasped, instinctively clutching her stomach to shield her son. The slightly crossed eyes of one of the large shaggy white cows stared in at her, its hooves planted firmly on the scrubby grass outside. Logan had raised the foundations of the house so that the high deck lined up with the bottom of the doors. The beast's head and shoulders were visible above the rail which ran the length of the deck, the only thing stopping the animal coming right up to the window.

"Get Daddy nen?" Phoenix asked. "Naughty cow not 'lowed in Daddy-garden."

Hana stood up slowly and the animal's eyes widened. Its ears flicked.

"Calfie!" Phoenix squealed and it snorted and jumped away from the window. Phoenix beat Hana to the ranch slider and put her hands and nose against the glass. Her nappy showed through the back of her elasticated pyjama bottoms. "Baby one!" she danced with happiness. The tiny animal tottered behind its white mother on pipe-cleaner legs which bent and wobbled underneath it. "Bootiful!" Phoenix sighed and beamed happily. She repeated herself over and over and then looked expectantly for Hana to open the door so she could go out and cuddle it. In the fading light, Hana saw the mucus dangling from the cow's shaggy tail.

"You can't go out," she said to her eager child. Phoenix's face crumpled in disappointment and her frown heralded the forthcoming objection. "No!" Hana said forcefully, reaching into her pocket for her phone.

"Photo?" Phoenix said and held out her hand. Hana squatted down to her level whilst dialling the number for the hotel.

"It's a brand new baby, Phoe. The mummy will get angry if you go near it. You can't go out. I need to get Daddy."

"Get Daddy. Daddy bwave. Not me. Daddy." Phoenix pushed her sincere face into Hana's just to make sure her mother understood and nodded her head with forced precision.

Hana nodded and sighed as her phone reception disappeared. She ran down the hallway to the kitchen and seized the wireless phone that connected her to the main house. Realising her daughter hadn't followed, Hana moved quickly back to her, finding her still watching the grazing dam, her hands pressed against the glass. "Baby dwinkin'," she smiled and pointed at the suckling calf. "He back and white."

Hana looked again, perplexed as the receptionist answered the phone at the hotel. "Hi Carrie," Hana started politely. "It's Hana. Please could you raise Logan for me? We've got a stray cow and calf in tow up at our place. It looks like she might have birthed it in the garden and..."

"More!" squealed Phoenix.

"...there are quite a few of them actually. I don't know where they're coming from."

The receptionist's voice sounded tinney through the handset. "I'll radio him. He went out with all the other Mr Du Roses a couple of hours ago."

"What - pardon?" Hana corrected herself. "Went where? What other Mr Du Roses?"

The woman hesitated, unable to sort the genealogy in her head sufficiently to list them as father, nephew and cousin. None of which were true. She resorted to names instead. "Logan, Alfred, Tama and Neville Du Rose. All of them. They rode out about four o'clock. Caused quite a bit of excitement in the car park on those mad horses of theirs." She laughed and then thought better of it. Hana heard lust in her voice and fleetingly wondered who she had been ogling. Early twenties, Hana figured it would be Tama.

"Oh. I'm not sure what to do then," Hana panicked. "How far did they go?"

"Back blocks," Carrie confirmed and Hana sighed.

"Ok. Thanks. Please radio him and let him know that some of the stock has come up here. They seem..." Hana watched Phoenix's face take on a look of disbelief as a large distressed dam raised her tail in a wiggly pencil-crayoned line and birthed a massive, cloudy bag of something from her back end. The sack slithered to the ground and the cow turned and licked it, uncovering the face of another calf.

"Mrs Du Rose?" the receptionist called, concerned at Hana's abrupt halt.

"Sorry," Hana sounded distant as she willed the little body to move. For a long time it didn't and then suddenly it wiggled, struggling to release itself from the constrictive natural sleeping bag. "The cows are upset. They look like they're spontaneously aborting. They're milling around and someone's going to get hurt. Look, if Logan's not there, please can you send someone else. Maybe Toby or Flick. They can't all have gone. It feels like something's wrong."

Hana squatted down next to Phoenix as the herd seemed to swell and grow, penning the newborns into a corner next to the house under stamping hooves. The child looked up at Hana wide-eyed as the throng increased, sure her mother would do something amazing and fix everything. Hana felt powerless. She put her hand over her mouth and prayed for the tiny, spindly bodies being forced back against the deck. "Oh

God," she breathed, "help them." She fought the urge to cry in front of Phoenix as the small bodies hid underneath their dam's stamping legs, moving as the herd swirled like water.

They were seconds away from being smashed and broken as the bullwhip sounded, cracking out into the dusk like an alarm. The herd shuddered and stopped. A dark horseman appeared at the edge of the garden, his hat masking his face but his body perfectly aligned to the white mare underneath him.

"Daddy!" Phoenix shouted and slammed her palm on the window.

"He can't hear you, baby," Hana said, relief in her voice. She put her arm around her child and cuddled her in close. She was desperate to pull her daughter onto the bed and close the curtains against the reality of their farming life, but knew it would cause more harm. She and Logan had argued about it frequently.

"Life sucks," he had said with passion. "I'm not sheltering her from it. She needs to see things resolved otherwise she'll be a runner, like you and me!"

"I have to let you see it finish," Hana breathed into her child's fluffy hair. "I need to let you see it all made better, otherwise you'll have bad dreams about it."

Phoenix pushed her bottom lip out and studied the scene before her with intense concentration, the hot bath and soporific story wasted in the aftermath. Sleep had gone from her eyes and her taut little body.

"Shed them!" Logan shouted to the other riders who appeared on the fringes and they moved around the seething mass, pushing their way through on fearless mounts.

"Sacha!" Phoenix pointed. "Luff Sacha."

Logan's white mare ducked and weaved, her head higher than usual as she avoided horns and flailing hooves. Logan sat solidly in the saddle, his body flowing with hers as he controlled her just with the touch of his reins against her neck. He was strong and powerful, no sign of his former weakness diminishing him as he did what he loved best. Instead of hiking up the panic, the riders dispelled it. They were the herd leaders and the cows relaxed under their authority, demurring to human instruction. The men used their bullwhips to hold and release the animals, checking them before sending them this way or that. Hana would have loved to see an aerial view of the display as the men channelled the beasts between them, their horses swaying on their front feet as they darted to thwart an escapee or drive the reluctant ones after the others. Sacha did a complete spin, effortless in its execution as she followed a straying heifer. She herded it successfully and it kicked its back legs in defeat in a mammoth bunny-hop and followed the others. In no time, the huge garden was almost cleared. The swell of bodies were gone and the night noises reclaimed their prominence once again; the cackle of disturbed tui and the growl of curious possums resonating alongside the clank of metal tack and the snort of tired horses. Logan kept the mothers and calves at the back near Phoenix's window, holding his whip out straight in front of him and putting Sacha's body between them and the disappearing herd. At first they panicked but then relaxed as Logan backed up a little.

Tama, Nev and Alfred rode up to him and Phoenix's face lit up. Alfred rode as though he sat in his armchair in the apartment, his body moulded to the stock saddle and his girth hanging loose under his mount. "I forget that Poppa Alf used to run the farm," Hana said quietly, mourning the man who had seemed so potent and all-knowing at their first meeting. Phoenix nodded enthusiastically.

"Nat Mefusa," she said, pointing at the horse and Hana remembered.

"That's right. Clever girl. Methuselah."

"Me wide 'im a Poppa Alfie," Phoenix said proudly and Hana shook her head. She hated the Du Rose men's disregard for safety or lifeblood in general, slinging her baby in the saddle from six weeks old and giving her mother numerous heart-stopping moments in the last, almost two years. *So much for waiting for the helmet to fit.* Nothing had ever happened. *But it could.*

Happy with the equilibrium, Phoenix was chatty. Her father had fixed everything, just like she knew he would. "Nonie Leslie not ride dough. She fat!"

Hana's eyes grew wide at her daughter's statement of fact. It was possible that Leslie herself had said it but Hana was saved the dilemma of reprimanding Phoenix, by the men outside. Their horses walked slowly backwards, controlled by imperceptible commands and the cows moved away from the house, trotting quickly past them. The tiny calves tottered after them making a strange mewing sound. "Bye calfies," Phoenix called and waved pleasantly. Then she turned to Hana. "My 'ungry."

The four imposing Du Rose men sat in Hana's kitchen, their socks fluffy and incongruous without their work boots. The other stockmen drove the rest of the herd back down the mountain and the noise seemed to shake the house on its pilings. The men's legs were long as they sprawled on the kitchen chairs and Hana found it hard not to fall over them as she delivered coffee and sandwiches to the table. The muffins she and Phoenix made together earlier were inhaled in a matter of minutes, the interesting bright red icing barely even touching the sides of their mouths on the way down.

"So, where are the calves and horses?" Hana asked tentatively, resting her hand on Logan's outstretched thigh under the table. Nev answered.

"We've shut the gate so the new calves and dams can stay up here for the night, if that's ok?" He asked the question out of courtesy, knowing Logan had already ratified the decision. "The others are driving the rest back down the mountain to JD's paddock near the road. It's got good grass. They won't be escaping anywhere else tonight."

Hana's eyes widened at the mention of the elusive *JD*, but she kept her ears open and her mouth shut for once. Her interest was piqued and she saw Logan studying her covertly from under his lashes.

"Where horsey?" Phoenix asked her father, her mouth covered in icing and her pyjama top stained with food colouring. She held her hands out to the side, palm upwards, questioning.

Logan leaned towards his daughter. He rescued a blob of icing from her chin and almost popped it into her mouth. Even though he washed his hands more than Hana did, the cracks in his skin bore ingrained dirt and his nails were permanently filthy. He changed his mind and wiped it on the inadequate bib around her neck.

"Outside, *moko*," Alfred answered with a smile. "Having a snack with the cows."

"I see...I see...Mefusa!" Phoenix struggled with her sentence, spraying crumbs onto the table and Alfred grinned.

"Yeah, the old boy's still got it!" he beamed. Hana wasn't sure if he referred to the horse or himself. The other men smiled at each other, except Tama, who worked hard to eat everything left on the table. He ravaged the plates like a starving man. *Castaway meets McDonald's.*

"What's the damage outside?" Hana asked. She had watched one of the cows kick down the deck rail near Phoenix's window.

"Superficial," Alfred answered. "Could have been worse. You might want to keep your gate closed in future."

Hana looked at him strangely. "It is closed."

"Not," Tama interjected. He waved his muffin at Phoenix and praised her with a mouthful. She laughed, red icing in her teeth like a vampire.

"It is!" Hana insisted. "I always close it." She felt abruptly under the spotlight as though the men wanted someone to blame and she was *it*.

"So why was it open?" Nev asked, his grey eyes shrouded and disbelieving. Hana was instantly defensive and it made her rude.

"Don't mistake me for some basket-case lunatic, thanks. The gate was closed when I drove through it at three o'clock. *I* opened it and closed it! I always close it because I don't want someone to blast through it and run Phoe over when we're playing outside. It's habit. I keep it closed all the time because then I will never forget! Look for someone else to blame." Hana's fire was on show for them all to see, her red hair seeming to glow with an inner burn and her porcelain face flushed and beautiful. Her green eyes lit up like display emeralds and flashed dangerously at her brother-in-law. Nev glanced at Logan and backed down.

"Well, anyway. That's how they got in. You can see their tracks all the way up the mountain and onto the road up. Good job you never got round to landscaping. They've dug up the ground proper. Thanks for raising the alarm though. We were already looking for them but would never have tried up here."

"It bite my mummy," Phoenix swallowed, her voice sounding muffled and strange. Hana pushed her sippy cup towards her, not wanting her to vomit on the table.

"What?" Logan said to her.

"Pardon!" Phoenix swallowed the water and admonished her father, waving the sippy cup and giving him an accidental shower. "It bited Mummy hand. Ouch!" She put her finger up to her mouth and sucked it. Logan looked at Hana, noticing the plaster on her index finger.

"Today?" he asked pointedly and Hana gritted her teeth. He still treated her like his mentally fragile mother sometimes and it infuriated her. She wondered if Nev treated his lovely wife the same way and saw in his eyes that he did. Anahera meant 'angel' in *Māori* and Nev's wife was exactly that. Gentle, patient and easy going; everything Hana Du Rose was not. She took a deep breath and reined in her temper.

"When I drove home this afternoon, the gate stuck and a sharp piece of metal under the catch snagged my finger." She held the plastered digit aloft, noting with satisfaction the blood speckling through to the outside from the cut. She turned away to avoid releasing the biting comment to her husband about getting DNA from the gate to prove it. It stayed unhelpfully at the front of her brain, still wanting to be said, sounding clever and witty in her head.

Phoenix did a spectacular sneeze and pink cake bits shot in a wide arc around her plate. She squeezed her face up and stuck her bottom lip out to catch the snot. Hana grabbed a length of kitchen paper and wiped her daughter's offered nose and face with its roughness, deciding that a proper face wash and change of jarmies was probably in order. She went through the teeth cleaning and story process for the second time, finding the men still sitting at her kitchen table when she returned. Logan had made more coffee and Tama stood with his nose in the pantry like a pig seeking truffles.

"Come out of there!" Hana chastised him and put her hands either side of his waist, moving him out of the way of the pantry. "What's wrong with you? Do you need worming?"

"*Ahakoa nui, ahakoa iti, Pūrangatia ko te aroaro o Taiawa,*" Alfred piped up and the other men tittered amongst themselves. Hana sighed loudly and Nev translated it for her.

"It means, no whether large or small, it will be heaped up in front of Taiawa. He was a gluttonous figure and would eat anything dished up for him, no matter what sort of food or quality it was. That's like our boy here."

"I'm hungry," Tama whined as he tried to get back to the pantry doors again.

"I'll make you something else," Hana said staunchly. "But then you stop." Tama scuttled back to his seat and sat down again. Hana handled two tins of pumpkin soup and looked across at the other men. "Are you guys hungry still?" They nodded as a unit and she turned away to hide her smirk. "Pumpkin soup it is then," she smiled.

The men ate the soup and another loaf of bread but in her quiet ministrations, Hana was able to glean knowledge that she otherwise wouldn't have.

"So who do you reckon's doing all this?" Alfred asked, beaming at Hana as she laid the steaming bowl in front of him.

"Insider," Nev said without doubt. "But why? Throwing a brick through a window at your missus was personal. The other stuff is about trying to ruin the business."

"So what exactly *is* happening?" Alfred asked with his mouth full. "I'm out of the loop nowadays."

Hana watched her husband raise his eyebrows at Nev. It was Alfred's choice to step back, nobody had forced him. After Miriam's death he had withdrawn from everyone and everything. It had been understandable but also made things much harder for Logan. Logan inclined his head towards his half-brother and Nev listed the things that had gone wrong over recent months.

"The first thing was that someone started cutting wire fences and mixing stock up," Nev began haltingly. "It seemed random but definitely deliberate. Then they cut the electricity to the main house and it cost a fortune to repair. That was when Logan and Hana were away and we had to pay to have it all reconnected. The power company said the line was deliberately cut. We've had native trees felled across bush tracks and electric fences turned off. The stock's been shifted round heaps of times and the mares have been let loose into crops that were meant to be for winter feed. Hana had the window smashed on her and now this with the stock being in your garden."

"Our water tanks were emptied too," Hana added. She leaned with her backside against the sink while the men ate, not wanting to intrude on their conversation. But she hadn't realised how bad things had got. Logan opened his mouth and Hana shook her head. "It wasn't Phoenix, Loge. I know you wanted to believe that, but I never leave her outside alone. I was there the whole time and she wasn't out of my sight. Besides, she couldn't turn the handle even if she'd wanted to, not how hard you tighten them. Sometimes I can't do them."

"I know it wasn't her," Logan admitted, looking contrite. "I didn't want to worry you. Whoever did it opened the taps at both ends of the house. They intended us to run out of water, but it's possible they didn't know we could also draw from the stream. So it can't be someone who was involved with building the house, or is familiar with the layout of the land." He laid his soup spoon in his bowl and sat back in his chair. All the men were at a loss.

"There's the window broken in your old bedroom with a brick and then there's also the cigarette ends," Hana said quietly. "Someone's been watching the house."

"What?" Logan looked at her aghast. "How do you know? Why didn't you say something?"

"I wasn't completely sure," Hana answered, "it was just a feeling at first. Especially at night. I kept closing the curtains because I thought perhaps it was me imagining things. But then one morning a while ago, I found a cigarette end outside the front door. The only people who'd been here..." Hana paused, suddenly nervous of mentioning that Flick had helped eject Logan from his marital bed. "The only people who'd visited us don't smoke. I walked around the side of the house and there was a whole patch of them next to the big Norfolk pine. And the ground was all dented."

"No point checking now," Nev said as he buttered another piece of bread to dip in his soup. "Stock will have destroyed it all."

Logan looked crossly at Hana as though she had betrayed him and she held his gaze. Her eyes contained a challenge and he got the message: *I couldn't tell you anything because we weren't talking!* Sadness crossed his face and he looked away, berating himself. He had let his wife down in so many ways.

Tama finally pulled his face out of his bowl and looked hopefully at Logan's. Hana's husband had lost his appetite. He pushed the bowl silently over to his nephew and Tama pinched Alfred's buttered bread as soon as he laid it on his plate.

"Bugger off!" Alfred told him and tried to pull it back. It ripped in half and he groaned and went back to the bread bag to begin again. Tama collected up the pieces and dipped them in Logan's cooling soup.

"So it's deliberate, possibly an inside job and there's a particular interest in what? Me and Logan or the farm?" Hana asked.

The men looked nervous. Nev turned in his seat and answered her. "We thought it was the business alone but we think it's you and Logan too. Someone wants to destroy everything you have but we aren't sure why. This latest...development is pretty ingenious and will do us a lot of damage financially and in terms of reputation, so we're fairly sure they won't stop until it's all over."

"What latest development," Hana asked, looking around at the men when nobody answered. Logan ran his hand over his face and exhaled.

"The calves, Hana. What did you notice about the calves?"

She shook her head feeling suddenly stupid. "I don't know. They were quite small, but you're already calving so I don't know if that means anything. One was born right in front of us. Is that it? Were they meant to die and freak me and Phoe out? Because they obviously didn't."

"One did," Alfred said blandly. "It got trampled."

Hana felt instantly sick and looked down at the floor. Hatred bubbled up in her heart for the person who would do this.

"What else?" Logan asked and Hana wanted to scream at him. He treated her as though she were a pupil in his English class, drawing answers out of her so she could pass an exam.

"I don't know," she said crossly. "Of the two we saw, one was pure white and the other was black and white. They were newborn calves. I don't know what you want me to say!"

"You just said it," Nev smiled with sadness in his glittering eyes. "One was black and white. We breed purebred Charolaise cattle for the meat markets. They're all white. And every year we hire a prize winning white Charolaise bull, which has been studied and researched and deemed to be compatible with our herds. Even with a recessive gene, we shouldn't end up with black and white calves that look like..."

"Bloody Friesians," Tama finished off for him, wiping his hand across the back of his mouth. "Someone's gone to a lot of trouble to put a bull in a paddock of heifers. And when could they have done it? And how? It's not like you can take a damn great bull for a walk in the mountains and accidentally let it loose with the cows and then call it back again."

Hana studied the tiled floor, admiring the tiny diamond-like sparkles in the black surface. It was eye catching and distracting but it didn't stop fear rampaging through her mind and creating monsters in her world. "Do you think...?" she couldn't finish the sentence. "Do you think it could be...?" She licked her lips, aware that the men watched her intently, perhaps hoping for some gem of wisdom to pop out of her rosebud lips. Hana touched the scar on her left wrist with her other hand, feeling the instant stab of pain from the shard of glass still lodged in her artery. Her attacker was dead, but he had wanted to hurt Logan so badly. "I wondered if Laval..." Hana gulped and instinctively moved her right hand up to touch the site of the pacemaker. She hardly thought about it these days, except in moments of great stress when she half expected it to go off.

"No, Hana." Logan's voice was gentle and he padded across to her in his socks. He wrapped his arms around her firmly and grounded her in his love and the scent of horses and leather tack. "It's not him, babe. It's nobody like that. This is why I didn't tell you. I knew what you'd think."

The men at the table shuffled uncomfortably in the face of the show of affection, so unusual within their clan. Alfred studied his hands with abject concentration and Nev stared at Logan's back with an air of interest. Hana linked her fingers behind Logan's back to stop her shaking and he slipped his fingers up underneath her tee shirt. "You're still beautiful," he whispered in her ear, making Hana squirm with the ticklishness of his breath on her skin.

"Hey, old people, can you not?" Tama interjected in a sing-song voice. He turned to Nev. "They're always at it. It's disgusting."

"Says you!" Logan answered him, turning round and pulling Hana in front of him. He leaned back against the sink with his legs splayed and Hana leaned her back against his stomach, slotting her feet neatly between his. Logan put his arms around her, hugging her into him, his long arms stretched across her chest. "Oh yeah," he smiled mischievously at Tama, "that's right. You're not getting any are you?"

Nev and Alfred fixed their slate grey eyes on the young man and he quailed under their scrutiny. "Lucy's a Christian," he said proudly. "And we're waiting."

Alfred's jaw dropped in surprise, revealing a set of false teeth at the top which clung precariously to his pink gums. Nev's head swivelled on his neck so fast it looked painful. Neither of them spoke and in the ensuing silence, Tama lost his nerve. He pointed at Logan and Hana accusingly. "They waited," he whined, "and it's turned out ok for them." Hana felt Logan's eyes burning holes in the top of her head as they bore into Tama's body. The tension in the pectoral muscle behind her communicated his anger. She stroked the hand nearest to her heart in warning, feeling Logan's fingers flex into a fist over her breast. A sigh escaped her as she wished heartily she had let her husband give the big mouth a slap, as it opened again.

"Lucy said God blesses you if you wait and look at them," Tama's voice went to a squeak at the end. "They're pensioners and turning out kids like…like…" he couldn't think of a suitable analogy.

Hana gulped as Logan's family as one, turned their grey eyes on her stomach. It was intensely embarrassing for her and she sucked it in as much as she could without being obvious. It didn't work. When Hana looked down, she still couldn't see her slippers.

Nev broke the silence. "Congratulations then." He smiled. "Another little Du Rose to add to the crew."

Logan exhaled with his nose and mouth on the back of Hana's head. It was warm and ruffled her hair. "Thanks," he said and the atmosphere became strained.

"You were a late baby, Logan," Alfred piped up, his face soft with the memory of the small boy who had captured his heart. "You were a little surprise too."

Nev looked awkward again and Tama snorted at the reminder of Logan's illegitimacy. "Er, yeah, I bet."

Logan blew out a quick breath, the same noise his beautiful Appaloosas made when startled or annoyed. It was heated and sharp on the back of Hana's head. "Are you done making trouble?" he asked his nephew coldly and Tama shrugged and handled the last crust of bread from the bag. The boy had no shame.

"You lot crack me up," he said, digging into the butter. "At least you've got each other. I don't got nobody of my own. I used to just tag onto other families and try and find my place for a while. Until I found Ma," Tama smiled fondly at Hana. "See, blood don't make family, it's the other stuff. Poppa Alfred had Logan all them years and Logan called him 'dad' and didn't know no different. Yeah we all lost Poppa Reuben who, for the record, was more of a father to me than anyone and Nev lost his dad. But Nev's got a brother now." Tama waved his knife dangerously in the other man's face. "You got Logan, like the coolest bro' you could ever imagine and Poppa Alf to ask stuff. I went to a house fire in Mount Eden last week. It was the poorest house I'd ever seen, I mean the thing was hanging together with string. It was this family and the mama was sick with cancer and couldn't work. It went up like a firework because one of the little kids thought he would make his mama warm and lit a fire in a blocked chimney. He found some dregs of petrol in an old can out back and saved it, he said, for a special occasion. He threw it on the fire and the damn house exploded. We got them all out. The mama and five little kids, even the baby in the cot. They've got nothing left and all she could do was shout at the top of her voice how lucky she was because they all got out alive. She kept shouting, 'Thank God, thank God,' and I thought, *thank him for what? You've got nothing*. It made me think about things differently. Family is everything, no matter what kind of family you end up with."

The room was silent, the air molecules banging together in their eternal dance and causing a static fuzz. Nev cleared his throat, "I should get back to my lot," he said and smiled his crinkly eyed smile. Alfred scraped his chair back too.

"Yeah, me an' all."

Tama licked his lips and wiped his mouth on his sleeve.

"Wait!" Logan said and everyone halted. "I'll radio the bunkhouse and get someone to ride up in the ute. Leave the horses here and get them tomorrow."

"What about water?" Nev asked.

"The old stream runs past here," Alfred said knowledgeably. "They'll be right with that."

Logan gave Hana a gentle push to make her stand up and padded over to the table to retrieve the radio. It crackled to life and he went outside to get a better reception.

"See you later *kōtiro*," Alfred hugged Hana tightly and kissed her on the cheek. He nodded in satisfaction and his eyes strayed to her belly. "Do we know when yet? You weren't sure."

Hana rubbed a hand over her protruding bump. "Beginning of December."

Alfred nodded happily again and patted her on the shoulder.

"Congratulations." Nev held out his hand to Hana and it seemed formal and awkward for a brother-in-law, even a half one. He laughed hollowly. "If you were anyone else I would give you a hug but I don't want your old man to kick my head in."

Hana snorted, wishing that it wasn't true. An image of Bobby's dreadful black eye wafted across her inner vision and her smile faded from her lips.

"Someone's coming up," Logan announced, coming back into the kitchen. He spun the radio carelessly in his hand and cuffed Tama round the back of the head. "I think we should all take a wee look outside at the damage and to see if those cigarette ends are still visible. Might give us an idea of what's going on."

The men nodded eagerly and put their hats on their heads and tramped back to the front door.

"Oh, there's one of the cigarette ends in the plant pot by the door," Hana remembered. "I picked it up and then forgot about it."

Logan returned to the kitchen for a sandwich bag to put it in and found Hana rubbing her eyes. "Go to bed, love," he said gently. "I won't be long." He kissed her on the forehead and then went off to play detective with his new sidekicks. Hana faced the food mess and sighed, clearing the bowls away and wiping the table. A knock on the front door was followed by the sound of it opening and closing. Hana went cautiously out to the hallway and looked at the visitor.

"Hi." She didn't know what else to say.

"Logan around?" Flick asked and his fingers writhed around the car key in his hand.

"He's out there." Hana pointed back the way he had come and returned to her task, a dreadful sadness winding its stealthy fingers round her heart.

"Hana."

She jumped as the voice came from right behind her. Flick had kicked off his boots on the mat and followed her. "I wanted to say, I'm sorry. I shouldn't have been like that with you the other day."

Hana looked at his eye, her brow knitting in sympathy. It still looked painfully swollen. Blue and purple had turned to a livid green that looked straight out of a paint palette. The man's eyeball was more visible and less bloodshot. It wasn't going to kill him. "That's ok," she said sadly. "It's your business." She turned away from the table with a cloth filled with crumbs and Flick caught her free hand in his.

"Please don't be mad at me," he whispered.

Hana sighed and looked at their joined fingers. "Bobby, if Logan sees you here, he'll kill you next time," she said with resignation.

"Logan?" he repeated and then wrinkled his nose in disdain as though the idea was ludicrous.

Hana's face was disbelieving. "If he gave you that shiner for helping me to the hospital, then imagine what he'll do when he finds you holding my hand in his own kitchen." Tiredness made Hana aggressive but Flick stood his ground.

"Not everything's about Logan bloody Du Rose," he said through gritted teeth. He pointed an angry finger at his eye. "This won't keep me away from you, Hana. I'm risking everything to tell you that I'm sorry for the other day. If he sees me come up here, he'll kill me for sure. He's done it before, I know that."

Hana's vision seemed to cloud. *Logan had killed someone.* "Logan has?" she whispered, her face ashen. Flick shook his head in irritation.

"Stop talking about Logan," he raised his voice and Hana was reminded of the power he had once wielded in his awful organisation. He had intended to hurt her and had succeeded once. She yanked at her hand to release it from his grasp and he shifted his fingers, contacting the ugly cut on her wrist by mistake. Hana cried out in pain and he dropped her hand and then didn't seem to know what to do. "Sorry, sorry," he said and ran his hand through his blond hair. "Hana, I need to shoot through. Please come with me?"

"What? Why?" she felt appalled. "But you haven't done anything."

"But he thinks I have and he knows how I feel about you. Please, Hana. Come with me."

Hana shook her head. "But nothing's happened," she repeated gormlessly.

"He thinks it *has*," Flick said again. "We need to get away from here."

Hana's brain struggled with Flick's words. *So* Logan knew how this man felt about her and thought that she'd been unfaithful with him. It didn't make sense, unless Logan was about to burst through the door and kill the man right there on the kitchen rug. Hana stepped back, understanding nothing. There came the abrupt sound of stamping feet and the front door handle clicked down. Hana turned quickly away and by the time Logan had kicked his boots off and walked down the hallway, she was rinsing the dirty cloth in the sink. Flick leaned against the centre island with his back to her, arms folded and legs crossed over at the ankles.

"Ah, cheers bro', thanks for coming up here," Logan said cordially and Hana turned to look at him in surprise. "The others are getting in the truck," he said and Flick followed him down the hallway with a single wistful look back at Hana. She listened to her husband chatting as they left the house, detailing a security watch over the property and issuing Flick with orders for the other stockmen. He was perfectly calm and unthreatening. Hana was completely confused.

Chapter 24

Hana cleaned the kitchen while Logan dealt with the men outside and when he returned, he whistled a gentle tune under his breath without stress. Hana looked at him curiously from under her lashes and he smiled at her and winked. "You seem happier," she commented and rinsed the cloth under the tap.

"Yeah," he said, leaning exactly where his stockman had been only a few minutes earlier. "I am actually."

"Have you solved the mystery then?" Hana asked and turned, drying her hands on a dish towel.

"Na, but we will." Logan held his arms out to her and Hana snuggled into his chest while he stroked her hair with tender hands. "Alfred apologised to me outside."

Hana leaned her head back and looked up at her husband. "Wow."

Logan caressed the skin on her chin with his thumb and stared intently at her lips. Then he bent forward and kissed them, his fingers straying behind her head and up underneath her hair. He inhaled like he did before seducing her fully and Hana battled to come up for air. "No you don't!" she exclaimed crossly. "I need details, you can't just say something like that and then move on."

"I'm not moving anywhere," her husband said softly and shifted his fingers under her shirt and into the small of her back. Hana pulled on his forearms, baring her chest as she reached back. Logan's eyes flickered and he focussed on trying to kiss her neck and the flat space of exposed flesh above her breasts.

"Stop it!" Hana giggled, her hands futile against arms strong enough to crack a bullwhip and halt raging cattle. "I want to know what he said."

"What do I get in return?" Logan asked, managing to kiss Hana underneath her jaw. She groaned in defeat, utterly outdone.

"Whatever you want," she squeaked. "Oh, hi Tama."

Logan whipped round and his grip relaxed slightly. Hana released herself and ducked under his arm, almost escaping but for a slap on the backside. "I'll just get ya later," her husband sniffed, pretending not to care.

"Logan!" Hana complained from the other side of the kitchen island. "Tell me!"

Her husband stepped forward quickly and Hana squealed and jumped, ready to run. Logan laughed. "Bedroom's that way, babe. You're heading in the right direction." He gave her the sultry look that melted her bones and Hana sighed.

"Fine. I don't care anyway," she said and sat down at one of the kitchen chairs. Logan planted himself in the one next to her and leaned back on two legs dangerously. He looked like a naughty teenager swinging on his chair in the classroom and his wife smirked. "I bet you were a nightmare at school," she teased him.

"Na, not me," he said, his face a picture of innocence as he raised his long arms above his head and stretched with a groan. His tee shirt rode up exposing his gorgeous stomach, toned from sheer hard work and the occasional workout in the hotel gym. Hana reached out and stroked the line of dark hair that plunged invitingly into his jeans. Logan smiled at her and squared his chair back on four legs, patting his knees and holding his arms out to Hana. She moved across and plonked herself on his knees, cuddling into his soft neck. He smelled of hay and horses and she breathed in the comforting scent. "He said he was sorry for being a dick," Logan coiled one of Hana's red curls around his finger. "He asked me to start calling him 'Dad' again and gave me a hug. He also said he loved me and he's never said that before." Logan sounded a little choked as he recounted the conversation with Alfred.

"Will you?" Hana said sleepily and felt Logan's body grow still under her. Then he nodded.

"Yeah. Reckon. Nothing's really changed has it? He treated me like his son even though I never was. The only difference is that I now know Reuben was my birth father. Reuben's dead and nothing's gonna change that. Yeah, I'll call him Dad."

"Good." Hana closed her eyes and pushed her face further under Logan's jaw.

"See what I mean?" Tama's voice sounded cross and Hana heard his bare feet pad across the tiles. "You're always at it."

"I'm holding my pregnant wife!" Logan was short with the young man, "And I don't appreciate you blabbing my family business to everyone. We weren't ready to tell people yet and now everyone will know."

"Poppa Alf knew anyway!" Tama argued.

"Nev didn't!" Logan's voice rumbled in his chest, lulling Hana soporifically and she relaxed and let her body go like a dead weight. Logan leaned back and adjusted his legs, wrapping his arms around her.

"Sorry." At least Tama sounded a little contrite.

"Yeah, well, love's-young-dream, when you've got your own house in order, you can go blabbing about mine!" Logan stared hard at his nephew. "Lucy returning your texts yet, boy?"

Tama darted a nervous look at Hana and then he changed the conversation quickly. "Wanna watch a movie with me?"

"Dunno," Logan kissed the side of Hana's face. "Hana?"

Hana sat up and inhaled, shaking her head. "No thanks. I'm too tired. You two spend some time together. I'm going to bed. I need a cup of tea so you just go. I'll sort myself out." She yawned and slithered off Logan's legs. He watched her go to the kettle and fiddle around. The boys shuffled off to the big lounge and set up the theatre system. They started looking through the DVDs in the cabinet and trying to choose something. They argued like school children.

Hana took her hot drink over to the double doors. She needed to tell Logan to shut the curtains in case their 'watcher' turned up again. She heard the rumble of the men's voices and saw them through the gap between the closed doors. They sat with their backs leaned against the sofa, DVDs scattered around them like wreckage. She turned away, leaving them to their choosing. It would only get them riled up again if she mentioned the voyeur. She was about to walk away when she heard Tama ask his uncle a question. "So what's with all your gear in the spare room?"

Hana froze in place and listened with her father's adage in her ears. *Those who listen at doors never hear good of themselves.*

"I behaved like an idiot and Hana moved me out."

"Really?" Tama laughed. "*Respect!* Good on her. What did you do?"

There was a silence and the sound of someone's jeans moving against the carpet. "You mean, what did I do to get thrown out or what did I do *after* she threw me out?"

"Both," Tama replied.

"Well, to *get* thrown out, I let this stupid English woman make me believe that if I wasn't nice to her, I wouldn't get the chance to see Ryan, who she told me was my son."

"Hmmn. He looks like one of us. Do you think he is your son?" Tama sounded guarded, but then he would. He was currently the resident son and his place could be in doubt.

"I dunno. I don't remember her but he looks like us. I just don't know."

"So how come she manipulated you so easily?"

"It was a bloody shock, having some stranger turn up and claim that we were an item. Everything was going so well with Hana at the time and all I could think was, *why me and why now?* She turned up one night and asked for me and my life turned to crap straight after."

"Did she ask for you by name then?"

"No, Tama. She asked for Elvis but he wasn't available." Logan mocked Tama as though he was thick.

"I didn't mean that. I meant did she specifically say *Logan Du Rose?*"

"What does it matter?" Logan's patience was running out. "Leslie said she wanted *Mr Du Rose*, so she got me."

"Is she hot?"

"What?"

"Is she hot, Logan? Would you have fancied her however many years ago?"

"Sixteen years ago, plus nine months or so. I don't know, Tama. I honestly don't know. Everyone I went out with, apart from...Caroline, was a redhead because I was looking for Hana. So no, she isn't and wasn't my sort at all. But then I look at the kid and he's pure Du Rose."

"So you still haven't told me why Hana chucked you out. I got a few texts from the boys saying you were messin' around with some English bird and Hana looked like she'd been kicked in the guts. That's why I'm here. I had time off, but I wanted to see if youse two were ok."

Logan's sigh was massive. It was unlike him to be so candid with anyone and Hana found it impossible to drag herself from the door, even though she knew she might hear something she didn't like. "I was so dumb," Logan said. "All I could think about was that I had a son and Sylvia, the mother, she dangled him in front of me like bait. She came on her own and didn't send for him until after she arrived and he came on the first plane out. But it took him a few days to get here. I felt trapped, like if I didn't tolerate her then she would call it all off and I would never get to meet him. The trouble was, she told Hana stuff behind my back and made her think I didn't love her anymore and wanted to set up with her and my new son."

"And Hana *believed* that of you?"

"Oh mate, it was awful. I came around the corner into the stable yard with Sylvia clinging to my arm and kissing my cheek and there's Hana and Phoe. I tried so hard to keep her out of the way so that she didn't see and there she was just standing there looking at me. I've never felt so crap in my whole life."

"Geez Loge. You sure know how to make life hard for yourself!" Tama exhaled loudly. "And don't say it. I know what I did with Anka and I really wish I hadn't. But all those years wanting Hana and then you get her and screw it up. Have you got rocks in your head?" Hana saw her husband tug at a tuft of the rug underneath him, his clever fingers twisting the red threads. "So what happened next?"

"I don't want to talk about it," Logan's voice was insistent. "It's been the worst few weeks of my life. I don't want to think about it."

"So Hana threw you out of the bedroom?" Hana heard Logan sigh deeply and Tama continued. "I know she did Loge. And why's all your crap still in the spare room? You look ok together now so why haven't you moved it all back in?"

"I don't know. I feel like I have to earn her trust back and I haven't quite managed it yet. I'm waiting for her to say that it's ok."

"What will you do if she never asks you to move back in properly?"

"I don't know! At the moment I'm just grateful for what I do have, can't you see that? I nearly screwed up my whole life!"

"You definitely did that, bro'. Talk about complicated! Why didn't you just tell her the truth from the start?"

"It...I don't know that either. I wanted to but when I got home she'd cooked this gorgeous meal and she looked so beautiful and...I couldn't do it. I was so angry with myself that I took it out on her. I'm an idiot."

"So how come you're back on track now?" Tama sounded strangely over eager. "How do you mend something that's so broken?"

"We had this awful argument. I kept her up here and told her that if she left she couldn't see Phoe again."

"Bloody hell!" Tama sounded angry. "That's what they did to my mum. How could you do that?"

"I know, I know. She had this hospital scan and was so scared to go, she got Flick to take her. It must have killed her driving out of those gates after what I said, but I get why she had to go to the hospital. *I did that to her*, I made her choose between our daughter and our son's safety and I will never forgive myself for that. Jack found the appointment letter in the stable yard and brought it to me. He hit me in the nose!" Logan sounded almost offended. "I forgot how hard he could hit. Bloody hurt. He told me to get after her so I did. We had this massive row in the motel room and she said she was leaving me and taking both kids and she would make sure they hated me...something like that. I felt like I broke."

"I don't think Ma would ever do that though, do you?"

"You didn't see her. I believed her when she said it. I told her I'd let her go but asked her to let me still see my kids."

"You caved?"

"Yeah."

"Why?"

"I just bloody told you!"

"Yeah but why? You can talk anyone round. Why give up?"

Hana had to strain her ears and concentrate hard to hear Logan's lowered voice. His unusual conversation with Tama had made her unutterably sad. Logan had never talked like this, not before the awful night in the motel. Her tea cooled in the mug.

"I made her a promise," he said, his voice laden with sadness. "About a year ago when we lived on the school site. I said that maybe if Alfred had let Mum go when she was so unhappy, she might still be alive now. I said if Hana ever got that desperate to leave me, I wouldn't hold on to her."

Tama swore, an unrepeatable word. "I feel for you mate. You're definitely a man of your word."

"But I'm not, see." Logan's voice cracked and Hana held her breath. "I've only ever told my wife one lie in our marriage and that was it. I've dodged stuff and omitted to tell her things but I've never outright lied to her face. Apart from that one time. I said it but I knew I would never be able to just watch her walk away from me. Then I sat in that motel room and those words came back to me and it's possibly the worst moment of my whole life. I bargained and begged for my kids and it was like I was emptied out onto the carpet. I felt like nothing."

Tama sighed. "Sorry Loge. Sorry I wasn't there for you."

"It's ok. I'm workin' it all out slowly."

"She didn't follow through; she didn't leave?"

"Not yet."

"What? You think she still might?"

"I don't know, Tama. I'm terrified. I walk in the front door and I'm thinking, *please God let her still be here*. Everything's fragile. I never thought I'd turn into a praying man but I bloody have recently. I feel like I need to be here all the time. Just in case. I really don't need all this crap with the property and the damage. Not now."

"What exactly did you say to Ma, you know, when you gave in?"

"Tama, I'm not going over it again. Are we watching a movie or not?" Logan sounded angry but something in Tama's voice arrested Hana's eaves dropping attention while a skin formed on the top of her tea.

"Please tell me. I need you to help me."

"Bugger off."

"Please, Logan?"

"Why?"

Tama sighed. "You know all that stuff about Lucy coming to stay here for a few days and everything being ok?"

"Yeah. Well, no actually. Hana might have swallowed that but I know she's not answering your texts."

"How do you know that?" Tama sounded cross.

"Because you keep looking at your phone, idiot! You're sending texts but it hasn't once beeped to receive one."

"Oh. Well, no she isn't talking to me, but I don't know why. Before I found out about you and Ma having problems, I was meant to go straight to Hamilton. I think Lucy might have dumped me."

Chapter 25

"Ryan's a great little worker." Hana smirked inwardly and tried to press down the warnings from her conscience which whispered that her behaviour was un-Christian. "They really love him in the kitchen. I've never seen anyone chop that fast."

Sylvia laid the cutlery down on her plate and glanced around the formal dining room at the other guests before hissing, "He's not here to work!"

Hana shifted her weight on the chair and pulled her little girl's pram towards her, so she could peer in at the sleeping pink-cheeked face. Phoenix lost her thumb and rooted for it, clutching Fluffy in a bear hug against her shoulder. She seemed fractious and disturbed.

Helena ventured over to the table, straight backed and attractive with her blonde hair pulled neatly into a bun. She looked demure and suitably maitre d' like until she turned so that only Hana could see her and beamed, giving the other woman a thumbs up. Hana smiled openly at her childishness. They had waited on tables together during Hana's last pregnancy, under the auspicious gaze of Logan's mother. It had been fun. Helena replaced her elated face with the demure one again. "Would Madam care for dinner?" she enquired, a picture of polite deference.

"No thanks, I'm all good. I only came for a visit and shouldn't really be in here dressed like a tramp. I ate with my nephew earlier. Congratulations on the promotion though. It's awesome."

Helena's eyes flashed out a coded message of bursting glee and then asked, "Is Tama back? I haven't noticed the young girls get that glazed-over look yet so he must be hiding his muscles somewhere."

"Not Tama, no. I ate with Ryan."

A look of consternation plastered itself over Helena's well-bred Swedish face and she nodded once and left, knowing better than to pry. Her new position also prevented her from adding to the cauldron of gossip and Hana's revelation burned like charcoal in the pit of her stomach, just as the cunning Hana Du Rose had known it would.

"Why are you telling people that Ryan's your nephew? You know damn well he's Logan's son!" Sylvia glared at the woman who stood in the way of affluence and rescue.

"Oh well, the DNA testing Logan's arranged for the end of the week will prove or disprove that, won't it? That's what the trip to Auckland is for." Hana rose to leave the small table and retrieved her pram from next to the wall. Phoenix stirred and sat bolt upright with staring eyes like something from a film about the undead, before laying back down and snuggling her soft toy harder into her stomach. The smile that the mother bestowed on her baby girl was maternal and loving and Hana's hand went instinctively to her stomach, smoothing the cloth over her son's firm outline. She hadn't meant to play her hand quite so quickly but it was too late now and she fixed her emerald eyes on Sylvia's face, noticing how sculpted with make-up it was. *Dear God, please forgive me in advance for cussing and being nasty.*

Sylvia's complexion had mottled with the realisation that Hana was pregnant with another of Logan's children and felt her claim on the handsome olive-skinned man diminish. What thread of hope remained, Hana smashed with all the grace and poise of Jack's old red Jeep going through a car showroom window. "Logan's never been a student in England, but I understand his brother, Michael was. He did an internship at a London hospital and the timing fits with your pregnancy. You can try tracking him down at Auckland General if you still want to seek paternity, but he's probably got more unclaimed offspring than a randy sailor. He's also an asshole, so you won't get anything out of him." She calmly turned to leave but Sylvia hadn't completely let go of her tenuous hold on Hana's branch of the Du Rose legacy.

"They're brothers you stupid woman! If I refuse to be tested it will be inconclusive because Logan has a family relationship with Ryan. It will prove nothing," Sylvia crowed, her voice growing louder and beginning to attract attention. One of the more fearless *Māori* waitresses made a move towards the table but Helena stopped her deftly with an outstretched arm.

"But she's havin' a go at the missus!" the girl said indignantly and Helena demonstrated the authority for which Logan had favoured her, holding onto the teenager and shaking her head.

"She's the new Du Rose matriarch," she hissed under her breath. "The *Kaumatua* told me. She'll be fine."

The women watched as Hana drew herself up to her full height and looked benevolently down on the painted doll seated alone at the table for two. Her protruding belly looked suddenly obvious and the eyes of the staff widened even as the guests waded through their food, oblivious of the drama unfolding nearby. Dressed in her grey sweatshirt and baggy tracksuit pants, Hana Du Rose easily outclassed the tart in the tight dress. All the formidable might and authority of the first Phoenix Du Rose and the stubbornness of Miriam coursed through her, inflaming her red hair in the romantic lighting as though she was a siren calling ships to their death. Hana said something as she dipped forward slightly from the waist and the other woman's jaw dropped grotesquely, the mask of elegance irrevocably broken. The staff strained to listen but only Helena's sharp ears caught the words, 'half-brothers' and '12.5% DNA.' She didn't know what it meant but the body language of Hana's opponent showed that she understood perfectly. And that was plenty good enough for the new Du Rose housekeeper.

Hana breezed from the dining room, her whole body shaking with adrenaline. She left a trail of devastation in her wake as Sylvia's dreams crumbled beneath her fingers and she had to be helped from the table to the lift reserved for the elderly and disabled.

"She's amazing! You were right," the teenage waitress concluded to Helena as they cleared the table of its detritus together. "What did the *Kaumatua* actually say?"

Helena pondered on her chance conversation that awful Christmas, with the elderly man who oversaw proceedings at the town's local *marae*, the place where *Māori* sub-tribes or *hapu* gathered to debate, celebrate or mourn. Reuben and Miriam Du Rose had finally been honoured together at a joint *tangihanga*, united in death, brother and sister-in-law, cousins, lifelong lovers and Logan's parents. The crinkled *kaumatua* had wagged his finger at Helena's brown husband, a drover for Logan's acres of beef cattle and declared authority over the slender British interloper who flanked her visibly distressed husband, clutching the tiny new-born baby girl to her breast. Helena paused, sounding out the *Māori* words badly with a hint of her Swedish accent. Her husband, Manu had translated for her. "The *Kaumatua* said, 'See her *mana*. She is the next *kuikui* in the Du Rose line,' something like that, anyway." She began to doubt herself, "Did I say it right?"

The *Māori* teenager who had grown up with the old language running through her veins widened her eyes in awe. She nodded. *If the marae elder had prophesied it, then that settled it. Hana Du Rose was queen.*

Chapter 26

"Do you want to stay down here tonight? I don't know if I can be bothered to drive home." Logan yawned on the double bed in his brother's childhood room, keeping his cowboy boots away from the covers. Phoenix sat next to his head and sulked.

"Not really," Hana answered, laying the sandwiches down on the bedside table. "I've put the pram in the truck so when you've eaten this, I'll drive us up the mountain."

Phoenix withdrew her thumb long enough to hold her hand out eagerly for the sandwich. Hana shook her head, "No, not on the bed. You can eat at the dressing table."

Phoenix looked accusingly at her father and Hana hid her smirk well. "Don't look at Daddy. He'll eat where he's told to as well."

The little girl rolled onto her stomach, becoming caught up in the petticoats of another of Aunty Liza's dresses, getting frustrated as she ended up on the floor with her knees stuck. Hana lifted her under the arms and allowed the layers to fall, unbuttoning the back and lifting it over the child's head. Underneath she wore a white vest and pair of woolly blue tights. Phoenix ran towards the table, diverting herself rapidly to the bathroom when the urgent need to use the toilet seemed more pressing. "No, don't want nappies no more!" she complained to her father. "My big girl now!"

"Oh, crikey!" Logan's voice echoed around the tiled ensuite bathroom. "Does Mummy know you've only got woolly tights on and nothing underneath? Where's your nappy gone?"

"Don't know. All gone."

"Yeah, I can see that!"

Hana sat against the pillows listening to her husband help his daughter flush and wash her hands, nibbling at a corner of one of Logan's sandwiches. Her appetite seemed to have miraculously returned.

"Hey!" Logan said, fake indignation on his face. "Take everything why don't you? Even the food out my mouth." He remained standing, watching his daughter fill her mouth too full as he did the same. Hana watched him silently. He blanched swiftly and swallowed. "Sorry, I didn't mean you would take everything. I was just thinking of..."

Hana reached up and placed the bitten sandwich on her husband's plate with a smile. Then she lay on her back, the creamy skin of her neat bump revealed as the sweatshirt rode inelegantly up. "Oh, it's fine really. I *am* taking over all of it." She smiled sweetly with a twinkle in her eye and looked at the ceiling. "As for Sylvia, don't give her another thought. I think she'll be moving on soon."

"But I've booked the DNA for Friday." Logan looked irritated. "What's she playing at?"

"Don't know," Hana said, rolling onto her side and inspecting a green stain on the sweatshirt. "You know all those boxes that came up from Culver's Cottage, do you think my maternity clothes will be in them?"

Logan put the plate on the bedside table and lay down on the bed next to his beautiful wife. He leaned towards her and planted a tender kiss on her rosebud lips, stroking her face with gentle fingers. His hand moved down over her clothing and up underneath the grey sweatshirt, playing sensuously over her sensitive stomach and irritating his unborn son. The child moved away with a kick, like a swimmer. Tracing the line of Hana's knickers as they folded away from the bump, Logan seductively flicked the straining elastic with his fingernail, just as Phoenix filled her mouth too full and barfed on the dressing table. The bed shook as Logan ran to rescue his daughter and Hana heard him talking to her in the background. "Don't be such a piggie, Phoe! That's how you choke yourself."

"Dat nasty," Phoenix complained and Hana heard Logan sigh.

"It is *now!* You smushed it up," he answered.

Hana smiled at the remembered sensation of her husband's fingers walking over her flesh and the thought of his hands reminded her of one very salient fact. Basking in the spirit of her recent reconciliation with Logan, Hana decided to put him out of his misery. "I'm guessing Michael visited you when you were in London."

"Yeah, a couple of times in the years I was over there. He interned at Guy's Hospital for a year and lived in hospital accommodation. When he wanted to go clubbing, he used my place for somewhere to crash. Not often though. We weren't really getting on at the time, not after his affair with my girlfriend back here. He had a real cheek turning up, to be honest. But family's family, aye?" The chair scraped on the wooden floor as Logan told his daughter, "Eat that one more slowly," and pushed her closer to the table. "Why?"

Hana smiled in satisfaction, not bothering to seek out her husband's face in the room as she dropped her bombshell. She had cared that Logan might be upset. It affected him deeply believing he'd condemned a son of his to the same fate; an absentee father. As she searched her soul she found she actually didn't care. In his own way, Logan had put her through hell. "Have you ever looked at Ryan's hands?" she asked, making her voice sound conversational. The image of Ryan's fingers clutching the plate floated before her eyes. "He has funny thumbs, just like Alfred...and Michael."

The absence of noise was as crashing and destructive as if a Greek wedding party had entered and smashed plates all over the room. Hana couldn't resist and rolled onto her side to peek at Logan's face. Her green eyes flashed with determination and the gunmetal of Logan's met hers, finding she didn't back down. He shook his head at her in disbelief and uttered his verdict, "You bitch!"

Hana lay on her back and inhaled, glad her husband had taken his punishment so well. A smirk played at the corner of her lips as Logan shook his head at himself, resting his backside against the fireplace as Phoenix bit into her sandwich, fortunately too busy to repeat the bad word her Daddy just said. "Does Sylvia know you worked it out?" he asked, his voice quiet.

Hana nodded. "She does now I've told her." Getting up to collect their things together for the ride home, Hana found Logan's eyes on her as he helped his daughter out of the chair. He smiled at her with a new found respect.

"I never knew you had it in you," he said quietly. Hana decided to capitalise on the moment and gave him a steely glare as Phoenix ran to wash her hands. Hana heard the tap running too loudly, evocative of her monkey-like daughter having climbed on the toilet seat to turn it on. Splashing followed.

"Yes, I do have it in me, Logan. Fortunately for you, it runs deep so don't push me again. You already *had* a son." She ran a slender hand over her belly as Phoenix found the tooth mug and started to fill the bath, accompanied by the sound of water sloshing on the tiled floor. "You weren't in need of a counterfeit!" The hard look she gave Logan almost took his breath away as he realised once again in their marriage; he had grossly underestimated his wife.

"*Kuikui* indeed," he said under his breath and turned to face his own reflection in the darkened windows. Hana retrieved her daughter, making Phoenix clean up her own mess with towels. The Du Rose men were fatally flawed. Phoenix Du Rose had written that in her diary, '*The men will be the ruin of this family.*'

Hana pushed at the little foot which dug into her ribs, the baby more active since the scan. "You won't be ruining anything, young man," she said sternly to him.

Phoenix stopped her ineffective mopping, which had now become more of a game anyway and said, "Wot?" attentively.

Hana confiscated the towels and corrected her, "Pardon! What's the matter with your generation?" Hana pulled the door of Michael's old room closed behind her as Logan carried his sleepy daughter down the corridor of the family wing.

"What do you think to me turning this whole wing into more hotel rooms?" Logan asked over his shoulder. Hana thought about Logan's room, the striking blue walls and the large bed in which she had probably conceived her daughter, currently being schemed in by Sylvia.

"I thought you were screwing Sylvia in your room," she sighed. "I won't be staying in there ever again."

"Well I wasn't," he said under his breath.

A deafening crash was followed by a piercing scream and Logan almost dropped his dozing daughter. Startled awake, Phoenix wailed and Logan handed her to Hana before whirling round on the spot and trying to pinpoint the noise. Sylvia catapulted from the doorway of Logan's old room and threw herself into his arms making a terrific howling noise. Broken glass sparkled in her hair and on her clothes. Hana's eyes narrowed at the sight of Logan's hands gripping the other woman's wrists and she wasn't satisfied until her husband had righted the woman on her feet and let go, stepping back to remove himself from her vicinity. His grey eyes glanced in Hana's direction once, as though seeking her approval for his actions. "Stop spreading glass everywhere!" Hana told the woman sternly and Phoenix looked at her mother curiously. "Get back inside."

Hana followed the sobbing blonde back into the bedroom and immediately saw the expensive billowing curtains and the ranch slider beyond, smashed into a million small shards. She turned back to Logan. "Take Phoenix downstairs and get someone to ring the cops. Ask Bobby...Flick to bring some board and we can cover the window for tonight. I'll get *her* sorted," Hana indicated the pathetic, trembling Sylvia and rolled her eyes. "Someone threw a brick. Look, it landed on the rug near the windows."

Logan stepped forward as though to check the location of the brick, but Hana indicated the child in her arms with annoyance at the same time as her eyes told him to leave. Sylvia needed to remove her clothing and Hana had no intention of allowing her to do it in front of him. Logan hefted the reluctant child onto his hip and left. Hana relaxed as the door clicked shut behind him. "I know it's unpleasant," she said to a shaking Sylvia. "It happened to me recently and it was quite a shock. Get into the shower and take your clothes off, then you can wash your hair and get it all out. Just be careful not to cut your hands."

"I can't wash my hair!" Sylvia protested. "It takes too long to straighten it. I don't have time."

Hana noticed the bags packed on the bed then, underwear and dresses flung into two neat, expensive looking cases. "You're leaving already?" she said in surprise. She hadn't expected Sylvia to take defeat quite so magnanimously.

"I'm going to Auckland, to see Michael," Sylvia tossed her blonde hair over her shoulder and the sound of glass tinkling onto the floorboards filled the room.

Hana sighed. She wanted the woman out and had no intention of dissuading her. "Then just take your clothes off and I'll try and shake them out enough for you to put them in your bag. Your hair's quite fine so perhaps you can brush the shards out. The cops have been called but they take hours to get anywhere out here and they'll need to talk to you. After that, do what you like."

Hana waited patiently by the ensuite door while Sylvia removed her clothes and handed them out to her. Her hands bore cuts and scratches as the razor thin shards attacked her fingers in the process. Hana shook the clothing out by the fireplace, trying not to contaminate the crime scene over by the sliding door. The brick lay in the centre of the pile like an accusation. *But of what?*

"Pass me the purple suit from the tan bag, will you?" Sylvia demanded through the partially open door. Hana finished shaking out the blouse and skirt in her hand and laid them on the bed while she dug inside the messy bag. The quality of the suit she pulled out was exquisite and the price tag betrayed its newness and hefty cost. Hana handed the lilac dress and matching jacket through the gap in the door, seeing Sylvia's lithe body clad in a bright red push up bra and thong. She had an excellent figure which instantly made Hana feel inferior. She tried not to think too hard about her favourite knickers currently clutching her bum under the ancient tracksuit pants, a dingy over-washed grey colour. In stark contrast, Sylvia's underwear was eye-catching, even down to the string of red dental floss that disappeared between her firm buttocks in the reflection from the mirror over the sink. Hana sighed and turned away.

"You put blood on my dress!" came Sylvia's shriek from the bathroom. Hana looked down at her hands. Her finger pads had been punctured in two places without her realising.

"Sorry," she said, "I've cut myself and didn't realise."

Now that Sylvia had Hana on the back foot and operating under a guilt reaction, she tried to press home her superiority. "You'll never hold onto him," she sneered. "It wouldn't have taken much more for your husband to have ended up in my bed. He was weakening."

"Maybe," Hana said, sucking at the cuts and tasting glass in her mouth. She picked it carefully off her tongue, feeling its grittiness on her skin. "But to really get under Logan's skin, you have to know him. He hates being touched and he cringed when you clung to him like you did. And he watches everything you say and do before he trusts you."

"Oh, I know all that," Sylvia waved her hand dismissively. "But we'd gone way past all that while you were sulking with that spiteful old woman upstairs. He loved my body and his is just flawless. We were great together."

Hana's heart constricted in her chest and the thought of Logan naked with this poisonous woman was painful. Her mind started to run overtime. Logan said he hadn't done anything wrong and getting naked with Sylvia was more than just wrong, it was the stuff of divorce. Hana closed her eyes and waited for the feeling of exhaustion to pass. They had struggled past it once but she knew she couldn't reopen it all and survive a second run.

"Flawless," she heard herself say, as though another being had taken over her speech capability. "Do you mean unblemished?"

"Oh yeah," Sylvia gushed. "He's absolutely gorgeous. Nothing wrong with him!"

"What about his scar?" Hana asked and Sylvia continued her appreciation of Logan's body.

"Oh that little thing. You can't even see it."

"Which one?"

"What?"

"Pardon! I said which scar?"

"Er..." Sylvia floundered. "Oh, he didn't have that back when we were together. But he's still gorgeous."

Hana shook her head sadly as the false, leggy blonde emerged from the bathroom in her finery. The woman was determined to try and cost her her marriage. Logan's haemophilia had riddled his body with scars. There was hardly an inch of him clear of marks from some minor cut which had struggled to heal. He hated his naked body, especially the long, ridged watershed that ran from under his right armpit to below his hip. It was his mother and father's gift to him, Miriam the carrier and Reuben the sufferer. The odds had been heavily stacked against Logan Du Rose in the haemophilia stakes. Hana had kissed and touched every inch of the worst scar, loving it as part of her husband's demi-god body. She held onto the certainty that this woman hadn't. "Goodbye Sylvia," Hana said politely. "You can leave after you've seen the cops." She opened the bedroom door and took one last look back at the viper in Logan's childhood room. Helena stood outside with her hand raised, just about to knock.

"Oh," Hana turned back to Sylvia. "Ryan can stay. We'll organise him a work visa. I can't imagine he'll want to be dragged around the country, while you try and find a suitably rich father for him."

Helena's face kept its professional veneer as she spoke to Hana respectfully. "The cops are too busy to come tonight. They said to take photos and clear it up. They'll come in the morning."

"Please can you organise that?" Hana asked, exhaustion leaking from every pore.

Helena smiled and nodded.

"There you go then," Hana shot her last comment back at Sylvia's angry face, "nothing to keep you here." She smiled at the housekeeper and walked towards the spiral staircase, meeting Logan on his way back up. "I just have to do something quickly," she told him. "You don't need to go back in there."

Relief crossed Logan's face like a mist moving across his eyes. "Ok," he said gratefully. "I'll get Phoe in the car. She's upset. We can try and get her settled and then spend some time together." His grey eyes were hopeful.

Hana left him in the lobby, calling into the kitchen to talk to Ryan.

"I don't want to go," the teenager told her wide-eyed. "I *do* want to stay here."

"Stay then," Hana told him and to her surprise, the dark haired young man seized her slender body and hugged her hard.

Chapter 27

Hana emerged from the bath feeling better. She wandered down to the kitchen in her towel, struggling to keep it closed over her rounded belly and following the happy sounds issuing from that end of the house.

Standing in the doorway, Hana observed her husband and daughter enjoying each other's company. They were alike with their dark wavy hair and olive skin, one a carbon copy of the other. Their grey eyes shared some private joke and Hana felt a flicker of envy at their closeness. She withdrew so that only her head peeked around the corner, watching Logan's long, capable fingers caress the guitar strings. One foot rested on the floor, the other knee bent to take the weight of the instrument. Logan's other foot pivoted on the rung underneath the chair next to him. He plucked at a few strings and pulled a face, turning a key and playing it again. Better.

"Nudey dudey," Phoenix giggled, fighting the buttons on her dress. "I be nudey dudey."

"No," Logan smiled. "It's not bath time yet. Mummy's in there."

"I dance," the little girl said and twirled with her arms outstretched. "Play it nen."

"Ok, Miss Bossy. What shall I play?" Logan asked and strummed his fingers over all five strings, creating a slow melodic sound. Phoenix began to sing, her small, clear voice already tuneful even though her brain muddled the words. "All right then. Just let me sort the chords out for that. Hang on Phoe, not so fast."

Hana recognised the tune as Logan bowed his head over the guitar and began to play. She watched his fingers work their magic over the bridge of the instrument, his long forgotten skill returning the more he played. His voice was a beautiful tenor, only ever shared with his girls.

"Pōkarekare ana ngā wai o Waiapu, Whiti atu koe hine, marino ana e.

E hine e hoki mai ra. Ka mate ahau I te aroha e."

Phoenix sang along, mangling the pronunciation in her sweet voice as she held the material of her dress out with delicate hands and twirled and danced with sure footed, bare feet. It was a lovely, lyrical tune from the annals of *Māori* history and washed over Hana like a soft veil.

"S'it mean, Daddy," Phoenix asked when the song's last note resonated through the room. She rested her tiny hands on Logan's knee and looked up at him expectantly, one hand straying to touch the shiny surface of his guitar with tentative fingers. Logan played the tune softly and translated it into English for his daughter.

"The waves are breaking, against the shores of Waiapu, My heart is aching, for your return my love.

" Oh my beloved girl, come back to me, I could die of love for you." He hummed the last few notes and Phoenix returned to her dance floor and readied herself.

"More Daddy. Again."

Logan played again for her, catching sight of his wife in the doorway as she slipped silently into the room. His eyes softened and kept contact with Hana's as he repeated the line just for her. "*E hine e hoki mai ra. Ka mate ahau I te aroha e.*" Then he sang it in English to make his point. "Oh my beloved girl, come back to me, I could die of love for you."

Hana smiled at him and kept her towel hitched up above her breasts. Logan's eyes strayed to her shapely legs and he shot her a covetous look filled with desire. "Hey, Phoe," he said to the child, without removing his eyes from his wife's face. "Tell mummy what *hana* means in *Māori*."

"Oh," she skipped with excitement, her grey eyes wide and twinkling. "Fame a wed hair."

Hana smiled encouragingly and looked to her husband for help and confirmation. The scar underneath his right eye crinkled as he narrowed them and fixed her with a penetrating intensity. "It means *flame, warmth*. It also means *radiance*." His eyes were sultry and alluring. "Phoe thinks it's because you have red hair," he smirked. "It means you're hot and your name is hot."

"Did you just find that out?" Hana asked him and Logan's eyes danced.

"No. I've always know what *hana* means to me."

Of course he would know. Logan grew up with *Māori* as his first language. It caused a strange ache in Hana's soul that her name meant so much to him and a piercing pain reminded her of what she had almost thrown away. Her face became thoughtful and her brow furrowed.

"Mummy," Phoenix's voice was a whisper and she put her hand up to cover her mouth before she told the secret. "Daddy say youse bootiful." Her eyes twinkled with mischief and she jerked her head comically towards her father without looking at him, sharing a joke with her mother. Logan smiled and laid his guitar gently on the table.

"Come on, miss," he caught his daughter up in strong arms and she squeaked. "Let's get you ready for bed before you give any more of my secrets away. You're a rubbish confidante." Passing Hana he leaned in and kissed her slowly on the lips. It held the depths of promise.

"I left the water," Hana said, stroking Phoenix's soft cheek. "But it's deep so you need to let some out and put more hot in."

"Hot in," the little girl repeated and placed a smacking kiss on Hana's palm. "Fanks. Luff oo Mama."

"Love you too, baby," Hana replied as Logan bore his daughter down the hallway to the bathroom on one strong arm. Hana's body froze in place at her child's next words.

"Who teached a song, Daddy? Who dun it?"

Hana heard the plug being pulled in the family bathroom and water gurgling underneath the floor as it travelled to the septic tank under the driveway. She held her breath as Phoenix persisted with her childish innocence. Then Logan replied, "My daddy taught me that and lots of other songs. Mainly old stuff because the chords were easy."

"Poppa Alfie?" Phoenix said with childish astuteness.

"Na, not Poppa Alfie," Logan said. His voice held no trace of emotion and Hana heard hot water tumble into the deep bathtub. "Poppa Reuben was my daddy."

"Where he? My see 'im?" Phoenix persisted.

"He died, darlin'," Logan answered. "Before you were born. But he knew you and he loved you."

"Luff me? Phoe-phoe?"

"Yep. Sure did."

"Nen, I luff 'im," Phoenix replied, reciprocal affection as natural as breathing. There was the sound of a grunt as Phoenix managed to successfully shuck her dress, stamping excited feet and a plop as she sat down in the bubbly water.

Hana stood with her head leaned against the wall, deep in thought. She deeply regretted the cruelty which had caused the thing in Logan to snap open, but the man he was becoming was so much more because of that single, traumatic event. She had never heard him acknowledge Reuben Du Rose before and it was a massive step for him, confessing his parentage to their daughter. Logan seemed softer and more open and it was intoxicating and heady. Hana ran her hand lightly over her stomach and felt the boy inside kick her hand. Perhaps there was hope for this family yet.

Chapter 28

"So, when's Lucy coming up?" Hana asked, faking innocence. "Would you be able to help me make up the spare room?"

Tama looked hard at her and then nodded. "Yeah I can, but it's got all Logan's stuff in it."

"Yeah, I wondered if you'd help me move all that back into our room. I think he's got the message. The spare bed and mattress are still in the garage and I haven't been able to drag it in by myself. Are you free to give me a hand or do you have places to be?"

"Yeah, I can stay." Tama looked wrong-footed but didn't venture any of his secrets so Hana used his brawn to carry the metal bed frame into the large spare room and begin assembling it. Hana took the drawers out of Logan's bedside cabinet and carried them into the bedroom one at a time and then came back for the frame. Tama worked busily with the spanner and screwdriver and Hana stroked his dark, wavy hair as she passed.

"Ma?" Tama fixed his grey eyes on Hana as she bent to retrieve a pair of socks that had fallen from one of the drawers. She stood up straight and smiled at him expectantly. Tama's fingers twisted the screwdriver nervously. "What do you do when you really love someone and things are getting in the way?"

Hana's face dropped and her green eyes dulled with instant sadness. "You're asking the wrong person, sweetie. I'm love's worst nightmare. I married a man who didn't love me because I was pregnant after a one night stand and punished myself for years for trapping him. He had an affair which he kept from me and then died. And I just nearly threw away my marriage to Logan because I was so quick to think badly of him. You should probably ask someone who married the love of their life the first time and made it work."

"There ain't nobody like that though, is there?" Tama sounded sad. "Not round here anyway."

Hana thought for a moment and then smiled, her eyes lighting up and her pretty face softening. "There is actually. Let's finish up here and then we'll go see him. I've got some things to discuss with him too, so that will work out great. I just need to see if Phoe wants to come with us or..."

"I stay a Wiri," Phoenix piped up. She had built a playhouse in the wardrobe and emerged with her hair tousled, completely naked.

"Phoe!" Hana looked shocked. "Will you stop taking all your clothes off, please?" Hana picked up the pretty dress and turned it over. "How did you get the buttons at the back undone?" The delicate pearl fasteners tumbled to the carpet as she spoke and rolled away. "Oh, like that. Well, you've wrecked it now. I'll have to stitch it."

"Stitch it," Phoenix repeated, holding up the Lego car she had been making in the wardrobe. It had five wheels. Hana squatted down in front of her and admired the car.

"Phoe, girls can run around naked, but it's not ok unless you're at home."

"At home," Phoenix smiled and looked around the room. "At Daddy's home."

Tama snorted over his task and Hana shot him a look at the same time Phoenix beamed happily at him. "Oh, come on!" He lifted his head and looked at the assembled females. "We used to run round nekid all the time."

"Nekid," Phoenix repeated and smiled at the word on her tongue. "Nekid." She bounced on the spot happily. "Nekid."

Hana groaned and hauled herself upright as Phoenix trotted off making car noises, her naked bottom wibbling as she moved. "Great, thanks for your input. Very helpful."

"Sorry," Tama smiled, not looking sorry at all, "but it's normal for kids to strip off. Clothes are really constricting and you can do more stuff without them."

"Yeah and you did a fair bit of that as I remember," Hana retorted crossly. "Anahera offered to have Phoe the other day while I did some work at the museum and when I got there to pick her up, her and Wiri were playing in a dirt pile outside the back of the house, completely stark naked." Tama snorted with laughter. "It's not funny!" Hana protested. "I felt really annoyed. I never did find one of her shoes. I think they buried it. My other children never did that!"

"You never brought your other children up *here*," Tama commented. "She's a Kiwi kid and half of us never had shoes to lose, even in winter. If you look at the adults around you, half of us would rather not be wearing them. Logan still walks around in bare feet when he doesn't have to wear shoes and I don't wear them in summer, even when I go out. How many restaurants have you seen signs in that say, 'Shoes must be worn,' or 'Patrons without shoes will not be served here,' and where else in the world would people need to be reminded that they've got nothing on their feet?"

"Fair enough about the shoes," Hana sighed, "but you don't see signs saying naked people won't get served, do you?"

"Probably in the rainforest you do," Tama joked and smirked at her. "Stop worrying, Ma. Don't make her self-conscious before she needs to be. She's a gorgeous little streak of loveliness at the moment. Don't ruin it. Anyway, half the problem is *what* she's wearing."

Hana looked down at the dress in her hand, the swags and bows and felt chided. "Maybe you're right," she conceded.

The spare room looked fresh and clean once they finished and potentially ready for Lucy's visit, although Tama seemed doubtful she would ever come. Leslie had Wiri at the hotel and he and Phoenix greeted each other with enthusiasm. "Are you sure you don't mind?" Hana said guiltily as the children skipped into Leslie's apartment hand in hand.

"Got pantsies on," Phoenix told the tousle-haired boy and he duly admired the leggings. Hana still hadn't been able to persuade the little girl to wear anything on her feet though.

"Got nothing else to do now, have I?" the old lady smiled, hugging Hana against her large body when her face dropped. "Get on with ya, Alfie and I love havin' them. They keep us young. We'll do some baking for when you get back."

"She just wants to be with Wiri all the time," Hana apologised. "She could have come with us but didn't want to."

"It's fine," Leslie said at the top of the stairs. "I'll be having Wiri most days until he goes to school in a few months."

"I didn't think Anahera worked," Hana commented and Leslie looked shifty.

"She don't, but she's not feelin' too well at the moment."

"Pregnant?" Hana asked but Leslie shook her head.

"No, no. Not pregnant. She won't tell me what's wrong but she's behaving a bit like...like Miriam used to before she got real sick sometimes."

"Bi-polar?" Hana asked and Leslie nodded.

"Just crying all the time and stuff. Nev asked me to keep the boy because she's not lookin' after him, or herself properly."

"Well, has she ever been like this before?" Hana asked and Leslie shrugged.

"Not to my knowledge. And I've known the woman her whole life. Her and her sisters lived up the road from me in the township. She always seemed like a happy little thing. Same age as my Nina."

"So she's not a Du Rose then?" Hana asked, "Some cousin twelve times removed or something?"

Leslie laughed. "No, definitely not."

Back in the car, Hana relayed the conversation for Tama. "Don't you think that's a bit odd?" she asked him and he shrugged, driving the expensive ute up the long driveway to the main road and turning left.

"I dunno," he sulked. "You women are all weird. I never understand what you're up to."

"What do you think of Asher? I saw him glowering at me from the paddock behind the house when I was trying to dig my daughter out of her rabbit hole. I get the feeling he hates me and Loge."

"He does." Tama made another turn onto a dangerous single lane road that ran clockwise around a mountain and Hana's stomach lurched as she looked down the washouts littered along the way. She stared a little too long at the plunging depths a few centimetres away and felt sick. Distracting herself, Hana pushed Tama for more information.

"What did we do?"

"You stopped Nev selling up. Asher's convinced there would have been a lot of money handed out once it was all carved up and he wanted his share."

"But it was all debts!" Hana exclaimed. "Doesn't he know that? Reuben hadn't paid any bills or taxes on that property for about ten years. Logan bought the farm for what he agreed with Nev and then still had to settle debts on top of that. Some of them only came to light when Nev handed him a court letter after the sale had gone through. They were going under, that's why Logan..."

"I know," Tama held up his hand to stop Hana's tirade. "But Asher won't believe anyone. He's convinced the developers would have cleared all that and he'd still have got a pay-out. He feels robbed and the idiot started spending it and now has some mighty debts of his own."

"Like what? And how do you know all this?"

"Like that flash car he's driving around and can't make the repayments on and I know because we grew up in the same house. He's a few years older than me and Anahera was the only female in the house, so she kind of brought us up together."

"Like brothers?"

"Yeah, sort of. Although it was different for him because he was proper family and I wasn't. I didn't know that; I genuinely thought Kane was my dad for years. But he wasn't and they all knew that. I spent too much time with Kane, smoking, drinking and trying to get close to him. Gradually they pulled back from me, I guess. I can see why now because I was out of control, but at the time it was just another rejection. Logan paid for me to go away to school and then made sure I had Michael's room down at the hotel when I came back. It saved me countless beatings. Miriam knew I was Michael's son so she treated me well."

"Did you know about Reuben and Miriam's affair?" Hana asked tentatively. Tama nodded, his dark wavy fringe bouncing on his eyelashes.

"The only people who *didn't* know were Logan and you," he said sadly. "Even Alfred knew but he didn't seem able to stop it. When she didn't see Reuben she was miserable and had one of her episodes and that was harder than them meeting and...well...having old people sex, I guess."

Hana looked revolted. "You have such a way with words!" she chastised him. "I didn't need that image in my head thank you!"

"You're welcome." Tama shot her a sideways grin.

"Shut up and drive," Hana yawned. "And behave when we get there. No saying anything stupid and embarrassing me."

"Oh I think you can probably manage that all by yourself," he complained. "I'm not happy about coming here without Logan knowing. He's gonna be dirty at me and I'm on his good side at the moment."

Hana snorted. "Logan doesn't have a good side."

"Yeah he does," Tama argued, "and for a few hours I was on it. Now you're gonna wreck it for me. *As usual.*"

"You're such a comedian," Hana replied sarcastically. "But I still think it's odd that Anahera should suddenly be so depressed without explanation. Do you think she knows something about all the vandalism and it's making her unwell?"

Tama let out an unattractive guffaw of laughter. "How the hell did you make a leap like that? She's maybe just a bit down or going through that thing you ladies go through later in life that makes you harder to manage than usual."

"Are you deliberately asking for a slap, Tama Du Rose? Because you're not too big for one!" Hana glared at him sideways and Tama smirked.

"Right, we're here." Tama pulled up alongside a white picket fence, pulling the truck up onto the grass verge to avoid the traffic speeding along the road. He turned in his seat to face Hana and wagged his index finger at her. "If you cause loads of trouble here, then I'll make sure none of it sticks to me. D'you get that, Ma? I've got enough problems at the moment. I don't need to be offside with Uncle."

Hana's face was unimpressed and she blinked extra slowly and looked like an insolent teenager. "Every man for himself," she said and launched herself out of the vehicle. Tama swore and followed her. Nothing good ever came of Hana's sleuthing and usually he got the blame from Logan for not taking care of her.

"*Kia ora!*" the old man grinned on the front porch, flashing pink gums and crinkling eyes. "What a lovely surprise. Come in Tama, good to see you." The kaumatua pulled Tama into him, pressing his nose to the young man's and holding him there. Then he turned to Hana. "Ah, two for the price of one!" He indicated her blossoming pregnancy and she felt as though she had been stripped naked and lumpy for the entire room to view. Tama read her awkwardness and snorted. Hana cringed inwardly and looked forward to slapping him. The elderly man pulled her into him and pressed his nose and forehead to Hana's. His eyes bored holes in hers and she gulped, knowing he had read everything about her there. *Mana* and power came off him like tidal waves and Hana felt safe and comforted for reasons she couldn't explain.

"Go find Tui," the kaumatua said and flapped his hand at Tama. "She's out the back in the sunshine. She's been baking, you're in luck."

"Oh what a good idea," Hana piped up, looking for revenge for the snort. "Tama can ask your wife about his love life."

Tama stopped dead in the doorway to the kitchen and looked horrified. Hana's green eyes danced and sparkled in a face alight with mirth. She might still slap him on the way home anyway. She hadn't decided yet. Tama did a rude hand gesture behind the kaumatua's back and Hana kept her face straight and gave nothing away, infuriating him further. "What's the matter, love?" Hana asked him. "Is there a problem with your hand?"

Tama's eyes bugged and he put his gesture quickly away as the old man turned to face him. "Er...no," he stammered, "I was just...waving goodbye."

Hana's face muscles struggled to stay in place as Tama high-tailed it out through the kitchen. She relaxed when the house juddered on its pilings with the slam of the back door. The kaumatua beamed at her and indicated the seat behind her. "Sit, sit, you are welcome in my *whare*."

"Thank you." Hana backed up to the comfy sofa behind her and sat down, sinking into its soft folds like an embrace. The seat cushion sucked her in so that her feet hardly touched the floor.

"That boy's still an egg!" the old man sat on an adjacent sofa and shook his head at Tama's antics. Hana looked confused and he pointed at the ranch slider behind her. "I seen his reflection. I assume it's at you and not me. He knows I would take his head off."

Hana shrugged. "Sorry, we've always brought out the worst in each other."

"Na, you've been the best thing in his life. *Ever*. Don't doubt that." He settled back in his seat comfortably and turned his perceptive brown eyes on Hana. "So, *kōtiro*, what brings you out to this side of the *maunga?*"

Hana felt overcome by a sense of futility, as she sat in the overstuffed chair in front of someone she had hoped would have all the answers. She struggled to know where to start and the embattled Du Rose legacy hung around her neck like a millstone, threatening to drown her under its weight. "The boxes," she said haltingly. "The family *taonga.*"

"Ah yes," the man smiled with enthusiasm. "I've seen the museum and met your curator. It's a very fine way of honouring a *whānau's* memories, even if your Will is from *Ngāti Maniapoto.*"

Hana looked momentarily confused. It had never occurred to her that Will's tribal affiliation might matter. "Erm...well, Logan..."

The elderly man threw his head back and laughed himself almost sick, ending with a guttural cough that Hana thought served him right. The sight of a plaster crucifix hanging over the ranch slider opening made her start with guilt and she wondered if she should bang the old man on the back. He blew his nose into a handkerchief with gusto and she glanced at Jesus again. *See he's fine*, she reasoned. The *kaumatua* collected himself. "Right, start at the beginning and tell me what's wrong with the *taonga.*"

Hana narrowed her eyes at him. "You know all of it, don't you? Everything I'm about to ask." She held his gaze, her stunning green eyes flashing her hope and expectation and the old man hated to disappoint her. But he did it anyway.

"No. Sorry, *kōtiro*. My father would have, but I only know rumour and speculation, same as most others."

Hana's shoulders slumped. "Didn't you read Phoenix's diaries?"

The man looked horrified. "No! They were in my safekeeping only. I would never damage my father's *mana* by doing that!"

"Fair enough," Hana sighed. "But I kinda wished you had. When I asked Logan what they were, he said they were a 'box of trouble' and they've certainly been that."

"History can do that," the old man smiled, "nothing like family secrets to blow relationships open."

Hana snuffed out a defeated breath. "Yeah, I saw that with Logan finding out Reuben was really his father. Will's brother from Hamilton was friends with Reuben and they wrote to each other. He gave Logan all his father's letters when we got back from Europe. They go back years, even before Logan was born. He's read them and I think he understands things a bit more now. He distanced himself from Alfred for a while but they seem to be getting on better and Logan's started calling him 'Dad' again."

The *kaumatua* nodded sagely. "Another's perspective can often help. I'm glad the letters were useful to your husband."

"I haven't read them. Logan hasn't offered and I'm not going to ask. I've got enough problems with his grandmother's musings to want to add Reuben's to the pile. The stuff she recorded...well, I actually wish she hadn't. No wonder she hid them with your family."

"So what specifically do you want to ask me?" the man asked, opening his hands in a universal gesture of acceptance.

Hana leaned forward in her seat. "I had all these questions, but now I'm here, I think it comes down to just two. Should I keep reading them and amassing all this terrible knowledge about the Du Roses and if I do, what should I do with the information?"

"Ah, then I'm afraid you've had a wasted trip," he replied. "My name is Arama, not *Atua*. Only God can tell you what to do. Some things are best left asleep and others benefit everyone by bringing them out into the light."

"I don't see any of this benefitting anyone," Hana said, biting her lower lip and holding the old man's gaze with frightening intensity.

"I disagree. It was painful and damaging for Logan to find out his origins and the way he found out was unimaginable. But look at the fruit of that revelation? The family is joined and the mountain whole again. If Logan had not been made to see his link to that land, the *whenua* would have slipped away. He may have just let it go and two complete generations of Du Roses would have been displaced. This way is better. Nev is a good man and like Logan in so many ways. They were allies as boys and now can be as men. We are none of us self-sufficient or without the need for family."

"But what about knowing things that are illegal, or morally wrong?" Hana pleaded, "What then?"

"It is a matter for your own conscience," the wise man replied.

"I'm just rubbish with secrets," Hana conceded, looking as slumped and defeated as she felt. "I knew about Reuben and Logan before he died. I worked it out when he appeared in Logan's bedroom and touched my stomach. Phoenix responded to him and I just knew. Reuben was like an older version of Logan and it felt overwhelming to know this awful secret and try to keep it here." Hana tapped her temple. "I didn't tell Logan and it weighed on me and made me depressed. Now I'm in the same situation. I know that two people who are now married, are actually half-brother and sister and they have no idea. It's burning inside my chest but I don't know what to do about it. If I say something, I cause devastation and if I don't, it just eats away at me. I sometimes feel like I have to make a choice about who to sacrifice and it's not fair! It's not *my* history!"

Arama, a man of immeasurable wisdom and *mana*, selected by his *iwi* for leadership, hefted himself out of his comfy seat and plonked himself down next to Hana. To her surprise he placed a firm arm around her shoulder and rested the other one on her writhing fingers. "You're asking all the wrong questions, *kōtiro*. It became your history from the moment you made your vows to your *toihau*. Logan is a noble leader and you come under his authority. What belongs to him is also yours. The mistake you're making is that it *is* your history, your *kōrero tuku iho,* but it is not your responsibility. Your part is to safeguard and add to it, which you are already doing." He smiled and lightly touched her belly with his finger. "It is not your place to judge, to dissect or to reason with the ghosts of our past. The weight you feel is because you cannot mend what was broken or stop its consequences reaching forward. That is not your role, it is your *toihau's* and he will do what he sees fit."

Hana nodded slowly. "So should I tell everything to Logan and let him deal with it? Because I learned something else about Reuben's father and I..."

Arama moved his arthritic finger from Hana's belly to her lips. "Sshhh, do not tell me. Does Logan know where the diaries are if he wants them?" Hana nodded. "Then your work is complete. Safeguard and keep them for him and your children. They will know when the time is right and *Atua* will give them wisdom to know what to do."

"But I believe in God," Hana said petulantly, "so why won't he just tell me?"

The old man hooted with laughter and squeezed Hana's shoulder. "Does he tell me how to cure cancer by mixing chemicals or what to say to men with guns pointed at the hearts of his children?"

Hana shook her head. The man was amazing but possibly not *that* accomplished yet. "No."

"Well then. That is your answer. *Atua* has other people already busy doing those things and doesn't require my expertise. He knows I would accidentally drop the important test tube and my big mouth would get everyone killed. There are those better suited than me. It is the same with you. You are reading about a woman's life. A very beautiful, talented and powerful woman, but still a faulty human being. Treat her writing like a soap opera, because surely it was." He chuckled heartily but his gaze on Hana as he stood up was serious. "But do not let it touch or influence you. You are not responsible for any of it. You are only the guardian. During the wars, when a *Māori* warrior was asked to guard a particular *pa* or fortification with his life; he did not ask why, he just did it. It's no different for you."

Hana exhaled, feeling easier within herself. The *kaumatua* was right. It wasn't her responsibility - none of it - and even with a century at her fingertips she wouldn't even begin to fix any of the consequences that the Du Roses had hailed down on subsequent generations. She smiled at the old man who stood warming the seat of his pants against the roaring fire like an old English gentleman and nodded happily.

"Do you think it's safe to find my wife now?" he smiled cheekily. "Do you think the marriage counselling is finished yet?" Arama led Hana to the kitchen window and they peered out at Tama and the *kuia*. The woman was in her seventies and sprightly, harvesting something from the loamy soil. A *ta moko tattoo* covered her chin and her white hair was pulled tightly back into a knot, a black beret resting jauntily on her head. Tama wielded the shovel in response to her pointing finger. Hana recalled the woman singing her onto the marae, welcoming her as part of their *iwi* and *hapu*, her beautiful, lilting voice lodging itself in Hana's heart with a sense of belonging. Arama was right. Logan's tribal *tikanga* was *her* history too.

"He's got his serious face on," Hana smiled, staring at Tama's nodding head. It bobbed prolifically. He looked like Phoenix's bobble head toy and it was comical. "Maybe we should wait a while."

"Help me make tea then." The old man pointed and Hana got cups and plates out of cupboards at his direction.

"I don't suppose you remember anyone on the Du Rose land who went by the name of JD?" Hana said, placing worn cutlery on the table next to a sumptuous plate of homemade scones. "He's been cropping up a lot lately." She faced the *kaumatua*. "I mean, am I supposed to try and make sense of this stuff, or just look after the artifacts and then leave them alone?"

Arama hissed through his gums. "It's about learning to live with what you find. *Whakamatemate* is a passion and a sense of mental anguish when one quests to find out a truth about something. It is a concern that seems to come from your very soul. But it can be all consuming. You have a naturally curious mind and your findings may help future seekers of truth. Just don't let it bite you harder than you can cope with." He smiled. "My father spoke once about someone named Jacob Du Rose. Perhaps it was him. He was the *rangatira's* first born and Phoenix Du Rose's elder brother. He was a sickly boy, but did not make it past his first decade. I remember my father saying he was deformed in some way. Latterly it was blamed on the Du Rose curse making itself known, but that's just township superstition. He could have been the heir to everything which passed to Phoenix. The Frenchman united the property under his daughter and the *rangatira*, Phoenix and Jacob's mother. There was a sister too. Leadership is passed to the most suitable candidate chosen and not always the eldest in a *whānau*. The *rangatira* may have favoured him but then again, maybe not. It would depend on his character. I can only think this JD might be him. When did Phoenix write of him?"

"On and off throughout. There's a lot of references to him just before Logan was born and especially around the time they were getting the breeding programme for the Charolaise started."

The *kaumatua* shrugged. "It must have been a paid employee then. It can't be Jacob. Perhaps search the names on the kauri tree on the mountain for another, but I don't recall anyone else of a similar name. Perhaps the 'D' is not Du Rose."

"That's true," Hana conceded and looked wistfully out of the window at Tama and the *kuia* chatting in the middle of what looked like a mini tornado. Leaves and soil whipped around them and they talked with animation and mutual pleasure.

"Hana Du Rose," the old man spoke her name gently and she jerked her attention back to him. "Hold it lightly, like the *koru*. If you uncurl it before it's ready, it loses its shape and will grow deformed. Let the stories unfold at their own pace."

She nodded. "Ok."

Chapter 29

Hana stood in the lobby of the hotel chatting to Tama. "They're incredible people aren't they?" she said wistfully. "I wish they were related to me and then I could justify popping in to see them all the time. I could adopt them like pretend grandparents or something." Hana sighed and Tama pulled a face betraying his complete lack of comprehension.

Something behind Hana snatched at his attention, his grey eyes widening in a fear reaction and Hana sensed her husband's presence in the room. His strong arms snaked around her shoulders from behind and she felt his powerful heartbeat through the thin material of her jacket as it beat against her shoulder blades. Logan locked his hands in front of Hana's breasts and pulled her body into his. She resisted the urge to lay back against him, knowing that Tama's eye-roll threatened to be unleashed. Logan's hands were dotted with healing cuts and scratches and dark lines decorated his palms from the constant outdoor work. He smelled of Sacha and Hana inhaled the heady scent of horse, hay and sunshine. "Where have you two been?" Logan asked with feigned casualness and kissed Hana's neck, the brim of his hat brushing roughly against her cheek. Hana opened her mouth but unfortunately, a little too late.

"She made me," Tama blurted, ignoring Hana's look of astonishment. He pointed a jabbing index figure at her, his betrayal almost complete. "I didn't want to go and I said you'd be mad."

"Go where?" Logan's voice turned icy cold and his chest became rigid against Hana's back. She watched the veins and sinews in his forearms flex and tighten as tension ran through his body. She sighed and shook her head at Tama in disbelief as he completed his manoeuvre.

"You tell him, Hana. I'm going to...up to..." Tama thought of a reasonable place to absent himself. "I'm going up to see Phoe and Wiri." He bolted to the left of the lobby to a small archway marked 'Private' and disappeared up the spiral staircase. Hana hoped he fell up the stairs in his hurry.

Without releasing his wife, Logan turned her slowly until she faced him, measuring the look of guilt in her eyes. "I think you and I need to have a little chat, don't we?" he said, raising one dark eyebrow in humourless expectation. Hana quailed as Logan took her hand firmly in his and led her after Tama's retreating footsteps. At the top of the stairs he turned left and headed towards Michael's old room. Holding the door open for Hana, Logan let her go past him and she cringed and tried not to touch his body as she went through the gap. A dull thud overhead told her that Tama was horsing around with her daughter in the upstairs apartment and she ground her teeth in anger at the injustice.

"Right then," Logan's fingers seized the lapel of Hana's jacket and he fixed his gaze on her firmly. "So what has my errant wife been up to now?" he asked sternly. To Hana's surprise, he fingered the material and then slipped it over her shoulders backwards. Her jaw dropped as he set to work on the buttons of her blouse, growing quickly frustrated with the small fiddly pearls and pushing his hands underneath and starting on her leggings, slipping them down over her hips.

"Are you kidding me? I thought you wanted to talk!" Hana exclaimed and Logan laughed, a gentle snuff that teased the soft skin on her neck.

"We can talk if you want?" His voice sounded husky and Hana shivered at Logan's lips on her bare shoulder as he shoved the flimsy material out of the way. "But you might be too busy for a while."

Logan enjoyed a perverse pleasure at making love to his wife on Michael's bed. "Serves him right!" Logan muttered when Hana complained. "Anyway it's our bed, our room and our hotel, so..."

Hana pressed her lips to his to prevent the rest of the sentence. "So am I still in trouble?" she asked, sounding cute and helpless. Logan shrugged. Hana looked at him curiously. "I thought you were mad."

Logan pulled her into his chest and wrapped his arms firmly around her, rubbing his nose and lips through the auburn locks at the side of Hana's head. "Mmnn," he sighed happily. "Stop worrying."

"I just hate it when you're mad with me," Hana breathed softly on his chest, ruffling his dark chest hair and Logan squeezed her in tighter to stop her.

"I'm not mad with you. Do you think I don't know what you've been up to?"

Hana pulled away from her husband and pouted. "How do you know?"

Logan snuffed quietly and pulled her back into him. "I know everything. It's my job to know and I'm not mad. So just lay here for a bit because I have to go back to the stable yard soon."

Hana snuggled into Logan's chest and lay her cheek against his downy olive skin. "Yes but..." she couldn't resist and he dug his fingers into her ribs just underneath her armpits. Hana squeaked in shock and then giggled as Logan tickled her. "Stop, stop!" she squealed as the tickle reaction became excruciating.

A loud hammering on the door made Hana jump and Logan stopped instantly. He quickly placed his index finger over her lips. "What?" he called, sounding stern and inhospitable.

Tama's voice came through the door, heavily muffled. "I'm taking Wiri home now and Leslie's giving Phoe her tea. So you can carry on with your old peoples'...activities."

"Thanks," Logan called gruffly, physically stopping Hana calling out by putting his palm across her mouth. "I've got a meeting with Jack soon. Are you coming back for the girls?"

"Yeah. Oh Logan, Carrie on reception asked if you'd given the message to Hana about her purse. Arama rang from his *whare* and said she left it there this afternoon."

"I haven't yet," Logan answered with the smirk evident in his voice. "But I will. Hey, when you drop Wiri off, can you stop by and grab it for her?"

Tama's answer was muffled by the door and the sound of a child bouncing around in the hallway. They moved away to the spiral staircase with Wiri's voice chattering about something in his high boyish voice. Logan took his hand off Hana's mouth and she immediately raised her voice in anger. "Why didn't you just ignore him? I feel embarrassed now, yelling to him outside."

"You couldn't go to the door, Han, you're naked and so am I. And you needed a lift home, didn't you?"

"But now they'll know what we were doing and it's humiliating."

"No it's not, I love you." Logan's grey eyes narrowed with his Du Rose sex appeal and he smiled at his wife. "I reckon we've got another half an hour."

It wasn't until Hana sat down in Leslie's apartment upstairs and watched her daughter spreading Marmite on bread with a child's plastic spoon that another fact occurred to her. She tutted at her own stupidity and shook her head.

"What's up?" Leslie asked her, noticing Hana's irritation.

"Oh nothing," Hana said crossly. "Just don't ever let me get desperate enough to rob a bank. I'd be rubbish."

Leslie stopped in the middle of the kitchen floor with a slice of bread in her brown hand. Phoenix reached out eagerly and moved her fingers in a pincer movement as Leslie ignored her. "For real?"

"No, no...I...no!" For some reason, Leslie's willingness to imagine a red haired mother of three, standing in a bank in her maternity leggings trying to rob it, caused Hana to snort with laughter. Phoenix and Leslie watched with perfectly straight faces as she first squirmed, giggled and then laughed hysterically at nothing in particular. Hana kept laughing until she realised that a trip to the bathroom was urgent and then she giggled at herself in the mirror for ages. "Oh, for goodness sake," she chided herself. "I think I'm so damn cunning and then I leave half my belongings at the place I'm not meant to be!"

Chapter 30

"What's the problem?" Logan put a finger in his ear to dull the sound of Phoenix banging wooden blocks into a shape holder with a plastic hammer. "Well how am I supposed to know? She said she was going so I assumed she'd gone." A pause made Hana look up from her book. "Then she must be coming back, mustn't she? Nobody just leaves their stuff. But look, pack it all together and leave it in the housekeeper's office. I want that room stripped and left empty from now on. If she turns up again, give her stuff back and tell her to get the hell off my property. If she won't go, call the cops." Logan's posture was stiff backed and synonymous with the word 'frustration.' He gritted his teeth. "Helena, just deal with it. Pack it all up and take it downstairs. I don't want her staying any longer, so when she comes back, make that clear. Get the cops and they can get rid of her." Logan waited for a second, his face filled with irritation and then said curtly, "Then change it!" He pressed the button to cancel the call and ran his hand over his eyes.

"Look Daddy!" Bored of whacking the blocks, Phoenix decided to smack herself on the forehead with the plastic hammer. "Not 'urting. Ouch!"

"No, babe. Don't be an egg," Logan told his daughter, absentmindedly removing the hammer from her small fingers. He picked her up in his strong arms and held her, his bottom lip pushed out in thought.

"What's up?" Hana asked, her fingers stalled on the pages before her. "Fine!" she rebuked him roughly as Logan began the makings of a half convincing head shake. He corrected himself.

"Sorry. Habit." He sat down next to her on the cream leather sofa and immediately Phoenix wiggled out of his arms and went to torment some of her other toys. She reached into the giant wooden box in the corner, obscuring the beautiful portrait of Benjamin Bunny that Hana had painstakingly painted on the wood and her feet teetered dangerously off the floor. She grunted with effort and then humphed with satisfaction as her hands appeared above her head waving a small red car. "Don't be like that," Logan whispered, putting his strong arm around Hana's shoulders and tugging her into his chest.

"Well, you're just doing your masking act on me, as per usual. Like I can't be trusted. I hate it. I'm not stupid. Why can't you understand that knowing the truth is infinitely less worrying than guessing at it?" Hana pondered the irony of her sentence, knowing that ignorance in certain matters was definitely better.

"Ok," Logan conceded. "That was Helena. Sylvia's not been at the hotel since dinner last night and wasn't answering her phone or door. One of the girls went up to take her laundry back and got Helena to open the room. The bed's not been slept in and all her stuff's packed ready to go. But she's not there."

"She was packed the other night," Hana replied from Logan's armpit. "I saw all her stuff after the brick went through the window."

"Apparently the cops turned up last night to talk to her about that and she wasn't around. Carrie left her a message but she's not shown up for it. Yet all her stuff is still there. What do you think she's up to?"

Hana snorted and the nasty thought was exposed before she could halt it. "Do you have any rich widowers staying in the hotel? Perhaps she's bagged herself one of them and spent the night."

"Then she can't be far away. But I've got Helena clearing the room out so she can get lost."

"You won't be able to make her go," Hana said, resignation tainting her voice. "And what about the DNA test?"

Logan smiled with grim determination. "I will make her go. And we don't exactly need a DNA anymore, do we? I told Helena to change the keypad so Sylvia won't know the room access number."

"But it's been the same number since your...since Reuben had that room," Hana said, sitting up and staring aghast at her husband. "You can't change it."

"I'm changing it," Logan said with a fire in his eyes. "We won't ever sleep there again now, so I'm turning that whole wing into guest rooms. Besides, she's the least of my problems. Her disappearance is no biggie, not like some others."

"What? Has someone else disappeared?" Hana asked, her interest piqued.

"Bloody Flick!" Logan's vehemence became evident with his next sentence. "We're due to run the stock in to check on calving and try to work this whole damn mess out and he's nowhere to be seen. All his stuff's gone from the bunkhouse and nobody's seen him since the other night. Selfish bugger!"

"Oh." Hana tried to disguise her unease. "I wonder why he'd do something like that." She looked hard at her husband. "You've been so good to him."

Logan's face remained veiled in irritation. "Yeah, it's really rats to run out on us like that. I liked having him here. He was someone I could trust. Oh well. Just goes to show that you don't always know people like you think you do."

"Won't the cops pick him up straight away?" Hana asked, keeping her question casual.

"Dunno, don't care," Logan replied, his mind already on a different track altogether.

Hana shrugged and settled back down. "Fair enough," she agreed. "Are you going to work?" She pointed at the rumpled white tee shirt adorning his torso and his brown legs stretching out of boxer shorts. Logan shook his head.

"Nope, not today. I'm spending the day with my girls." He smiled at his wife and snuggled her into him on the sofa.

"What about the problem with the cattle? Don't you need to sort that out?" Hana's eyes widened in surprise and Logan laughed.

"What's done is done. I can't change anything. We're gonna have to wait and see which of the heifers births a flamin' Friesian calf. It's a nightmare for our breeding programme, reputation, everything."

"But we only saw one black and white calf last night. The other one was white. So could it be ok?"

Logan snorted. "Who knows babe? Black is a dominant gene so you would think it came out immediately, but I've done a bit of research this morning and apparently that might not be the case. It could come out in subsequent generations and then the bloodlines are screwed basically."

"Oh," Hana sighed. "I wish I understood it all."

"It's fine, we need to get the vets in and do some genetic testing. I have no idea what we're going to do right now. But I'm sure as hell not gonna waste today worrying about it. We'll wait until all the dams have calved and then see what we've got. It can't be the whole herd because they're kept all over the property in different areas, so it's just a case of working out which of the groups the rogue bull got to. Then we need to understand how!"

Hana looked at her husband with a furrowed brow. "Why are you so calm? You would normally be out there checking fences and raging around looking for a culprit. I don't understand."

Logan stretched out gentle scarred fingers and touched her stomach tenderly. His hand brushed the cloth of Hana's tee shirt gently before lifting it up. He exposed her rounded tummy and distended belly button, his fingers light and sensitive. He shifted his body and dipped his head, placing his lips gently over the dark pigmented line that ran from Hana's breastbone deep into her trousers and Hana held her breath as she felt her husband's kiss. Logan sat up and looked into Hana's green eyes. "Maybe I've realised there are more important things," he whispered and kissed her soft lips.

"Ooh, Daddy!" Phoenix jumped to her feet as Logan's phone rang and she brought it over to him, tripping over her own feet.

"Thanks, honey," he replied with a fondness in his eyes which caused his daughter to beam and bite her lower lip. Logan answered the call abruptly. "What?"

A long conversation ensued in which Logan did a great deal of listening, nodding and grunting. "What did Jack say?" he asked and waited again while the tinny voice chimed in his ear. "Ok so keep the herd we drove down from our place the other night, completely separate. Don't let them mix. See what they birth in the next week or so. It's possible that it's all contained within that group. There's no way anyone could have gotten to the lot. Check the ear tag numbers of the dams and work out where they were being kept. I think I know which ones they are, but it'll be interesting to see if I'm right."

Hana studied her husband with concentration in her green eyes as he hung up the call. "You want to go don't you?"

Logan bit his lip and smiled at her confusion. "No, I don't want to go. I want to stay here with my wife but she doesn't appear to want me. Have you got some other dude turning up or what?"

Hana looked affronted. "Why on earth would you ask me that?"

"Joke!" Logan soothed. "Hana, what's going on with you?"

She sighed. "I just feel really jumpy at the thought that somebody's been standing out there watching us. I keep closing the curtains and then thinking how unfair that is, shutting out this beautiful view. But I'm scared as well and I'm finding myself awake in the middle of the night far too often." She shook her head and her red hair tumbled out of its clip. Logan stroked her cheek and snuggled her in tightly to his chest.

"I know. It's pretty sick. If I ever find out who it is, I'll kill them myself."

Hana wrapped her arms around Logan's waist and breathed in the comforting scent of him. She felt a gentle touch on her leg and looked down to see Phoenix rubbing her eyes. "I go bed now," she asked with casual politeness. "I tired. Fuffy tired."

"Want me to take you?" Logan asked and the child nodded. He stood and scooped her up in his strong arms and bent so that Hana could kiss her daughter. Phoenix puckered up her lips and kissed her mother, bowing her head onto Logan's shoulder as he bore her away to her cot.

"I should probably get some lunch ready, the day's disappearing," Hana declared as Logan came back into the room. He shook his head, gently removed the book from her hands and picked her up bodily.

"It doesn't matter, babe. It's a day with me so it's not a waste and I'm looking after you today. You look tired."

"But...that's odd because I feel fine..." Hana trailed off as she caught his meaning and slapped his arm. "You bad boy! I don't look tired at all. What if Tama comes back?"

"He won't. He's doing some stuff at Nev's place. They're digging the footings for the new barn behind his house. We'll keep all the heavy gear in there while we strip the area that's all scrubby. It's gonna take a few months to get it in shape for grazing or crops."

"I thought Lucy was coming to stay," Hana said as her husband negotiated his burden through the door frame.

"Mmnn, yeah," Logan replied without committing himself to betraying his nephew's heartache. "Now stop talking." He kicked the door closed with his foot without letting go of Hana's arm and began to peel her clothes off and drop them on the chair. "I love you, Hana Du Rose," he whispered, kissing her neck as his hands roved under her remaining clothes.

"You're utterly impossible," Hana sighed as Logan's bristles rasped against her soft skin and she heard him give a low snicker. When he placed his hands either side of her face and looked at her, his eyes danced, alight with mischief and lust. She opened her mouth to chastise her husband further but he took full advantage and planted his lips over hers, searching with his soft tongue and pressing his hands into the small of Hana's back.

Chapter 31

The bath later was hot enough to make Hana's skin mottled and blotchy. Her head swam horribly as she tried to get out. She stood for a moment wrapped in her towel and debated calling Logan for help. The front door slammed and Tama yelled out. "I'm back. Anyone home?"

Phoenix shot down the hallway in full flight shouting, "Tama, Tama!" and Hana heard a grunt as she evidently flung herself at his legs.

"Well I don't get many naked women throwing themselves at me," he joked. "Where's all your clothes?"

"In a woom," Phoenix replied seriously.

"Well don't you pee on me!" Tama attempted to exact a promise from the toddler.

"Pee on me," she repeated, "Ok."

Hana heard Tama pass the bathroom door on the way to the kitchen. "No, *don't* pee on me," he said with a nervous edge to his voice.

"I goin' Mama barf," Phoenix said conversationally and their voices lowered to a hum as they went out of range.

Hana stood on tiptoe and unlatched the window, feeling the cold breeze nuzzle over her skin and raise goose bumps. It soothed and relieved her after the heat of the bath. The window opened sideways and Hana pushed her face out, gripping her towel tightly against her breasts. A pair of red eyes startled her near ground level in the darkness and she stifled a shriek. The possum stared her out, its unblinking eyes fixed on her, downy ears alert and flicking. "Don't even think about it," Hana whispered and the creature stared as the breeze disturbed the fur around its long back. A shuffling emanated from the trees at the far end of the property and Hana froze as the beam of a flash light flicked off so quickly that she doubted her eyes. The possum's face turned towards the noise and then the animal was gone, responding to danger in a silky fleeting movement. Another pair of red eyes observed Hana from the possum's back as it fled, the young marsupial clinging to its mother's back with an expert grip. Hana stared towards the origin of the light, seeing and hearing nothing.

Feeling exposed in her towel, she slammed the window and yanked on the blind, hearing the comforting rumble as it dropped into place. For an instant she wondered if the intruder could be Bobby, his recent behaviour seeming so out of character. Or was it? Perhaps he had simply reverted back to type.

Hana sat on the side of the bath and waited for her blood pressure to return to normal, ignoring the pounding in her head and the dreadful sick feeling. Logan's gentle knock on the door was a welcome relief. "Han, can you leave the water for Phoe?"

"Ok," she breathed and ran a hand over her face.

Her husband, astute as ever was through the locked door and over by her side in a second.

"How do you do that?" she complained, pulling her towel firmly around her breasts. "I just feel a bit odd, that's all."

"Misspent youth. Want me to get a doctor?" Logan squatted down next to her and his grey eyes darkened with worry.

Hana contemplated the poor doctor who had been summoned to Alfred's apartment after she fainted and shook her head quickly. "No way! I'm fine. I just need to cool down."

Her incapacitation made Hana irritable and she regretted it instantly. "I'll get dressed and if I still feel unwell, I'll make an appointment tomorrow and go...somewhere."

"What's wrong with the local doctor?" Logan pushed and Hana paled.

"Last time I saw him, I was a complete raving lunatic. I told him you'd get rid of me by murdering me when I became inconvenient. Don't you remember the look on his face? I never want to see him again and I'm certain he won't want to see me!"

Logan smirked and bit his lip. "Yeah that was pretty radical," he snorted.

"Who's killing who?" Tama asked from the doorway, holding a naked, wiggling Phoenix in his arms.

"Mama barf for me!" she squawked happily and kicked her chubby legs.

"Come on then, baby," Hana relented. "And I'll just sit here and watch you. But no splashing tonight."

Tama stood the olive skinned bundle up in the bath and she sat down with a plop and a giggle. She rolled onto her stomach in the soapy water with her eyes shut comically and her little legs kicking. "I swimmin'!" she called.

"Any food going?" Tama asked and Logan nodded.

"Yeah, I made roast chicken and veggies. Be about half an hour. That ok?"

"Only if I can grab some bread now," Tama negotiated and Logan nodded. The young man disappeared into the kitchen and Hana heard the sound of the pantry opening and closing. She eyed her husband and raised an eyebrow and he shrugged.

"Just leave him. He'll sort it out."

"I don't understand though. He made me get the spare room ready for Lucy to visit but now she's not coming."

"I think they broke up," Logan whispered. "It was the distance got too hard for her."

Hana watched her daughter doing her pretend swimming in the tub, arms and legs flicking like a beached turtle.

"Hana, what's wrong?" Logan's voice cut through her attempts to numb her brain and Hana fought an irrational flash of anger.

"Nothing! Stop!"

Logan jumped back as though bitten. "Sorry. I just care."

Hana looked back towards the window, guilt etched into her knitted brow. "It's ok. I'm tired and fed up is all. Every time I think my life is settling down, there's some new disaster. Logan, did you ever find out who the smoker was? The person who lurked up here and left the cigarette ends?"

"Na, sorry. The cows mashed the evidence and there's no reason for anyone to be doing that." Logan rested his slim backside on the corner of the sink and folded his arms, crossing his feet over at the ankles. Hana saw a hole in his sock and fixed her gaze on it.

"Do you think it could have been Flick?" she asked, working to keep her tone casual. When Logan didn't answer, she looked up, sighing as she failed to cover her concern quickly enough and knew he saw. She glanced away again but a hardness made its way across his grey eyes.

"Now that's a strange question," he said in a low voice. "And I'd quite like you to qualify it, please?"

Hana squirmed under his glare, her husband's stance making her feel guilty and frozen out. "I don't know." She attempted to fudge her way out of the uncomfortable trap and Logan's eyes narrowed in response. He kept her pinned to the side of the bath with his eyes while oblivious, Phoenix tumbled around happily in the water like a mermaid.

"Hana!" Logan snapped and the little girl sat up quickly and stared at her father and then her mother. "Tell me why you would think my stockman would be lurking around outside my house?"

"He's just been behaving weird lately." Hana's words came out in a rush as two pairs of penetrating grey eyes watched her halting progress. "Since the hospital appointment. He's been acting oddly, like...scared. And now he's gone." Hana stood up, attempting to display more confidence than she felt. "I don't know, Logan," she said. "But if you're trying to insinuate something inappropriate, you're hardly in any position to do that. So don't!"

Hana stalked into the bedroom still in her towel and closed the door behind her. She went quickly to the huge ranch sliders that occupied one whole wall and stared out into the darkness, leaving the light off. The view outside was spectacular as the Milky Way soared overhead like a riotous white stripe of activity. A prickling sensation began at the back of Hana's neck, creeping up into her hair and causing an involuntary shiver to ransack her sensibility and reduce her to nervousness again. She saw the light over in the trees once more, a cursory flash of yellow artificial glare against the milky moonlight, gone as quickly as it came. Then the red blaze of a cigarette, turning slowly to orange as the smoker drew in the cancerous mix, throwing it carelessly down onto the scrubby ground.

Hana's breath caught in her chest and she yanked the cord to close the curtains, fumbling in her haste and hearing the weight on the end of it bash against the wooden architrave. The material met in the middle with a comforting hiss and Hana shrieked as she felt strong hands on her shoulders and she whirled round.

The back of her head hit the glass, muffled by the sound of the curtain and her husband hissed. "Geez woman! What's with you? I only came to say sorry!" Logan reached out one-handed and flicked the light switch next to the window, flooding the room with a comforting yellow glow. With his other hand he kept Hana in place, his fingers pinioning her shoulder as she shivered and shook with the withdrawal of adrenaline. "Have I lost my touch?" He finished with an injection of humour that seemed wasted on his wife, although doubt lurked beneath the surface.

"No, sorry." Hana sank into his strong arms, gasping with relief and exhaled fear like a noxious poison. Loyalty to Bobby prevented her telling Logan the watcher was back; in case it was him.

Logan's hand snaked under her jaw and into the hair at the back of her neck, grounding her in his solid confidence. Hana breathed out slowly through pursed lips that were instantly covered by Logan's softness and seeking tongue. "Phoenix?" she whispered against his skin and he sighed with contentment.

"Tama's giving her backstroke lessons and playing duckies."

"What?"

"He's throwing bread to her." Logan's laugh rumbled gently inside his chest and Hana smirked at the image of Tama sitting on the side of the bath eating a sandwich. She let her husband release her twisted fingers from the towel between her breasts and drop it gently to the floor.

Logan's expert thumbs roamed across her hips in a downward spiral and his stubble on her neck distracted Hana temporarily from the threat outside in the darkness, as the man watched the entangled silhouette. The watcher raged inwardly. "Bitch!" he mouthed to the night and used the fleeting light of the torch between his teeth to light another cigarette.

Chapter 32

Hana walked into the police station, her heart pounding with the effort of remaining calm. She gave her name at the front desk and endured a short wait.

"Mrs Du Rose, thanks for coming in," the officer smiled at her as he shook her hand. His manner was gentle and his dark *Māori* features added to the official uniform, giving him a handsome quality to rival her husband's. "You're a hard lady to reach."

"Is Detective Inspector Odering here?" Hana asked, looking around the south Auckland station. The furnishings and paint work smacked of government institution. "He left a message for me earlier. I came as soon as I could but I've left my daughter with my in-laws, so I can't be long."

"No, ma'am. He asked me to show you." The officer stepped back smartly, holding the heavy door open with a long-armed reach so that she could proceed ahead of him. "Through here."

Five minutes later, Hana stood in a small darkened room with a huge glass window in one wall. Six blond men lined up on the other side of the pane underneath a number spray painted on the wall. As a group, the men were dressed casually with blue jeans and chequered shirts, a light growth of stubble adorning the lower part of their faces. Tears pricked behind Hana's eyelids and nausea gripped her stomach as she watched Flick stare straight ahead, his gaze fixed on the glass. It was as though he saw her there, the intensity of his blue eyes superheating the window between them so that it trembled with the power of him.

"They can't see you, Ma'am," the officer reminded Hana, touching her lightly on the forearm. "Are you ok? Can I get you a drink of water? You can sit here for a moment. There's a chair behind you if you step back."

"I'm fine," Hana gasped. "I built it up in my mind and it's just an anti-climax."

The officer's head whipped round so fast that Hana's eyes widened in fear. "So the guy who attacked you isn't here?" His face registered a heady mix of irritation and fear. "But Detective Inspector Odering said..." He changed position, shuffling his smart work shoes on the tiled floor. "I have your statement here. I know it was a few years ago now but if you want to have a read of it, I can give you a moment. You identified Robert Dressler from a photo identikit. So did another witness..." he reached for his clipboard and shuffled through the sheaves of paper fixed to it. "Your husband was the other witness I believe? We should get him in. I wonder why Odering didn't..." He stared at Hana again, warm brown eyes channelling confusion. Hana made a show of looking down the line as the men on the other side of the glass struggled to maintain their wooden pose.

Hana turned to face the policeman, who flicked his paperwork and let the sheaves shudder to rest beneath his fingers. "I wasn't married to Logan back then and his identification wasn't as certain," Hana lied. "Officer, the man who attacked me was wicked. He had a hard face and I'll never forget the hatred in his eyes." She looked back at Bobby's tortured face, his forehead lined by resignation. His eye had healed to a light green hue underneath and the cut on his eyelid had left a pink scar. Hana breathed in, breathed out. "I don't see that awful man here." Hana smiled, comfortable with her level of honesty. "May I go now? I have to drive home - I promised my daughter I'd do baking with her."

The cop nodded. "Yes, Ma'am. Thanks for coming, we appreciate it. I'm sorry you've had a wasted trip."

"It's fine. I'm sorry I can't tell you what you need to hear."

In the car park, Hana maintained her casual stance and waved at the perplexed face of the officer as he watched through the glass fronted station. She drove away feeling sick and at the first opportunity, pulled over and used her cell phone to dial an unfamiliar number. "Hi, please can I speak to Judge Liza Du Rose?"

Within a few short minutes, her sister-in-law's clipped voice came across the line. "How did you get this number?"

"I took it out of Logan's phone."

"Why?"

"I need your help."

"Ask your husband."

"I can't," Hana sighed. "It's complicated and I'd like you to trust me." Hana explained her predicament to the judge, pausing to plug her ailing phone into the dashboard charger. "Logan saved Bobby once and although I suspect they had a fall out recently, I want to honour what he started. I'd like to engage a lawyer on his behalf, anonymously and pay for it."

"But he'll get Legal Aid."

"I want him to have a proper lawyer, who'll put his best interests at heart, not someone who'll get dragged out of bed and arrive not knowing who he is or giving a damn!"

Liza laughed. "Nice, well, thanks for that glowing appraisal of my colleagues. I'll be sure to pass it on. I'm guessing you want to stand bail for him too?"

"Yes please," Hana conceded. "I have money put away from my late husband's estate and the sale of my houses. I'll use that."

"It won't be millions!" Liza snorted. "He's a low grade criminal, who I suspect they now have no reason to hold, seeing as you just removed their justification. Odering must love you!"

"I don't care! Will you do it for me? And make sure the lawyer you engage can't be traced back to me or the Du Roses. It's important."

A silence greeted Hana and she peered at the phone and then shook it slightly. But it hadn't cut out. Liza's voice came out of it, as bold and forceful as ever. "Respect, Hana Du Rose."

"Pardon?"

"Respect! You have mine. You sound more like a Du Rose every time I speak to you. I have to admit that I wrote you off initially. But maybe my stupid brother knew what he was doing after all."

"Thanks?" Hana was unsure about the compliment but didn't have time to weigh it against her conscience. "So you'll sort it out for me?"

"Leave it with me. I'll call you on this number when I know something."

Hana made the journey back to the hotel, taking it slowly around the sharp turns. She called into Alex's restaurant on a whim and purchased a number of his specialty chocolate snails for Logan. The cousins were thrilled by the impromptu visit and delayed her further, so that she was already on the long drive down to the hotel when her phone rang. "Hello?" Hana kept her voice level, not recognising the private number showing on the screen.

"It's me," Liza said. "The cops let him go. There's nothing to pay. You said it wasn't him so they had no reason to keep him. He's gone on his way apparently."

"How did you find that out?" Hana risked asking.

Liza gave a hollow laugh. "Best you don't know. Cheers." The phone clicked and then disconnected. Hana heaved a sigh of relief and allowed herself a few tears.

"I didn't lie, God," she justified her actions, seeking to placate her own screaming conscience. "I told the truth when I said the man who attacked me wasn't there. That man doesn't exist anymore. Bobby's changed. He's different now. I would trust him with my life and I owe it to him to return the favour."

Hana mopped up her tears and reapplied her eye makeup, returning home to deliver the snails to her husband. "That was a long drive just for some chocolate," he commented, eying her with curiosity.

"I know you like them and you're worth it." She smiled, the strain in her face thinly disguised.

"Thanks. Chef's improved them since last time." He bit ruthlessly into a shell.

"Yum!" Phoenix squealed as hers slithered out of her warm fingers and slid across the plate. "He 'scapin' me!"

"Catch him quick!" Logan laughed and helped her retrieve the slimy object from next to the fruit bowl. "Want one?" He held out a white chocolate snail with mottled brown markings and Hana's eyes watered.

"No, thanks. I really thought I would, but now I've got them, I actually feel quite sick." She pulled a face and left the room, fighting down the tide of guilt, but knowing her husband would eventually hone in on it like a heat seeking missile. For now Bobby was safe. And that was something Logan didn't need to know.

Chapter 33

"Wiri, Mama. Look, Wiri!" Phoenix skipped on the spot and with great concentration attempted to leave planet Earth altogether. "Oof!"

"Oh dear, never mind." Hana retrieved her daughter from the concrete with a smile, hauling her up one-handed. "You're nearly there. Jumping's hard isn't it?"

Phoenix knitted her brow and sulked, her bottom lip shooting out. "Wiri do it."

"Wiri's bigger," Hana said, dropping the last of the pegs back into the basket. "Jumping with two feet is the sign of a big girl," she encouraged her daughter.

"Wiri do it," Phoenix said again and Hana turned from the washing line with a look of confusion.

"My feet hurt," the little boy said, his face dirty and sad. "I can't do jumping now."

Hana gaped at the sight of the dishevelled visitor, the knees of his jeans ripped and flapping in the breeze and the edges of his feet smeared with brown clay and blood. "Wiri! What are you doing here? Where's Mummy?" Hana asked, unable to hide the shock in her face.

"She's crying," the child said, his tone heavy. "She's scaring me."

"Beedin'!" Phoenix squealed in horror and gulped back a wail. "Wiri beedin' feets! Oh no!"

"It's fine, we'll deal with it." Hana injected confidence into her voice and with a smile, lifted the child onto her hip. She abandoned the washing basket and worked her way around the deck, Wiri clipped around her body like a peg and Phoenix bobbing next to her, looking up at her friend with concern. They kicked their boots off in the garage and Hana took her charges through to the kitchen and sat the small boy on the centre island. Then she surveyed the damage.

The boy's grey eyes were listless and sad and a heaviness hung over him like a veil. His body language was one of defeat and resignation and he shivered uncontrollably.

"How did you get so many cuts?" Hana asked and tenderly smoothed the dark wavy hair away from his forehead to examine a growing bruise.

"Kept falling," he said, without emotion. "It's a long way."

"Does Mummy know you're here?"

A shake of the tousled head and Hana smiled, keeping the anxiety at bay for now, not wanting to make him fearful of trusting her. "I'll just let her know and then I think the best thing for you would be a nice hot bath to warm you up and let me see where the damage is."

"Baff!" Phoenix squealed with excitement and Hana stopped her with a raised hand as her daughter's tee shirt flew across the kitchen and she attacked her leggings with eager fingers.

"No babe. Wiri's hurt. He needs to go in by himself."

"Oh." Phoenix saddened straight away.

"Would it be ok if Phoe came in the bathroom with you?" Hana asked the child, respecting his privacy. "But not in the bath."

Wiri nodded and looked as though he didn't much care. "I'm not going home though," he said with determination. "I'm living here now."

Hana used an intermittent signal on her cell phone to text Logan and tell him Wiri was with her, in case they were looking for him.

'*Didn't know he was missing! Nev's gone home to check what's going on,*' came the reply.

The child's body was as damaged as his clothes. His knees bore decent scrapes and a cut on his hip yielded a spiteful splinter. He made no complaint as Hana pulled it out with a pair of tweezers but Phoenix winced and gripped the side of the bath with fingers white from the effort. The water stung the cuts but the child didn't cry or make a fuss. The foamy bubbles soothed and the herbal horse chestnut acted as an antiseptic and a balm. "Nonie Leslie made this bubble bath." Hana chattered as she kneeled on the floor, one of Wiri's feet in her hands as she examined the injured skin. "She gave me a *panipani* for this exact thing, made from native leaves."

The child nodded and Hana stopped wasting her breath, knowing with a sad realisation that she couldn't comfort him. Instead she massaged the muck from his toes and the balls of his small feet and tried to infuse him with love. She remained silent as he lay back so she could wash the winter filth from his hair and then she pulled the plug and swaddled him in a giant, soft towel. She cradled him snugly and carried his inert, shocked body through to the lounge and lay him on the sofa, placing a gentle kiss on his clean forehead.

He smiled at last. "Thank you, Aunty Hana."

"You're welcome, Wiremu. I'll just go and swill the bath out and then how about I make you both a lovely hot chocolate?"

Wiri nodded and battled to retrieve his arms from the towel and sit up more. Hana put a cartoon on the television to occupy both children and left the room as Phoenix snuggled up to her friend and pulled a throw down over them from the back of the sofa. "I lookin' after you now," she informed him with authority and made her body so small she was able to tuck herself between his hip and the back of the sofa. Then she laid down and put her head on his chest, drawing comfort as much as she gave it.

Hana cleaned the bath and then inspected Wiri's ruined clothing. Had they been Phoe's she would have thrown them away, but it wasn't her decision to make. *What is going on? Why would Anahera let him leave without raising the alarm? And why did he have no shoes or coat against the cold?*

Without a ready answer, Hana set the washing machine going with a load of dark clothing which included Wiri's. She produced the promised drinks and the children settled on the floor at the coffee table to drink them, happy with the bowl of naughty sugary snacks and crisps that each received with a look of gratitude, their thanks muffled by eager mouthfuls. While the children vegetated in front of endless reruns of SpongeBob SquarePants, Hana hung out the washing in the watery winter sunshine and clattered around lighting the big fire in the lounge.

The men arrived a few hours later, pulling onto the driveway as Hana retrieved the washing from the line. Logan's expression was casual as he swaggered over to his wife and took the heavy basket from her, but his brother's was not. "I'm sorry about this, Hana," he said, agony in his eyes. He ran a hand over his face and Hana heard the bristles against his palm. "Ana's losing the plot. She's not making any sense."

"It's fine." Hana reached out and touched her brother-in-law's writhing fingers and saw Logan's narrowed look from the corner of her eye. "He's a bit cut up. It looks like he fell a few times and picked fights with fence posts. But he's ok. There's no serious harm."

"But how the hell did he manage to walk all the way from our place to here?" Nev raged, his anxiety driving his body into jerky, uncontrolled movements. "He could have got lost in the bush or anything! Stupid boy!"

"It's in his blood," Hana said with wisdom. "He's a Du Rose. But he's upset, Nev. If you go raging in there like this, you'll make it worse. I don't know what's happened or why he's run, but being angry won't help." Hana placed herself in front of the garage door, effectively barring entry to the furious man.

She saw Logan smirk and look away, cuddling the laden washing basket awkwardly.

Nev postured and his grey eyes flashed with danger. Hana stood her ground.

"Hana," Logan said and she looked at her husband. He raised his eyebrows at her, warning her not to get involved in another man's business but she disobeyed, gritting her teeth and remaining in place. Logan placed the basket on the ground with precise movements and then looked at her with a pointed mix of admiration and interest.

"I want to see my son!" Nev blasted at her, his breath ruffling Hana's fringe and Logan took a step towards him.

"I'm not stopping you," Hana replied, not moving an inch.

"I'm taking him!" Nev leaned closer and Hana didn't flinch.

"He's naked. I've washed his clothes but they're badly ripped. Have you brought some others for him to wear?"

Nev gulped and Hana knew he'd been home but not given it a thought. Guilt dulled the gritty grey eyes and Nev worked his jaw. "No, I didn't."

Hana's expression softened at the formidable man a few inches from her face. "Nev, I'm not telling you how to raise your child, but Wiremu's frightened of something. I'm not stopping you from seeing your boy or taking him home, but he's calm now. Lose the anger and then I'll let you in."

Logan gave a hearty smirk and rolled his eyes, his body tensed to defend his wife if Nev became any more of a threat. He shook his head at the nerve of his fearsome wife and bit back a snort. But Hana had guessed right and Nev shared the tenderness of his mother, Antoinette and only the looks of Reuben Du Rose. The violence of the Du Rose males had missed him out and the gentle giant buckled under Hana's astute study. "Is he ok?" he whispered.

Hana nodded and smiled. "He's in the lounge watching TV. Come on." She jerked her head and kicked off her boots. Logan retrieved the washing basket and left it on the garage floor as the men trooped down the hallway behind her in their socks.

The children lay entwined on the sofa, the woolly throw pushed off onto the floor. Cartoon characters squawked at their own antics in the corner but their audience slept soundly. Both sucked their thumbs, Wiri still shrouded in his towel, his hair fluffy and damp near his skin. Phoenix had squished herself between him and the back of the sofa and her nose was pushed up against Wiri's shoulder, a line of dribble glistening against his bare skin. They looked peaceful, the strain finally absent from the little boy's face. His feet poked out of the bottom of the towel, the skin raw and painful from prolonged contact with rocks and bush material and Nev winced.

In silence, the men followed Hana to the kitchen and she clattered around with the kettle, making tea. Logan pulled himself water from the cold tap but Nev slumped at the table in defeat. "Sorry," he said, sounding ashamed as Hana laid the steaming mug in front of him and placed the sugar bowl and a spoon within reach. "I'm just a farmer. I can't do all this emotional stuff. I wasn't raised that way."

"What's going on?" she asked, her voice soft and enticing.

Nev shook his head. "I dunno. I've been trying not to see, I guess. Something's been wrong for months, since just before we moved into the new place. I thought it was what she wanted, us to stay here and farm. She says it is, but then she's so depressed all the time."

"It's been a harrowing couple of years," Hana ventured and Nev nodded with enthusiasm.

"Yeah. Losing my *matua* was...horrific. I thought we'd never get over that. But this fresh start, it was meant to make it all right. I dunno what's gone wrong."

Logan slumped down into the chair next to Hana and sniffed. She stifled a smile at the ready tell, which told her that talk of emotional issues was making him uncomfortable. He reached for her hand under the table and squeezed her fingers, seeking an unknown reassurance. Hana squeezed back and saw him receive whatever it was he sought. His grey eyes relaxed and lost their stormy hue, his fingers caressing hers with a heady seduction. "Would Ana talk to Dr Seuli?" Hana asked and Nev shrugged.

Then he looked up and a flicker of hope lit his face. "Would you ask her? She might listen to you."

Logan's jaw worked and his fingers clamped harder over Hana's. She knew he didn't want her to get involved. For once, she respected his wishes. "I can't just rock up and tell her to go and get help," Hana said, trying not to sound dismissive. "It would be rude. It definitely wouldn't encourage her to trust me."

Nev's shoulders slumped. "But she's not listening to me," he said. The man shrank before their eyes, receding in stature and presence and shocking Logan, whose love for his half-brother reared itself unexpectedly.

"Why don't you leave Wiri here?" Logan suggested, surprising his wife. "Just for tonight. Maybe Hana could take him home tomorrow and assess what's going on."

Nev's gratitude felt painful to the others as it oozed from him as relief and the sense of a burden shared. "Thanks!" he gushed, his eyes sparkling bright with unshed tears. "That'll really help."

The tall *Māori* kissed his small son tenderly on his scratched forehead and left, heading home with reluctance, to a situation way out of his control. Logan made dinner while Hana sat at the kitchen table and darned the many holes in Wiremu's clothing. "I think I'll patch the knees," Hana mused, fitting different sized squares of material over the tears. She held up two pieces of light denim from her work basket. "What do you think to these?" she asked Logan. "They're from that shirt of Tama's that he wanted the sleeves cut off."

Logan shrugged. "I guess so. They've only got to last until he gets home tomorrow. Why bother?"

"I don't want him to put the same clothes on in the morning and be reminded," Hana sighed and Logan smiled as he mashed the fluffy potatoes.

"You're gorgeous," he said.

Hana pressed the lighter material over the first rip and slipped the needle through the double helping of tough fabric. "I'll stitch it on the outside and then let the edges fray a little. It'll look trendy then."

"It took balls to stand up to my brother like that," Logan said, his voice low and expressionless. Hana felt the veiled warning cross the room in a black wave.

"I don't think so," she replied.

Logan turned sharply. "Kane would have given you a slap for that."

"Nev's not Kane," Hana replied with confidence. "And anyway, you were standing right there. I felt perfectly safe. You exuded enough threat and menace for the both of us."

Logan turned back to the potatoes with a shake of his head, knowing he would never understand his wife as long as he lived.

Wiremu ate well, coached by Phoenix, who mothered him without shame. He slept in one of Tama's tee shirts, the hem reaching almost to his ankles. The child rejected the spare bed, opting instead to sleep with his hero and he lay passively in the double bed while Hana spread the *panipani* onto his feet with care.

Tama crawled into bed later and tried not to disturb the child. Hana popped her head around the door and asked him if he was ok. Tama nodded. "Yeah, I'm just thinking about how different my life has become in the last two years." His mind strayed to memories of huddling in a bed with pilled and ripped elderly sheets, a tiny Wiremu clinging to his teenage frame while Nev tried to protect the rest of the family from a drunken, brawling Kane. "I forget how hard it was being brought up on the other side of the family. Nev and Anahera had it real hard. Having Wiri here reminded me."

Hana made her way over to the bed in the darkness and pressed her lips to Tama's forehead. "Love you, babe," she whispered.

"That was my eye!" he complained, but Hana heard the smile in his voice.

"Liar! Oh my goodness! Who's this?"

Tama snorted as Hana's groping fingers touched another hot little body, contacting a fluffy head resting against Tama's shoulder. "That's why I had to get in the middle," he hissed. A grunt from the Wiri and the rustle of a nappy, identified his other bed partner. Tama stifled a squeal as a pair of cold bare feet with twinkling toes, pushed their way underneath his thighs.

"Gosh I'm sorry. Do you want me to take her out?" Hana asked and heard Tama shake his head, his hair swishing against the pillow. He smiled with contentment and sleep claimed him, as the children cuddled deeper against their favourite adopted brother.

Chapter 34

"What's *she* doing here? Oh yeah, that's right, she owns everything now, doesn't she? Happy *Mrs Du Rose?* ould you like to look around, maybe move your stuff in?"

"Asher, stop!" his mother pleaded. She sat on the sofa with her head in her hands. "You have to stop this. I can't take any more. *Please?*" Anahera looked frighteningly fragile and tears welled up in her beautiful brown eyes. Her eyes seemed massive in her face, the weight dropping off her even as she sat there.

Hana felt a stab of fear in her heart, acknowledging the very real possibility that the woman might be desperately ill. She fought the urge to make a biting remark at the arrogant Du Rose male in front of her but only for Anahera's sake. Wiri looked anxious and gripped Phoenix's hand as she stood next to him. She sucked her thumb and stared watchfully in that intense way she had, missing absolutely nothing but not understanding either. Hana felt sure the child possessed an incredible filing system in her brain which stored data for future reference. It was exactly what Logan did. He was a mine of information.

Hana took a deep breath and stepped into the role of peacemaker. "I'm sorry you don't like me, Asher. But your mother's obviously not well. Can't we just agree to disagree for her sake?"

"For *her* sake!" he exclaimed and Hana realised with dismay she had only inflamed the situation. "When have you and that jerk husband ever done anything for our sake?" He said Logan's name and swore viciously and Hana's redheaded temper flared. She struggled visibly, her green eyes flashing. Asher put the boot in, turning his spite on the innocent. "What are you lookin' at?"

Undaunted, Phoenix stared the young man down, only her lips moving gently against her thumb. Sensing danger to his friend, Wiri gripped her hand tighter and turned his beautiful face towards Hana's daughter, whispering confidentially. "Phoe, d'ya wanna see my cars?"

The little girl turned to him wide-eyed and nodded. Then she glanced at her mother and Hana managed to nod once.

"No way!" Asher hadn't finished. "We don't need you snooping around our place."

"Snooping?" Hana couldn't keep the sarcasm out of her voice.

"Yeah, snooping!" Asher's grey eyes flashed with a latent danger that was instantly more threatening. Something behind his eyes appeared unhinged and reminded Hana of Kane Du Rose. Hana looked across at Anahera, who watched her with an undisguised sense of fear. Hana didn't know what to say. She fixed her eyes on her daughter's dress as she swished down a long hallway to Wiri's bedroom. The little boy hadn't once let go of Phoenix's hand.

Anahera got unstably to her feet. "Asher, you're being ridiculous. Don't you understand that Reuben lost *everything?* We had nothing left. Logan bought your dad out and gave him a job and us a home. Why can't you accept that?"

Asher shook his handsome dark head violently. "Lies. All lies. The developers offered Dad millions for the land. Logan didn't pay half that. They offered us a fortune and Dad turned it down. He wanted to keep it in the family. He sold out and we got nothing."

"How do you know what the developers offered Dad?" Anahera fired the question at her son and a red rash began on her neck, spreading outwards until it blemished her jaw and chin as well. "Who told you, Asher? Is it whoever's making you do this to us?"

Asher blanched, his olive skin paling on his lovely features. Hana struggled to catch up, knowing she had just missed something fairly major. "Sod off, Mum!" Asher shouted at the woman who had birthed and raised him in a warzone, without thought for herself. "Just shut up. You're useless!"

His mother's face crumpled in grief and Hana was instantly appalled. She had worked in an all-boys school for sixteen years and the angry young man reduced himself to the level of a mardy fourteen year old in her eyes. Hana's face burned with righteous indignation. "Don't you dare speak to her like that! Who do you think you are?" She faced him down, a furious banshee with flame red hair and eyes the colour of emerald gems. Asher was tall like all the Du Rose men. He turned his spite and sense of injustice fully on her instead.

"Who do I *think* I am? Oh, I know who I am, lady. I'm the rightful heir and you're a bastard's wife."

Before even considering her actions, Hana slapped him straight across the face. He recoiled with a sneer on his lips and worked hard not to touch his bristled skin to check for damage. Hana's palm stung from the action and the scratchy sensation from Asher's beard.

Idiot! Her inner voice reprimanded her. Hana's pounding heart ached in her chest and she touched the pacemaker under her left collarbone with the tips of her fingers. Her right hand shook as she rested it on her blouse, feeling the comforting bulge under her skin. Asher's jaw worked furiously in his face, the bone appearing and disappearing through his stubble. "You're a bitch!" he said but his tone was less frightening and his eyes held a flicker of respect for Hana. Something inside her head snapped with the increased blood pressure and she sought an end to the awful situation.

"You know what?" she bit at him. "If my husband's so distasteful to you, why don't you just leave like Kane did? Why are you sticking around? Go and make your own life, do your own thing. You're big enough and ugly enough to make your own legacy and do a better job of it than us."

"What?" Asher's jaw dropped and his mouth hung slackly open. Anahera's eyes bugged as though they were going to pop out of her head and Hana gulped. She had just done exactly what they expected. Inwardly she kicked herself for her own poor judgement. She had forced herself into a corner and didn't know how to extricate herself from the situation without doing more damage. She was like a serrated knife, plunging herself into a crisis and turning it into a tragedy on her way out.

Without losing any of her credibility, Hana shook her head and smiled sadly at the conflicted young man, softening her tone. "What do you want from me, Asher?" She opened her arms, palm up in a gesture of exasperation. "Do you want me to tell you to leave? I can do that if you want and my husband will back me up, whether he agrees with me or not. What do you want?"

The young man's jaw worked some more, grinding his nice teeth without mercy. Hana waited and then shook her head at his lack of reply. "Whatever," she said dismissively. "You think what you like. My husband paid a fair price for this land and cleared other debts you probably weren't even aware of. He gave your father the opportunity to stay on *whānau* land and work the *whenua* as he always wanted." Hana turned to leave, the destruction already complete. "I'll give you two choices, Asher. Change your attitude around my family and stop bad mouthing my husband, or you can go. Personally, I don't care which you choose. It's entirely up to you, but if I ever hear you use that word for my husband's heritage again, I'll throw you off this property myself. Do we understand each other?"

The young man ground his teeth some more and Hana waited, determined to see this out even if she had to wait all day. She raised her eyebrows expectantly at him, her heart beating a tattoo in her chest and sending the blood way to fast to her brain. When he still didn't reply, she shrugged and turned. "Phoe!" she called pleasantly down the hallway and her voice echoed off the newly painted walls and ceiling of the homestead. Out of the corner of her eye, Hana saw Anahera slump back down on the sofa again and put her face in her hands.

"Mama!" Phoenix sounded excited and trotted into the hallway from a bedroom to the right. Her curls bounced with her ungainly run and she held a small object out in her hand. Wiri sauntered after her casually, his hands rammed into the front pockets of his jeans. He exuded pure 'Du Rose' with every fibre of his being. "Look what Wiri gived me!" Phoenix ran into Hana's legs and held the object aloft. A small blue toy car sat in her hand, teetering on the tiny palm as though parked there and left to its fate.

Hana squatted down to look, biting her bottom lip and wondering how to extract herself from a situation which seemed to get worse by the second. She felt Asher's eyes boring into her back and heard the victory trumpets in his heart. *Here they go again, taking what belongs to others*. Hana could imagine his thought pattern. "It's beautiful," she told her daughter.

"Like Tama's," Phoe cried, only really interested in the similarity.

"It is, clever girl," Hana praised her daughter. "So how about we borrow it for tonight to show Tama and then put it back in Wiri's room with its brothers and sisters? Then when Wiri comes to play with you, he can bring it again? Like a game. Yes?" Hana worked hard to sell the story and Phoenix knitted her brow in concentration. *Please don't kick off. Please don't kick off,* Hana pleaded inside her head, fully prepared to deal with it if she did, but really not wanting to with her current audience. Phoenix looked at Wiri for confirmation and he smiled generously at her.

"K," she said happily. "Showin' Tama. You come my house, Wiri," she said and pointed her finger into his chest.

"Ok." He smiled.

Hana closed her eyes and swallowed while her back was still turned. Stress waves rolled over her whole body. "Awesome! Maybe Wiri would like to do baking at our house one day this week?"

Both children's eyes lit up and Phoenix licked her lips exaggeratedly. "Makin' Tama cakes!" she cried and bounced on the spot. She wasn't yet competent at completely leaving earth and wobbled slightly on the downward. Wiri smiled and looked thrilled with the invite.

"Great then," Hana said with false bravado. "Wiri can come for his car and bake cakes." She looked across at Anahera but the woman kept her head down. Feeling awkwardly and with her heart still thudding in her chest, Hana left the house. She pushed her feet into her boots and did up the zips but Phoenix, frustrated with her tiny trainers, stripped off her tights on the doormat and carried it all in her arms. Wiri stepped out onto the gravel like all New Zealand children, without shoes. Phoenix was rapidly becoming one of them.

Hana strapped Phoenix into the car seat in the back of the truck while Wiri stood patiently next to her, one hand resting on the arm of the car seat. He looked wistful, as though he wished he could come with them and Hana felt torn. She bobbed down to his level. "Darling, please don't run away like that again, will you? It scares me that you walked so far on your own." The child nodded and looked sad. "Wiri, the house telephone can ring the hotel, did you know that?" He shook his head. "Do you know your numbers yet?" Hana asked him and he nodded. In the dust on the truck door, Hana wrote a zero with her finger. "That one. Press that one and you'll get through to someone on reception. Tell them it's Wiri and ask them to find Hana. Do you understand?" He nodded.

"Look for the circle and ask them to find Hana," he sighed. She nodded. He was a bright boy. So much of his situation reminded her of all she had heard about Logan's upbringing. He had been a small, dark haired boy trapped in a lonely, unhappy life, with no understanding of the wars which raged around over his head. Hana wanted to scoop Wiri up and take him home and fought the maternalism that screamed inside her head on his behalf. *No*, she defied it. *I need to stop collecting other people's children to love better.*

"Hana," Anahera's voice sounded strangled as her feet crunched across the gravel in her slippers. "Thanks for bringing Wiri home. He just gets really fed up of all the upset." Her eyes welled up with tears again. "I'm sorry about Asher. I never realised until now that it's all about the money with him. I thought it was about the land but it's not." A sob escaped her throat and Hana sighed and put her arms around the other woman. "He's not a horrid kid," Anahera cried. "Please don't think badly of him."

"I won't," Hana promised. "My son can be a total jerk sometimes. I've lost count of the number of fights we've had recently. It'll all be fine, I'm sure."

Anahera shook her head. "I don't think it will. Not unless he..." The woman stopped and pulled away from Hana's kind arms. "Thanks for bringing Wiri," she said again and dried her eyes on her sleeve. She reached for the little boy's hand and he gripped hers placidly, smiling up at Phoenix with a look of failed nonchalance that was far too old for his years.

Phoenix reached out with her arm and stretched towards her little friend. She pretended to be chatting like the women. She opened and closed her mouth and tossed her head as though having a silent conversation. Wiri laughed and she sniggered. "Luff you Wiri," she said softly and he crinkled up his eyes, the weight of the world for that single moment, no longer bearing down on his wise, four-year-old shoulders.

Chapter 35

"Aye? What? Can you say that again?" Logan's brow furrowed and he stuck his index finger in his other ear and listened intently to the voice coming out of his phone. "So you've stopped work why?"

Hana stopped plating up the sandwiches she had made for lunch and watched her husband, sensing trouble. He disconnected the call and turned to her with a strange look on his face. "What is it?" Hana asked, her voice laden with fear.

"Nothing. It's fine. I'll sort it out."

"Logan!" Hana slammed the plate on the table and the sandwiches jumped off and landed on the stripped wood. "You're doing it again!"

Her husband hovered in the doorway, evidently pursuing the latest crisis and skipping lunch. "I have to go, babe. I'll explain later."

Hana took a step towards him. "No! You tell me now and start treating me like an equal or there's really no point me being here. I'm not prepared to live like this anymore. I'm not a child and I've had enough."

"Please let me go?" Logan implored her but Hana stood her ground, fed up of the shroud of mystery she had existed in for the last two years. She put her hands on her hips in a show of defiance and faced her formidable husband, refusing to quail at the dark flash of anger that lit his grey eyes in warning. Her rounded belly made her feel ridiculous, poking out in front of her like a comic stomach. "Hana!" he snapped, his teeth gritted.

Hana sighed in defeat once again. She put her hands down by her sides and shook her head sadly. A wave of misery crossed her face and she turned away, giving up the idea of ever being an equal partner in her marriage. "Don't take the ute," she shot over her shoulder at Logan. "I'm going out."

"Hana, please?" Logan's tone had changed to one of irritation. "I need the car, I have to go *now*."

"Fine, I'll get a taxi and charge it to you," she called from the hallway. "Come on Phoe, let's get your coat on."

Hana heard Logan's footsteps padding down the hall after her and shook her head in frustration. She sensed him in the room and when she glanced up, his face was dark and unreadable. "Where are you going?" he asked, biting his lip and Hana's chest stabbed with guilt at what she'd caused. She was calling in at the museum but realised Logan imagined a more non-returnable journey. She cursed herself as the spiteful part of her sought to capitalise on his insecurities.

"Mind your own business and I'll mind mine!" she bit, regretting the look Phoenix gave her, a silent reprimand of solidarity with her father.

"Hana, I have to go but I promise I'll tell you later." Desperation littered her husband's words.

"Don't bother," she retorted. "I'm quickly losing interest in everything to do with you and your business dealings."

"Don't be like this. I'm just trying to protect you." An edge of begging had crept in too and Hana felt cruel but at the same time powerful.

She did up the buttons on her daughter's coat and waited while Phoenix bent down to collect her squashy pony. "Grab your shoes, sweetie," Hana told her with a reassuring smile and Phoenix toddled off to retrieve her boots. Hana rounded on

Logan. "I don't need your protection, I need your honesty. Your secrecy is what got us into this mess of mistrust in the first place! Can't you see that? Have you actually learned nothing?"

Logan pursed his lips and exhaled slowly. "You're really gonna wish you didn't know this."

"Whatever Logan!" Hana pushed at her husband's strong chest as he blocked the doorway into Phoenix's bedroom but her slight fingers contacted a rock hard surface that didn't move an inch. Placing one arm across to completely prevent her exit, Logan dug his other hand into his jeans pocket and retrieved his phone.

"What?" he said to the caller with a definite edge of antagonism. Hana used the opportunity to try and duck under his arm and with a smirk, he anticipated her move and lowered his arm to in front of her bowed head. "I'm coming now! Oh and Tama, keep everyone away from it until the cops get there. Look I won't be long, I promise. Just manage everything for me please mate?"

Hana stood up straight, her face awash with enough confusion and guilt to betray a woman who had badly misjudged a situation. "*What* is going on?" she asked.

Logan placed both hands on her shoulders. "Are you leaving me?" he asked, biting his full lower lip.

"No!" Hana almost shouted. "I didn't leave you! I went to a hospital appointment and we argued. *Because* of all the secrecy. If you don't start levelling with me then we really have no future. But right now, I'm going down to see Will."

"Oh." Logan's jaw worked and his face looked chastened. "Sorry." He took a deep breath and secured his hands on Hana's shoulders. "I have to go to Nev's new place. The construction company are there assembling the new barn in the paddock behind his house."

Hana nodded, remembering the discussion about a new barn for equipment needed to reclaim areas of Reuben's neglected old farm, which had been taken over by scrub. Logan took a deep breath and swallowed while Hana looked up at him impatiently. "They dug the footings out the other day and now they've come back and...there's a body in the hole."

Hana's face tilted as though she needed to let his words percolate into a different side of her brain. She narrowed her eyes against her husband's impatience. "A what?"

"A body, Hana. A dead person. I *need* to go now. The cops are on their way and I need to be there!"

"Ok." Shock wiped all expression from Hana's face but as Phoenix appeared waving her favourite pair of red wellies, her mother seized control. "You drive to Nev's place and then I'll take the ute to the hotel so that I can get home after I've seen Will."

Logan huffed in irritation but Hana's look stopped him in his tracks. "What's your problem? You have a ride to the site and you still have me. Is there something else I don't know about that's irritating you?" Her tone was strident and demonstrated a backbone that Logan hadn't credited her with. He shook his head and Hana gathered her handbag from next to the front door. She lifted Phoenix bodily and the child inserted her feet into her boots and waited for the door to open, chatting happily to Fluffy in her arms. Hana slipped her feet into her ankle boots and then turned back to her husband with a look of pure arrogance and raised her eyebrow. "So are you coming, or what?" she asked and stepped over the threshold.

"Bloody women!" Logan complained as he jogged into the garage to grab his cowboy boots. As he emerged from the house, hopping to fit his feet into his boots, Hana noticed a definite smirk on his face and turned to watch the tui going about his business from the passenger window. Logan's nature meant he had to be king but Hana felt she was finally learning to best him, slowly but surely. Her husband climbed into the driver's seat and slammed the door. But instead of inserting the key and starting the huge diesel engine, he leaned over the gearstick and pulled Hana into him. The seatbelt felt tight across her breast and belly but she didn't resist, allowing Logan's forehead to touch hers. His hair tickled her skin in a feather light touch and he sighed deeply. "I love you, Hana Du Rose," he whispered and kissed her with soft, enticing lips on hers.

Hana leaned back, confused as Logan started the car, not understanding the smirk of satisfaction on her husband's handsome face. As the ute roared out of the driveway and jerked to a halt so that Logan could close the wide metal gate, Hana spied the kauri tree nearby, its high branches stretching out like wide embracing arms. The history of names scored into its elderly bark called to her, issuing words of wisdom and comfort to the outsider she had always been. Realisation trickled over Hana like cold water down the back of her neck and she abruptly knew Logan's game. The strong Du Rose male loved a challenge and his wife had just become *it*. Hana sighed and shook her head as the tall man got back into the ute and released the handbrake. She observed him sideways through slitted eyes as he rode the breakneck track with confidence, his hat pushed back on his head and his dark wavy hair escaping from underneath. A day's beard growth graced his cheeks and his long black eyelashes flicked in concentration. Hana watched his capable hands control the steering wheel, pausing to bend the gearstick to his will and back again, cuts and scars littered over his fingers like a pattern. She reached out a tentative hand and placed it on his strong thigh, feeling the tension in the muscle under her palm. Without looking, Logan removed his left hand from the steering wheel and placed it over Hana's. He caressed her fingers at the same time as making horrendously tight turns and it was at the same time, sensuous and dangerous.

The vehicle flew behind the hotel, slamming onto the seal with a bump. Logan needed both hands at the top of the road to make the turn onto the highway. He gunned the five kilometres to Nev's new place at the front of the Du Rose property, near the main road at breakneck speed. He kept both hands on the wheel but Hana deliberately left hers on his thigh. She twitched her fingers over the hard material of his jeans, causing him to feel distracting sensations that made him almost miss the turn, jerking the vehicle round it too quickly to have been safe.

Chastened by the presence of her daughter already asleep in the seat behind Logan, Hana removed her hand but smirked with satisfaction at her vague reflection in the side window.

Chapter 36

"Just go back to the hotel, babe. I'll call you as soon as I can. I'll get a ride back with Tama or one of the others." Logan's kiss on Hana's lips was far too lingering for either of them. He spun out of the driver's door and slammed the heavy metal behind him, striding quickly over to a knot of gathered males.

The construction workers wore bright fluorescent orange vests and stood out like beacons amongst the farm staff. A teenager wearing the fluro uniform sat with his head between his knees, vomiting periodically onto the muddy ground. Logan squatted down next to him and said something, rubbing his back in a tender motion. He looked up, spoke to Toby and jerked his head and the stockman strode off towards Nev's house.

Hana shifted her rounded belly across the divide between the seats, narrowly avoiding the jutting gearstick in her back. She adjusted the seat from Logan's long-legged position and lowered the steering wheel. By the time she got the seatbelt around her and plugged in, she saw Toby appear from the house with a mug of liquid, which he bent down and gave to the boy on the ground. The teen passed a shaking hand across his eyes and took a sip. Logan recoiled as the liquid shot straight back out again, splashing the boy's clothing and spattering against the ground.

Hana checked behind her and began to reverse the huge vehicle along the track from the paddock gate. Eventually it would be fenced off from Nev's property but for the moment, it was a sea of heavy wheel ruts, many of which turned in a large arc onto what would be Nev's garden. Hana braked sharply as a police car with strobing lights pulled silently in behind her and jerked to a hasty stop. Irritated at her blocked exit, Hana followed the wheel ruts and did a U-turn, trespassing onto her brother-in-law's property.

As Hana came level with the police car it remained in place, blocking her exit and the driver wound the window down. "I'll have to ask you not to leave the property, Madam," he said politely, inclining his head towards the space behind the ute. "Please reverse over there and someone will be along shortly to speak to you."

"I just dropped my husband off," Hana said with a whine in her voice. She glanced around at the sleeping toddler behind her. "I need to get back next door. I have a meeting."

"Sorry Madam, nobody on and nobody off. Those are the orders. Are you the householder?"

"No!" Hana said, irritation creeping into her voice. "I just dropped my husband off here."

Her eyes widened as the policeman got out of the car and stepped towards her. He flipped open a pocket book. "What's your name?" he asked, still polite.

"Hana Du Rose," she sighed. "And my husband owns all of this and the site next door. I just dropped him off. He's over there." *And he's going to be absolutely loving this,* she thought crossly. This was her punishment for disobedience. The reason for Logan's haste to get there became apparent to Hana as the policeman eyeballed her with professional detachment.

"What's the problem?" Logan's voice out of Hana's view sounded authoritative and the cop turned smartly on his heel.

Hana's heart sank and she refused to look at her husband. She could hear the slight veins of, '*I told you so,*' in his tone.

"I'd like this lady to park over there on the grass. The detective will want to speak to her when he arrives," the cop replied, his voice still polite and business-like.

"My wife is co-owner of this property with me and gave me a lift here. I just arrived," Logan stated in challenge. "But I can provide her details and she'll be happy to be interviewed later. As you can see, she has my daughter in the back and is heavily pregnant. If you want to detain her, that's fine but please suggest somewhere more appropriate than here." Logan's arm moved to take in the mud, the wheel ruts and the impossibility of Hana exiting the vehicle without either slipping over or getting filthy.

The policeman hesitated. "I have my orders, Sir," he intoned, still polite but forceful. Another police car pulled up behind his, further blocking the gateway. The civilian vehicle which followed it, had its rear end half on the fast road behind it, looking dangerously vulnerable. A tall figure unwrapped himself from the passenger seat and eyed the filthy ground with distaste. Seeing the mud bath in front of him, he stayed where he was.

"What's going on Du Rose?" he shouted and Logan visibly stiffened.

"Oh, for f..." Logan eyed his wife's raised eyebrows and stopped the expletive's casual escape. "What?" he shouted back instead.

"Get these vehicles shifted!" the man demanded and Logan looked pointedly at the cop. Reluctantly the uniformed man seated himself back in the car and looped it round behind Hana, clearing the way for the following cop car and the civilian vehicle. The tall man folded himself back into the grey Mondeo and it drove through the ruts and stopped in front of Nev's front door.

Logan stepped up onto the ute runner board and leaned his elbow on the open window. He peered in at Hana with an amused look in his eyes. "Just say it!" she snapped crossly. "Say, *it's your own fault* and get it over with."

Logan tipped his hat back on his head and stretched his long arm behind Hana's head. His strong fingers massaged the tension out of the back of her neck with capable skill and she almost moaned. "Do you want me to say it?" he asked, his voice husky and Hana shook her head.

"Not really. I should have just stayed home."

Logan's other hand slipped a long red curl behind Hana's ear and he let his fingers trace the line of her cheek, running his thumb underneath her bottom lip on the soft skin there. "Oh, I don't know," he smiled. "I quite like having you around."

Hana tutted in exasperation and tried to bite his finger. Logan laughed but the mirth disappeared from his face at the sound of the familiar voice behind him. "How come all murder cases involving you, result in me being knee deep in mud?" Detective Inspector Odering appeared in Hana's peripheral vision and she smiled with insincere pleasure.

"Hi, Detective," she said. "Would you be able to interview me real quickly? I need to use the bathroom."

Logan stepped down and Odering pulled open Hana's car door, immediately spotting her rounded stomach through her tee shirt. "Ah, congratulations once again," he intoned pleasantly. "My young sergeant here will just do a cursory check of your vehicle and then I'll send someone to take all your details."

Hana's son's face appeared next to the inspector and he looked embarrassed as he gave a cursory wave. "Hi, Mum," he said lamely.

"How come you're both here?" Hana asked, shaking her head to clear her confusion. "Aren't you based in Hamilton?"

"Yeah," Bodie replied, examining his brown, caked work shoes with disdain. "We've just been seconded up here for a few weeks to..."

"When the family reunion is over, could I trouble you to check this vehicle?" Odering huffed and Bodie pulled a face at Hana and rolled his eyes.

"Hang on, why would you be checking my ute? I just got here and Hana turned around and was on her way out when your man stopped her. What's the point?"

"Just do it!" Odering growled at his subordinate and then eyeballed Logan. "Because I said so."

"Mum! What happened?" Bodie shrieked suddenly, drawing attention from the crowd by the gate. He pointed at Hana's rounded stomach in horror and she blanched under his critical stare. Logan laughed with an unhelpful snort.

"Well, it's like this. When a man and a lady have a loving hug..."

Hana shot her husband a chastening look and he shrugged and wandered back to the vomiting construction worker, who had moved onto heaving up his lunch.

"How could you?" Bodie hissed crossly. "This is embarrassing!"

Hana's face fell and she felt swiftly older than her years, the pleasure dying in her green eyes at their chance meeting. Detaching from her son, she sought the sympathy she saw in Odering's eyes and asked him politely, "Please can you get on with the search. I really need to go."

The detective nodded and reprimanded Bodie with a jerk of his head and a sharp instruction, "Send Hawera over here and you get on with cordoning off the area."

Bodie hesitated and shot his mother a look of disgust before leaving. Odering shifted awkwardly in the mud as it spread gleefully up his dark trouser legs. "He'll calm down," he said with uncharacteristic gentleness and Hana nodded, momentarily lost for words.

"Am I really such a disgrace?" she whispered, dangerously close to tears, aware that a few minutes ago she had been a sensuous temptress to her gorgeous husband, abruptly reduced to the status of *scrawny-old-woman-embarrassingly-pregnant-again.*

"No, Hana, you're not a disgrace." Odering stood in the gap close to her and lowered his voice. "You're the same age as my wife and our youngest is four. Her older children reacted exactly the same as your son, but they do come round, I promise."

"Thanks," she acknowledged his kindness, pressing her finger and thumb over the bridge of her nose to prevent the threatening tears of disappointment. Hana sniffed and inhaled deeply. "What are you searching for?" she asked the detective in a small voice.

"I don't know," he answered honestly. "But we got a call an hour ago to say a body was found on these premises and we drove in and caught you leaving..." Odering held up his hand in supplication. "I know, Hana, I know. But I'm doing this by the book, love. So my officer will check your car and then you're free to go. If you could just let us do our job and I'll look around with him. It's about continuity. What kind of detective would I be if I let a vehicle out of the crime scene with the murder weapon inside - whatever that might turn out to be?"

Odering opened the rear door and searched around inside, running his hand around all the nooks and crannies and peering into the pockets behind the seat. He was quiet and gentle around the sleeping child, not wanting to alarm her if she woke to an unfamiliar male face and Hana felt strangely grateful. The boot of the ute crashed closed with less care from the other officer.

"I don't even know what's in the boot," she grumbled as Odering returned to her side. "The pram I think, Logan's tack maybe." Her brow furrowed as she tried to think what the copious space might contain and Odering smiled genuinely.

"There's nothing there that I wouldn't expect, Hana. So go home and someone will be along in a while to ask a few questions of everyone there; if we need to. Your husband's boring holes in the back of my head, so just smile and nod nicely and be on your way."

Despite herself, Hana did smile and her pretty green eyes sparkled mischievously. She opened her mouth to speak and Odering laughed. "Don't even think about it Mrs Du Rose. Arresting Logan is on my bucket list. Making the charges stick is an item by itself and occupies a whole line."

"Fine," Hana snorted. "See you later then maybe." She put the ute into gear and drove slowly through the gate as another strobing police car tried to squeeze past her. Being the bigger vehicle, Hana held her nerve and forced it to back out onto the highway and drove off with a smirk, tempered by the sadness at her son's reaction to her pregnancy. *Again.*

Chapter 37

"Oh, let me take my little *moko*," Leslie cooed as Hana struggled through the front doors of the hotel carrying a sleeping Phoenix. She went easily to Alfred's wife and snuggled into the voluptuous neck with a sigh.

"I wanted to see Will," Hana said, not wanting to get caught upstairs in the apartment right then.

"Yes, yes, you go on. Come up when you're done and we'll have a snack."

"Nack," Phoenix said, popping her head up immediately interested. Her drooping eyes and tousled hair smacked of a child that should still be sleeping.

Hana thanked Leslie and burst through the museum doors, making far too much noise for the serenity of the place. An elderly couple, examining a glass case containing postcards and personal letters, jumped in fright and Will glared at her. Hana bit her lip and fidgeted.

"Henri Du Rose fought in the second world war with the *Māori* Battalion," Will continued. "The postcards are from his wife, Phoenix to him at the front. He returned injured in 1941 and they married. But he wasn't the same man who left this mountain, sadly. He had shrapnel in his head that moved continually and he suffered from depression. Nowadays we would say he had Post Traumatic Stress Disorder, but not then."

"That's so sad," the female guest commented in a drawling American accent. "Mind you, we don't treat them any better now, do we? The number of homeless veterans in our country is a disgrace. At least he had a family to come home to." She bounced her curly white hair in emphasis and Hana's impatience made itself known in the agony on her face and her pent up body language. Will nodded to her and jerked his head towards the work room at the back of the museum.

The whole area had once been an enormous guest sitting room with games facilities and the space towards the back had contained a toilet and washroom. Logan had ploughed money into the renovations to please his wife and the ensuite area had been converted into a workroom to Will's specifications. Hana walked briskly to the sliding door and entered, throwing herself roughly down into a swivel chair that objected to her upset with a groan. Will appeared shortly after, wheeling himself across the wooden floor noisily.

"What's got youse?" he asked, dropping the carefully crafted speech he used for the guests. "Yous in a hurry? We can do this another time." He stared at Hana's foot jiggling on the floor with curiosity.

"We've got a massive problem!" Hana exclaimed. "The cops are crawling all over Nev's place. They've found a body."

"That's bad," Will agreed. "But why's it our business?"

"Because it has to be the blond drover. *That's* where the Du Roses buried him after his affair with Antoinette. He went missing remember and his brothers came down from Auckland searching for him. For all we know they're in there too." Her voice rose with a squeak, "It could be a mass grave, right behind Nev's new house." Hana clapped her hand over her mouth and paled. "Ugh, Phoenix and Wiri played in the mud from the footings the other day, while the builders were stopped after the wet weather. What if the children had found the body? They would have been traumatised. *I* could have been traumatised!"

To Hana's horror, Will let out a hoot of laughter. She was infuriated. "What's to laugh about? This is serious. I thought you were my friend!" Her pretty eyes narrowed and her face crumpled unattractively. Will snickered.

"I am your friend, but youse also my entertainment."

"But don't you get it? Now they've found the body, there'll be a massive investigation and they'll want to take the diaries away..."

Will's eyes bugged horribly. "They's not takin' them diaries anywhere! They won't have climate control or wear gloves. Na. Not gonna happen."

"So what do we do?" Hana panicked. "We've got the evidence to show that one of the Du Roses killed Caroline's father. Phoenix *said* it wasn't Reuben, but she must have known the body would be found one day. She might have been lying to protect her son in case he was still alive when there was an investigation. She was very far sighted. I wouldn't put it past her." Hana tapped her fingernails nervously on the bench in front of her. "Are any of the diaries out on show?"

Will shook his head. "No, they're all in the safe for now until I get through the history of 'em. Then I'll decide. I'll keep 'em there."

"But what about the cops?" Hana dropped her voice to a whisper. "If they come looking, we'll be deliberately withholding evidence. Phoenix seemed to think the drover's disappearance was something to do with this mysterious JD and from something Logan said recently, I think that man's still alive. He owns that strip of land at the front of the property by the main road."

"That's ridiculous," Will scoffed. "He's long gone now. Tell you what I'll do. I'll call up my niece in Hamilton and see if she could digitally scan all the diaries we have in the cradle she's got. I'll get them down to her and at least then if the cops come wanting their evidence, I can give them a digital copy. They'll have to accept that 'cause they ain't gettin' the originals."

"But then everyone will know that Caroline's married her half-brother." Hana ran a hand over her eyes and noticed mascara on her fingers when she examined them. She tutted in irritation.

"Not our problem," Will reassured her and placed a gnarled hand over Hana's.

"Well, it will be when she turns up here strutting around and causing trouble!" Hana spat crossly.

"Youse have a habit of turnin' 'ifs' into 'whens' girlie," Will sighed. "There's no whens yet. We don't know enough. So let's not be worrying before we have to, hey?"

"Bloody diaries! Why did the *kaumatua* have to bring them back? Logan said they were a box full of trouble. Thank goodness he doesn't know how much yet! I don't want to be an accessory to murder and I don't want Caroline back here," said Hana, panic making her green eyes flash like precious emeralds.

Will patted her hand. "I know, *kōtiro*. But right now, the way youse behavin', them cops gonna be arrestin' you as look at ya. Youse look guilty as hell. Just say nothin' and it'll be fine. Them's all in the safe and tomorrow they'll be sorted out."

Hana looked up startled as the sound of soft footsteps came to her through the partially open sliding door. She opened her mouth to speak and Will looked at her curiously. "That sounded real close," he said nervously in a low voice. "I think someone was listening." He swore and Hana jumped up quickly and ran to the door. She was just in time to see the heavy fire door to the museum closing slowly on its mechanism. Hana shook her head at Will.

"They're gone. Could it be the American couple?"

"Nope. They were done when I came in here."

"Do you think they heard?"

"If they stood outside then definitely, yeah." Will ran his hand across his face. "Now you have to tell your husband."

"I can't, I can't!" Hana cried, reacting instantly to Will's admonishment to keep her voice down. "Because then I have to admit I know he's not a Du Rose. And he hated that I worked out Reuben was his father and didn't say anything. He won't forgive me a second time. How do I say something like that? This is bad, really bad. And if the cops get the diaries, then they'll know too. What am I going to do?" She burst into tears.

It took Will a full fifteen minutes to calm her down. "It's ok, they didn't hear none of that. Stop worrying, it's a fool's game is worrying. Say *nothin'* to anyone and we'll see how this all pans out."

"Unless the cops send my son to interview me," Hana sighed. "He'll see right through me. He already hates Logan and when he saw my baby bump earlier, he just freaked out in front of everyone." She ran a hand sadly over her son. "He said I was embarrassing."

Will tutted and pulled Hana's limp hand up to his mouth and kissed it, his wheelchair rendering him unable to get any closer to comfort her. "*Te mate o te tangata rā, he rūrūwai noa iho, he pōrangi,*" he hissed. Hana looked at him blankly and he translated, "The problem with that man is he's a fool."

Hana nodded miserably. "He was fine until I married Logan."

"No he wasn't!" Will scoffed. "He was fine while he could make youse dance to his tune. Now you've a *tāne* and it don't go down well. He's a brat."

"It's because he knew about my first husband's affair for ages before Vik died. He admitted it last year. He adored his father but then he saw his flaws and it affected him."

"A decade ago! He's had time to get over it, Hana. Stop makin' excuses for him! He's got two kids of his own and needs to grow up!"

"I guess so. Do you think the cops will accept digital copies?"

"They ain't getting no choice! Leave it with me and I'll sort it all out. I've got some time off coming, so me and the boy will have a ride down into the Tron for a day. I'll shut the museum and you stay away, don't cover for me. Right?"

"Thanks, Will." Hana kissed his wizened cheek fondly. "I don't know what I'd do without you to rant to."

"And plot with," he snorted. "Get on with ya! That old lady's been hanging around waiting for ya for hours now. Your youngun's the light of her life. Go drink some of that foul English tea youse like and act normal!"

Hana used the private spiral staircase up to the first floor and then the apartment stairs. In the kitchen area, Alfred and Phoenix sat at the round dining table and dipped spoons into bowls of steaming food while Leslie bustled around serving them. Her face lit up when she saw Hana. "Come, sit your *nono* down," she grinned. "Get some *kai*."

Hana plonked herself down onto a chair and smiled at her daughter, who waved her spoon happily. "Boy up," she said and smacked her lips happily. Hana looked momentarily confused and Leslie plonked a plate of mixed vegetables in front of her. Hana peered at it.

"Don't tell me youse never had a *Māori* Boil-up?" Leslie asked aghast and Hana shook her head.

"I've heard about them but not really. Is it casserole?"

"Kinda. Kumara, puha, spinach and other veggies and this one's got prime beef in it. Full of iron and vitamins. And my family recipe for butternut doughboys. Get tryin it." Leslie provided a spoon and fork and stood with her hands on her hips expectantly as Hana tasted a morsel of beef.

"It's really nice!" she said and dug her spoon in again. "It's got heaps of flavour."

Leslie humphed and dished herself a bowl "Youse can't be married to a *Māori* man and not give him boil ups!"

Hana felt in disgrace and ate the delicious meal quietly. Alfred winked at her when she looked up and pulled a funny face. She smiled wistfully at him like a naughty child, at the same moment as her phone chirped from her pocket. "Sorry, everyone, please excuse me. I have to take this." Hana rose and answered the call, moving away from the sound of scraping bowls and Phoenix asking for more.

"Hey babe," Logan's comforting voice spoke into her ear. "I promised I'd call. Is everything all right?"

"Yeah, me and Phoe are just having tea with Alfred and Leslie," Hana replied, struggling to keep the sullenness out of her tone.

"Have you said anything?" Logan asked.

"Does he want some boil-up saving?" Leslie called, guessing at who she was talking to and Hana repeated the question.

"Ooh yes please, definitely. I love her boil-ups." Logan's enthusiasm chastised Hana further by implication.

"How long will you be over there?"

"I'm coming back now with Toby. The cops have stopped the build - obviously and set up all their gear. The coroner just arrived so there's nothing more I can do."

"How's the family?" Hana asked, trying to enquire after Anahera without being obvious.

"Yeah, not good. Very shaken up, understandably. I've offered to let them move over here for a few days, but I'll sort that out with Helena and Carrie."

"Ok. See you soon," Hana replied, feeling shaky at the sense of relief that washed over her at the thought of her capable husband arriving soon. She fought the urge to publicly collapse into his safe arms the moment she saw him. Hana went back to her food and although she chose her words carefully, Leslie was as sharp as a knife.

"What's goin' on?"

"Nothing," Hana smiled and shook her head, but tiredness made her unconvincing.

"Don't youse lie to me!" Leslie started and fortunately, Alfred intervened.

"Leave the girl alone, woman. She looks knackered. The boy'll be back soon. Youse can interrogate him instead." He smiled at Hana from under his eyelashes, his grey eyes sly and full of meaning. *If you dare!*

Logan breached the stairs to the loft apartment half an hour later. He was in his socks and had rolled his muddy jeans up on his calves. Phoenix beamed from her plate of suet pudding and custard. "Funny, Daddy!" She waved her spoon towards his unusual turn-ups and a blob of custard hit her in the eye. While Alfred and Leslie dealt with the mishap, Hana managed to cling to her husband and infuse herself with his strength. He looked tired and fed up and fidgeted overly much to be of much comfort. Warning vibes radiated out of him like electrical pulses and Hana was instantly on red alert. She eyed him anxiously as he dug into his food, less enthusiastically than Leslie was prepared to accept.

"What's with you, boy? Youse love my cookin'!"

"Yeah," Logan wiped his mouth with the back of his hand and smiled at his daughter. "I've got a bit of a problem."

Alfred studied the man he had raised as his own and waited patiently, but poor Hana felt the butterflies begin in her stomach, knotting it up and threatening to reject the lovely stew. She fought to hold it together, not least because Leslie would never speak to her again if she chucked up her prized boil-up. Logan ate and talked. "The contractors found a body behind Nev's place. The cops are all over it like an infection. Nev's moving Anahera and Wiri into a room downstairs for a few days. She's gone to pieces totally. Nobody seems to know where the hell Asher is."

Leslie tutted and shook her head in wonder at the news, but Alfred's body was rigid with expectation. His grey eyes bore into Logan's face with concentration.

"Do they know who he was?" Hana asked in a whisper and Alfred's eyes widened to show the whites. Logan swallowed his latest mouthful and looked at Hana curiously.

"It's not a he, Hana. It's a woman. It's Sylvia. Someone's killed her."

Chapter 38

Hana gaped at her husband, but still noticed Alfred's sigh of relief as he sank back into his chair.

"Bloody hell!" Leslie exhaled and Phoenix went into a paroxysm of indignation.

"Om er! Om er, naughty Nonie. Not wearin', vewy bad!" The child's face reddened in horror and Hana beckoned to her.

"Come sit on Mama's knee, baby. Nonie didn't mean it. Come here."

The little girl slithered from her chair and padded across, holding out her arms to Hana. Once settled on her mother's knee, she humphed in satisfaction and pushed her spoon into Hana's food. With a sly look at the adults, she popped a piece of succulent beef into her mouth and chewed happily with her baby teeth, her eyes closed in appreciation. Leslie smiled fondly and shook her head at Hana, evidently thrilled that one of the females liked her food enough to go back for more. "You want another portion, girl?" she asked Hana hopefully but the other woman shook her head.

"No thanks, Leslie. It was delicious but I just lost my appetite." She sighed and ran a hand across her eyes, knowing she must look dreadful. A sickly greyness shrouded her inside and out. "Sylvia!" Hana sighed into the back of Phoenix's fluffy head, her face disbelieving. "I can't take it in. And I feel so mean because thinking she'd left for good was the best part of my week! What kind of person does that make me?"

"One that probably shouldn't repeat that to the cops," Alfred said wisely. He regained his composure immensely quickly for a man over seventy. Hana stared at her husband, tucking into another portion of dinner and narrowed her eyes.

"How can you just sit there calmly eating?" she asked.

Logan smacked his lips with contentment and his face gave nothing away. "Because I'm starving. And because the cops will be round in a bit to see me. Nothing half as nice as this in an Auckland jail."

Hana exhaled loudly and the room spun before her eyes. She concentrated on taking calm, shallow breaths and Leslie grew concerned. The old lady was at her side in seconds. "Stupid boy!" she chastised Logan roughly and he had the decency to look guilty.

"Not again, not again!" Hana fought the urge to cry and Leslie patted her back with force, as though the woman was choking and not just falling apart at the seams.

"Hey," Logan turned towards his wife and reached for her hand. "I didn't know about it, I haven't been across there for days and they honestly can't pin anything on me. Don't worry. It'll be fine."

"Poor Sylvia," Hana breathed. "Why didn't she just leave that night when she said she was going to? She'd be happily hunting down Michael for paternity and leaving us alone. At least she'd be alive."

"Michael?" Alfred was instantly alert. "What's Michael got to do with this?"

"It's complicated," Hana began. "But Michael is Ryan's father, not Logan. I broke the news to her the other night and she didn't take it awfully well."

"Maybe don't tell the cops that either," Alfred intoned, his voice laden with doom. Hana's breathing became even more frantic and Leslie grabbed Phoenix quickly off her knee. Another stolen chunk of beef hit the floor beneath the table and the child groaned.

"They'll think I did it," Hana hissed, her voice laden with misery. "She threatened everything I had. I'm going to end up having this baby in prison, I know I am. Innocent people get convicted all the time. What am I going to do?"

"Run!" Alfred stood up quickly. "You can go to my *whānau* in the north. They'll help you…"

"Dad!" Logan's voice cut through the panic like a shot of reason. "Quit it! Nobody's running! We didn't kill her so we're going nowhere. We just have to play the game and let them work it out."

"Er…hi. The receptionist said it was ok just to come up." Bodie's tone betrayed awkwardness and guilt at disturbing the family. "Oh, you're eating. Sorry." He stood at the top of the apartment steps having climbed them quietly and avoided detection until he chose to be seen. His dark hair was damp and he waited on the top step for a formal invitation to enter their space.

Hana glanced at Logan and found his expression unreadable. Her son was intruding and the mother in her ached at his evident awkwardness. She turned and smiled. "Come in, Bo. I'm sure there's plenty if you're hungry."

Relieved, Bodie pressed his feet out of his shoes without bending down to unlace them. He padded across the space between the landing and the kitchen, leaving damp footprints on the wooden floorboards. Leslie humphed and turned away still carrying the child, bustling over to the simmering pan and clattering with crockery one-handed. Alfred sat down.

"Sit," Hana indicated the empty chair next to her. Bodie lowered himself carefully into its wooden embrace.

"Should you be here?" Logan asked, with a directness that bordered on rude.

"It's fine," Bodie countered. "Odering knows I'm here. But you hardly helped yourselves did you? I don't know how you always seem to get mixed up in this kind of crap."

"Does Odering think we did it?" Hana's green eyes were wide and fearful. Leslie plonked a laden bowl of stew in front of the unwanted guest and slapped a soup spoon next to it.

"I'm gonna take my *moko* for a warm bath," Leslie snapped, challenging Hana to disagree.

"Thanks, that's a great idea," Hana replied with a small smile. "It's probably best she doesn't hear too much."

Leslie humphed again and left the room. Hana heard the child getting excited over the bath and the option of bubbles. Bodie tucked into his dinner and the gathered company waited in silence.

"How'd she die, boy?" Alfred asked eventually and Bodie looked up with a small smirk. Logan rolled his eyes at the young man's minor victory.

"Shot at close range in the face." The answer was given without emotion but Hana recoiled and clapped her hand over her mouth.

"I think I'm gonna be sick," she whispered.

"Yeah, not real nice," Bodie replied. His mouth was full and Hana saw the food swirling like a washing machine and fought sickness valiantly. "The contractor who found her is still ill. He's ended up in the hospital on a drip, heavily medicated. Only a young lad. It's his first week with that company. He left school last Friday. Ironic hey?" Bodie glanced round at his audience as though he related nothing more than the state of the weather. "He shot puke right over the crime scene so DNA will be fun. Not that there was a clean site to get any, to be honest. She's been there a couple of days. It was a mud bath, it's been raining and every man and his dog traipsed all over it before we turned up."

Logan shook his head slowly and glanced at Hana. She detected a flicker of a smirk in his eyes and wondered what was wrong with her men. They cared so little about serious things in their ego-laden relationships.

"We thought she'd left," Hana said quietly. "As far as we were concerned, she'd gone."

"Well, she had," Bodie said callously and Hana shuddered. "In spirit, just not in body."

"That's enough!" Logan's reprimand was loud and pointed. Hana sighed. *Here we go.*

"There's a sixteen year old boy downstairs who just lost his mother. Are you gonna tell him? You're gonna wander down all casual and let him know that she's laying in a muddy trench with her face blown off are ya?" Logan stood up and Bodie tensed. "Ah man, you're about as unprofessional as your other buddies. Finish your food and sod off!" Logan scraped his chair back under the table and strode down the apartment with long-legged steps, the muscles in his back tensing under his shirt.

"Daddy! Bubbles!" Phoenix's excited voice travelled back to the group around the table, innocent and unburdened.

"He's right. You should go." Alfred stood up and left, hauling his stooped body after Logan. He passed the bathroom and headed to his bedroom at the end of the apartment. The sound of game show laughter permeated the gloom.

Hana slumped in her seat and sighed heavily, resting her elbows on the table and cupping her eyes. "Why do you feel this need to wind him up?" Her voice carried a perceptible whinge.

"Odering told me to." Bodie lowered his voice. "I think he gets some perverse thrill out of it."

"And you always do as Odering tells you, don't you?" Hana observed her son with sadness. "Whatever the personal cost."

Bodie looked ashamed, the first glimpse of honesty since he'd entered the apartment. "He's my boss. He's going places and hopefully taking me with him."

"He sure is," Hana mused. "I just worry about where that might be."

"Look," Bodie's tone became urgent and he laid his spoon down in the empty bowl. He turned his body fully towards his mother. "I'm glad they've all gone. I need to talk to you. The local doctor came to certify the body as dead. The coroner was too far away. He said some odd stuff as soon as he saw the body. He made a statement about coming up here about ten days ago to see you after you had some kind of fainting spell. He said you asked him for help. You stated..." Bodie reached into his pocket and removed the ever present notebook. "*My husband's having an affair with an old girlfriend who turned up yesterday. If I should die unexpectedly, please could you make sure that everyone knows I was disposed of? The Du Roses do that, you know. They dispose of their problems.*"

"Oh no!" Hana's eyes filled with tears. "Oh my goodness. I was angry with Logan. I didn't mean it!" She ran a shaking hand across her face. "What have I done? You all think Logan did it, don't you?" Her voice rose with anxiety and Bodie leaned in to his mother, putting a hand quickly over her mouth.

"Mum!" he hissed. "Shut up! I'm not meant to be telling you any of this. It'll cost me my job if someone finds out! But yes. On the basis of that, it certainly looks like it."

"You don't understand...I..."

"Mum, I'm only telling you what a well-respected local medic said. He actually stepped into the hole and said, '*Oh thank God! I thought it was going to be Hana Du Rose!*' It's too late now. The investigation's heading this way. I think Odering wanted me to wind Logan up so he made a mistake. They have a long history, Mum. They can't stand each other and this isn't gonna end well. You need to explain some stuff and quickly!"

Hana took a long breath in and told her judgemental son the whole sorry story. Bodie was appalled. "Geez! So he was knocking off this woman?"

"No! I told you he wasn't. I just *thought* he was. He can't have killed her, Bo. He's been with me for days now. He's stuck to me like glue. I've really needed him and he's been there. There's been a handful of times when we've been separated but he hasn't been by himself. He'll have been with the other guys on the farm. I'm sure he can get an alibi for all his time over the last week or so."

"Well, you'd better hope so." Bodie's face was serious. "Mum, why don't you come back to Hamilton? You can live with me and Amy as long as you want to. You don't have to stay here."

"I'm fine!" Resignation dawned in Hana's eyes. "You're never going to believe me, are you?"

Bodie shook his head. "No, sorry. And nor is anyone else."

"How come Odering doesn't think I did it?" Hana asked. "I had more to lose than anyone. I'm sure one of the waitresses from the dining room could verify I sat with her a few nights ago and Sylvia seemed upset towards the end of the conversation."

Bodie leaned back in his seat. "See, you're the only person who's mentioned that. We've had cops downstairs for the last hour taking statements and not one of them heard anything about you meeting with the deceased. Your husband runs a very tight ship, Mum. Nobody will dare say anything against you or him. Which is why any alibi he gets here is worthless. Not one of the staff will speak out against him. Can't you see that?"

"But Logan didn't kill her!" Hana maintained and Bodie shook his head.

"I'm sorry, Mum. But I think you're deluded. And you've got one hell of a nasty wakeup call coming your way!" The young police officer stood up and scraped his chair back under the table. He kissed Hana lightly on the forehead and dumped his bowl and spoon in the sink. With a wistful smile he walked away, turning as he fitted his feet back into his shoes and bent to tie the laces. They were streaked with loamy mud, despite Bodie's efforts to clean them. A flake of stained tissue stuck to the heel. "You know what, Mum? I was so jealous of anyone ever replacing Dad that I saw off every guy who showed an interest in you. I made a mistake. Any of those jerks would have been better for you, than this." He waved a uniformed arm expansively to take in Alfred's apartment and the life that Hana had chosen for herself and he was gone, clattering down the stairs to the floor below. Hana heard the fire door at the bottom hiss closed behind him, leaving her with a heaviness nothing would dispel.

<h1 style="text-align:center">Chapter 39</h1>

"Hey, babe. Don't cry," Logan crooned, pulling Hana's tearstained face into his chest. "It'll be ok. I didn't do it and nor did you. These things always work out. It's just gonna take time for the cops to work through everything. We have to wait."

Hana sniffed harder and a sob struggled free from her throat. Logan's body tensed. "What did Supercop say? Did he upset you?" His voice hardened and Hana gulped.

"No. He just spelled out the facts and it made difficult hearing."

"Yeah. It's pretty rats. I mean, the woman was a pain in the ass but it's a horrid way to go. And then there's Ryan. What happens to him now?"

A clatter in the stairwell made the couple jump apart hurriedly, greeted by the sight of Ryan running full pelt up the steps. He tripped at the top and Logan jumped up in a defensive stance. "My mum's dead!" the boy screeched. "She's dead!" Tears streamed down his face, spattering on his white chef uniform.

"Oh, I know darling. I'm so sorry." Hana stood and held her arms out to the boy and he rushed forward, almost overbalancing her. She stroked his hair as he sobbed over her shoulder and down her neck, unashamed grief pouring out of him in loud, guttering heaves. Logan retreated to the bathroom and relieved Leslie, who surged into the kitchen oozing capability and comfort.

"Poor baby," the old woman cooed to the boy, including Hana's tears in the wide sweep of her affection. "Youse both been having a terrible year." She rubbed hard on Hana's back and then bustled off to make the ever present pot of tea. Ryan's grip on Hana's upper body lessened and after a few sniffs he reluctantly released her.

"Sorry," he whispered and swiped a hand across his eyes. "You're the last person I should expect sympathy from. She made your life a misery. How can you be so nice to me when she was such a bitch to you?"

"Because I know what it's like to lose a parent, Ryan. And so does Logan. Even if you didn't particularly like them much in life, it doesn't stop it hurting once they're gone. She was still your mum."

"I've got nobody now." The boy's eyes brimmed with tears and several of them plummeted downhill and splashed off his shirt.

"Don't be daft," Hana said softly. "You'll always have us. Family is family."

"Yeah, but I'm not family am I?" Ryan said with resentment and Leslie half turned from the sink. "Mum came to see me, Hana. She told me. Logan's not my dad."

Hana saw Leslie's body tense, her back growing rigid and stiff. "I know, sweetheart," Hana soothed, "but if it helps, I know who is."

Ryan shrugged. "No matter. Now I know it's not Logan, I don't really care anymore. I wanted it to be him so bad." The boy plunged into sobs again and Hana embraced him, letting him bury his sodden face in her hair. Leslie plonked the teapot down on the table and raised an eyebrow at Hana, who shrugged. Leslie had already guessed. Hana wondered how, but both women knew Michael wouldn't be interested in the boy.

"It might not be as bad as you think, honey," Leslie said in a gentle voice. "We think Logan's half-brother, Michael is your daddy. So that means Alfred is your poppa and Tama's your half-brother."

Ryan's head shot up, abruptly interested. "What, that big guy who was here before? The fireman?"

Hana nodded. "Yeah, Tama. He's Michael's son too. So you're still family."

Ryan sniffed hard, a snot-gobbling snort that sounded vile. "Do I have to leave here and go back to England?" he asked, fear and confusion in his face.

"I'm not sure," Hana replied. "Honestly, I'll look into it for you but surely if we can prove that Michael's your father, you should be entitled to citizenship. Either way, Logan will know how to sort you out a visa to work here even before that."

"Already underway." Logan's voice was clear and gruff as he ruffled Ryan's hair on the way past. He grabbed himself a glass and filled it from the cold tap. "Liza's sorting it out for me."

Leslie rolled her eyes and Hana bit down on her smirk at the older woman's distaste for Logan's sister. "Would you guys be ok if I nipped downstairs? I need to see Will about something."

"We'll be fine. Alfie's just gettin' Phoe out of the bath," Leslie smiled. Logan looked at his wife curiously.

"Will's gone back to his unit. I saw him wheeling himself over there as I got home."

"Oh, that's ok. I'll call by his place. I won't be long." Hana left quickly before Logan could voice an objection. She gathered her boots into her arms at the top of the stairs and skipped heavily down them.

At Will's ranch slider, Hana rapped hard. "Will, it's me, Hana. Please come to the door. I need your help!"

"Wait up!" the old man's shape wheeled towards the door, dodging the furniture in his way. "Where's the fire?" he intoned crossly. "It's bloody open, get yerself in here now you've made all this fuss."

"I'm sorry, I'm sorry." Hana tripped over the lintel and almost pitched herself into the old man's chair with him.

"What's with you, woman?" he bellowed and Hana jumped and added sadness to her agitation. "Na, sorry love. Ignore this old man. I just need to take a pain killer and I'll be right."

Hana followed Will to the kitchen, suppressing the urge to push his chair faster in desperation. She watched him pop a tablet out of a blister pack and slip it between his lips with shaking fingers. Hana grabbed a glass out of an eye level cabinet and filled it with water, handing it to the old man. She shifted her weight from foot to foot with great impatience. "Will, I have to give the cops the diary about Caroline's father really quickly," Hana said, trying to keep the tremor out of her voice. "It's all gone wrong. The body they found isn't the blond drover. It's *Sylvia!* And now, because of what I said to the doctor about the Du Roses burying their problems, they think Logan got rid of her. I'm such an idiot!"

The child kicked out and Hana gasped as her bladder took the force. She ran a hand over her rounded stomach and groaned. Will's expression shifted from obstinate to concerned. "Hey, let's go sit in there. Take the weight off your feet, love. Tell me what's goin' on. And slow, mind!"

Hana ran through her tale and Will listened with avid concentration. "Youse certainly know how to complicate your life, child," he chastised her when she'd finished. "But I agree. Youse need to go and speak to this policeman and tell him everything. They's bound to want to dig up that whole area lookin' for another body but at least they'll know why you said what you did. Otherwise they's gonna think the worst of your *tāne.* He don't deserve that."

"Thank you," Hana breathed with relief. "I know we didn't want this, but that was before Logan got put in the frame for murder. I don't see what else we can do but let them have the artifact."

Will nodded and patted Hana's writhing fingers. "Right, you go and find this detective inspector and I'll fetch the diary from the safe and find you. Truly, it'll all be fine."

Hana nodded and stood up. The old man waved off her offer of help to exit the building and sent her on her way, shaking his elderly head after her. "Geez woman! Thank the good Lord I haven't known too many like you," he commented gruffly as he struggled with the door key and then the ramp. "For sure I'd be dead already!" He waved a gnarled hand at Hana as she looked back at him, her cardigan flapping around her legs in the wind. His gesture of reassurance soothed her and she headed back to the house with determination in her step.

Chapter 40

"So that's why I said what I did about the Du Roses," Hana concluded. "I feel really guilty about it now. I was under an incredible amount of pressure and I'd just read in the diary that the blond drover disappeared and nobody seemed to know where he'd gone. If you go back through the police records for then, there might be a missing persons' report."

Detective Inspector Odering eyed Hana with a look of utter bemusement and faint annoyance. "So you knew there'd been a murder on this property and actively concealed it?"

"No! Not at all!" Hana cried. "For all we knew, he took himself off somewhere and had a perfectly nice life. Phoenix Du Rose wrote that he disappeared and she didn't know where he'd gone. But there's a problem with handing the diary over." Hana's green eyes flashed with concern and she held Odering's suspicious gaze so hard, he couldn't look away. "There are things in the diary which would be very damaging to the family. Only Will and I have read it. As curators of the Du Rose Museum, we'll permit you to take it away for a limited time and copy those parts of it that are relevant to your investigation, but if you ever make any of it public and damage my family, I'll go as high as I need to make you pay. Do we understand each other?"

Odering's gaze faltered and then renewed its determined, piercing effect. "You have no control over what I choose to do, Mrs Du Rose. I'll issue you with a receipt and reserve the right to conduct my investigation however I see fit. This is a murder inquiry." He smiled woodenly to accentuate his point. Hana gritted her teeth and took a step towards him.

"I repeat, Detective. If you do anything to hurt my family, I'll make sure you suffer too."

"Are you threatening me, Hana? For goodness sake, woman. This is almost comical!" Odering laughed and Hana fought a wave of humiliation.

"Laugh if you will," she said, a hardness taking over her pretty face, adding angular lines and contours. "But making an enemy of Judge Du Rose would be a stupid thing to do, even for you. I could imagine the fun she'd have, legitimately turning over your shoddily presented cases in her court and making you look an absolute fool every opportunity she got. And there're other family members who I'm sure would wade in quite happily. So laugh at *me* all you want, Detective. But don't make the mistake of underestimating *us*."

Odering gulped visibly and Hana struggled to hide the violent tremors shaking her body. They started inside her core, condemning her mafia threats and her offence against everything she believed in. The voice in her head cried, *who are you?* Hana ignored it and maintained her attacking stance, keeping her pregnant body still and from the outside at least, composed.

Clattering sounds against the heavy dining room door made her turn and she wrenched the handle with relief. Will stared up at her from his wheelchair and Hana stood back wordlessly to admit the old man. He settled himself in the room and put the brake on his wheels and then Hana's friend eyeballed the tall detective. "We got problems," he announced and Hana's eyes widened.

Odering rolled his eyes and dragged a dining chair from behind him, slumping down into it with apparent frustration. "Do we really? Why am I not surprised?"

Will bristled. "Don't be so damn disrespectful you young buck. I might be a cripple but I outrank you in age and genealogy and don't you forget it! Be careful how you speak to the *whānau* of the *Kīngi*." Will's voice held an edge of steel that Hana always understood existed, but the force of it petrified the occupants of the room into stillness and Odering into shame.

"I'm sorry, sir." He rose to his feet again. "It's been a long day. I'd like to see the diary Han...Mrs Du Rose told me about and then I'll be on my way. I can assure you both I'm only interested in the parts relating to this investigation and any others that might come about *because* of the contents of the diary. Nothing else."

"See, that's the problem," Will stated huffily. "Someone's robbed the safe. The whole damn lot's gone. All eight of 'em!"

"What?" Hana whirled on the spot. "How?"

Will shrugged. "Someone opened the safe. I unlocked the museum door and wheeled in like always and the thing stood wide open. All gone!"

Hana gaped like a fish, her bottom jaw hanging loose. Odering sighed audibly and she faced the policeman down in fury. "Oh, right, I get it. You think we've done this on purpose do you?"

"Well, it is a little convenient," he sniffed.

"How?" Hana shouted, no longer caring that her voice carried a hint of hysteria. "How can it be *convenient*, you silly man? You would have been able to read about the blond drover and understand why I said what I did to the doctor. Now there's nothing and you'll carry on thinking my husband killed Sylvia. How convenient is that? It's all I had to give you. And now it's gone!"

"Hey, hey honey," Will reached out a wrinkled hand to the distraught woman. "Calm yourself, *kōtiro*. This is no good for your *pēpe*. Sit, sit!" He indicated the seat next to Odering. Hana shook her head.

"I can't sit down. This is terrible!" She ran a shaking hand over her eyes, failing to hide her distress from the two men. "I don't understand! *You* set the combination and were the only person who knew it, apart from Logan."

"Er, about that. Mr Du Rose din't know either. It was only me. I asked him if he wanted it and he said no, he wasn't bothered." Will snuffed with a small laugh. "I asked what he'd do if I died in the night and he said, he'd tie the safe to the back of his mare, tow it up the mountain and drop the whole damn thing off the top where it belongs. Said he din't care for his *tipuna wahine's* troublesome ramblings."

"Oh. Great." Hana looked crushed. "So why are we even bothering?" She shook her head slowly from side to side, doubting Logan's enthusiasm for her latest project and wondering if it was simply his way of keeping her occupied. "Fantastic." Hana sensed the fight leave her and she wobbled on her feet. Will reached out a hand and placed it in the small of her back.

"Sit down, woman! Youse makin' me *anipā*."

"You're not doing much for me either," Odering relented. "You look sick." He took Hana by the forearm with a firm grip and led her to the chair, not letting go until she was safely seated. He turned to Will. "So the safe was open and only you have the combination? So it's been burgled?"

"Yep," Will's sigh was heavy and defeatist. "I had some coins and a money pouch in there and some other bits that were quite valuable. They's all still there. Just the diaries, every last damn one." He perked up and looked at Odering with a hopefulness in his eyes. "Could your guys do fingerprinting and DNA or something? We really need them diaries. I hadn't finished cataloguing them. I was meant to take them into Hamilton tomorrow and get them digitised. Damn, I'll have to contact my niece and tell her I won't be there now." He tutted, a promised treat denied him.

Hana tried to put her head between her knees and groaned as her protruding stomach prevented the action. "I feel sick!" she stated, the force of her misery communicated through her tone. Odering appeared with a glass of cold water, his shiny shoes resting next to Hana's socks on the quarry tiled floor. Hana sat up and took the glass, thanking him with her eyes. "Why does this stuff always happen to me?" she complained and Odering screwed up his face in sympathy. "As if my life isn't complicated enough!" Hana slurped the water unattractively, rivulets running down her chin and splashing onto her cardigan.

Hana heard the door open and peeked up, seeing Odering's heels disappearing through the gap. She turned to Will with her eyes wide. "You have to let him have the books!" she said to him. "This isn't funny. Logan could go to jail for killing Sylvia because of what I've said."

Will's jaw dangled slack and ugly, displaying the gaps in his gums where teeth used to be. He shut his mouth and a grin spread across his face. "You think I made that up? Geez woman. You are one hell of an actress!"

A horrid foreboding snaked across Hana's chest and the colour drained from her face. "The diaries are really gone?"

"Yes!" Will looked appalled. "I don't tell lies, woman! Course they's gone!"

"Oh that's terrible." Hana looked genuinely sick and then a flush of hope lit her cheeks. "Or maybe it isn't. If they've been destroyed, then that's awesome. No more of Phoenix's tales to hurt everyone. Oh, but what about Logan." Her expression became sour again. "The one about the blond drover could have helped him. Damn."

"Youse missin' one very important point," Will said softly, his eyes studying Hana with fierce intensity. "Whoever has them diaries...well, they've got power over this family. *Lots of it.*"

Chapter 41

"Fingerprint guys say the safe's been wiped. No new prints. There's a few of Will's on there but nobody else's."

"Figures," Hana said, keeping her tone level. "I've never touched it. No point. Will wouldn't give me the code. Logan doesn't really go in there. So whoever took the diaries covered their tracks."

"How come?" Odering sipped his hot tea with care, observing Hana over the rim of his mug.

"Oh, I didn't like what I read. It's amazing how a little knowledge can be such a dangerous thing. I read four volumes in total, not in order but they were damaging enough."

"In what way?"

"Mainly parentage. If I hadn't already known that Reuben was Logan's father, I'd have found out through the diaries. Other people had affairs and fathered children who've grown up thinking they belonged to someone else. Just one big mess really. I threatened to burn the one about the blond drover and Will confiscated it. He put it in the safe and promised he'd catalogue it and leave it there."

"Why that diary in particular?" Odering asked, making himself sound deliberately conversational.

"Not because of the drover, if that's what you're asking." Hana smiled at Logan's old adversary. "Rueben's wife had an affair with the drover before he disappeared. Then she had a child. It was the ramifications of that which shocked me, nothing else. The child's grown up thinking she was abandoned by her family, when the truth is that she arrived here because her birth mother couldn't live without her."

"But surely that'll help her with closure?" The detective looked confused.

"It won't, I promise." Hana gave a heavy sigh and defeat stampeded across her face. "For every ounce of comfort that might offer her, it has to be balanced against the distress it'll also bring." Hana leaned forward in her seat and lowered her voice. "Because that child recently married her half-brother and is apparently blissfully happy."

"And committing incest. I get it." Odering set his mug on the table. "Ok. I understand now."

"So do you promise to be careful with everything I tell you?" Hana asked with sincerity. "And I'll refuse to disclose her name, whatever you do to me."

Odering smiled. "I'm not gonna bloody torture you, Hana. Keep your secret, unless it's relevant to the investigation. But this business about the drover that went missing is of interest. Don't suppose you have a name for him?"

"No, sorry. That would have made life a heap easier because then Will and I could have looked for him and reassured ourselves. The trouble is, the diary only said he disappeared and his brothers came looking for him months later. It doesn't say he was killed or who did it, just that he suddenly wasn't here anymore. Phoenix had her suspicions but that was all we had to go on."

"Ok." Odering stood. "I'll get one of my officers to take statements from you and the curator and for now, they'll have to account for your odd comments to Doctor Seuli.

Unfortunately your statement counts for very little as the wife of the suspect, but Will's should help. I can't clear Logan though, Hana. I hope you understand that. From what I'm already hearing, he had good reason to get rid of the deceased, more than most!"

"Thank you," Hana breathed, her heart filled with foreboding. "If you could also find out who took those diaries - that would be a weight off my mind too. I have a very awkward conversation brewing with my husband that I'd really rather not sit through."

Odering patted Hana gently on the shoulder and smoothed his slender hand across her back. "You'll be fine sweetheart. Your husband's not an idiot. He'll understand."

"Yeah." Hana didn't sound so sure.

She hauled herself out of her chair after Odering left, finding the short journey almost insurmountable. Will waved to her from the end of the ground floor corridor and she acknowledged him, both of them tired and overwrought at the latest development. The old man kissed the palm of his hand and blew it towards Hana with care and she struggled to prevent the ready tears falling. She raised a smile for his sake alone and continued on her journey, using the spiral staircase off the main lobby and arriving in the loft apartment puffing for breath. The space seemed airless and Hana felt lightheaded.

"Hey, gorgeous." Logan sat in the lounge reading a bedtime story to a dozing Phoenix. He kept his voice low as her eyelids drooped and she cuddled into his chest, thumb tucked in her mouth and rosebud lips periodically twitching. "If I snuggle her up tightly and sit in the back, would you be able to drive home?" Logan whispered. "I think she might stay asleep then. The olds have gone to bed already. No stamina."

Hana slumped into the chair opposite. "There's no point me driving us up the mountain tonight. Odering wants to talk to you. Now." Hana's body language was defeatist and Logan's eyes widened in alarm.

"What's going on, babe?"

"He's letting me talk to you first. Then he wants you to go downstairs. He's using the family lounge to take statements." Hana found it hard to look at her husband. She exhaled and tiredness swamped her. "I tried to help negate the stupid comments I said to the doctor a few weeks ago. He's made a statement to the cops saying I appeared scared for my life. He's reported that I claimed you got rid of people who got in your way. It puts you squarely in the frame for killing Sylvia." Hana's voice stayed monotone as she struggled through the speech she prepared on the way upstairs. "I didn't say you specifically at the time, I said the Du Roses. But there was a reason why I thought that and I should have shared it earlier. I read in your grandmother's diary about a blond drover who had an affair with your Aunt Antoinette. She had a child, a baby girl who was very obviously his. She had bright blonde hair and...it doesn't matter anyway, but the child arrived here when she was two and Reuben allowed it. When your aunt died, he brought the girl up..."

"Caroline?" Logan's wide grey eyes registered horror. "Geez, that's...weird. But it still doesn't explain why you thought I'd kill you." He looked hurt.

"Because the blond drover disappeared mysteriously and nobody ever saw him again. Family came looking and went away disappointed. Phoenix thought someone on the property disposed of him."

"You should have told me, babe. Bloody diaries. I never wanted the damn things opened." Logan shook his head, his eyes dulling with sadness. "So Odering wants me now?"

Hana nodded. Tears sprung from her eyes. "Yes. Will went to get the diary to show Odering why I said that comment to the doctor. And I went to see Odering to explain. But..." Hana's voice adopted a frantic note and a sob escaped. Logan's face softened and he stood up, laying Phoenix down on the chair and swaddling her up in the sweater he yanked over his head. He took a stride towards his wife but she held up her hand to halt his progress. "Someone broke into the safe and stole all the diaries. So now I can't show him and he's only got mine and Will's word for it. So instead of making things better for you, I've just made it worse..."

Logan ignored her resistance and with one stride, scooped her into his arms and held her tightly. "Shhhh," he whispered, supporting her with his hands in the small of her back. "It's gonna be ok. None of this is your fault. Don't cry, Hana, please. We've both shed enough tears over this family."

Hana's breath came in stilted gasps as the weight of her misery buried her underneath its cloying fingers. She tried to speak but nothing sensible came out. Logan kissed her damp cheeks and ran his thumb under her eyes, smoothing the delicate skin with gentle strokes. "I'm going downstairs now," Logan said, sounding more confident than he felt. Stress raised the livid scar under his right eye, making it look white against his bronzed complexion, but Logan smiled at Hana and tried to infuse her with love. "Babe, can I just ask you one question?"

Logan pushed Hana away from his chest, keeping her upper arms in a firm grip. Her face was blotchy and puffed from crying, snot and tears dotted around her cheeks and chin. "What...?" she sobbed.

"Do you think I killed Sylvia?"

"No!" Hana's face expression changed to one of incredulity. "What a stupid question!"

Logan laughed. "That's my girl. I can face anything if you believe me."

Hana shook her head. "Idiot! Of course I don't think that. Sylvia was leaving. She'd done her worst. If you were going to bump her off, you'd have done it when she first arrived or when our marriage hit the rocks."

"Oh, so not complete exoneration then? Just bad timing."

"You know what I mean," Hana sulked and hiccoughed from her crying. "I'm just saying."

Logan shook her gently. "Fair enough. Right, I'll go down and see my mate Odering now." Logan let go of his wife's hands and leaning in, gave her a last, smouldering kiss. "I love you, Hana Du Rose." His smile was tight."

"We'll wait here for you," Hana whispered.

"Might be a while," Logan shrugged as he walked away from his wife, glancing back once over his shoulder with a wan smile.

"I'm praying it won't be," Hana answered and slumped into the chair as her husband stepped down the stairs, his cowboy boots clicking on the treads. "I'm really praying it won't."

Chapter 42

Hana woke with a start as a cool hand ran across her forehead. She tried to sit up and groaned, "Oh, my back!"

"Shhhhh," Leslie's voice was hushed. "*Moko's* sleeping. I put her in the spare bed. You wanna go too?"

"No. I'm waiting for Loge."

The big woman tutted. "You had an argument?"

Hana sat up, every bone in her body sending darts of pain into her brain, in punishment of her disregard of its comfort. "What time is it?"

"It's after three. What you doin' still here? Where's Logan?"

"The cops think he killed Sylvia."

Leslie's eyes widened to froglike proportions. "Truly?"

"Of course he didn't!" Hana's irritation escaped without control and her eyes lowered with guilt. "Sorry, Leslie. It's been a long day."

"Get some sleep, *kōtiro*," the old woman urged and Hana shook her head.

"Would you keep an ear open for Phoe, please? I'm going downstairs to wait for Logan in the lobby. I can't settle and I need to walk around a bit. I'll take my phone. Text me if you need me and I'll come straight up."

"I'll get Alfie to text," Leslie replied. "I'm too old for them tricks, honey."

Hana rose with difficulty and kissed the woman on her cheek. On impulse she wrapped her arms around the voluptuous body and rested her head on Leslie's shoulder. "I love you, *Kōkā*."

Leslie sighed loudly and gathered Hana into her, squeezing her tightly and infusing her with affection. Hana's use of the *Māori* word for mother, or aunty, secured their relationship and moved it onto a different level. Leslie sniffed with emotion and kissed Hana wetly on the temple. "Don't be long. And leave the bottom door unlocked for yourself."

Hana used the spiral staircase to the ground level and slipped out into the lobby without making a sound. Soft lamps lit the area and the heavy front doors stood strong against the winter chill, the kauri wood dark through the glass of the inner doors. All external doors were locked at midnight by an efficient security team. The reception desk stood empty, all keys secured in the adjoining office that had been Miriam's and the hotel was devoid of human noise, most sensible guests asleep. Hana looked around her, knowing the space intimately in daylight but confused by the shadows encouraged by the surrounding darkness. She lightly fingered the back of an armchair, intending to sit and wait for her husband's return but thirst built in the back of her throat and exited as a dry cough. "Cup of tea," she said to herself and walked towards the kitchen instead. "Then I'll sit and wait."

The kitchen door creaked on its hinge as Hana pushed it open. It sat in darkness but for the lamplight sneaking through from the family dining room. Male voices hushed at the sound of her entering. Hana scurried towards the light, the burgeoning hope crushed in her chest at the absence of her husband and her face fell. "Sorry," she said. "I thought Logan might be back."

"Na, not yet," Tama said, his voice muted in tones more suited to a library. "Liza met him at the station with the big guns. Last I heard anyway."

Hana observed Tama's companion, who pushed a glass of water back and forth across the knotted wood. "Sorry, Ryan. This must be really hard for you."

The boy shrugged and his fingers forced the glass into a dangerous pirouette. "It's ok. I know Logan didn't kill her. Wouldn't have blamed him though. She was poison."

Hana knitted her brow and winced. She flicked her eyes towards Tama who rolled his eyes. "Would either of you like a hot drink?" she asked, dropping easily into the role of mother. Tama smirked.

"I wouldn't mind some of that hot chocolate you make, Ma. Granny Miriam kept a secret bottle of brandy on the top shelf."

"Fetch it down for me then," Hana conceded. "And I'll make some."

Tama's long arms reached easily up to the top shelf of the pantry and retrieved the dusty bottle of expensive brandy. There was a decent gap at the neck where it had been used but the liquid sloshed happily inside as Tama placed it into Hana's hands. "I remember this," she said. "We had some on my wedding night when Alfred cut his finger. Miriam poured it." Hana stroked the label with reverence, her resolve to using it dissipating.

"It's just a bottle of booze, Ma," Tama breathed and kissed Hana's forehead. "Hurry up, woman. I like your special hot chocolate. Get on with it!"

Hana clattered around with a saucepan and milk from the chiller. The clock ticked on the wall heralding the arrival of the half hour between three and four and she sighed. The staff would begin appearing around five for the breakfast preparations. With a shrug, Hana stole a goodly amount of the milk for her cause, shirking the inevitable rising guilt. She boiled the milk on the immaculate industrial stove, adding the chocolate powder and brandy and watching the liquid pearl with the extra ingredients, occupying herself and sparing her brain the futile exercise of worrying.

"Here you go," Hana placed two large mugs on the dining table and went back for her own.

"You shouldn't be drinking alcohol," Tama chided her as she returned sipping her own.

"Whatever," she replied rudely. "I'm not meant to be having sleepless nights or worrying either. What's one more sin at the moment?"

"True, true," Tama conceded and smiled, pulling his face out of his drink with a brown, milky moustache adorning his facial hair.

"How did you know Liza was with Logan?" Hana asked, defeatism creeping into her tone.

"She texted me earlier," Tama replied.

"Oh. I didn't know you and she had any kind of relationship."

Tama reached across and grabbed Hana's hand. "We didn't, Ma. But when I moved up to Auckland she asked for help with some jobs at her place on my days off. Then I started staying there when she was in Wellington. It gave me somewhere to go outside the bunkhouse. Her place is real posh, ya know. She's grown on me. She ain't so bad really."

"Yeah," Hana kept her opinions to herself.

"Anyways, in times of trouble, family sticks together."

Ryan waggled his eyebrows and then turned to Tama. "Why do you call her, *Ma?*" he asked, pointing at Hana.

Tama wiped his spare hand across his mouth, dislodging the creamy foam from his upper lip. His other fingers stroked Hana's, like the consolation prize for Liza's replacement of her. "She just is. She loves me for what I am, the good, bad and the ugly. I can talk to her about anything and she gives me good advice and sometimes runs interference with Uncle Logan...if I'm really persuasive." Tama gave Hana a cheeky look and she scowled.

"I do not!"

"Na, not often. Only when it's serious." He pulled a face and bit his lip.

"My mum wanted me to go with her when she left," Ryan said sadly. "The last thing I said to her was, '*Go away. I hate you.*' Why did I have to say that?" A solitary tear plopped onto the table and began to soak into the bare stripped wood. Hana reached sideways and took the teenager's writhing hand in hers. Ryan gripped onto her fingers with a ferocity she hadn't expected, embracing the lifeline with a sobering verve. Tama stared at their joined hands and a curious look passed across his features. Spotting the root of jealousy and insecurity, Hana increased her pressure on Tama's fingers, clasping their hands together and breathing permanence into their relationship. Tama relaxed and the smile in his grey eyes was a mixture of relief and adoration.

"This a private party?" Logan's tone was dull as he forced the dining room door open faster than its automatic closer desired and it gave a grating clunk.

"Yeah, bro. No ticket, no cuddle," Tama quipped, unfazed by the warning look in his uncle's dark, grit coloured eyes. Logan noticed the mugs of hot chocolate on the table and his expression changed to one of longing.

"Is there any of that left? I'm guessing it's my wife's brand of *hot-chocolate-for-alcoholics-anonymous?*" He slumped into the seat next to Tama, smiling at Hana and trying to inject humour into an otherwise terrible situation. She abandoned Tama's hand and slowly pushed her mug towards him.

"Have mine. I shouldn't be drinking brandy really."

"We'll share." Logan reached for the handle and took a decent slug. "Oosh, woman! This blows your head off."

Ryan snickered. "I'm not old enough to drink either."

Hana smiled at Ryan and let his hand go, resisting the look of anxiety that crossed his face. Logan winked at her and she understood his coded message. He didn't want her to ask about the police station with the boy present. "I'm going up to check on Phoe," Hana said and disengaged herself from the table. Her rounded belly caught on its edge as she made a mess of standing up, wobbling like a child's toy on unsteady feet. Anxiety crossed Logan's face.

Hana left the room with as much dignity as she could muster, going first to the kitchen to clean the milky saucepan. The scent of brandy washed up in the soapy water and caused a wave of nausea to take her by surprise. She suppressed a decent retch by putting her hand in front of her mouth and waiting for it to pass. Hana replaced the saucepan and crept from the kitchen, hearing the men's low voices beating a steady hum. Ryan's sobs came to her as the door closed behind her and she moved down the corridor using the wall for support.

The vacant downstairs toilet provided the stricken woman with relief finally, as Hana sat on the floor and cried painful tears. *What did you expect?* Self-derision was the hardest critic as Hana vented her misery at Logan. She wanted him to hold her, gather her up and take her home to the house on the mountain. She needed to know what happened at the police station. Traces of the old secrecy haunted her with darkened threat. *I can't live like that again,* Hana told herself. *I won't.*

"Hana, what are you doing here?" The female voice was curt and unforgiving, asking a question and stating the obvious. It *was* a weird place for a pregnant woman to be found in the early hours of the morning, alternately crying and retching.

"Making Christmas cards." Hana's answer was deliberately rude, her animosity towards her sister-in-law poorly disguised. *Not disguised at all,* her inner voice chided her.

"It's good to get organised early." Judge Liza Du Rose folded up her long legs and sat down next to Hana on the spotless tiled floor. "Have you seen Logan yet?"

Hana glanced sideways at the other woman's beautifully styled black trousers and felt self-conscious about her maternity slacks hanging around her knees in lumps and ridges. Hana pulled her legs up underneath her. "I just saw him in the kitchen."

"And you're sat in here why?"

"Because I can't take any more!" Hana snapped. "I've had enough of all this!" She wafted her arm around the room and Liza bit back a smirk. "Don't laugh at me!" Hana yelled and Liza shook her head.

"Sorry. But you have to admit it's a bit random. My brother's sat in the kitchen after being interviewed for most of the night and his wife's sulking in a hotel toilet, waving her arms and throwing a fit."

"I'm not throwing a fit!"

"Well what do you call it then?"

"You texted Tama. Nobody texted me! I've been worrying all night."

Liza rolled her eyes. "Logan was a little busy and I'm not meant to have your number. *Remember?* Besides which, congratulations on the baby and we kind of assumed you might be sleeping."

"Whatever!"

"Well, nice chatting but I'm shattered. I've managed to postpone today's very important fraud case until this afternoon, but I still need to be back in Auckland by midday. Are you coming?"

Hana looked up at her lithe sister-in-law as Liza elegantly pulled herself up from the floor like a ballerina, all stomach muscles and poise. "I can't get up," Hana grumbled. "My legs have gone dead."

Liza laughed and held out her hand. With great reluctance, Hana placed her slender fingers with her untidy nails into the judge's moisturised, manicured hand. "Thanks for sorting my problem out before. I appreciate it."

"Oh, no worries," Liza smiled and her beautiful face mirrored Miriam's. "You'd pretty much taken care of that by yourself."

"What happened with Logan?" Hana asked, breathing in shallow pants over the sink as nausea rose again. "He wouldn't tell me in front of Tama."

"Are you ok?" Liza asked. "Warn me if you're gonna puke. I've got a really delicate stomach."

"Just tell me," Hana groaned. She ran the cold water and filled her hand with its satisfying freshness, lifting it to her mouth and spilling half of it down her shirt.

"They interviewed Logan for a few hours and got his take on everything. They've made a timeline and will now go away and check it all out. I'm guessing they'll be coming your way very soon."

"I gave my statement last night. To Odering," Hana said, slurping the water and getting some up her nose.

"Well, they'll need to hear it all again." Liza leaned back against the sink unit and crossed her feet at the ankles, her lethal looking stilettos clicking on the tiles. "You'll have to back up Logan's story, particularly with regard to times and dates. Conversations will be really important too." Liza examined an expensive acrylic nail. "And just so that you know, it was stupid to tell Sylvia to leave in front of witnesses when she was in a state of distress and her son heard you say that it was biblical to take hits out on people. You haven't helped your own cause, or Logan's. You had a couple of public run-ins with the woman by all accounts. I'm surprised they're bothering with my brother at all!"

"Oh. Does Odering seriously think Logan did it?" Hana splashed water on her face and patted it dry with a paper towel.

"Do you?"

"No! Of course not!"

"Good. Then everything will be ok. What about this kid of hers? Ryan. He'll be a suspect too."

Hana turned to face Liza. "He admitted he saw her before she died and they had an argument. Apparently she wanted him to go with her when she went up to Auckland to find Michael. He told her he hated her."

"Hmmmn." Liza tapped a pointy heel on the tiles. "Well, someone killed her. It's probably best if it's him."

"But he's family!" Hana felt appalled. "He's sleeping in your old bedroom!"

"Logan's *whanau*," Liza smiled. "And if this kid has to be thrown to the lions to save my brother, then so be it!"

Hana quailed and felt the world shrink in front of her at Liza's words. It wasn't just that she would be willing to sacrifice Michael's son to save Logan. It was that she clearly wouldn't do the same for her.

Chapter 43

"Wait!"

Hana curled her lips in distaste at the sight of the young man on her doorstep and turned away. His knock interrupted a well-deserved nap while Phoenix slept in her cot and the woman was crotchety and irritable. "We have nothing to say to each other."

"No!" Asher jammed his foot in the door to prevent Hana slamming it in his face and her expression registered fear.

"Go away or I'll call Logan."

"Please, don't do that?" The young man's face paled in fear and his brows knitted and relaxed continuously, clown-like and strange against his dark complexion. He looked sick and ill and his vulnerability pulled at Hana's maternalism. "I really need to talk to you," he pleaded.

Hana glanced behind her, suspicion making her usually accommodating nature reticent. "Have you been watching my house?" she asked, with a directness that made the young man blanch.

"No. I promise I haven't." Asher's eyes widened, grey orbs in a frame of dark eyelashes. "It's not me."

Hana stared at him and a quizzical look grew on her pretty, sleep-kissed face. "What do you mean? Do you know...?"

"Please!" Asher begged and glanced behind him at the driveway, empty but for his beat up blue ute. "I need your help."

Hana had been around Logan far too long and she made no attempt to hide her suspicion. She indicated a wrought iron bench sheltered under the eaves and showed with a sweep of her hand that Asher should sit on it. "This is nice." He stroked the coiled metal of an intricately shaped leaf and sought Hana's approval by admiring her stuff, as though it would overwrite his previous aggression. His fingers shook. "Where'd you get it?"

Hana leaned her back against a sturdy brick pillar and eyed the young man with an intensity that made him squirm against her green eyes. "Logan asked a man in the township to make it from a drawing he had." Hana kept her face emotionless and inquisitorial. "What do you want, Asher?"

The young man dipped forward so that his elbows rested on his knees and he used the backs of his fists to knead his eyes. He possessed the captivating Du Rose looks and physique and Hana watched him with interest. When he raised his head, he looked wrong-footed and exhausted. "I don't know where to start."

"Try the beginning," Hana stated and examined a chipped nail on her left thumb. "But please hurry up. It's cold out here."

Asher looked at the front door, a slither of warmth dusting them from the small gap. He looked back at Hana and she rolled her eyes at him. "You must think I'm stupid after our last meeting," she told him. Asher had the decency to drop his eyes and bite his lip in shame. He wouldn't be going inside after all.

"Yeah. Sorry about that. I got a lot of things wrong. I'm an idiot."

"Asher, why are you here?" Frustration leaked from Hana's voice as her well-deserved nap eroded before her eyes.

He shifted in the seat, betraying his awkwardness. "Mum thought you might be...more understanding than *him*. I wanted her to come with me but she can't face it."

"Face what?"

Asher sighed. "I've got myself into a big mess with the developers and I can't get out of it. One of their foremen came to see me when Poppa Rueben died and Dad refused to sell to them. At first it was all nice and we met in the township and he bought me drinks. Then he told me how much money his bosses offered my dad to sell up and it was a fortune. He said Logan had cheated my parents and stopped me getting my inheritance. I believed him. I genuinely thought they offered Dad millions for the land and that we'd be rich. I didn't know about the debts until you said the other week and...I thought you were lying to shut me up. I asked Dad later and he got out all the paperwork and showed me. There would have been nothing left if he'd sold to the developers and he also showed me their offer of sale. It was nothing like as much as they said. I know now that Uncle Logan paid way over the odds for the land and then paid off heaps more debt after that, even though he never agreed to take responsibility for debts at the start. My dad said we were going under and Logan stopped us being declared bankrupt. He discharged all the debt and gave me and Dad work on the farm. I was wrong."

Hana shifted on the spot as her legs numbed and her fingers rubbed against the brickwork behind her. She bit back the snarky retort which came readily to her lips, with difficulty. "That's great, Asher. You've had a eureka moment. Congratulations. Is that what you came to say? Surely you could have apologised to my husband as easily. I didn't need to hear it."

Asher bit his lip. "It's not just that though, is it?" His dark eyes bore the heavy weight of fear, his pupils dilated and obscuring the colour of his stunning grey irises. "It's not just that. They paid me, the developers, to do stuff. They wanted me to help drive you off the property and then they promised they'd pay my family what we were owed. The foreman gave me instructions and I got paid when I'd done whatever they asked. I was saving it for Mum and Dad but then I dipped into it to get my car. But it was a big mistake and I needed more to run it because it's a bit of a money trap and…it's all a big mess. My mum's having a nervous breakdown and it's because of me. Now there's that body and everyone's gonna think I did it, especially the cops. I've sold the car but I didn't get all the money back on it. I don't care. I just need this whole thing to be over."

Asher was in his early twenties but his face was that of a much younger man, as foolishness robbed him of arrogance and pride. He looked up at Hana through long dark lashes that blinked away tears and she shook her head, annoyed at herself. "I need to sit down and something tells me I'm going to want a drink in my hand." She exhaled in a huff of displeasure and pushed the red front door open and then stood back. Asher got shakily to his feet and kicked off his work boots before entering Logan Du Rose's castle.

"Wow!" Asher exclaimed in the lobby, looking up at the apex ceiling with its ornate skylights and glinting chandeliers. "This is awesome."

Hana stopped and spun around, seeking his disdain but seeing only childish delight. "We work hard for what we have," she warned and Asher lowered his eyes.

"I know that now."

"Here." Hana handed the man a cold drink of water, laced with ice cubes as he had requested. "Now tell me what's going on. And in particular, what did you do?"

Asher stumbled through his story for a full twenty minutes and Hana's hand shook with so much violence, she was forced to lay her mug of tea on the coffee table. A winter sun streamed in through the long windows, warming the day and bathing the occupants of the lounge with welcome light. "I don't believe this!" Hana gulped a mouthful of her cooling drink and lay the cup back down. Then she ran a shaking hand across her eyes. "How could you?"

"I'm sorry!" Asher leapt to his feet and Hana jumped in fear. "I'm sorry," he said, calming himself and sitting back down on the sofa opposite her. "I know how it looks. If I could take it back, I would."

"Take it back!" Hana's anger burst from between her pretty pink lips and her green eyes flashed emerald. "I'm pregnant! You threw a brick through the window and I was showered with glass. You've caused so much trouble on this property that I don't know where to start. You've cost Logan thousands of dollars with having to get electricians, glaziers and the trick with the water up here was mean! We've got a child. To run out of water this far out would have been miserable."

"I know. I know." Asher sat with his head low, work worn fingers covering his eyes.

"The herd!" Hana leapt to her feet. "You put the Friesian in the herd, didn't you?"

"I just unlocked the gate for them and distracted the stockmen by letting the horses loose on the other side of the mountain. They had to go and round them up."

"When did you do it?"

"End of last year. You and Logan left for Europe and I felt so angry. I'd love to go to France and see where my genealogy started, but I'll never afford that. I thought Logan had ripped us off, so it was one of the first things the developers convinced me to do. I managed to do it before Toby brought in the Charolaise bull. He got it to cover cows that were already pregnant without realising. The ones they were artificially inseminating were held further up the mountain, which is a good job, otherwise the vet would have picked it up straight away."

"Yes, what a *good job* for you!" Hana's comment sounded snarky and full of irritation.

"I only did the ones on the front block!" Asher's eyes bugged with injustice. "I picked the least important ones. They aren't the main breeding dams. They're the beef herd that the hotel uses. It could have been worse!"

"Gee, thanks so much." Hana rolled her eyes.

"Look, I know how bad this all is. They put me under a lot of pressure once I was sucked in. They don't care who they hurt;

they want this mountain and will do anything to get it. They haven't refunded their clients yet, did you know that? They've delayed the build but they're still promising buyers that the development's going ahead."

"No, I didn't know that." Hana looked Asher in his fearful grey eyes. Her gaze was steady and intimidating, channelling Du Rose Matriarch with an unbending stare. "I'll get you a pen and paper. Make a list of everything you did. Everything! With dates and times. Logan will be the final judge regarding what happens to you. He might involve the cops and that's up to him."

"That will kill my mum," he said softly. "And Dad, when Logan tells him."

"You should have thought of that then, shouldn't you?" Hana raised one eyebrow and cocked her head at the young man, as she reached into a drawer underneath the coffee table and retrieved a refill pad and pen decorated with the lacing of baby teeth. She slapped it on the table in front of him. "Get on with it!" she ordered him. "I'm going to make another drink and a sandwich for my daughter. Do you want one?"

To her surprise, Asher nodded his head slowly. "Yes please," he said and it was almost inaudible as the weight of his crimes began to take shape in a series of blue biro scribbles on the top page.

Hana returned with another cold water and a beef sandwich. The irony was not lost on the man. He embellished a large full stop next to his listed adulteration of Logan's prize Charolaise herd, making it into a hang man as his sub-conscious worked overtime. "I'm sorry," he said quietly as Hana lifted the pad.

"You did all this?" She sounded astounded as she examined the list of over thirty misdemeanours, including broken windows, sabotaged equipment, fence breaking and leaving gates unlocked and open. Asher had the decency to look ashamed. "I need to call Logan and probably your father." Hana walked through to the kitchen and lifted her cell phone from next to the sink. She sighed with exasperation at the lack of reception. Lifting the handset on the wall, she pressed zero for the hotel receptionist. A noise behind her startled Hana and Asher squeaked and lurched for the notepad in her hand.

"Wait!"

Fear lit Hana's eyes as their fingers contacted and she released the pad and leapt back. The handset dropped floor-wards, breaking into two parts on the tiled surface. "Damn!" She looked at it with horror, all hope of help gone.

"Sorry! I just forgot something else I did." Asher laid the pad on the centre island and stared at Hana. "Please don't be scared of me. I know I did some awful stuff, but please, don't be like this with me?"

Hana couldn't prevent the sneer which deformed her beautiful face. "Are you for real? You covered me in glass! You were the reason my little girl had to watch cows aborting in our garden! I suppose that's what you forgot to write down, was it? Item number thirty-one: I let out the cows with the calves that nobody wants and drove them up to Hana's house!"

"No, actually, I'll write that now." Asher's hand shook as he detailed the afternoon's work in a slanting left handed script. Hana picked up the broken phone and tried to fit the two parts of the handset together. Her fingers shook with fury and her breathing came fast and irregular. Asher laid the pen neatly on top of the paper and put his hand out for the handset. "I'll do it," he offered.

Hana ignored the proffered hand and laid it on the bench next to the paper, but curiosity got the better of her and she peered at the second to last item on the list of Asher's sins.

I threw a brick through Logan's bedroom window at the hotel and smashed it.

Hana pointed a shaking finger at the offending item and stared at Asher in horror. "That was you? About ten days ago?"

Asher nodded, his shame hanging like a necklace around him, dragging him into a torturous oblivion. "Yeah. I saw the light on and you were moving around in there. I could see you through the window..." He looked at Hana in horror. "Not like that! I wasn't perving or anything. It was just your silhouette!" Asher smirked at the memory of the fantastic overarm, which made him good at schoolboy cricket. "It was a great shot," he lavished misplaced praise on himself. "Went right through the middle and you screamed." His face dropped with an appropriate degree of contrition. "Sorry."

"I'm getting Logan." An urgency crept into Hana's tone as Asher placed the mended handset on top of the bench. "This is even more serious than I thought." Hana pressed zero on the handset a couple of times before anything happened and the urgency was still there as she spoke politely to the receptionist down at the hotel. "Hi, love. This is Hana. Please can you get Logan and Nev for me? I need them here quickly." A female voice issued from the device, garbled and distorted. "I know," Hana replied, the veneer of calm slipping as misery took over. "But this is urgent, like, really desperate. I want them here within the next ten minutes."

Hana bit her lip as she laid the handset down. "That was stupid!"

"I know," Asher began and she silenced him with the raising of her hand.

"Not you. Me. The cops are crawling all over the hotel still. What if Odering gets wind of this and follows Logan up here?"

"I'm happy to take my punishment," Asher replied bravely. "Look." He lifted his sweatshirt to reveal a stunning set of abdominal muscles, honed by years of hard work and riding horses. Hana gasped, but not at the beautifully sculpted masculinity in her kitchen. Asher's skin was a mass of bruises and purple welts, cutting into his flesh and leaving a trail of destruction.

"Are you a haemophiliac?" Hana asked and he shook his head.

"No! Bloody good job too or they would have killed me. After Dad showed me the paperwork and listed the debts, the foreman asked to meet me. He turned up with four other guys and wanted me to put stuff in your water tanks to make you and Logan sick. But you were kind to Wiri and I knew he'd slept here. He likes you." Asher gave Hana a tight smile. "I told them no."

"They beat you up?" Hana pursed her lips and her eyes widened.

Asher nodded. "Yeah. But only on my body, not where other people would notice and ask me about it. They're clever."

"They're evil!" Hana spat. "How could you get mixed up with men like that?"

"I'll go to prison, it's fine. I know I deserve it." Asher nodded his head like a toy, his dark curls bobbing comically on his head.

"You'll go to prison for murder, you silly boy!" Hana said, shocked at his complacency. "That's game over for you!"

"No, not murder." Asher looked confused. "Just criminal damage for the property and probably actual bodily harm for throwing bricks through windows at you."

"Murder!" Hana stressed again, wishing her husband would arrive quickly and take this latest problem off her hands. "You'll go to prison for murder."

"Na, I won't. I never killed nobody!" Asher's face betrayed confusion and disbelief. His old scorn at Hana resurfaced as he shook his head at her and pulled a disdainful face. Hana gritted her teeth and blew out an exasperated breath.

"So how come the woman you threw a brick at, was found dead in the paddock behind your house a few days ago?"

Asher's face morphed from disbelief and confusion, through to realisation and terror. "Was that her in Logan's room then? Not you?"

Hana nodded. The foolish youth whistled through his teeth and exhaled with a smirk. "So it was true then? Uncle Logan *was* knocking that bitch off. Well, what-da-ya-know."

Hana rolled her eyes and shook her head, washing her hands of the stupid idiot in front of her. Logan could deal with his own family. She was done. "You know what, Asher?" Hana said with a smile. "The developers saw you coming. I hope you get what you deserve."

By the time Logan arrived up at the house on his blowing horse, Nev cantering up behind him; Hana was finishing loading a grumpy Phoenix into the ute. Logan hurled himself from the sweating beast and ran over to his wife, his face a mask of confusion. "Babe, what's happened? I got your message. What's up?" His fingers were tight on Hana's upper arms and she wriggled to shake them off. Nev's face looked strained and full of tiredness. Hana pitied what was ahead for him.

"Ok," Hana addressed the Du Rose men with fake confidence. "There's something in the kitchen you should see. It's a list, written by the man who's been doing all the damage to your business and property." Both men bridled and looked towards the house with naked, righteous anger in their familial faces. Nev flexed his fists, the Du Rose temper obviously only hidden skin deep. "Before you go inside, I would take big, deep breaths, because you'll need them before you talk to him. He's an idiot. I'm going out for a while and when I come back, I want him gone. If he's still here when I get home, I'll commit a few murders of my *own!*"

Hana raised her voice at the startled men to highlight the overt threat and climbed up into the truck. She started the engine with a roar and made the huge wheels hiss on the gravel, at the same time as the men set off for the front door at a run.

Chapter 44

At the house, Hana carried Phoenix into the museum. The little girl rubbed her nose on Hana's shoulder and settled down for a nap.

"She's heavy. Give her to me," Will insisted, grunting as Hana lay the spindly bundle of child on his thighs.

"I don't want to hurt you," Hana worried.

The old man guffawed. "Nothing left to hurt, *kōtiro*. And I'm sitting on my *nono* all day so it makes sense." He patted Phoenix's back gently with his arthritic fingers, the dark hair standing up on each bent finger like fur. Comfortable in his presence, the child snuggled into his lap and lay back like a queen, her thumb finding its way between her lips and her eyes flickering closed. Will patted her chest in a rhythmic pattern and Phoenix sighed with contentment.

"When she gets bored, please can I get on?" Hana slumped into a nearby chair and the old man snuffed a gentle laugh. "I'm knackered!"

"You do too much," Will chided softly.

"Has Odering had any luck finding the diaries?" Hana asked, her expression confused as she failed to process her feelings about the troublesome manuscripts.

"No, girlie. You got your wish. We won't see them again."

"That's not fair, Will. I was perplexed about their content, but I was fine as long as you kept them safe. *Which you didn't!*"

The old man's jaw snapped open, making him look like a stunned mullet. "Did you take them?" His question shocked Hana in return and hurt radiated across her pretty face.

"No!" She screwed her face up and narrowed her green eyes. "I don't know the combination to the safe, remember? You wouldn't give it to me!"

"For valid reasons, woman; not that it did me much good. I've been wondering if I should resign. What good is an archivist who can't protect the artifacts? Probably about as much use as a man with no legs." Will's face dropped and his facade of geniality was replaced by the man underneath, vulnerable and sensitive.

"Idiot!" Hana slid forward on her seat and clasped the old man around the neck in a crushing embrace. "Don't you dare leave me! You're more to me than just the keeper of all the damaging Du Rose secrets. I need you here. You're my confidante and my friend and the closest thing I have to a dad on this side of the world."

Will snaked his spare arm around the woman's back and pushed his face into the hair at her neck. Hana heard him sniff and squeezed him harder. Phoenix grunted in the small space between their bodies and turned on her side, wedging her button nose into Will's armpit. "*Matua kēkē* squishin' Phoe-Phoe!" she grumbled.

"Grumpy baby," Hana chided her daughter and used the edge of her sleeve to wipe the rolling tears from Will's crinkled cheeks. "What did she call you?" she asked him.

"Uncle." Will's tears rolled more readily and Hana smiled down at her child, whose eyelashes fluttered in irritation.

"Well, you can't leave then! You're obviously family," Hana chided the old man. "We just have to sort this out ourselves."

Hana made tea in the kitchenette at the back of the long workroom and Will rocked the toddler in his arms with tenderness. He smoothed a dark curl from Phoenix's forehead and included her in the blanket covering his ruined legs. She slept deeply, emitting only the sound of an occasional suck on the peachy-pink thumb. Hana put the tea down on the table and Will pushed himself across, resting his hands over the tyres of his chair and rolling it forwards. Hana knew better than to humiliate him by taking over. She sat down on an office chair and subconsciously rubbed a hand over her son, feeling the knotty bones of his spine and the back of a firm head pushing up into her ribs. "This baby's so long," she mused to herself and Will smiled.

"Lookin' to me like someone got their dates wrong." He sniffed and sipped his dark coloured drink - builder's tea - he called it.

"Nope, definitely not. This boy's French, a little gift from Paris." Hana's face took on a wistfulness and her cheeks pinked at the thought of just one of her nights of passion in Europe with her randy husband. Muscle memory caused her fingers to twitch as she recalled the feel of her palms moving over Logan's strong, muscular back and the whiteness of her skin against his olive tones. Her lips remembered his deep kisses and the way he maintained eye contact with her as he...

"Earth to Hana Du Rose! Am I in this conversation by myself?" Will's face held a knowing that made Hana squirm in her seat with embarrassment. "Dirty girl!" he chided her and Hana bit her lip, badly stifling a smirk. Will saw it anyway and shook his head. "I asked you what we can do to sort this out. You said we should sort it ourselves."

Hana sat up straighter and banished the image of her naked husband with difficulty. Contact with Logan left an inner glow in Hana's soul that radiated out as a disgusting satisfaction with life. She forced her mind back to the moment and wrangled it into submission. "If we write a list of what we know, then maybe we can work some things out and hurry up the investigation. You know what this family's like; the cops won't know anything helpful." Hana thought of her persistent son and cringed.

"It must be like trying to floss a shark's teeth." Guilt lit her green eyes as she imagined the Du Rose shark snapping off her son's dark-skinned fingers. Conflict danced in her heart, leaving muddy footprints in her sobriety.

"What's with you and lists, woman?" Will groaned. Hana's mind strayed back to Asher's handwritten confession and she shuddered.

"I'll tell you later. That's a whole other story but it works for me and we've nothing to lose." She reached behind her and snagged a pad of notepaper with the hotel logo printed on the top. Hana's search for a pen was futile as Will had banned such offensive-leakers-of-acid in the museum and she settled for a 2B pencil, which she had to sharpen first. Then she sat poised, looking at Will with expectation.

"Don't you look at me like that!" he bit at her. "You want to solve this, not me. I just want the *taonga* back safe. I don't care about the rest of it. And stop chewing my pencils! I knew it was you."

Hana removed the end from her mouth and dried it on her trouser leg. "The first question is whether or not you think the missing diaries are anything to do with Sylvia's death or something separate?"

"How would they link to her death?" Will scoffed. "She won't be in them. Nobody except your husband knew she existed until recently."

"Logan didn't sleep with her," Hana informed him with a snip in her voice. "She lied. His brother is Ryan's father."

"Well, he should be more careful where he...it don't matter. He's a *kaumatua*. He should know better."

Hana's brow furrowed and the pencil strayed to her lips again, before a bug-eyed glare from Will halted its progress. "I think it's all connected. So let's start with Sylvia's death. I'll list all the people who could have done it and then we'll work from there."

Will shrugged and grumbled, "I just want the diaries back. Don't care about no nasty dead *wahine kairau.*"

"Om, did you just say a rude thing?" Hana leaned forward in her chair with her eyes wide. Will pulled a face.

"Get on with it, woman. My bloody knees are goin' to sleep!"

Hana's jaw dropped in confusion. Will's knees were long gone, victims of diabetes and the surgeon's operating table. She opened her mouth to speak and he glared at her, making her think better of it. Hana stared at the pad. "The list of possible suspects is too long," she moaned.

"Then start with yourself and your *tāne* then!"

Reluctantly, Hana wrote her own name at the top next to a number one and added Logan's. She wrote it small and faint, as though it wasn't properly there and Will rolled his eyes and shook his head. Phoenix snored and farted, belying the seriousness of the adults' deliberations. Will looked disgusted and shifted the little girl so that he could examine his pant leg through squinting eyes.

"Tama," the old man suggested and when Hana shook her head, he lost his temper. "If you're just goin' to challenge every name, then this is pointless, girlie! Just leave it to the cops."

"Sorry, sorry." Hana scribbled Tama's name on the pad under Logan's.

By the time Phoenix woke up, fluffy haired, pink-cheeked and smiling, Hana had produced a list of some twenty five names. "Do you think I need Jack and the stable workers on here?" Hana's pencil hovered over the list, ready to strike through some of the names.

"I reckon so," Will nodded, amusing Phoenix with the soft toy on his key fob.

"Even ranking them in importance leaves me and Logan at the top," Hana groaned.

"Well, move the older employees up there with ya," Will suggested. "Especially them what's been 'ere years, bro."

"Right, here goes. We've got me and Logan, Alfred and Leslie, maybe Nev, although he has no motive..."

"He does for wantin' the diaries though," Will stated. "If you think the two things are linked then you have to leave him up there."

"I suppose he might know that Caroline is his half-sister. If he really loves Kane, then it's worth keeping it secret that they're half-brother and sister too. And if he doesn't love Kane, then lighting a fire under him will only bring him home. That will cause more trouble than you could imagine, especially if he wanted to live on the property. Logan won't allow it."

"So if it's both things - diary and murder - well, I was scared of the diaries *and* wanted Sylvia gone. Logan didn't know what the diaries contained and honestly doesn't care about them, but he wanted Sylvia gone. Nobody else knew what was in the diaries but pretty much everyone was sick of Sylvia. Oh no!" Hana wailed. "I'm the only one who knew about the diaries and wanted Sylvia to leave!"

"Prime suspect then. Arrest that woman!"

"You're not helping!" Hana complained. Will snorted.

"Lists are like the Bible. You can make them say anything."

"You can't make the Bible say anything!" Hana was affronted. "It's the Word of God. People misquote it, that's all."

"Say bye bye to Mama," Will told Phoenix, their heads bowed over a stain on the battered looking dog dangling from his keys. "I think that might be pickle."

"Bye Mama." Phoenix offered a lovely smile and a wave that involved more wrist than hand.

"I'm not being arrested. Ignore the silly man." Hana glared at Will, ignoring his smirk. The thought entered her brain in a rush, the memory faint but important. "Will, remember that day we talked about what was in the diaries and we heard someone moving around outside the door?" He nodded. "Well, what if the murderer heard what we said and felt as though the diaries implicated them in some way?" Hana's eyes lit up in response to the catharsis.

"So who was it?" Will asked without looking up.

"I don't know. I didn't see." Hana's body deflated in the chair like someone had let the air out of her. She sighed. "This is too hard."

"So leave it to the cops! It's their job. The *taonga* will come back. I can feel it. They are linked to this place. They'll find their way home. Until then, I'll dedicate my life to stopping that stupid old woman dressing your daughter in clothing from the 1800's so she can spill food on them."

"Yeah, I don't know where she's getting all those from."

"Well, ask her!" Hunger made Will snap as his blood sugars altered his mood. Hana raised her eyebrows.

"Tell you what. I'll see where Leslie's getting the clothes from." She handed the curator a blue pencil case and opened her arms to Phoenix. "Come here, babe. Will, do your bloods and I'll go hunt you up a sandwich from the kitchen."

Hana returned an hour later with a ham and cheese sandwich for Will. He grumbled and moaned at her. "Good job I'm not dying! I thought you forgot me. I think you're secretly the murderer and you was tryin' to bump me off because I know too much."

Hana looked horrified and Will laughed. "Give me the bloody food, or I'll wheel over your feet!"

"Sorry, Helena made you the sandwich." Hana reached into her pockets one at a time and produced a bag of potato chips, an apple and an orange. The old man smiled with genuine pleasure and sat them on the table next to his plate. "I called up to see Leslie but then couldn't persuade Phoe to leave. They're baking some weird cookie-thing together, although my daughter's eaten most of the raw mixture. Apparently there are three more apartments on the top floor like hers, filled to the roof with family junk from when they converted to a hotel. Everything went up there. She said there's clothes and well...loads of stuff. And, I'm going to try and find JD. Logan says he's still alive, because he collects the rent from the paddock near the road every year. But he was there when the blond drover died, he's possibly Reuben's father and he must know about Caroline being a Du Rose."

"Do you think he killed this woman?" Will asked, spitting sandwich onto his lower lip. He sucked it back in, much to Hana's disgust and laughed at the prim look on her face.

"Not really," Hana conceded. "He's probably up north somewhere. The *Māori* side of the family were a mix of Waikato and Ngapuhi tribes so he may have headed home - if he was even *Māori*. I'm having to make that assumption. And he might not even be a relative. Maybe he was a worker, or someone Phoenix Du Rose trusted. I think it's fairly safe to assume they were lovers at some point, because of what she said."

"Does the lift go all the way to the top floor?" Will asked abruptly, his mind straying to the treasure trove above his head.

"No. But I wonder if your son could carry you up there. Would that be too humiliating for you, if we could organise that?"

Will looked at Hana in wonderment and she felt the soft glow of his approval. It was misplaced. His amazement was at her stupidity, not her planning expertise. "The boy wipes my bloody ass every morning, woman! What's more humiliating that that?"

Chapter 45

Hana left Will to his diet of sandwich and sarcasm and headed for the stables. The clatter of unshod feet drew her to a loose box in the corner and Sacha's dappled head poked over the top, at the sound of Hana's soft tread. "Hey, gorgeous." The woman responded to the soft wicker and kissed the downy spot just above the mare's lips. "Nice whiskers," Hana giggled and Sacha shook her head, causing the long, curly mane to swish from side to side. "Don't worry, it's an age thing. Logan would freak if he ever saw mine."

The huge head pushed at Hana's stomach and she stepped back defensively. Sacha's blue eye narrowed in a wink and the brown one blinked slightly later as she scented the apple in the pocket of Hana's hoodie. "I forgot about that." Hana extracted it with difficulty, its shiny redness glinting in the sunshine. "I was going to give it to Will, but he's being a pig. I gave him the sour green one. Sour like him." Hana pushed her bottom lip out like a child and Sacha blew gently on the woman's face. Hana released the apple, rewarded by a torrent of apple juice and slobber as the mare snipped the fruit into pieces and left them in her hand, eating them one by one with long, delicious crunches. When she was done, Hana wiped the mess on the mottled forehead. "Why are you in? I thought Logan was going into the back blocks today. I saw him just before he left and you're not even tacked up."

Sacha nuzzled Hana's hand and then put her head back over the half-door. Hana peered in and saw a long cut trailing down the mare's front leg. Blood and gore oozed from it.

"Hey, Miss." Rawhiti appeared next to Hana and glanced over at the horse. Sacha bared her teeth.

"What's happened?"

"She went for Jack earlier. Mr Logan's worried. He thinks she might be having mental problems. She shied up at him when he tried to tack her."

"She shied up at Logan?" Hana's face paled.

"No, she was fine with him. It was Jack. She kicked out and caught him on the arm and then scraped her leg down the wall as she landed. Never heard a horse make that kind of noise either. I swear she was screeching. Mr Logan looked devastated. He borrowed Toby's bay gelding. They needed to go."

"Are you waiting for the vet?" Hana observed the dappled backside as it faced the door, loaded with veiled threat.

"Na, don't need him. He hates her anyway. Mr Logan said to bathe it, but she won't let anyone in with her. She'll have to wait until the stockmen get back now."

"Won't it get infected?"

"That's her lookout. She's played up once too often I reckon. Think she's about due for the bullet."

Sacha's sturdy kick to the wooden door shuddered it on its hinges and Rawhiti stepped back.

"How's Jack?"

Rawhiti shrugged. "Says he's fine."

"I'll go see him. He's getting too old to be knocked around." Hana leaned over the door and spoke to the mare's bum, watching the flesh creep and the ears at the head end flick back and forth. "Sacha, I'm going to see Jack. Then I'll come back and bathe that leg."

The piercing noise split the air as the horse whirled round. Her eyes were staring and crazed and Sacha rose up on her back legs and smashed her front hooves into the wooden door. The wood split half way down and a hole appeared, revealing the other stamping feet. Rawhiti swore and ran backwards, almost pitching himself over an abandoned wheelbarrow. "Stop!" Hana shouted and the mare sank to her hooves, her mismatched eyes fixed on the woman. "That's enough!" The shock in Hana's voice wasn't just from dealing with rowdy teenage boys over the last decade and a half; some of it was genuine. The mare put her head down and blood dripped from a cut on her poll from contact with the high ceiling.

"Just stay away from her," Hana ordered Rawhiti and she set off for the stable office.

Jack sat behind his usual mountain of paperwork, examining a livid bruise on his forearm. He saw Hana knock and enter, even though he couldn't hear the courteous sound in deference to his authority. "What's going on?" Hana splayed her arms for the deaf man, hands palm upwards. He shrugged and pointed two fingers at his temple. Hana blanched as he mimed pulling the trigger. "No!" She shook her head frantically. "No." She tapped her chest and pointed up the mountain. "I'll take her home. Don't shoot her!"

Jack sneered and pulled his sleeve down over his arm. He shook his head, mocking her. Anger flared in Hana's heart, easily matching his. "What have I done to you?" She mouthed the words carefully. "Why are you being so rude?"

"*Get out!*" The words were grunts but the gesture and the menace were clear. Hana took a step back, horrified.

"Why?"

Jack cast around him for his pad. He located it under a sheaf of invoices but a working pen was harder to find. The scribble on the paper came as a bitter blow to Hana, who had tried so hard to befriend the oldest Du Rose employee and respect his position in the hierarchy. "*Stop digging up the past. Do us all a favour and leave us alone.*"

Hana's hand shook as she read the words scratched into the page. She looked at the old man in confusion. "You know, don't you? You know all about the Du Roses." Confirmation shone from the wizened face and the pursing of his lips. His eyes were so hooded by elderly, sinking eyelids that their colour was no longer distinguishable. But there was hatred there, oozing out like black liquid. Hana took a step forward. "You know about Kane and...Caroline, don't you?"

Jack squinted in concentration while he read Hana's lips and then his face broke into an eerie grin. His mouth opened wide with hilarity and Hana spied a flash of pink, toothless gums as he let out a roar of laughter. He clutched his sides with mirth and enjoyed the illegal union of half-siblings, both of whom he clearly hated with passion. The old man had never been able to form words that were foreign to his deaf ears, but he could laugh with abandon.

Hana took a step towards the elderly man, searching his face for the respected employee that Logan revered. Jack's guttural noises slowed and he followed her silhouette against the bright sunshine outside as Hana approached. "Jack," Hana put her hands on his littered desk and leaned forward. "Jack, do you know how I can find JD?"

There was a momentary delay and then the old man detonated. The shout that issued from between his lips was feral and terrifying. Hana leapt back covering her belly with her hands and tripped over a stricken saddle lying on its pommel near the door. She managed to save herself on the doorframe, slicing her hand open on a spiteful splinter of wood and gasping in pain. Bulbous veins stood out on Jack's neck and forehead as he howled unintelligible noises in her direction. He seized a dirty mug from the desk next to him, toppling a pile of papers that slithered onto the aged rug. Hana ducked as it smashed on the lintel above her head, showering her with stained ceramic chips that tumbled past her like heavy snowfall. Defeated, Hana r an.

Chapter 46

"He's gonna kill me!" Rawhiti complained as the quad bike laboured up the endless driveway to Hana's house.

"Stop moaning!" Hana snapped. "At least you get to ride the quad. I'm five months pregnant and having to walk miles!"

"Well, if Jack dunt kill me, Mr Logan definitely will!" the young man vented, examining a rip in the handlebar of the quad.

"If you don't shut up, then *I'll* kill you," Hana retorted and he pulled a face and looked down at the steep drop on the other side of the narrow road. Hana stopped for a moment as Sacha tugged on the lead rope and rubbed her face along the cut on her leg. "Don't do that, honey," Hana pulled on the rope and used her sleeve to rub the transferred gore away from the mare's eye. Sacha blinked and snuffed at Hana's zipper, chomping her great teeth and licking her lips. "Not far now. Nearly home."

The quad bike engine strained at the low speed it took to maintain walking pace alongside Hana. Rawhiti drove dangerously near the edge in his determination to stay away from Sacha's dinner plate sized hooves. He eyed the mare with a wariness born of experience. "How come she responds to you?" he asked over the noise of the complaining engine. "I couldn't believe it that day when you rode down the mountain on her, with your wee one asleep in front of you. She's such a..." Rawhiti bit his lip as Sacha made a low sound in her chest that resembled a threatening growl.

"Oh, we didn't always like each other," Hana said, running a gentle palm over the noble forehead as Sacha plodded next to her. "The first time I rode her up here, I spent the whole time complaining. I tried everything to get Bobby to swap with me, but she wouldn't carry him."

"Who's Bobby?" The engine spluttered and grumbled and Rawhiti fiddled with the throttle.

"Flick," Hana replied, sadness creeping into her voice.

"Yeah, he took off, aye?"

Hana nodded.

"Do you reckon he killed that chick? The one they found over at Nev's place?"

Hana stopped immediately and Sacha halted behind her, as Logan had trained her to do. The mare's face was peaceful but Hana's was tortured. "Why would you ask me that?"

Rawhiti braked and his muscular pectorals wobbled under the impact of the sudden stop. Hana wondered why the young man never wore a shirt against his silky olive skin. He turned his pretty face to meet Hana's eyes. "Well, it just looks real dodgy dunnit? She gets knocked off and then he shoots through."

"I suppose." Hana's brain worked overtime. "I never thought about it like that." She chewed her lip and looked thoughtful.

"He might have been protecting you," Rawhiti offered.

"Why me?" Hana's eyes narrowed and she started walking again, towing the huge blonde mare after her. Rawhiti started the quad moving forwards again, kangarooing on the spot for a heartbeat.

"Coz he was in love with you. That's why. He knew you was upset about that chick bein' here and he might have done something about it. I would have."

Hana looked at Rawhiti with a horrified intensity. He moved quickly to iron out any misunderstandings. "Oh, like...not because I'm in love with you...oh, not that you're not gorgeous because you are...like all the boys say you are...but if I was him."

"I'm bored now." Hana decided to put him out of his misery and the dark-skinned young man looked relieved to be let off the hook.

"Don't tell Mr Logan," Rawhiti begged as he pulled alongside. Sacha turned her blue eye on him and squinted spitefully. He veered the bike to the right and Hana smirked.

"There's nothing to tell him! You put your foot in your mouth and choked on it. What's he gonna do about that?"

"Rip my f...head off," Rawhiti gushed. "He's real protective over you. The slaps he's given people are legendary around here. Apparently his dad, Reuben Du Rose could box too. Mean left hook, both of them."

"Does Logan hit people very often?" Hana fished for information, Flick's black eye occupying her inner vision and the oblivious young man opened his mouth and his brains rolled out.

"Na. I've never seen 'im do it. I just heard about it, bro. I wouldn't mess with 'im. He'd flatten me. I'm a bit scared of him actually, but not as much as Jack. He gives me the sh...he frits me bad." Rawhiti winced with the effort of squashing his volley of expletives, in front of a woman who looked as though she'd never heard such vile expressions.

"Nice people you work for," Hana mused and Rawhiti put his head back and laughed. The mare snuffed and he shut up instantly.

"Are we nearly there?" he asked as Sacha skittered sideways, faking fear as a tui burst from the trees. Her blue, wall-eye glistened with mischief as she lined the quad up with her hind feet.

"Sacha!" Hana chastised her and the mare breathed out a huge, wet sigh of defeat. "Not far now. Don't you like working for Jack?"

Rawhiti pulled a face and tried to pick his words carefully. He looked at Hana with fear in his face. "I don't know how to answer that. Well, not to you, anyway."

"Why?" Hana asked.

Rawhiti exhaled in a quick snuff, very much like Sacha's annoyed huff. "Because stuff always gets back to him. He knows *everything*. I will end up *tū-ā-kiko*."

"He would hurt you?" Hana's mind strayed to the deaf old man who had welcomed her into the Du Rose stable yard the first time. His face had creased with a grin at the completeness that the redhead offered his employer. He attended their wedding reception, hanging near the back of the room to avoid pointless conversation and he had been ecstatic at the news of Hana's first pregnancy. Phoenix adored him and Jack was firm but loving to the horses. Hana shook her head. "I don't want to disbelieve you but..."

"You're gonna anyway." Rawhiti's face hardened as he gritted his teeth, his jaw line showing through the stubbly young face.

"I don't think he's himself at the moment," Hana offered, feeling pathetic as she saw herself handling the situation all wrong. "Why don't I talk to Logan and..."

"No!" Rawhiti's shout was full of betrayal. "Don't you dare!"

Seizing her opportunity, Sacha masked her dislike of the young stable hand as defence of her mistress. She dragged the lead rope from Hana's hand, leaving a burning line across the woman's palm and aggravating the splinter's nasty trail. With a terrible squeal, she lurched for Rawhiti with teeth bared and ears flattened against her head. The quad surged forwards with a horrific backfire and the pair set off up the mountain, the lead rope trailing as the white horse chased the terrified man on the bike.

Hana stood on the single-lane track and ran a painful hand across her eyes. "Fantastic!" she said out loud. Her feet ached from the climb and she felt tired enough to lie in the undergrowth that spilled from one side of her. The darkened native bush with its ferny floor covering looked inviting. Hana peered over the edge that Rawhiti had hogged, looking down on the paddocks below. Nev's house was a tiny dot on the landscape, Sylvia's resting place still marred by the presence of a white tent even though the body was now in the morgue. The weight of the world and the awful montage of Du Rose secrets pressed down on her head. Hana tutted in irritation and forced her legs to crest the final incline to the gate.

Rawhiti was nowhere to be seen but the quad bike ticked over to itself, its nose pressed to the railings of the gate. Hana flicked the throttle back to silence it and removed the key. Sacha nosed in the undergrowth nearby, her brown eye covetously eyeing the green grass around the house. "That was very naughty!" Hana bent at the waist and snatched up the lead rope. "Stop winding him up!" The mare snickered and rubbed her forehead on Hana's sleeve as the woman wrestled with the gate catch. "It's not funny!" Hana warned her. "I don't want people to feel like that about you. Logan listens to the stable guys, *especially* Jack. It will break his heart, but he will have you destroyed if you become a danger."

Sacha hung her head and looked down at the ground. Hana stroked the rough hair on the wide cheek and laid her forehead against the mare's. "I'm talking to you as though you understand," Hana sighed. "But you probably don't. If by some small miracle you know exactly what I'm saying, then please behave up here, Sacha?"

The mare snuffed at Hana's hand and licked at the remaining scent of the apple. She sighed wetly and Hana kissed the hard bone of her long nose. "Come on." Pushing the gate open, woman and horse squeezed past the abandoned quad bike and stepped off the black tarmac and onto the lush grass. Sacha's head went down immediately and Hana pushed the gate closed behind her with her foot. Hana's stomach got in the way and she bent down to unclip the lead rope, before walking towards the house, retrieving her door keys from her pocket. Sacha munched happily behind her, eyes closed in ecstasy as she ripped long lengths of grass from the ground. Rawhiti peered down at Hana from the apex roof overhanging the front door.

"Why did you just let her go?" Incredulity laced his voice. "She's a bitch. She chased me!"

"No she didn't," Hana replied, tiredness overwhelming her as the door handle turned under her fingers. "She was playing with you. I've told her off."

"Playing?" Rawhiti's voice went up a few octaves. "She wanted to kill me!"

"Rawhiti!" Hana stepped backwards so that she could see the young man's face. Exhaustion made her tone sharper than she intended. "I've seen her herd cattle. She could have passed you and faced you down in a heartbeat. She jogged up the road behind you. It looked ridiculous!"

The young man looked ashamed for a moment and then leaned forward, his face level with the expensive spouting under the overhang. "Mrs Du Rose? I don't suppose you've got a ladder?"

After a great deal of hassle, Hana extracted the ladders from the garage and set them against the edge of the tiles, abandoning the infuriating stable lad when he looked secure enough not to kill himself. Hana sank into a kitchen chair and raised her bare feet onto another, listening to the sound of the kettle hissing behind her. Sacha moved slowly around the outside of the house, raising her head occasionally to chew and observe her surroundings. The long windows near the seating area framed the dappled white body, the regal Arab tail and proud head mixed with the strength of an Appaloosa and the cunning of a quarter horse.

"I put the ladder back in the garage." Rawhiti's voice broke through Hana's tiredness and she nodded. "I hung it up where you said."

"How on earth did you manage to get up there?" she queried and Rawhiti looked embarrassed.

"Probably 'cause I was shi...scared." He bit his lip. "Did you know that a terrified man could scale a ten foot wall without equipment?"

"Well, it's a great pity that a terrified man couldn't come back down again, isn't it?" Hana rubbed at the base of her back, which ached after carting the ladders around the front of the house. She sensed the young man's need for forgiveness and forced a smile onto her lips that resembled a grimace. "Please could you make a pot of tea?" Hana indicated the kettle as it clicked off the boil and he shuffled over in his socks to oblige. "There's a glass jug with salt in the bottom. Please could you pour some water into that? I'll use it to bathe Sacha's cut. It's still oozing."

Rawhiti plonked the chipped brown teapot on the table and went back for the tray containing cups, milk and sugar. He hovered next to Hana, unsure of whether he should sit or not. "Sit and have tea." She smiled, working it into something less horrific and managing a half decent expression of welcome. "Or if you'd rather, there's ice and juice in the fridge."

Reassured, Rawhiti rifled around in the fridge and produced a carton of orange. He had fun working the ice dispenser on the front of the stainless steel refrigerator and Hana hid her smirk. She would wipe up the splashes later. He returned to the table with a glass packed with ice cubes. "That's more ice than juice," Hana laughed and he grinned.

"That thing's fun!" he replied.

"I'll go back out to Sacha when the water's cooled," Hana said, raising her hand at the immediate protest on Rawhiti's face. "You don't have to help me. I'll be fine."

Eager to change the subject, the young man pointed to Hana's belly. "When's your baby due?"

"Not for ages yet." Hana poured herself tea and sipped the hot liquid, wincing as it burned her tongue but desperate for the refreshment. "I'm not sure why I feel so knackered."

"Were you real sick and stuff?" Rawhiti seemed interested, unless he was a good actor.

"No, I wasn't this time. I was with Phoe and it went on for months. I obviously carry boys better, because I was fine with Bo and terrible with Izzie. I threw up a couple of times, but I felt fine. Mind you, with Phoe I kept fainting too, so this baby's been way easier."

"Fainting?" Rawhiti looked nervous.

Hana laughed, unable to mask her mirth at his discomfort. "I had a heart condition and didn't realise. The pregnancy messed with my heart - increased blood flow and the demands on my old body." She patted the pacemaker over her left rib and smiled, trying to offer reassurance. "I'm fine now. I've only fainted once and that was..." Hana's voice trailed off at the memory of her awful showdown with Logan. It seemed like a lifetime ago.

"I don't know CPR. I'm crap at first aid!" Rawhiti's eyes bugged with terror.

"Then I promise not to die anywhere near you," Hana offered.

Her guest looked nervous still and sipped his drink, bashing himself in the nose with all the ice cubes and getting very little liquid.

"Do you think Logan will shoot Sacha himself?" Rawhiti slurped at his drink without elegance.

"No. She's his favourite and she's just taken offence at something. He'll train it out of her. She'll be fine. I'll keep her up here for a few days until her leg heals and then we'll see what's going on."

"She'll be an excellent guard dog," Rawhiti commented, rubbing a stray ice crystal out of his eye. "She's obviously got a thing about you."

Hana bit her lip and observed the feisty mare, pulling grass and wandering the property without a care in the world. A beautiful smile lit her face as the realisation dawned. Hana beamed at Rawhiti. "You're right, she will. Nobody will dare come onto the property with her around."

Sacha stood like the meekest of riding school hacks, while Hana huffed and puffed over her distended belly and attempted to clean the wound on the mare's leg. "I forgot how hard it was to bend down," she said, standing upright with a red face.

"Want me to do it?" Rawhiti sat on the top of the gate, holding out the jug of salt water in one hand and the bag of cotton wool balls in the other. His buttocks clenched and relaxed as he fought to balance on the thin metal rung.

"Na, this looks clean now." Hana scooped up the pile of used, fluffy balls on the ground next to her and then washed her fingers in the left over water. It felt warm and gritty. She seized the tub of manuka honey from the ground next to her and unscrewed the lid. "This is the good stuff, no expense spared on you, girlie." Hana dipped her finger into the creamy, tan honey and handed the pot to Rawhiti. He juggled with his other items and screwed the lid back on, watching as Hana smeared honey into the long gash on Sacha's front leg. The mare snuffed at Hana's hair and kept her eyes closed, looking relaxed. Hana managed to avoid banging her head on the underside of the huge face as she stood up, puffing with the effort. "It's not hot enough for that to melt and run off, so it should reduce any inflammation and stop infection. I can't see any more splinters so I must have got them all out down at the stable yard. Time will tell."

"You must love her if you're spreading twenty bucks' worth of honey on her miserable, rotten leg," Rawhiti commented and Sacha opened her blue eye and stared at him with a sentiment that made the man cringe.

"I do love her," Hana said and patted the broad forehead. "And so does my husband, so that makes it worth it to me."

"She'll get the shits if you let her have the whole section," Rawhiti commented, waving the jug so that the water slopped onto his jeans. He pulled a face and dabbed at it with the side of his hand.

Hana looked around the huge expanse of grass, left over from the hot summer. "Yeah. The cows weren't really here long enough to make a dent in it. I'll get Logan to bring up some standards and tape and we'll break feed her for a couple of days."

"What about water?" Rawhiti swatted at an imaginary fly and spilled the rest of the salt water.

"There's a stream that runs down the side of the house. She knows where it is. I'll leave her for now and Logan can sort out buckets later if he wants to fence her away from it."

"True. Can we go now?" Rawhiti held out the jug, cotton wool bag and honey towards Hana.

She took it and rolled her eyes, replacing the items in the house and locking up after her.

Down at the hotel, Hana sought her husband. After several false starts, she found him in the equipment shed, looking for something in a cupboard near the darkened rear. His eyes showed tiredness, their grey diminished against pin-prick pupils and a layer of dust filmed his face and body. "Hey, gorgeous." Logan reached for his wife and pulled her in close. His stubble scratched her chin in the kiss and his lips felt dry and gritty. It would have bothered Hana once, clad in her stiletto heels and pristine suits. But the twists and turns of life had changed her outlook and she clung to her husband's strong frame with eagerness, ignoring the dirt that tumbled from his clothes to hers.

"I took Sacha home and bathed her cut," Hana said, peering into the cupboard. A shadow board with tools stared blankly back at her, most of the slots occupied.

"Oh, thanks babe." Logan's interest turned wholly onto his wife, his errand forgotten. "I had to leave her. I felt bad but everyone was mounted up waiting. I don't know what's wrong with her at the moment. Jack had a rant when we got back. He wants me to put her down. He's had enough." His eyes filled with sadness and Logan ran a dirty hand over the skin above his mouth, giving himself a black moustache. "I dunno what to do." The scar underneath his right eye twitched and Hana reached up and stroked away one of her husband's stress-tells.

"Don't worry," she whispered. "She's happy for now."

"I love you, so much." Logan's breath tickled Hana's face, the faint scent of his familiar spearmint gum wafting over her like a comforting, warm blanket. His body relaxed as relief seized him. She smoothed her hands across the dusty skin of his cheek and stretched up for another kiss. He inhaled and ran his fingers across the base of Hana's spine, her stomach protruding between them. Logan lifted his wife, holding her tightly under her buttocks, his long arms stretching round so that his hands settled under her thighs. It put their lips level as he pressed his to hers and closed his eyes. The kiss deepened and their breath came in quiet puffs filled with passion.

Hana's eyes shot open and she gasped as Logan's body tipped and swayed with the motion of him walking backwards. "No!" she hissed as he grappled one handed for the door handle. He pushed the door roughly and the small office opened out behind him, relatively tidy in the absence of their resident mechanic, but still full of greasy, blackened pieces of broken equipment.

"Do as you're told woman!" Logan's eyes sparkled with a diamond quality as he smiled at her, worry and disappointment abandoned in favour of the excitement of dangerous lovemaking. He sat Hana gently on the littered desk and before she could hop down, turned the key in the lock and appeared in front of her again. He slipped his tee shirt over his head, leaving his dark hair sticking upwards in a curly, static-filled tumble, his huge arm muscles flexing with the action.

Hana sighed and shook her head, running her fingers over the strong wall of chest. "I said no." Her green eyes narrowed as her body betrayed her and Logan smiled that sexy half-smirk that he kept just for her.

"I heard ya," he whispered as his stubble ground along the tender skin of Hana's neck. "I just don't believe ya."

Hana sighed, deliberately letting it sound like resignation; but as Logan's rough cheeks grazed her shoulder, she smirked and pursed her lips. Her hands strayed over the ugly raised scar - the one that Sylvia had never touched with her perfectly manicured fingers, but thoughts of the other woman were rapidly dispelled by her husband's expert attentions.

Chapter 47

Hana woke in the plush bedroom with tortured thoughts of Bobby coursing through her brain. It was yet another disturbed night fuelled by rampant worries. *What if she had helped a murderer to escape?* Too many things crowded in on her and sleep evaded her after the first thoughts leaked through to her consciousness.

Hana turned to her sleeping lover, his face turned towards her and his right hand resting on her stomach as he snoozed. His face looked peaceful, a rarity nowadays. The idea of confession left her as quickly as it came and Hana bit her lip and extracted herself from the four poster bed backwards. She laid Logan's hand gently on the mattress and it crept for a moment, looking for her. He stilled. Satisfied, Hana left the room.

Phoenix slept on her back with her chubby arms raised high above her head, tiny snores issuing from her rosebud lips. Hana moved quietly down to the kitchen to make a cup of tea and found Tama sat at the table. His body seemed rigid and uncompromising and his hair was ruffled and unkempt. "Hey, boy," Hana ran her hand through his dark curls and Tama relaxed his two-handed grip on the mug in front of him.

"Hey."

"What's the matter? It's five o'clock in the morning." Hana knew the signs instantly and a part of her shrugged in annoyance at herself for asking.

"Lucy." The one word answer contained a swirling pit of buried emotion, which threatened to break through into the young man's controlled expression. "She dumped me."

"Oh. Sorry." Logan had warned her, but Hana managed not to convey that in her sympathy. For Tama's sake, it needed to sound genuine. "Where have you been? I got worried about you, right around the time Odering started looking for you for your statement."

Tama shrugged and his nonchalant response was reassuring for Hana. A man who seemed so unbothered by a cop's interest in him, could not have committed the murder. "I drove to Hamilton and she said a friend of hers saw me with another girl in a nightclub in Auckland. So we're done."

"What girl in Auckland?" Hana felt wary.

"I have no idea. I get home from work and I'm knackered. I go home to sleep and then within minutes of my head touching the pillow, it's time to get up again."

"Did you tell Lucy that?"

Tama rolled his eyes, an epitome of the rude teenager and Hana felt herself withdraw. Years of being drawn into conversations like that with Bodie, had left her expecting to be blamed or her advice labelled as stupid or irrelevant. She made tea with the avid interest of a connoisseur, despite the fact it was regular decaf. Hana made a show of dipping the bag in her mug and adding the milk, buying herself time to find the right wise words to say. Nothing came to her, so she admitted defeat and turned to leave the room.

"Sorry." Tama's apology sounded more sincere than grudging. Hana clutched her drink and observed him, still not sure whether to stay or go. "I'm just really upset. I did everything she wanted and this is what I get for it."

"What did she want?" Hana kept her voice light and soft.

"No sex before marriage, me to do all the romancing and stay on track with my training. That worked didn't it?"

"Would you like me to speak to Lucy?" Hana ventured. Bodie would have pitched a fit like a Tasmanian devil at the suggestion but Tama was different. She risked it. The young man turned to her with a stricken look, his grey eyes turning to a gritty shade and he shook his head.

"Thanks, Ma, but you can't now."

"Did you delete her number? I can probably find it somewhere..."

"No!" Sounding more insistent, Tama shook his head. "I have deleted it. I don't ever want to speak to her again. It's over. I'll move on. I'm due back at work at the weekend so I'll head out this afternoon."

"Why don't you get some sleep first? You look done in. Did you argue until late?"

Tama shook his head. "I don't want to talk about it anymore."

"Fair enough. Want a hug?" Hana laid her drink on the table and the young man nodded with a slight inclination of his dark, glossy head. She wrapped her arms around his strong neck, feeling the tension of his body and the grief of emotional loss resonating out of him.

"I was gonna ask her to marry me. I finish my probation soon and I'll get stationed at a fire headquarters somewhere. It could have been local. They offered."

"Poor baby." Hana kissed Tama's head and held him for a second longer. "It's her loss. You're gorgeous."

"Yeah. So much for that."

Hana left the young man in peace and went into the lounge to curl up on the wide sofa to think. She heard him scrape his chair back and put his mug in the dishwasher, recognising the shushing sound of his socks on the tiles as he left the room. Hana tutted to herself, wishing God would give the poor boy a break. As it turned out, Tama's troubles were self-inflicted. A familiar chirping sound came from the kitchen and forced her to shift herself to answer it. Hana yanked her phone from the charger on the side and opened the new text.

'Hey, Hana. It's Lucy. I need to talk to Tama and he's not answering my calls. I've accused him of something and it was a huge mistake. I need to apologise.'

For once, Hana engaged her brain before she replied and padded down to Tama's room to give him the good news. He didn't respond to her gentle tap on the door but she heard him moving around in his ensuite bathroom. Water swilled as he cleaned his teeth in the sink. "Tama," Hana whispered as she pushed the door open, aware of Phoenix snoozing in the room next door. "Sweetheart, Lucy's texted me because she..."

Tama stood in the tiny bathroom in his boxer shorts. His muscular frame was built like Logan's; firm and well-defined, work-hardened and strong. Raised veins covered his muscles and belied the sheer power of a twenty-year old, who could carry an overweight man safely up a flight of stairs and out of a burning building.

Hana gasped. "Tama Du Rose! What did you do?"

With a wistful smirk, Tama turned towards her and shrugged. He touched one of the raised, bruised areas with a flicker of pride, a woman's lips standing out on his flesh like an emblem. "If I'm accused of it, I thought I might as well be guilty of it."

"You idiot! You slept with a woman *that* quickly? She only broke up with you last night!"

"Actually, I slept with three women and I forgot how much fun it was."

Hana's mouth gaped until she realised how unattractive the look was. She closed her lips with a snap. "Please tell me you're kidding and you were...careful." She struggled to keep the horror out of her voice. Tama shrugged and in frustration, Hana turned to leave, cannoning straight into her husband, who leaned casually against the door frame in his boxer shorts, arms folded. His grey eyes observed his nephew with a glint of amusement. Tama acted up to the testosterone laden audience like a player in a bad scene.

"Yes, Ma. I was careful. And yes, it was three at once. It was awesome. They were hot and fun and I'm not sorry. Lucy can stick her ideals and her beliefs. I've done everything she wanted and yet the first opportunity she gets, she turns me over *that* fast." Tama clicked his fingers to demonstrate his irritation.

"You silly boy," Hana breathed. "Lucy's sorry and she wants to talk to you. She held her phone up in the air, Lucy's text still backlit on the screen. How can you come back from this, now?"

Tama shrugged again and rolled his eyes. "Maybe I don't wanna. I'll get some sleep and then head home. I'm a bit bushed."

Logan snorted and Hana glared at him. She left the room and hissed, "*Don't* encourage him," at her husband. She was half way down the hallway when she heard Logan's low voice.

"Three? At once. Geez mate."

Hana didn't hear all of Tama's reply but her husband's laugh at the next sentence wound her up, at the men's blatant disrespect of foolish women. "Yeah," Tama boasted. "I left the fat one till last."

She shook her head and her eyes bugged as Tama's voice came again. She halted with the realisation of the trouble his words would cause and heard the painful grunt as Logan's body landed on his nephew's. She almost went back to break it up and then thought better of it. Tama had pressed the self-destruct button yet again, but telling her husband how much he enjoyed himself with the redhead first, was not a clever idea.

Chapter 48

"**D**on't come to me for sympathy!" Hana held her hand out palm upwards as the men wandered into the kitchen, jostling each other through the door.

"He's just jealous," Tama commented, pulling a face at his uncle. "When was the last time you managed…?"

Logan raised his hand to slap the younger man and Tama ducked away. "Want another split lip, Uncle? I'm more than capable of doing you some serious damage - then you can kiss my ass goodbye for good!" Tama's grey eyes flashed with danger and both powerful men squared up to each other.

Hana turned to see an oozing cut on Logan's lower lip and blood trickling down his chin. Tama had an open wound above his eyebrow and her heart sank. "So we're back to this, are we?" she asked them both. "Lucy falsely accuses *you*," she stabbed her finger at the silly boy in front of her, "so you go off and use some dumb girls to make your ego feel better! Then you come home and wind Logan up to make him want to finish the job. Was that your intention? Is it total self-annihilation you're looking for, or just to alienate everyone who loves you? For goodness sake, how many times do we have to go back here?" Hana slammed her palm down on the table, enraged by the pain that shot through her wrist. As an attempt to make her point, it was an epic fail.

"*You* should know better!" She jabbed a pointy finger at her husband. "And what's next Tama? You're leaving for good are you? How do you want this to end? You storm off back to Auckland and then make it so that you can't come back here? You tell me that we're the only family you've ever known and then you deliberately wreck it for yourself. I will never understand you Du Rose men. You know what? Phoenix Du Rose said over and over again in those diaries, '*The Du Rose men will be the ruin of this family.*' I've watched you both do this so many times, I'm losing the will to live with it anymore." Hana pushed her chair back roughly from the table and thrust her mug away from her. Cool tea slopped onto the wood and made a puddle in a formerly hidden dip. She stalked from the room and slammed her bedroom door, feeling the old lady's words wash over her like the curse it was.

Hana slumped onto the bed and put her hands over her ears to block out the matriarch's whispers.

"Mama, lemme in." The toddler's voice came from near the bottom of the door and Hana leapt to open it. Phoenix waddled in with Fluffy in her arms, one of his ears bent inside out. "Mens shoutins. It scary me."

"Sorry, baby." Hana picked her daughter up and cradled her. "Come for a cuddle?" Phoenix nodded her fluffy head against her mother's chest and then snuggled down with her underneath the covers. The bed was still rucked up from Logan's exit and Hana felt his warmth lingering in the sheets.

"Bad boys waked me up." Phoe pouted and pushed her face into her mother's armpit, squeezing her eyes tight shut and showing all the signs of wanting to return to the safety of sleep. Hana stroked the slender back with gentle hands and felt her daughter slumber easily, as only carefree children could. She sighed and thought about Sylvia again, the woman's death weighing heavily on her mind. She was no nearer to solving the mystery. With each pass through the list of possible murderers,

Hana found it surprisingly easy to discount all prospective subjects. No one person had a greater motive than any other. The whole thing seemed futile. Whichever way she looked at the problem, she and Logan were the most likely killers. To her surprise, Hana dozed off in the silent bedroom, the sound of Sacha's continuous munching outside the window providing the only distraction.

Logan was absent when Hana woke later and a note on the kitchen counter in his neat, left-handed scrawl told her he was sorry for his behaviour and had gone to work. Hana felt his disgrace leaking from the tatty page. She went outside in her nightdress and wellington boots to bathe Sacha's leg with more salt water, replacing the honey and working it into the wound gently with her fingers. "It's looking good, old girl," she mused, squatting down to check her work. "But once it's all better, you'll have to go back down the mountain. You can't hide up here for the rest of your life. You know Logan's rule, hey?" Hana looked up at the bristly chin and the mare eyed her calmly. "*Everyone has to earn their keep.*" She mimicked the dictatorial mantra of her husband in a low voice that hurt her throat and Sacha thanked her for the reminder, by snuffing snot all down the back of her nightdress.

"Euwgh!" Hana stood up and pulled a face and the mare winked her blue wall-eye. Then she did it again, spattering the front with warm breath and green blobs. "If that's your idea of thanks, then it rates with Tama's. *He's such a stupid boy!*"

Sacha pushed her white forehead into Hana's arm and rubbed against her in a quick, up and down motion, satiating an itch. Hana giggled and reached for the hard poll between the horse's ears, scratching it for her. "The one place on your body you can't scratch," Hana crooned. More grass-laden snot issued from the huge nostrils, signifying happiness and peace.

The woman looked down at her clothing and wrinkled her pretty nose. The granny nightie had been dragged from her packing boxes at the start of the winter. Pale mauve with a tiny flower pattern, it was flannelette and warm.

"That's the unsexiest piece of clothing I've ever seen in my life!" Logan complained frequently, his amorous attempts thwarted by the tiny buttons at the neck and the voluminous length of it. "It's like a bloody fortress!"

Hana ran her fingers over the worst patch of snot and sighed as the remaining honey and clumps of horse hair added to the mess.

Without warning, Sacha's head shot up at a sound only she had registered. Hana took a step back, protecting her stomach by instinct. The huge mare fixed her eyes on an area at the side of the property, where the bush was held back from encroaching by a sturdy wooden fence. Sunshine made the canopy appear darker beyond the trees and Hana saw nothing to be alarmed about. Sacha's eyes became wild and the whites showed around her irises as she stared with an alertness that was frightening and threatened catastrophe. Her muscular frame tensed, veins rising out of her powerful shoulders like watersheds and pressing against the white skin. She made an awful noise. Not a gentle snuff, but a snort of anger as the Arab in her breeding roused. The horse moved but not her usual, graceful, floating gait. She charged at the fence.

Hana squeaked and stepped back, kicking over the jug with the remainder of the salt water. Her rubber boot sent the manuka honey spinning in a different direction and she stumbled, managing to right herself at the last minute. Sacha snorted in fury and ran at the fence numerous times, jarring to a halt and skidding in the mud. She was terrifying. With teeth bared and eyes rolling, the mare lost patience with the barrier and barged it with her shoulder.

"Sacha, no!" Mindful of her own safety, but concerned that the mare would do herself further harm, Hana ran over in her boots, the granny-nightie flapping and her red hair streaming out behind her. "Stop!"

Hana reached the fence and gripped it for reassurance as the mare turned towards her. Sacha's breath came in short gasps and her ears lay flat against her head. Hana's chest tensed in fear as the mare took a few steps backwards and then reared. She was sideways on to Hana as her enormous hooves pawed the air and head back, she let out a terrifying call. The timbre of it was ear splitting and even to Hana's untrained ears - it was a warning. When the heavy front feet made contact with the ground, they sent out a splat of mud to further embellish poor Hana's nightie. Sacha's body remained perfectly square and she stared into the bush with menace in the brown and blue eyes.

Hana gulped and stood still. Turning her head without further spooking the mare, she peered into the bush. "There's nothing there," she whispered, her breathing tight and her body shaking from the receding adrenaline.

Then she saw it, on the floor of the bush a few metres in and as soon as she spied it, she smelled the familiar scent. The ground was moist and the risk of fire slight, but Hana clambered over the post and rail fence and picked her way towards the thin trail of smoke. The hand-rolled cigarette lay on the ground, discharging its poison fruitlessly. Hana stepped on it with her boot and then reached through the vines to retrieve it. She held it between thumb and finger, careful not to touch the spiralled end which had recently been in someone's mouth. Long and thin, strings of brown tobacco floundered at its end, blackened by the last of the burning. Peering through the vines, Hana spotted the pressed area, revealing footprints in the soft earth and then her keen eyes, accustomed to the gloom, saw the trail of damaged supplejack vine left by the owner of the cigarette as they made their escape.

Tripping and stumbling, Hana ran for the boundary fence and the angry mare, desperate for the protection of both. Bush lawyer's hooky thorns snagged at the nightie and the thighs beneath. Hana wrenched them away with fingers that bled. But she held the cigarette aloft, determined not to lose her evidence. Hana climbed awkwardly over the fence, aware that the watcher may still be there. She hurried around to the front door and hurled herself on the bench to remove her boots.

"Oh God!" Hana appealed to her maker, staring at her pink toes on the cold concrete as she put her head between her knees to stem the panic. The scraping of hooves in front of her revealed that Sacha had followed. Her white body blocked access to the woman as she stood guard over her and a wet nostril reached out and sniffed Hana's messy red locks. Hana raised green eyes that were wide and frightened. "Who's watching me?" she asked the mare. "Sylvia's dead, they've dealt with Asher and even Flick's gone."

Sacha rested her chin on Hana's head, offering comfort as one mother to another, but it was uncomfortable. "Rawhiti said you'd be a good guard dog," Hana sniffed, fighting ready tears. Sacha whickered softly and rubbed her forehead up and down Hana's arm. "Ooh, watch out." Hana gripped the cigarette between shaking fingers and kissed the downy hair above Sacha's nostril. The mare stepped back as Hana stood up, grateful for the heavy shoulder to lean on. "I wish you could tell me who it was."

In the kitchen, Hana lay the precious evidence on a saucer and turned around. Tama stood in the doorway observing her. His brows knitted in confusion. "Strange running clothes, Ma." His smile was wistful and sad. He pointed at the clumps of bush lawyer adorning the hem and the unfortunate rip in the side. "Logan will be gutted." His manner made Hana suspicious and she watched him carefully. Tama shrugged. "I'm just packing up and then I'll be out of your hair. Thanks for everything." He left the room with his shoulders hunched and the weight of the world pressing down on his head.

"Don't you dare run away, Tama Du Rose!" Hana's sharp rebuke made the young man jump as he attempted to stuff too much clothing into a small rucksack.

"Geez! Don't *do* that!" Guilt made him tetchy and easily unnerved.

"Then what's all the, '*Thanks for everything,*' rubbish? Yeah, you screwed up. Why make it ten times worse?"

"Please don't make it harder for me?" Tama begged. He threw his backside onto the bed and it groaned in protest. Tama rubbed his fists into his eyes and kept them closed, even after he finished and his hands lay twitching in his lap. Hana sat on the bed next to him and put her arm around his neck.

"Stupid boy! You think you can't make a mistake and be forgiven? I spend my life apologising."

"No, I can't. I'm like Liza; completely ruined. I just need to live by myself and stay away from people, like she does. I'll throw myself into firefighting instead of relationships and do the world a favour."

Hana turned his face towards her, disturbed by the hopelessness in Tama's eyes. He resisted and the movement was strained. "Then I've done a very poor job with you, my love." Tender fingers stroked the rough skin of the young man's cheek, undaunted by the tear that trickled over them. "I love you, Tama Du Rose," Hana whispered, deliberately repeating the precious name that Logan had paid to bestow on him. "You're *my* boy now. You're irritating and you eat everything out of the pantry. You open your mouth and put both feet in and I love you. I'll always love you. You're my friend and confidante and the day you graduate from fire service training, I want to be there. I'll be the proudest mummy in the crowd and won't be able to stop myself crying and making a show of you. You've come so far, babe. Don't cut yourself off from us. Please?"

"But I don't deserve you. I've messed up!" Angry fists formed on rigid thighs and Tama turned away embarrassed, as another tear coursed over Hana's fingers. She moved her hand to his shoulder and lay her head on it, feeling him tremble beneath her contact.

"Can I still see you?" Her voice sounded heavy with sadness and disappointment. "And what about Phoenix? She adores you. Can she still see you?" Hana's eyes filled with tears at the finality of the moment - and her own failure to redeem this lost young man.

Tama inhaled and sobbed at the same time. It took him by surprise and he failed to get control before the egocentric wall collapsed as rubble. His raw brokenness was exposed and terrified, he reached for Hana. Weeping obscured his words as Hana provided a lifeline for his grief, not for the first time. "Shhhh," she soothed. Sobs shook his strong body, reducing it to that of a frightened child and Hana let her own tears mingle with his, stroking his back and feeling him sweat in anguish. His misery soaked her shoulder and collar.

When he was done, Tama lay limply over Hana, his arms wrapped around her body and his face pressed into her saturated hair. His body shook with the aftermath of his crying and his chest hitched sporadically, as his lungs fought to restore equilibrium. The air molecules seemed to ping with the sound of silence, until Hana heard the thud of tiny feet on floorboards next door. "You're not going anywhere today." Hana kissed the side of Tama's head. "You can leave tomorrow when you feel better about things. Today, I'm keeping you close. I want quality time with my son." She smoothed away the remaining wetness from his face as right on cue, Phoenix poked her fluffy head around the door frame. A sweet riser, she beamed and bounced across the room, dangling her soft toy by one hoof.

"Me do cuddles," she sang, clambering roughly onto Tama's knees and pushing herself up between the adults. Tama groaned as a bony knee crushed a delicate part of his anatomy and Phoenix looked up with mischief in her eyes. Her face clouded with pain as she saw the trail of tears on Tama's cheek and with a tiny hand she reached up and touched it. "Oh. Why you sad?" she whispered, compassion and fear causing her own grey eyes to fill.

"He needs lots of cuddles today." Hana knitted her embrace around both children. "We need to love him heaps."

"I love 'im heaps," Phoenix's sincerity was touching and Tama gulped.

"Well, let me get both of you breakfast and then I've got some things I need your bro's help with."

"K, nen." Phoenix slid off Tama's knees backwards with eagerness rooted in the word *breakfast*. She padded off to the kitchen, all bare feet and bulging night-nappy. Hana stroked Tama's damp hair back from his head.

"Everything will be ok," she promised with a kiss to his cheek.

Tama shook his head. "Try telling that to Lucy," he sighed.

"Yeah, about that. She texted me. Apparently there's been some huge mistake and she knows it wasn't you at the nightclub. She's been trying to contact you. That's what I came in to say earlier when I saw the..."

"I know." Tama ran his palm across his eyes. "I read her texts. I've been ignoring her calls too."

"Maybe don't make any decisions today," Hana soothed. "It was her error in the first place, so it's fine if you make her wait."

Tama shook his head. "I don't want to see her again. I need to put it... and her...and the other thing behind me." He grimaced, possibly at some pornographic memory and Hana winced. Tama caught the fleeting expression and smirked. "You've led a very sheltered life, Ma."

"Thank goodness!" she exclaimed. "I don't think foursomes are really my style. Far too many pairs of eyes to hide my stretch marks from. I've only got two hands."

Tama snorted, his familiar twinkle restored in the fathomless grey Du Rose eyes. "Do you think it's possible to be forgiven for something...you really enjoyed?"

Hana frowned and pushed at the firm bicep under her hand. "Horrid boy! You can't say sorry if you're not. It's false."

"I'm *sorry* about the consequences," Tama confessed. He smirked again and the lovable rogue was back. "But it was quite good fun..."

"La, la, la," Hana put her fingers in her ears and stood up. "I don't want to know." She reached the door and then turned back. "But Tama, that kind of sex is quite disrespectful to women, sweetheart. Love isn't meant to be like that. It's what concerns me most about this. I know it's probably what Kane encouraged, but it's not right."

Tama nodded slowly. "Yeah, it's not my usual. To be honest, if anyone came off worse, it was me. They were vicious." He rubbed at the site of one of the raised love bites and grimaced.

"Well just don't end up like us," Hana mused with sadness. "You don't want to be happily married with a couple of nice kids and have some woman turn up at your door with a long-lost son or daughter." Her eyes held a faraway look and Tama nodded.

"Message received, Ma."

Chapter 49

Phoenix slurped milk from her cereal bowl like a piggie, putting it up to her face and spilling most of it down her pyjamas.

"Phoe, no!" Hana snatched the bowl away before the rest of the liquid ended up in her lap.

"Tama dun it!" Phoenix Du Rose looked indignant and pointed an accusing finger at her cousin.

"I don't make that kind of mess, woman! I'm way more skilled."

"Don't you dare!" Hana thumped the plate of toast on the table between the pair and confiscated his bowl. Phoenix's eyes bugged with happiness. She waved her spoon in the air and pointed to a jar of Marmite.

"Mmmmmmnnnn!"

Tama spread the disgusting treacle on the bread, licking his fingers afterwards. Hana clamped a hand over her mouth and fought a rising sickness. "I thought you'd be over that by now," the young man said, looking at her with curiosity.

"Not where that stuff's concerned. I never really had morning sickness this time. It's been great. Apart from...that."

Phoenix smiled with it in her teeth and Hana turned quickly, needing to excuse herself. Without removing her hand from her lips she said, "I'll get a shower and when I come back, I need your advice with something important."

"That thing on the side?" Tama pointed the brown knife towards the saucer containing the cigarette, his observant nature already a step ahead. Hana nodded and left the room before the smell of Marmite completely unpicked her.

Phoenix played with her Lego on the floor, trying to ram some poor little man's backside onto the rounded point of a train carriage. "Won't go on!" She tipped him back into the carton in frustration and reached for another victim.

Hana kept her voice low and conversational. "If it wasn't for Sacha chasing them off, what would have happened? Would they have approached me or just kept watching? And who is it? It must be something to do with Sylvia's death but when I mentioned it to Odering, he brushed it off."

"What did he say, exactly?"

Hana tutted and did an impression of the stuffy detective. "Tell your husband about it, Mrs *Du Rose*. I don't think your farm problems are anything to do with me."

"Farm problems?" Tama snorted. "What an idiot. He's such a townie! You've got a bloody stalker!"

"Do you know anyone on the farm who smokes these kinds of cigarettes?" Hana pushed the saucer across to Tama with her index finger.

"It depends what's in it," Tama said honestly. "If it's weed, then yeah, a few. But not openly. Logan would fire their asses."

"Open it then." Hana fetched a sharp knife and plonked it on the table in front of him.

"But it's evidence!"

"Of what? And nobody's interested. Just open it and tell me if it's got weed in it."

"I could probably light it and tell you that."

"Be serious!" Hana slapped Tama's hand. "Do this properly. I'll take photos on my phone."

Exasperated, Tama opened the flimsy white paper and the long tendrils spilled out into the saucer. He flicked through them with a ratty nail. "Yeah, it's definitely laced with marijuana. But tiny amounts, not enough to get a kick from."

"The people you know who smoke it - who are they?" Hana pushed her face forward in eagerness. "I want to know."

Tama sat back in his seat and shook his head. "If I tell you, then you tell Logan and he fires them. I'm not doing that."

Hana's jaw dropped. "But it's wrong! They're driving machinery and vehicles. Anything could happen. So he'll be within his rights."

"So, I'm not telling." Tama pushed his chair back and tipped the spliff into the dustbin, before loading the saucer into the dishwasher.

"I needed that!" Hana complained. "It's evidence."

"You said it wasn't. Now you're contradicting yourself."

"Who is it, Tama? This is scaring me. I need to know so I can stop them. I can't live like this; feeling like someone's always watching me." She stood up, wringing her hands together in fear. Phoenix stopped playing and watched the adults.

Tama embraced her within strong arms. He rested his chin on the top of Hana's head. "Ma, they smoke socially, with a beer at night. This is different. It's such a small amount, that it's...almost like a top up. Maybe the person watching the house is sick and it's medicinal."

"What if they're a junkie and they kill me?" Hana pressed her face into Tama's sweatshirt and felt him shrug.

"Na. I'll go down to the bunkhouse and talk to the guys tonight. But I'm tellin' ya, when they use it, they get hammered on it. No half measures."

"Om er!" Hana bit her lip and looked indignant.

"If you tell Logan I told you that, I won't help you!"

"Tama!"

"I mean it!"

Phoenix looked at the Lego lady in her delicate fingers and brought the plastic doll right up to her nose. "Mean it!" she said with violence and Hana chose to stop her debate.

"Trust me," Tama whispered and Hana rolled her eyes. Whenever Logan said *that,* it meant trouble.

The trio spent the day baking - well Hana and Phoenix baked and Tama ate non-stop. They chilled out with movies, snoozed on the sofa and enjoyed each other's company. At the end of it, Hana felt quite rested. "What should I do?" Hana asked Tama, as Phoenix dozed on his chest with her thumb in her mouth. "Lucy keeps texting and ringing me. It's getting embarrassing."

"Give it here." Tama held his hand out and Hana extracted the vibrating device from down the side of the sofa cushion. He peered at the screen over Phoenix's fluffy hair. "The reception's crap up here. I thought Logan let some guys put an aerial up in exchange for free coverage."

"He did. But there's problems with it."

Tama's fingers flicked over the keys and curious, Hana tried to peer over his shoulder. "Are you texting her back?" She took the phone back from the young man's long fingers and stared at the blank screen. "You weren't rude, were you? She'll know it's not me."

"I blocked her number." Tama's voice sounded flat and Hana rubbed the flat of her hand over his thigh.

"Sorry, darling," she whispered and he nodded.

"Not as sorry as me."

Tama drove Hana's ute down to the bunkhouse just as Logan appeared in the old farm ute. He looked shattered. "Where's he going?" he asked Hana, as the elderly driver's door creaked shut behind him and Tama gunned his newish Holden Colorado towards the top of the driveway.

"Down to the bunkhouse to say goodbye to the stockmen." She cringed at her partial truth.

"Well, Odering wants to see him before he leaves. That guy's getting on my nerves. I know he thinks I did it. He's spent a lifetime wanting to lock me up and now's his chance."

Logan refused Hana's baking and went for a shower after kissing his little girl goodnight. "No singing tonight, *e taku ipo*. Daddy doesn't feel like celebrating his ancestors at the moment. They're all a bunch of..."

"Logan," Hana interrupted him. "I'll read Phoe a story, it's fine."

Logan kissed his wife with dusty lips in the doorway and Phoenix was entertained by two read-throughs of Hairy Maclary from Donaldson's dairy. "I don't know why I always read it in a Scots accent," she mused to the dozing girl. "It's how I read it to Bo and Izzie in England, not realising it was written by a New Zealander. Weird hey?"

Phoenix didn't answer, so Hana kissed her on the forehead and left the room, pulling the door against the doorframe. Logan intercepted her in the bedroom, a towel wrapped around his midsection and leaving very little to the imagination. "Stop!" she giggled. "Tama will be back soon."

"I'll be really quick," her husband teased. "You won't even know what's happened."

"Whatever!" Hana burst out laughing. Logan pinned her against the bedroom wall and stripped her clothing off piece by piece until she stopped giggling and complaining and sought him out with hands and lips.

"Now I have to get dressed again," she grumbled later, struggling to untangle one of her legs from the bed sheet.

"No you don't. Stay with me." Logan wrapped his arms around her and pinioned Hana in a firm grip. "You don't have to get up." He pushed his face into her hair and rested his leg across hers.

"It's Tama's last night and he had quite an upset last night. I want to make sure he's ok."

"Yeah. Hell of an upset." Hana heard Logan smirk in the darkness.

"You shouldn't encourage him! What if one of those girls had been your daughter? If wouldn't be so funny then; even if she was consenting."

Logan's body stiffened next to hers and he shuffled with guilt. "I never thought about it like that."

"Well start to," Hana chided him. "Your mother taught you better than that. Tama didn't have a mother, so stop undermining me."

"Sorry." Logan's silence was foreboding and Hana relented, turning to face him and pulling his head onto her chest.

"What's wrong?"

"Everything," he replied and his voice sounded heavy. "This business with Asher has really got to me. Ungrateful little..." Logan sighed. "The damage that kid's done is crazy. Oh look, we can come back from it but part of me wonders why I should bother."

"Do you just mean the financial damage?" Hana kept her voice light.

"Not really. Anahera is a mess and Nev looks like he's gonna bawl every time he looks at me. At least I know now which herd he stuffed up so if I can keep them separate, we should be ok. It's the hotel dams so we'll just keep Charolaise off the menu and call it home grown beef. If he had wrecked the lot, I would have chucked it all in, sold up and gone."

"What happened about the developers?" Hana asked, still seeking her watcher.

"Gone," Logan said with confidence.

"How do you know?" Hana asked, seeking his reassurance.

"Because the joker pushing through the mountain development just settled damages to his clients, an hour before Che bought him out."

"The Triads made him sell?"

"Don't be sorry for him, Hana. He doesn't deserve it. "

"You know, one day, Logan, Che is going to demand a favour of you that you really can't do," Hana sighed. She felt Logan's hair shuffle against his pillow as he laid back."

"Other way, babe. He'll owe me until the day he dies. Ain't nothin' gonna change that."

Hana rolled onto her side and felt for Logan's body as he receded away from her. "Why?"

She heard his brain ticking inside his head as he sought to either dodge the question, or tell her the truth. She wouldn't know which, until his mouth opened. All she was certain of, was that he wouldn't lie. "Remember I told you that Mrs Che took over the 'firm' when Che had a heart attack a few years ago?"

Hana nodded on her pillow and waited, blocking out the memory of Mrs Che's threats and her gimlet eyes. The bed shuddered under her quivering body and sensing her angst, Logan reached for her hand.

"Well, I was there. Their base was a nice restaurant in downtown Auckland. It was a front for all their work. It's where I first met Che. About seven years ago, after I came back to New Zealand, we had a meeting and he just keeled over onto the floor. His guys jumped me. They thought I did something to him. Mrs Che screamed and screamed, this awful high pitched wail. His lips went blue and I could tell what was wrong. My grandmother died the same way when I was five. Everyone thinks I don't remember, but I do. I was shouting 'heart attack' and 'ambulance' but so many of Che's men don't speak English. Mrs Che made them let me go but he'd already gone. I did CPR on him for ten minutes before the ambulance came but the cops knew what the restaurant was and wouldn't let the ambos in without them. I carried him outside to them and Che lived. There was some damage to his brain. His speech was odd for a while and Mrs Che stepped up. They sold that place and moved over the bridge. I don't think anyone could face being there anymore."

"When I had my heart attack..." Hana's words were cut off by Logan's lips landing hard against hers. He hadn't shaved and a day's stubble scratched at her chin.

"Don't," he whispered. He loved her for a second time, so different from earlier. He felt like someone else in her bed and Hana enjoyed this rare outing of a more tender Logan. He was the man from the motel, vulnerable and needy and made her feel powerful.

"I suppose you're going to get into that hideous nightie," he groaned later, his words slurred with sleep.

"Na, I threw it away," Hana whispered. "Too much stuff on it."

"Thank God for that," Logan breathed. "It was like being married to Leslie between the sheets."

"Gee, thanks."

On the pretext of being thirsty, Hana slipped into her dressing gown, equally unattractive in her husband's opinion. She went to the kitchen and waited for Tama. He returned just after eleven, jovial and loud. "You drove my new car up that mountain drunk?" Hana raged at him.

"I'm not drunk," he hiccoughed.

"How many did you have? Actually, don't bother! Just tell me about the weed."

"Oh yeah!"

For a moment, Hana considered physical violence. "You forgot why you went down, didn't you?"

"Nope." Tama swayed on his feet and observed Hana gormlessly. "They can't get it anymore. The guy in the township that used to sell it, was taking the money off Leslie for her husband's debt. Remember? We all went down there and beat him up!" Tama did a fist pump to empty air and overbalanced. "Logan made him eat his own teeth and he split not long after. Gone north."

"Why does everyone in your world, *go north?*" Hana exclaimed and Tama laughed.

"That's very funny."

"No it isn't. And nor are you. So nobody grows it and nobody buys it here? So whoever keeps turning up to watch the house, isn't from the property? It's not someone I know?"

"Oh, you're hurting my head," Tama complained.

"You're such an idiot!" Hana's frustration was on show, but wasted on the young man.

"I know," he hiccoughed again and a sob leaked out. "But I love you so much. You're all I've got in this world."

"Oh great! *Loving Tama*. Only narrowly preceded by *Horny Tama*."

"Will you sleep with me?" The tall man swayed on his feet. "I need help into bed." He attempted a lascivious smile that failed, making him look more like a comic strip duck.

"I'm not sleeping with you. And I'm definitely not helping you to bed." Hana skirted the room trying to look threatening. "And if you try and get into bed with Logan and me again, I'll let him take your head off."

Tama put his head down and started to cry. Used to his drunken antics, although much less so in the last year, Hana made her escape, knowing that when she awoke she would find him exactly where he was, only hopefully in a more horizontal position.

Chapter 50

"I'm too bloody old for this!" Hana raged at Tama the next morning. He sat with his head in his hands, a giant mug of black coffee in front of him. "You were meant to drive home today and you're probably over the limit. If you dented my car, Logan will kill you and if you survive that, I'll finish you off!"

"Ooh, please stop shouting. It hurts. You should have seen the state of Ryan. He fell up the stairs. The last I saw of him, Leslie was whacking him around the butt with a broom." Tama laughed and then groaned. "Ow!"

"You took Ryan drinking?" Hana's voice rose an octave and Tama winced. "I am so fed up with you!"

The sound of the front door slamming sent Tama into a tail spin of agony and he laid his head down on his forearms. Leslie bustled into the kitchen, instantly putting her hands on her hips as she spotted Tama. "I want a word with you, *moko*."

"Please, not now." He pushed his chair back and staggered from the room, clutching his head. Leslie maintained her angry demeanour until both women heard his bedroom door close and then she giggled. "Oosh, he was a state. Been drinkin' with the bro's. They were only gone two hours, bloody lightweights."

"I'm so sorry," Hana began, dropping into the role of disgraced parent. "I sent him down on an errand and he came back like that."

"Well, I'm here about that other boy, Ryan. He's livin' downstairs in Liza's old room but he's got no mama now and he's alone in a strange land. Alfie says Michael don't want to know, so I wanna take him on."

"But...aren't you and Alfred shipping out soon anyway? Won't that be setting him up to get hurt again?"

"Oh, Alfred went up north to his *whanau* to check it out and he didn't like being around them. That *hapu* has always been a bit weird so for the time bein' youse stuck with us."

"Oh that's wonderful," Hana breathed, relief in her voice.

"Ah, *kōtiro*. Youse my *whanau* now." Leslie almost snapped Hana's neck in a stranglehold embrace.

"You having Ryan would be a relief," Hana sighed. "We do have five bedrooms here, so if it gets too much, he could fit in."

"Na, we'll be fine." Leslie smiled. "What did you send the boy down for?"

"Pardon?"

"The errand. What did you send Tama down for?"

"Oh that." Hana bit her lip and considered her options, but Leslie was sharp as a diamond and waited expectantly. "Well, I found a cigarette with...marijuana in it. I thought maybe it was one of the stockmen so Tama went to find out. It didn't have much in it, but...well, anyway, he got hammered instead. With Ryan." Hana exhaled in exasperation.

"That'll be Alfie's."

"What? Pardon?" Hana found it hard to keep her face under control.

"It's Alfie's. He smokes it for his arthritis. It controls the pain. He don't get...you know..." Leslie rolled her eyes and swivelled her head on her neck, whilst waving her arms. Hana had never seen a pot user do that, but figured it might make them easier to spot if they did.

"Does Logan know?" Hana asked.

"Noooooooooo! And you don't tell him!" Leslie punctuated her sentence with a light punch to Hana's upper arm. It stung. "Your Logan hates the stuff. Says that was half the problem in them London schools. He'd go mental."

More secrets. Fantastic. Not only did Hana know that her husband was not a Du Rose, she also knew that his half-brother had married a random half-sister. Now she was also party to the fact that his father - who wasn't really his father - smoked weed on Logan's property and was also possibly stalking their home.

"I think I'm going to shoot myself," Hana said out loud and Leslie looked at her curiously.

"What?"

"Would you like a scone? I made some yesterday."

Leslie smiled and shook her head. "Na thanks, daughter. I'm watchin' my weight."

Hana snorted and bit back the rude comment, unable to stop it playing out in her brain anyway. Quite what Leslie was watching it do, beggared description. Perhaps she was just watching it increase on the scales.

"I've got Wiri coming up. Anahera has a doctor's appointment. Is Phoe ready? He loves to see her."

"She's actually the only member of my household who's dressed," Hana smiled. "So yes."

Leslie narrowed her eyes and pulled an interested face. "So how did Logan go to work then? Did he *whakahahake?* I would pay good money to see that body on a horse."

"You've lost me...I...oh." The meaning of the *Māori* word dawned on Hana abruptly and she smiled sweetly. *To strip naked.* "Yes, I've heard that a lot of people would. Not likely though. My husband's a complete prude."

"Not like that Tama!" Leslie guffawed. "I'm glad I'm not the housekeeper down at that hotel anymore. Helena had complaints about him after the other night. Bit too popular for his own good!"

"He was at the *hotel!*" Hana put her hand over her mouth. "I assumed he went drinking in Hamilton."

"Oh no, he didn't. There was a bridal shower and he did a full striptease in the bar. Poor Lofty dint know what to do with him. He couldn't kick him out because he's *whanau*. Tama went up to a hotel room with a big group of them."

"He said there were three..." Hana couldn't keep the shock out of her voice.

"Lofty said there was more than three! Between six and ten. And they all looked like crap at breakfast. I stuck my head round the door after ten and they all had eyes like pee holes in the snow."

"So what was the complaint?" Hana closed her eyes and regretted asking. Leslie stood up to leave, her eyes sparkling brightly as she cast her eyes around for the child she wished to kidnap.

"Apparently he entertained quite a few of them and was somethin' of a stud. They left him a massive tip at reception and wanted his phone number."

"Oh, what? They thought he worked here as a...as a..." Hana couldn't bring herself to say it. Even whispering it could get them shut down. "Don't let Logan find out," she panicked. "He'll kill him." She ran a shaking hand across her face and blinked rapidly a few times. "So what was the *complaint?*"

Leslie leaned forward to hear her better and then stood up, her voluminous skirt flowing back into place around her large hips. "Oh yeah, that. The bride-to-be wanted her knickers back."

Chapter 51

Hana pushed her hands underneath Logan's shirt and groaned at the feel of his soft skin under her fingers. "Leslie was fantasising about you naked on a horse earlier. Is it possible?"

"It would be painful. And the thought of Leslie with the hots for me does very little for my ego." Hana's husband tipped his hat back and kissed Hana underneath her jawline, sighing with desire. "You, on the other hand..."

"What are you doing at the bottom of the driveway?" Hana asked, her voice muffled. "I could have run you over."

"Waiting for a hot woman to come pick me up."

Hana jumped as though shot and shoved at Logan hard, stepping back in irritation. "Not funny. We already did that particular drama. I don't need a repeat."

At first, Logan looked confused and then realisation crawled across his beautiful features. "Don't do this, Hana. Stop throwing Sylvia back in my face!" Logan held onto her forearms and wouldn't let her withdraw from him. "We need to get past this."

"I can't." Hana exhaled and pulled at her arms, a fruitless action against Logan's work-strengthened hands. His grip was fixed and it frustrated her.

"Why, Hana?"

"I don't know. It feels like her influence stretches everywhere sometimes. When you say things like that, it makes me feel vulnerable. I promised myself I would never feel like that again."

"What can I do?" Logan's face was stripped of desire and lust, leaving pain in its stead. Hana felt bad.

"I don't know. I don't want to know why you're waiting here; I don't care. Just let me go, please. Wait for whoever you like. Leslie took Phoe for a few hours and I need to see Will and...sort some other things out."

"You think I would be standing at the bottom of our drive, *waiting for a woman?*" Logan sounded aghast. His dark eyes clouded over.

"You *said* it."

"I meant you. *You're* my hot woman. Ah, geez Hana." Logan let her hands drop to her sides, wincing as her stomach protruded through her shirt, her jacket hanging either side of their son like theatre curtains. It brought him to his senses and Hana saw sensitivity flicker across his expressive face. "I love you, babe. I treated you badly and it damaged your trust in me, I get that." Logan reached for his wife as the sound of a heavy engine droned up the first part of the hill. A trades van came nose to nose with Hana's abandoned ute and stopped. Hana read the signage of the telecommunications company on the paintwork and dropped her eyes to the ground.

"Hey bro," a heavy man climbed from the passenger side. "You Du Rose?"

Logan nodded without taking his eyes from Hana's face.

"We're here to check out this mast. We've got some parts to replace, but it's off track. Boss said you'd be here to meet us."

"Later?" Logan inclined his head towards Hana and raised his eyebrows. She didn't respond, watching as the men loaded equipment onto Logan's quad bike and another one, which Hana hadn't noticed parked just off road.

Hana ground her teeth as the men drove off the road and plunged into the bush, following Logan's lead. Her husband didn't look back and she chewed her lip and watched him disgorge his tall frame from the bike and open a gate. Back in the ute, Hana rubbed her hands across her face, annoyed at her senseless outburst over nothing. It took some considerable manoeuvring to reverse and then drive around the work van, slewed across the widest part of the bend.

The museum was closed and the receptionist informed Hana that Will had gone back to Hamilton for a hospital visit. She felt at a loose end and texted him to apologise for not being more attentive. His reply was curt and told her to stop being so stupid - he was fine.

Hana climbed the spiral staircase and then the next set of steps up to Leslie's apartment in search of her daughter. Only Alfred was home, reading the newspaper with his bifocals resting on the end of his nose. He observed Hana over the top of their metal frames as she slumped into the chair opposite him. She rolled a crumb under her index finger until it was too squashed to roll properly and then looked around the open space. "Where's Leslie gone with Phoe?"

"They went down to the township to play on the swings."

"But there's swings on the camp ground," Hana mused out loud and Alfred watched her.

"True, true," he said. "They wanted an outing. Nice to go somewhere different."

"Oh." Hana squished the crumb into a splat, wrinkling her nose when it wouldn't move anymore. "When will they be back?"

"They'll be back, when they're back, love. What's eating you?" Alfred placed his newspaper on the table, gathering the sports pages into the centre and eyeballing Hana. She felt uncomfortable under his glare and rose to put the crumb in the dustbin. Choosing to remain standing, Hana leaned back against the counter, forcing Alfred to turn. "Come on girlie. Tell me?"

"I just had an argument with Logan," she spilled, hanging her head and pushing her bottom lip out. Alfred raised one bushy eyebrow, dotted with grey and white hairs. "I started it," Hana conceded. "Something he said just tipped me over the edge and I freaked out. It made me think of Sylvia and how she made me feel. I flipped and he got upset."

"Yeah. I get that." Alfred's voice was soft, the misery of decades of living with an adulteress colouring his words and offering Hana sympathy. "I remember." He ran a hand through his hair, touching a thinning spot at the crown. "It stinks." He patted the chair next to him and beckoned to Hana. "Sit," he told her.

Hana thumped her bottom into the padded seat and eyed the old man, recognising a kindred spirit. "It never goes away," Alfred whispered. "But it does get better."

"My first husband cheated; it makes me wary and suspicious. I don't need much cause to go loco. The Sylvia thing brought it back. And now she's dead so I have guilt added to that as well."

"Why guilt?" Alfred's expression was curious.

Hana bit her lip and spoke, fearing judgement. She lowered her voice, looking for a confidence bearer. "Because I'm glad she's dead. How awful is that? She can't come back to try and take Logan again, but that means Ryan has no mother and a woman's dead! I'm a nasty person."

Alfred snuffed and reached out a gnarled hand, touching Hana lightly on her knee. "No, *kōtiro*, you're normal. You have no idea how many times I wished my own brother dead. I even thought of killin' him myself. That makes me worse. That night we walked down the mountain after the fire, you and me, remember? All I could think was, '*It's over; the pain is over.*' But it wasn't, was it? It was a different pain, is all."

Hana nodded. "I just wanted to drag Vik back out of death and then kill him myself!"

"So where does that leave you and the boy?"

"Vulnerable," Hana smiled. "The first woman who bats her eyelids at him and I'll be packing my bags, even if Logan doesn't respond. He's damned if he does and damned if he doesn't."

"Even with your children?" Alfred reached out a tentative hand and his fingers caressed Hana's burgeoning stomach. She watched his face as the old man strived to connect with the tiny boy, jerking backwards as the baby kicked out at his hand. Hana giggled at Alfred and took his hand, placing his palm firmly over her son and holding hers over the top. The child disturbed, moving around and settling down for a nap, his head shoved down and his feet kicking Hana's ribs.

"Wow!" Alfred's face was alight as he withdrew his hand, the rolling earthquake in Hana's stomach stilled and calm. "He's a busy wee fulla."

"Another *moko* for you," Hana said and the old man's expression changed to one of sadness.

"Not mine. Reuben's."

"Yours!" Hana placed her hand over Alfred's writhing fingers, bent, distorted digits, twisted like twigs by age and work. "They have nobody else."

"True," Alfred smiled. He put his hand on Hana's cheek and stroked it gently. "You know, I love you more than my own daughter?" His eyes watered and he ended the moment abruptly. Hana kept hold of his hand and looked at his fingers.

"Alfred, do you take pain relief for your arthritis?"

The old man looked at his useless fingers. "It don't work. I started...on some other stuff recently. It's good. It dulls the pain heaps and I can even ride Methuselah."

"Marijuana?" Hana whispered.

"Shhhh!" Alfred's eyes widened and he looked around the empty apartment for spies.

"Where do you get it from?" Hana asked. "If someone wanted to buy some, where would they go locally?"

"You can't take it when you're pregnant!" Alfred exclaimed. "I don't want you takin' it at all. I'm desperate, is all. Bloody desperate!"

"I'm only asking," Hana reassured him. "I heard that the loan shark Logan saw off was the only supplier and he's gone."

"I don't need no supplier." He looked proud of himself. "I'm growin' my own." Alfred laughed at the look on Hana's face. "Close your mouth, girl. Flies will go in." He stood up and held out his hand. "I'll tell you, but Logan mustn't know."

"No, no, it's fine. It's probably best I don't know."

Alfred scrunched up his face in disappointment. "But I wanna show youse."

"Fine!" Hana huffed and followed him. Alfred pulled up short in the centre of the apartment and faced a blank wall. Confused, Hana stared at the wall and then at him. Alfred touched the side of his nose like a magician and pressed the wall at a point just above the waist high architrave. With a click, the wall moved inwards and the whole panel from the architrave downwards, popped out. "A hidden panel?"

The historian in Hana jumped for joy but the hotel-proprietor's-wife cringed. "Where does this go?"

Alfred giggled like a small child and bent down, entering the doorway with his chin on his knees. Hana had no choice but to follow. "Pull it closed," he told her and clicked the panel shut behind them. Hana panicked. "It's fine," Alfred reassured. "We can get back out." He continued ahead, drawing a small torch from his trouser pocket and lighting their way. The route continued at half height and Hana tripped over the first low step as it presented itself."

"Where are we going?" she whined and Alfred's whispered answer echoed in the dark expanse around them.

"Roof," he hissed backwards.

"I don't like heights!" Hana exclaimed and Alfred ignored her, climbing upwards in the uncomfortable bent position. The baby kicked and protested at the prolonged squashing administered by Hana's ribs and she chuntered to herself, until running face first into Alfred's bottom. "Oof!"

Alfred drew back a bolt by the light of the torch and opened a door in front of him. Light flooded into the space. Blinding light, green mountains and blue sky.

"Far out!" Hana stood up straight in the outdoor space. Concrete slabs covered a square area, twenty metres by twenty in the middle of the vast hotel roof. At the very centre stood a glasshouse, integral to the original building. Apexed on four sides, there was very little vertical edge to it, creating the aerial illusion of a glass skylight for a lower level. Only it wasn't. The area was sheltered by its well-like construction and the roof rose up around it on every side, forming a pooled oasis within solid, brick walls. Hana stood on tiptoes and peeked over the edge of one side, watching the slate roof slope away from her. Potted plants decorated the outdoor space and the glasshouse was covered from the inside by green shade cloth. Alfred smiled at Hana's reaction. "You've got deck chairs!" Hana giggled pointing at two striped green and white chairs leaned inside the glasshouse door. "Does Leslie come up here with you?"

Alfred nodded. "She finds it hard but yes, she's losing some weight so it's gettin' easier."

Hana shook her head. "Doesn't anyone know this is up here?"

Alfred shrugged and sniggered like a naughty boy. "I don't think they remember."

"But what about Logan? I thought he had the plans for this place."

"This just shows as an empty space on the plans. The apartment belonged to my mama. She showed me this when I married Miriam and Ma moved downstairs to the ground floor because of her heart."

"So Miriam knew?"

Alfred shook his head. "No. She had her secrets, so I kept mine."

"So who maintained all the plants and the slabs?"

"Me," Alfred said proudly. "But Leslie's been bringing up seeds and plants to make the place look pretty. We raise 'em in the glasshouse."

"Ah yeah. And the marijuana too?"

Alfred nodded. "Yep and the shade cloth stops the cops seeing it when they do aerial sightings in the bush. It just looks like a covered skylight."

"So have you always grown it?" Hana asked, uncomfortable with the realisation that her daughter spent a great deal of her life downstairs, metres away from a stash of illegal drugs.

"No, no, surely not. I came off the doctor's pills when I married Leslie. It interfered with…things. I knew someone who took marijuana as pain relief and decided to grow it up here. It helps me."

"Does Leslie use it?" Hana's face betrayed her concern for Phoenix and Wiri, at the mercy of the woman at the wheel of her car.

"Never!" Alfred said with determination. "She don't like it but she understands. And don't be worrying about my *moko*. I come up here to smoke it, never near the babies. I don't drive no more so I'm not a fool; my licence ran out last Friday." Alfred looked sad at that. "End of an era. I won't apply for it again. And I don't take care of the children without Leslie anyways. I'm not a danger, I promise. I'm just in pain, Hana."

"Alfred, how will this work if Ryan comes up here to live with you?"

The wily old man smiled and squinted in the daylight, like a man on top of the world. He shrugged. "I lived with Miriam for more than forty-five years and in that apartment downstairs for twenty of 'em. She never knew about my secret wee garden. The boy won't either."

"Where do you dry the marijuana?" Hana asked, curiosity getting the better of her. *Repeatedly saying the name of the drug might make it more acceptable*, Hana reasoned. But it didn't; it still felt wrong.

"In the passageway. There's a bit to the left that's higher. I string it up there. Wanna see?"

"Alfred, I already know too much," Hana sighed. "Logan has a way of getting things out of me, without me realising."

Alfred smiled and nodded, a regal motion filled with *mana* and nobility. "But not *everything*, Hana. Some cards you play very close to your chest." The old man winked at her and she cringed, hating how that gave her away. Alfred laughed. "We need to go downstairs. Your baby will be home soon."

"Alfred?" Hana had almost forgotten her question for him. He halted at the doorway and waited. "Have you ever smoked it up at our place?"

He pulled a face. "No, never. Only up here." Realisation dawned. "Oh, those cigarette butts you found in your garden? Na, thems was different papers to mine. Thems was real thinly rolled and fine. I need the bigger, thicker stuff with my old hands. Want to see?" He turned back towards the glasshouse with eagerness in his face.

"No, it's fine. How could you tell that? Weren't they all trodden by the cows?"

"Not all of them. Logan just said that to stop you worrying."

A sound like a wind chime came from just inside the open doorway. The area was sheltered from the wind and the sound carried easily.

"Girls are home," Alfred said and hurried towards the stairs. The downward journey was over in seconds and the pair emerged through the half door before the clattering of children's shoes made it up the second of the wooden flights. "Mama!" Phoenix exclaimed, waving the wooden stick from an ice lolly in her face as Hana sat down at the kitchen table. She smoothed her red hair behind her ears and smiled at the child, receiving her on her knee with enthusiasm.

Hana glanced backwards at Alfred and Leslie, just in time to hear the loving wife ask her husband, "Are you feeling any better, *makau?*"

Chapter 52

"You took my bloody keys and wouldn't answer my texts!" Tama raged, as Hana put the wiggling infant down in the hallway. "What are you playing at?"

"How's the head?" Hana asked, sarcasm spilling from her tone.

"Painful!"

"Well it serves you right!" Hana watched Phoenix skip over to her carton of Lego and start building again, her dark fringe flopping into her eyes. The little girl bashed it roughly out of the way with a delicate hand. "And it means you're still over the limit and not fit to drive."

Tama gritted his teeth and rolled his eyes. "I needed to get back today."

"No, you need to be ready to go on duty on Sunday. You can leave tomorrow."

"I have stuff to do."

Hana slapped a fat envelope on the table. "Well, I guess you can spend your wages," she smiled, but it wasn't a pleasant expression. Tama narrowed his eyes at the package.

"What's that?"

"It looks like rather a lot of cash, from a grateful bunch of women numbering around ten apparently. They'd quite like to see you again, especially the bride - who wants her knickers back, please."

Tama paled. "Oh."

"So if the fire service doesn't work out, you can always make a living as a stripper and a gigolo. You're obviously very good at it."

"Does Logan know?"

Hana turned to him with fury in her eyes. "I *know!* Doesn't it matter to you what I think? Why does everyone care what Logan does or doesn't know? Who made him the big *kahuna?*" Hana heard her voice take on an irritating screechy quality but couldn't seem to stop herself. "Everyone tells me things and then says, '*Don't tell Logan.*' I should go into blackmail; I could make a fortune." She stormed off towards her bedroom, ripping her jacket from her shoulders and hurling it onto the bed. It clipped one of the four posts and caused the voile to cascade down around her side of the bed, coming to rest on the carpet. Too tired to bend down, Hana walked over to it and flopped onto the bed, nestling into her pillows and turning on her side.

Tama's face poked around the doorframe, misted by the pretty green voile that enclosed Hana. She sighed. "Go away. Your keys are in my bag by the door. Do what you want, Tama. I'm fed up of all of you."

He ventured into the room, as though approaching an unpredictable filly, each footstep carefully planted and considered. "When you stormed out, Phoe said, '*oops*' and giggled. She's got your sense of humour."

"Well, let's just hope she's got more sense full stop!"

Tama carefully pulled the green shroud from in front of Hana's face and pinned it back to the corner of the four poster bed. "That's wonky!" Hana grumbled.

"Tough!" Tama budged her with his hip. "Shift over, Miss Grumpypants."

Hana humphed and moved backwards to the middle of the bed. Tama's long frame settled next to her in a sitting position and he put his arm around her shoulders and pulled their bodies together. He ran his long fingers through her hair, massaging Hana's scalp and making her want to purr. "I'll leave tomorrow," he agreed. "You're probably right."

"I'm always right. It's just that nobody ever listens to me." Hana's attitude of ugly self-pity was intoxicating, her voice muffled with her face pushed into Tama's hip.

"Yep. True dat." His fingers rubbed and stroked absentmindedly, soothing a headache that Hana hadn't even realised was there in the background. He stopped as his mind wandered and Hana slapped his hand to make him start again.

"Did you ask Bobby to leave?" It had been bothering her. Tama shook his head.

"Flick? No, you told me not to. I get the feeling he shot through of his own accord."

"Ok," Hana sounded grumpy.

Tama spoke in a conciliatory tone, "Seeing as I was stuck up here with no car keys and a banging head, I went for a little walk through the bush. I started where you found that cigarette. Wanna know what I discovered?"

Hana turned to face him, her green eyes reaching into his grey ones eagerly, "Yeah. What?"

"Well, somebody's tiny gumboot steps had overwritten everything from the fence to a point a few metres in. She'd moved around a bit and stomped about and ruined most of the evidence there." Hana groaned. "But fortunately, Poppa Rueben could track like the bushman he was. So he passed on his considerable skills to moi…"

Hana slapped his leg and Tama laughed. "Ok, so I tracked someone away from the house, two people actually. There's been a fair bit of traffic that way and they've worn a track."

"Two people?" Hana's voice sounded small, remembering another time when two men had hunted her without mercy. One of them was Bobby.

"Yeah," Tama pulled her in closer. "One overwrites the other and vice-versa. So they either come together or at different times. But then this is what's interesting. There's actually three tracks down the mountain. There's the central one, with both sets of shoe treads, and then there's one either side, far enough away from the central one to be undetected. One side has one set of treads, but the other side shows the other ones. It's weird."

"So they come up together, but then they also come up separately and stick to their own track? That's bizarre."

"It is, hey?" Tama conceded. "Thing is, as you stand at the top and look down, the footprints in the central track are the same as the ones I followed in the track to the left and that track, is old. It hasn't been followed for maybe a week. It's overrun by animal prints and bush debris. There's stuff growing back over it. The prints in the track to the right, do show up in the central path, but underneath, fainter and only partial. But the track to the right is fresh."

"So what are you saying?" Hana's brain whirled from the information, going round in a washing machine-type cycle and staying dirty.

"I think that at first, maybe two people came up together or separately and used the same central track. Then for some reason, they came up on their own and didn't want the other person to know and created different tracks simultaneously either side. The person using the track to the right, has kept coming up but carried on using their own track. But the other guy, used the left hand track for a while and then for some reason, reverted back to the central one and overwrote that man's tracks."

Hana groaned. "That's too confusing. What if they came up together and walked side by side and liked to walk on a particular side of their friend? Like a habit?"

Tama shook his head. "Na. Definitely not. There's about ten metres between the left track and the central one, and about thirty metres between the central and right tracks. The right one goes through some really dense supplejack and deep undergrowth."

"How did you find them?" Hana asked, her voice betraying a new found respect for Tama.

He glowed under her admiration. "Just by sweeping the area and knowing what was there before. I've been hunting up here with Logan since I was a kid, before there was a fence or a house. There's not many landmarks in there but I know most of them. Tracking's in our blood." He said the last wistfully, missing a previous life and pastimes that were pleasurable once. Hana heard the longing in his voice.

"Have you left tracks?

"Of course," Tama replied with confidence. "But whoever uses the tracks won't care. They don't deviate, they just come up and down. They won't see mine. I was smart."

"So both tracks lead from down the mountain straight here, to our house?"

"That's the interesting thing." Tama settled, like a man with a decent tale. "The track on the right, comes up the mountain and mainly comes here, but I followed a fork to a different location further in. Then there's a definite track from that location to here, but not to where you found the cigarette. That person goes to a different observation point near the cliff and he stands and watches the back of the house. That's quite well used."

"No!" Hana buried her face in Tama's hip and put her hands over her ears. "This is too scary!"

"It's gonna be fine. I'll talk to Uncle Logan and he'll sort it out."

"You can't!" Hana protested. "Because he'll go looking for whoever has the marijuana and I promised!"

"What?"

"No, no, the person who has it, didn't leave it there. He...they don't smoke it up here. But if Logan goes looking, he'll find the same person I did. And they aren't our stalker. But it will cause so much trouble, it's not worth it."

Tama sighed in exasperation and ran his hands through his hair. "Why do you never leave things alone, Hana Du Rose? You're like a one-woman-car-pile-up!"

"What's at the other location? You said that the track on the right went somewhere else and then back to our house. Like a triangle? So what's at the end?"

Tama raised his hand. "This is why we need to tell Logan. There's an old wooden hut that we used to camp in years ago, when we hunted for more than a night. It's ancient and just about had it now. It's got sides and a roof but a good wind could blow it over."

"So one of the people watching the house has been there?" Hana asked.

"No, they've been living there!"

Hana's eyes widened in terror. "What? How far away?" She pushed herself up in the bed, her hair cascading over the pillows behind her. "What are we going to do?"

"We're going to do nothing. I'm going to tell Logan."

"How do you know they're living there?"

"*Were* living there. He hasn't been back for a few days. Put it this way, Ma, he has a liking for pig roasted over a spit and he hunts with a crossbow. There's marks in the dust inside the hut from a very large shotgun being leaned up against the wall, but he would know not to use it up here. The sound would echo off the ridges and we would all hear it. Remember?"

Hana's mind drifted back to Phoenix's birth. She recalled Tama's panic and his whispered words as he pulled the trigger. *'Three quick shots in succession. Hunter in distress.'* The sound had rolled and reverberated around the mountains, deafening Hana as she laboured in the dirt. Logan had found them. Her hand strayed to her son and fear lit her eyes. "I don't want to do that again," she whispered. "I want to be in hospital; with midwives and lots of drugs."

Tama laughed. "Then you need to stop lying to your midwife about still living in Hamilton," he chided her. "Or else that's exactly what's gonna happen. How come she hasn't visited you at home yet? That's hardly gonna work is it?"

"She keeps texting me and I told her I was on holiday," Hana hung her head.

"Ma!"

"I don't want to have the baby in Auckland. I had my heart surgery in Auckland!"

"It's hardly the city's fault! Get real, Ma. You must be about due to pop soon!"

"Ages! I've got ages!" Hana raged. "It's just a big baby, they said. Paris, I conceived him in Paris! I do know when I..."

"Enough!" Tama raised his hand and screwed up his face. "I have a good imagination and I really don't want to know why that one time sticks in your mind, thanks." He kissed Hana's forehead and smoothed out the angry lines with his odd shaped thumb, Alfred's gift of genealogy. "I won't ask if Logan knows, because I don't want to see you go up like a firecracker!" Tama laid down fully and pulled Hana's head onto his broad, fireman's chest. "Now shut up and relax, or I'm telling."

Chapter 53

"That damn midwife keeps ringing the house. You need to call her back."

"Oh, I didn't know that."

Bodie picked at fluff on his uniform shirt and shrugged. "She turned up and Amy told her you didn't live there anymore. She asked you to call her."

"No! Why would you do that to me?" Hana raged and Bodie jumped back in surprise.

"What did we do?"

"You just got rid of my midwife for me. Now I'll have to start again and find another one!" Hana ran her hands over her face in irritation and tried to bring her redheaded temper under control. She took deep breaths and tried to count to ten.

"Oh, she said there was nothing wrong. You're fine, the baby's fine, she just needed to speak to you. She told Amy that it's nothing to worry about."

Logan took that moment to walk into the family dining room, his perceptiveness picking up the tension in the room within a heartbeat. He strode over to Hana and took her in his arms. "What's wrong sweetheart?" He glared at Bodie sideways.

"Nothing!" Hana pushed his arms away in frustration, suspecting that the two men tied to her by blood and marriage were working up to a fight. "I'm going up to see Alfie," she snapped and left the room quickly. Half way down the corridor, her heels clicking on the quarry tiled floor, Hana remembered why she went into the dining room in the first place. "Damn," she swore. In search of the drink she had promised herself, Hana walked back the way she came, passing the door to the dining room and the males she suspected were already arguing. She entered the kitchen via the main door and snuck past the wide archway, catching sight of Logan's rigid back as he faced her son. Bodie leaned against the windowsill, side on to him, ignoring whatever spewed from Logan's mouth.

Hana sipped from the glass in her hands, trying not to slurp and draw attention to her presence. She stood in a relaxed pose, one leg bent at the knee as she contemplated the difficulties in her life. Bodie's sneering laugh brought her back to a miserable reality. "Are you even sure that baby's yours?" he asked. Hana froze in shock. "She's a bit adamant about her dates. Amy says that's what the midwife is panicking over. Maybe Mum's got something to hide."

"I'm going to smack you out in a minute!" Logan's voice cracked with a menace that made Hana's blood chill.

"Go for it, I'll arrest you. I can't wait, Du Rose. One day you'll slip up big time."

"All this because you don't wanna pay back the money I lent you?" Logan sounded incredulous. "I lent it in good faith and you promised."

"I don't have it." Bodie's voice took on a whinging quality and Hana squirmed. That was guaranteed to wind Logan up more.

"Your mother told me she released a trust fund for you and your sister. I know where Izzie's went; it's currently floating that damn church they work for. But you? What did you do with it? One minute you've got enough to play the 'big I am' and buy expensive gates for Culver's Cottage and the next, you're broke. What did you do?"

Hana waited with interest, knowing from experience that Logan's teeth were gritted.

"I can't tell you," Bodie griped, his tone insipid, making Hana feel ashamed of him.

"Gambling? Another woman? A tribe of illegitimate kids? What?" Logan's voice softened. "You don't deserve it but do you need my help?"

Hana wanted to rush in and hug her husband until his bones cracked, at the same time telling him not to bother helping the stupid boy. Bodie hesitated and there was silence. Hana put the glass down gently, the condensation on it making it likely she would drop it fairly soon anyway.

"I made a dumb investment and lost the lot. Amy thought I still had it, so I've had to follow through and buy Mum's old house. We had Hope and Amy's still on extended maternity leave. We're living hand to mouth and the strain of it is killing me. She wants stuff and I'm terrified she'll find out. She thinks I'm just a miser and don't want to spend my money on her. We argue about it all the time."

"What was the investment?"

"I thought it was a dead cert. I was wrong."

"Stock market?

"Yeah."

"I wish you'd come to me. It's how I made most of my start-up cash."

"I know that now," Bodie sighed, a trace of frustration speckling his tone.

"Forget the grand for the auction," Logan said. "It's forgotten." Then he laughed, "It's probably not good for the leading cop on a murder case to owe the prime suspect money. So let's forget it ever happened."

Hana heard her husband's cowboy boots move towards the door and his hand contact with the handle, his wedding ring clanking against the metal with a faint 'ting.'

"Logan!" Bodie's voice sounded frantic and Hana listened to the strain in it with a mother's ears. "You're not the prime suspect."

Logan's boots grated on the wooden floor, sounding gritty as he turned. Hana thought about Tama's statement to Odering. He knew nothing and was out drinking in the township with most of the other stockmen, including an underage Ryan between the estimated times of the murder. They had alibied each other, down to a man. Hana waited with bated breath for Bodie's exciting revelation. She hadn't expected that!

"It's Mum, Logan. Mum is the prime suspect."

Chapter 54

Hana managed to escape from the kitchen before sickness overcame her. She ran down the corridor towards the lobby, almost bowling over a giggling group of guests who stared at her wild green eyes and parted to let her through. Outside on the front steps, Hana shoved her head between her knees and took deep breaths.

The scuffle of feet sounded behind her and a strong arm snaked around her shoulders, as Logan sat down on the step next to her. "You're avoiding me," he said, gentleness in his voice making Hana's tears spring to the surface. "You faked tiredness last night when I wanted to talk and you hid in the bathroom this morning. It used to be me that played the role of serial avoider. We seem to have swapped."

"Sorry." Exhausted and sick, Hana couldn't think of anything else to say. Her brain obscured whatever it was they had been fighting over.

"I haven't cheated on you, I won't cheat on you and I need you to start believing that. Otherwise we're heading nowhere in this marriage." Logan's voice maintained its even keel, a steady, comforting rumble. Hana turned and threw herself into his arms, burying her head in the collar of his shirt. When Logan tried to talk to her, pulling her away by her upper arms, she kissed him on the mouth to stop him.

"I love you," she said between kisses and Logan wrapped her in his arms and held her.

"Good job really," he replied softly. "Otherwise I might be a bit afraid of you."

Hana sat back on the step and looked at her husband, searching his eyes for meaning. "You would never be scared of me," she said with honesty. "You're really powerful and I'm...weedy and pathetic."

Logan threw his head back and laughed, his hilarity infectious. His shirt, open at the top, showed the start of his magnificent chest and his grey eyes sparkled like gems. A passing couple stepped carefully around them and the woman looked back a few times at the handsome man in the cowboy hat. Hana gritted her teeth. "What's funny?"

"You could do more damage with one of your glares than you realise, woman. You're formidable."

Hana sulked and Logan leaned in for another kiss, touching Hana's tongue with his and causing her to feel sensations she would rather not in a public place. "You're a rubbish eavesdropper," he said, pulling back from her blazing green eyes, which opened wider in surprise.

"I don't know what you're talking about," Hana blushed in confusion.

Logan eyed her sideways through eyes that were dangerous and perceptive. "No?" He used his hand to shield his eyes from the low glare of the sun that sneaked underneath the brim of his hat. "Good job I don't think you did it then, isn't it?" He looked back at his wife, his handsome face filled with the glow of amusement. *And superiority*; a man enjoying his own joke. "Creeping up on people is a skill. I learned it out of necessity. My life was so confusing that I needed to be one step ahead of the game."

"That worked well. You didn't even know who your father was." Hana cursed her vicious tongue but Logan eyed her with respect.

"Touché." He brandished the French expression with a casual air, disarming Hana easily by not rising to her foolishly placed bait. He smiled at his wife and twisted his wedding band on his ring finger. Hana gulped. Logan Du Rose only ever played the game to win. She felt herself crumbling inwardly under the force of his personality. Tasting victory, Logan took Hana's fingers in his, caressing the knuckles and lifting her hand to his lips to kiss, with a seduction he had mastered just for her.

"How did you know I was there?" Hana grudgingly conceded, catching Logan's smirk even as he tried hard to conceal it.

"I sense when you're around. I automatically look for you. Coupled with the fact that you creep like a small elephant in clogs."

"Is that why you let my stupid son off with the money he owed you? Because you knew I was listening?"

Logan looked at Hana with sexy crinkles in the corners of his eyes and grinned. "Hell yeah! If it had just been me and him, I'd have taken it out of his face!"

Hana snorted, "Liar! If you were going to do that, you'd have done it months ago. I didn't even know he owed you. You're nothing but a big softie!"

"Shhh!" Logan put his hand over Hana's mouth and a man pulling a large suitcase up the hotel steps looked at the couple in alarm. "Don't go spreading that around. I've got a reputation to uphold."

The smile dropped from Hana's face, landing somewhere near her boots. "Do you think I killed Sylvia?"

Logan studied her as sadness and a flicker of guilt settled in her face. "No, Hana. I don't think you killed her?"

"Is it because you're my alibi?"

Logan struggled with his wife's sincerity as the answer left his full lips, reluctantly crushing her naive illusion of his trust.

"No, baby. It's because you couldn't work out how to get the safety off a pistol like that. And it takes you so long to aim, Sylvia could have run a half marathon and left you stood there fumbling."

"Oh." Hana's bottom lip shot out. "I thought you were impressed with my shooting. Are you not then?"

Logan slipped his arm around her shoulders again and cuddled her into his armpit. She smelled his deodorant and wished she was safely at home in bed with him. "For a townie who shuts her eyes when she fires, I think you're doing awesome."

Hana opened her mouth and Logan put an index finger over her lips. "I know what kind of pistol it was because Bodie accidentally-on-purpose let it slip. And no, I don't own one."

Hana sighed and shook her head. "Logan, I'm keeping a secret from you..." she began, her heart constricting in fear.

"Yeah, I know," her husband replied.

Hana sat up and stared at him open mouthed. "You know?"

He nodded and gave her a lazy smile. "Yeah, you're also a rubbish liar and an even worse secret keeper."

Hana hedged her bets, not sure which of her many secrets he had guessed. She went for the least damaging. "I went to an identity parade at the police station a while ago. They caught Bobby and..."

"Yeah, me too."

"What?!" Hana turned on the step and eyeballed her husband. "Oh for goodness sake!" she folded her arms and sulked. Her tantrum was wasted on Logan.

"They got me in after you. I enjoyed the chocolate snails from Alex's place though. That was a nice touch. I would have just told you, but you seemed intent on turning the whole thing into an intrigue so I thought I'd play along. Flick walked free anyway and I had fun."

"So you think I'm a rubbish secret keeper?" Hana sighed and thought about the diary contents and her burden of knowledge. *You're not as clever as you think Du Rose.*

"Pretty much." Logan shoved his hat back on his head and smiled at his wife, smugness creeping into his expression. "I'd say you were worse than average."

"Do you think this baby's yours?" Hana's mind dragged her back to Bodie's cruel accusation. Logan reached his other hand round and stroked the baby bump sticking out of her dress. The material stretched taut under his palm and he smiled at Hana's attempts to break away from the track-pants and sweater image; *for him.*

"Of course he's mine," he whispered. "I remember Paris. Don't you?"

Hana smirked and lifted her lips for a kiss. Logan ran his hands up underneath her hair, touching the sensitive skin at the back of her neck. His lips felt soft and his cheek smooth from a hurried shave that morning. He tipped his hat back and rested his forehead against Hana's.

"That's perfect!" The unfamiliar voice made Hana jump and she turned to see a woman wielding a camera. Logan's body stiffened and Hana rested a warning hand on his knee. "I just wanted a few more pictures after our interview." The woman strode over to them, silhouetted against the sunshine. She was small with long curly dark hair and purple framed glasses rested on a neat nose. "Mrs Du Rose, I presume." She smiled and stuck her hand out for Hana to shake. "I interviewed your husband recently for our blog, *The Bowes Library Corner-*. We write about all sorts of things including New Zealand attractions and holiday destinations."

Hana glanced sideways at her husband. Logan's eyes were gimlet hard, more black than grey and a vein pulsed in his neck. Hana stood up, her polite English reserve in attendance. "Nice to meet you."

Logan rose to his great height, accentuated by his position on the steps. "You don't use that photo," he warned. The journalist shrugged and smiled.

"Whatever." She turned and walked back to her car, satisfied with the intrusion into Logan Du Rose's life. He had been curt and closed during the interview and the editor wanted more. Despite snooping around for four hours without the businessman spotting her, the journalist had uncovered little about the recent murder.

"Is that the journo you met a few months ago?" Hana asked in a low voice and Logan nodded, his hat brim moving up and down as he watched the woman start her car and leave with a casual wave. "She did a nice write up after the tourism awards. She definitely painted you as the dark, foreboding millionaire with a soft spot for his wife." Hana smirked. "Why did she come back?"

"Sylvia's murder, Hana." The woman's name on his tongue wiped all humour from Hana's face. Her shoulders drooped once again. "She was snooping. And if I find out any of my staff spoke to her, there'll be another death!"

"Can't you complain to Odering about journos snooping around during an investigation?"

Logan snorted, sounding like Sacha when she was cross, "He already wants me to shut the hotel! That would give him the excuse he needed."

"I think I should go and talk to him," Hana mused and Logan turned to her sharply.

"Stay away from him, Hana!" His thumbs rested in the front pockets of his jeans and he stood with his legs slightly apart. He looked like a king, standing on the steps of his throne room surveying his kingdom. *Or a Maori chief*. The *rangatira* in him cried out from the depths of his genealogy, powerful and magnificent.

Hana stretched up on tiptoes to kiss his cheek and gave him a smile. Logan watched her climb the steps and go into the hotel lobby, his eyes narrowed. Hana saw him shake his head, just a fractional movement but enough to make her cringe. *She never did as she was told; surely he knew that by now.*

An hour later, Detective Chief Inspector Odering stood and eyed Hana through a blank expression that successfully obscured all emotion. It was etched perfectly onto his angular face and Hana suspected it took years of practice to achieve that level of apparent detachment. Hana sat on Nev's new sofa in his abandoned lounge, seeing the struts from the unfinished barn waving through the window like abusive fingers sticking up into the air. *Screw you*, they mocked, behind the policeman's suited back.

"When can Nev move back in?" she asked, making conversation.

"We never said they had to move out," Odering replied, his face straight.

Hana pushed her knees together as a flick of his eyes suggested he was looking up her dress. Her tights had rolled down over her growing belly and bunched up at the crotch. Not attractive. "How's your wife and children?"

Odering's face dropped its blankness for a second, replaced by anguish and then gone again, pushed back behind the mask. "Divorcing me."

"Oh." Hana cast around for something helpful to say but found nothing.

"Why are you here, Mrs *Du Rose?*" He said her last name as though it tasted bad.

"I brought you cookies." She smiled and held the ice cream container out towards him like a *koha* - an offering. She leaned forward, crushing her stomach under her ribs and laid it on the floor in front of her. Odering smirked.

"We're not at the *marae*, Hana. Am I meant to twirl a broom handle like a majorette and dance across to get them?"

Hana bit her lip at the overt disrespect for her husband's culture. "There's no need to be rude." She stood up, bent with difficulty and retrieved the cookies. Odering observed her with interest as Hana stalked across Nev's expensive carpet in her boots and pushed the container into the man's stomach. His lips parted in a smirk and he grabbed it with one hand whilst lurching for her wrist with the other.

"Why did you do it?"

Hana looked down at his fingers, the knuckles white as they gripped her slender wrist. She winced as the pressure disturbed an old wound, a shard of glass hidden in her vein, so microscopic her surgeon-brother couldn't find it. Odering registered her pain and lessened the force, but he didn't let go. "I didn't kill Sylvia!" Hana protested and the man cocked his head like a bird.

"I *meant* Flick! Robert Dressler. Remember him? He hunted you like a dog for a year, stalked you and threatened you." Odering held Hana's wrist up in his hand like a trophy and leaned into her face for emphasis. "*Hurt you!*"

"He didn't do *that!*" Hana's denial was too quick and Odering's brown eyes flared in anger.

"I knew it! He was here the whole time!" He flung her wrist back at her and stepped away, a vein pulsing in his forehead like it was about to blow. "You pick and choose, you people! How can I do my job?" Odering turned his back on Hana and raised his hands to his head, linking his fingers behind so that his elbows protruded like wings and his suit jacket exposed dark, hairy wrists. The ice cream container lay dropped on its side on the ground, emitting a clunk as the last cookie succumbed to gravity.

Hana examined her wrist, the long, raised scar awoken from its slumber and smarting. She touched the tender skin, engrossed in her task as she fought to mentally switch off the pain. Her mind dredged up a buried memory - *blood spurting in the sunshine like a rainbow - armed response cops in balaclavas and vests - get down on the ground - get down on the ground now - the ground coming up to meet her - darkness*. Hana breathed through pursed lips as she overplayed the mental tape with an oft rehearsed and better one of her own. *It's over. I'm safe. I'm loved.*

"I'm so sorry!" Odering's long arms pinioned Hana to him, a lapel pin sticking into her cheek and his unfamiliar male scent clashing with Logan's aftershave lingering in her nose. "I shouldn't have done that, I'm sorry. I didn't mean to bring it all back. Hana, I'm sorry."

Hana's waxy, paleness alarmed him further as she pulled away and the torture in her face spiked the conscience of a good man struggling with a rotten life. Hana stepped back and Odering's hands fell limply by his sides. "Don't tell Logan?"

Hana rolled her eyes at the growing list of things *not* to tell her husband. Soon she would need to tape her mouth closed in order to be around Logan at all. Hana experienced the sudden urge to seek her husband out and tell him absolutely everything. All the secrets, lies, problems and offences that she currently safeguarded for other people. She could dump it all on him and absolve herself. "Get lost," she replied to Odering and turned to leave. The cookies lying on their side, probably broken, offended Hana's sense of propriety and she bent from the knees to retrieve them. It was an elegant, ladylike manoeuvre, little more than a curtsey and she managed it with dignity. She placed the container with precision on the coffee table.

"I didn't kill Sylvia." Hana's voice held nobility and grace and her face was hard and unyielding. "You've had this house for your investigations long enough. Get cleared up and get out!"

Hana stalked across the gravel to the ute, her low heels crunching in the stones beneath her. She ignored her son, who exited the marked police car to her right as she climbed into the high vehicle. It gave her huge satisfaction, revving the powerful diesel engine and emitting the throaty victory roar. For the first time since she began struggling with the massive size and opulence of a vehicle which Logan had purchased with childish delight, she understood why he liked it. It represented power and supremacy and Hana wrenched the heavy vehicle into an impossible arc, peppering Bodie's cop car with stone chips like bullets, as an alternative to the rude gesture her fingers struggled to suppress. She flew down the driveway to the road, her face blank as the ute bull bars intimidated another cop car into reversing out onto the fast road backwards. Hana didn't acknowledge the young, spotty policeman's look of disgust as the ute ate up the main road under its immense wheels. The Du R ose *kuikui* had spoken.

Hana brushed angry tears from her cheeks as Logan's grandmother's written missives came home to bite her. *'The curse isn't that they sleep around, have secret children and act like hypocrites - and oh yes, they certainly do that! It's that they hold their women in a death-grip, they crush and destroy them from the inside like parasites.'*

"Well, it's too late!" Hana screamed into the empty vehicle as it droned down the hotel driveway like a hive of bees. "They're my family! And they're all I have." The last sentence emerged as a hiccoughed sob and Hana pulled over onto the grass verge, as tears hindered her driving. "The Du Roses are all I have left," she whispered. "It's all or nothing."

Chapter 55

Tama passed his fire service training three months later and a heavily pregnant Hana cried her eyes out at the ceremony as promised. He stood tall in his dark uniform and stared straight ahead, his life finally beginning at the tender age of twenty-one.

Odering removed his makeshift command centre from Nev's house and the family moved back in. Flick was not seen on the mountain again and Sacha recovered enough to go back to work. Hana stayed away from Jack and the stable yard, throwing herself into her daughter's care and playing *housewife* with enthusiasm. But she still felt watched.

"Do you ever get this feeling that somebody's observing you? It's this flesh-creeping sensation that makes the hairs stand up on the back of your neck." Hana used the iron on the delicate fabric with extreme care, watching the beautiful French linen lie flat under her ministrations.

"No!" Will scoffed.

Afraid to mention it again, Hana lifted the dress up for Will to inspect.

"Yep, that'll do," he smiled and held out a plastic coat hanger. "We'll display this one in that nice new cabinet out of the sun. The glass should protect it though."

Hana sighed and rubbed a hand across her stomach. Will laid the dress on his thighs and observed his companion with interest. "That girlie of yours is runnin' you ragged. Take a break."

"No," Hana picked up the iron again and checked the setting, making sure it stayed on a low heat. "I've only got three more to do. The blue one's quite pretty. I can't believe Liza used to wear these. The thought of her in anything except stilettos and business suits is hilarious."

"French, 1700s. Bloody criminal!" Will complained. "Your girl's purple juice stain won't even dry-clean out!"

Hana ignored his rant, having heard it many times before. Her son lashed out with his feet against her ribs and she groaned and almost dropped the heavy iron.

"Watch the fabric!" Will screeched and lurched for the iron from his wheelchair, missing and almost pitching the ironing board over onto Hana. She managed to retain the hottest object but the dress slid to the floor.

"Will!"

"Turn the damn thing off and sit down!" he ordered her and Hana conceded with reluctance.

"I'm a bit sick of this pregnancy now," she grumbled. "I always seem to do the end part in the heat of summer."

"Well, that's your bad planning, then," Will said and Hana stuck her tongue out at him behind his back.

"Saw that," he chided her.

"Do you think the diaries will ever come back?" Hana asked, sipping the tea Will made and pulling a face.

"When they're ready," he said, his tone ominous and Hana shook her head, her red hair cascading down her back and tickling her neck.

"That doesn't make sense."

"When's that baby due?" The old man pointed a teaspoon at Hana's enormous stomach.

"Six weeks. Izzie was two weeks late though, so I could be ages yet." Hana slurped her tea with all the finesse of the builder it would have suited. She shuddered at the bitterness of it. "I don't like my new midwife. Bodie kindly screwed up my grand plan to have the baby in Hamilton. I swear he did it deliberately!"

"Ah yep," came Will's diplomatic answer, aimed at keeping him out of trouble.

"She's called Pam, she's got a voice like a cheese grater and fancies the pants off Logan. She practically dribbles at the sight of him. He says it's like being mentally undressed by one of those waste disposal units you have in your sink." Hana snorted with laughter and reached for a biscuit. "She keeps going on and on about how big the baby is. The scans show that he's fine; we're both fine! My husband's six foot four inches and it's a boy. He's hardly genetically disposed to be a midget is he?"

Will stared at Hana with a curious look in his eyes. "What?" she asked him, waving her cookie in the air and dropping crumbs she would never be able to retrieve.

"I'm just wonderin' what a cheese grater sounds like," he mused.

"Come to my next appointment with me," Hana suggested, putting her hand up to cover a yawn.

"Right woman, ring that Leslie upstairs and ask her to keep your girlie for a few hours. You look like crap. Go have a lie down. Or grab a room upstairs. I'm sure they could find you one."

Hana's face clouded. "I'll never sleep down here again. Not after..." She bit her lip and reached for the phone, discovering from Alfred that Leslie was out anyway. Phoenix and Wiri were being treated to another trip to the zoo.

Hana kissed Will on his bristly cheek and used the ute to drive up the hill. She opened and closed the gate and parked the huge vehicle on the driveway, feeling a horrid pressing between her legs. "Ouch, baby!" she exclaimed and rested one hand on the truck's bonnet. "Nice of you to engage your head, but I can think of more appropriate moments!"

She waddled to the door clutching her stomach and fumbled with the key. The small white cigarette end on the doormat made her gasp in horror and she bent to pick it up, overbalancing against the bench and banging her face on the metal. "Oh, please God, no!" she groaned, sensing danger. Hana shoved at the door with terrified abandon and then pushed it behind her as a wave of pain shot through her bladder. She turned the key, panting with relief at her perceived safety.

As Hana stepped over the doormat, water cascaded down her legs, soaking everything in its path. Fury added itself to fear as she bent double and let out a roar of frustration. "-*Noooo!* Not again!" A contraction joined the imminence of her labour as pain tore at her insides like a hot knife. The forewaters seemed relentless in their gravitational tumble, making a decent puddle on a previously welcoming rug and Hana sank to her knees in misery. With difficulty, she wrested off her tights and underwear, wincing at the uncomfortable sensation of the cooling water. Another contraction bit half way through and she had to pause, panting for breath and swearing out loud with the effort of not crying out. "This is not fair!" she complained as, unable to stand, she was forced to crawl to the bedroom on her knees.

The toilet was a welcome seat and caught some of the mess as Hana grappled around in the small bag across her body. She sat still and typed a gentle message to her husband, explaining the problem and whilst urging him not to panic, suggested he didn't muck around either. In an attempt at light-hearted humour, she mentioned that he might like to step over the doormat in the hall to avoid breaking his neck. Then she pressed the button that would summon the cavalry.

"No, no, no! Don't do this to me! Not today. Send you stupid thing, *send!*" Hana peered at the screen, seeing the revolving icon that showed the phone searching for signal. Her heart sank at the same moment as a violent contraction drove her to the tiled floor. "Oh, God, please help me? Not like this! Not again!" She seemed hardly able to take a breath between contractions and memories of Phoenix's hurried entrance into the world failed to help. At least that time she hadn't been alone. She had Tama.

Hana crawled out of the bathroom and across the bedroom floor, stopping at regular intervals to leak more mess on the rimu wood floorboards and hug her stomach in agony as it threatened to rip clean open. "I just wanted you to be a Paris baby!" she wailed to her busy son. "Why couldn't you just do as you were told? I'm not ready for this yet!"

The bedroom door seemed a long way away and the kitchen even further as Hana's forehead rested against the floorboards of her bedroom. Her only source of help was the intercom with the main house, but it may as well have been a gap of miles to bridge. "I'm too old for this!" she raged as the pain intensified and the dreadful urge to push her guts out onto the floor began in earnest. At the end of a spiteful contraction and in the moment's lull between that and the next, Hana caught a dark shadow in her peripheral view and shrieked. The steady knocking she had mistaken for her pulse beating in her temple; was actually a man's hand thumping the bedroom window.

"Jack, help me!" Hana wailed as the threatened contraction bit. The elderly man cast around him, looking for something to smash the glass with and settled on a plant pot. It bounced off the toughened glass and hit him comically in the stomach, bending him double to match Hana's stance. She heard herself laughing like a maniac at the hilarity of her situation, dissolving into tears at the unbearable pain of the next contraction. Jack stood upright again and resumed his steady drum beat on the window and Hana relented.

In the seconds between the next few contractions, she managed to cover the distance between her and the ranch slider but it took her a good five minutes to be able to reach up and unlock the catch. Jack came quickly inside and hunkered down next to her, trying to communicate words with his hands. Hana made the action of a telephone and he looked at her askance and spread his hands wide, mouthing, '*How?*' His inability to speak made ringing anyone impossible.

Hana writhed, alternately sitting and then kneeling and then sitting again. Nothing helped. "I need to sit against the bed," she decided, pointing frantically to the side nearest the bedroom door. Jack pointed to the side nearest her and she shook her head and motioned to the ranch slider. "Lock it, Jack. Please, lock it. It's not safe."

Understanding, the old man pressed the catch on the door and then transferred his efforts to helping Hana get to where she wanted to be, dragging her the final few metres as she groaned and railed at the injustice of her circumstances. When she peeled the soaked dress away from her skin and felt between her legs, her probing fingers contacted the baby's fluffy topknot and she knew then. It was game over.

Chapter 56

The baby bellowed lustily from lungs that couldn't possibly be under formed. Exhausted, her breath coming in heaves, Hana pushed herself into a sitting position, her back against the hard wood of the four poster bed. The sharp angles cut into her shoulder blades, offering a different focus from the pain between her legs.

Jack knelt on the floor on his rickety joints and Hana saw a pair of pale, kicking legs, chubby and streaked with blood, flailing around between his hands. With competence and grave calm born of years of farming experience, Jack snatched up Hana's discarded cardigan and swaddled the crying boy into it. With difficulty he pushed himself across to Hana on his old-man's-legs and handed her the child. Hana looked down at the source of her previous agony and her first contact with her son brought an unladylike hoot of laughter. Jack looked at her curiously with his brows knitted.

"Oh my gosh!" Hana exclaimed, looking at her unusual midwife with green eyes that leapt and danced with pleasure. "Not Paris at all. This little chap is pure McGillivray. He's a little gift from Belfast."

The child stared up at the sound, unfocussed eyes following unseen light and tone, watching angels dance near the ceiling as only newborns can. His eyes were darkest blue, with no intention of staying the familiar baby colour. His shock of downy auburn hair told Hana exactly what colour they would become. He was a tiny replica of her and would share her mother's emerald eyes and red hair. He knitted his brow and pursed his tiny lips, already fighting the cardigan with clenched fists. Judith McGillivray's bright face and determination lived on in her daughter's child.

Hana felt self-conscious about her splayed, naked legs and the mess on the rug beneath her. Her eyes flicked curiously in Jack's direction, looking for disgust or some other kind of emotion. He held her gaze, his hooded eyes blank and expressionless. Hana shifted with the baby clasped firmly in one arm and tried to pull her dress down. The lusty wail started again like a claxon, rising and falling. It was the sound of frustration and dismay. "Ok, baby. Let's see if I can remember this," Hana spoke to her son, who crinkled his face and wobbled his bottom lip. She undid the buttons on the front of her maternity dress, hearing one skitter across the wooden floor as she pulled too hard. "Thank heavens for maternity bras," Hana wittered as the arms and legs flapped again. Eventually she sorted herself out and put the child to her breast. Like an angry lamprey he latched on, causing Hana to groan with the intensity of the let-down. The instant rush of flowing milk confirmed her earlier revelation. The child wasn't early at all. "My dates were wrong," Hana said to Jack, mid groan. "I'm an idiot!"

Jack said nothing but his face had changed. He looked at the child with something akin to hatred. A wave of evil doused the room and hung cloying and heavy over Hana and her baby. Her body involuntarily reacted, flexing her muscles in a fear reaction. "Jack?" she said slowly, mouthing the word precisely for him to follow and forcing a questioning look onto her face.

His eyes narrowed but not before they had flashed unmistakeably. The hooded eyelids fractionally revealed the grey Du Rose eyes and Hana's jaw dropped. *How could she never have noticed?* The man put his hands up in front of his face and signed something to her in his strange variation of the familiar deaf language. Hana recoiled in shock and clutched her child closer to her breast. "No!" she cried and her face filled with horror. Jack pushed his hand towards the child, jabbing his index finger with the same bland look on his face and then signed the awful word again. *Bastard*.

"No!" Hana slapped at the gnarled hand and tried to shift backwards away from him. "No he isn't! How *dare* you say that!" She held the baby in one arm, feeling him tug on her nipple as she disturbed his relentless feeding frenzy. She pushed at the floor with her free arm and slithered away from the old man, horrified at the streak of blood she left behind. A dull warning ache in her stomach reminded her of what was still to come and the child's feeding hastened its process. "*Oh, God no!*" she wailed, moving backwards but getting nowhere of any significance. "Please, Jack why? Why are you doing this? I don't understand."

The old man's eyes were gimlet hard and he shrugged as though he didn't care. He pointed at the child again and signed the wicked word. Hana shook her head, not understanding. Jack's face hardened and he moved from his uncomfortable stance, half leaned on one thigh and buttock, to a kneeling position again. Something fell from his inside jacket pocket in the motion, a small rectangular package. The cigarette papers skittered across the smooth floor and lodged in her sticky blood like a thwarted snowboarder. Hana's breath caught in her throat as divine clarity flooded her muddled brain and she knew *everything*. The faint scent of tobacco wafted across to her, not unpleasant like the filtered white sticks but musky, slightly sweet like her Irish grandfather's pipe smoke.

"Don't you dare touch Logan's son!" Hana shouted, hearing the smacking sound as her treacherous phone fell off the bed behind her and landed on the boards. The battery went one way and the sim card another. Unable to hear the noise, Jack didn't flinch, standing awkwardly and pausing with a look of pain on his face as the blood reoccupied his stiff legs. He shook his head again and pointed at the child. "Get away from me, get out!" Hana screamed, hearing with disgust the heightened pitch that made her sound panicked and betrayed her terror. It was pointless. Jack didn't need the words to tell him what she was saying. He could read it in her face.

Jack shook his head sadly and signed the incongruous sentence to her, *"I thought better of you."*

"I've done nothing wrong," Hana sobbed, gripping the child tightly with both hands. "I've done nothing wrong." her legs felt ineffectual and wobbly and she knew what would happen if she tried to stand. Hana's only defence was to hang on to her baby and make it difficult for the old man to wrestle with her. But she had seen him with the horses, his will of iron always beating them in a tussle.

She breathed out loud jagged breaths into the silence, feeling a sudden familiar pressure. "No, no, no!" she gasped as a sharp tug pulled in the centre of her chest, spreading ominously left. Labour and shock played their part in overworking her delicate heart and for the first time since its implantation, Hana willed the pacemaker to administer the promised kick. "Do it, just do it," she begged, gripping the child and understanding that the electrical impulse may temporarily incapacitate her more.

"Hana, sweetheart, look at me." The voice was calm and capable and infused her with a sense of hope.

"Bobby!" she gushed, "He's going to kill my baby!"

The blond drover stood at the bedroom door with a loaded shotgun, aiming with practiced precision at the old man's body. He moved the barrel's aim from the man's chest to his forehead with a tiny, steady upward movement, its dark twin eyes lethal. Jack followed Hana's gaze and his face clouded with malice. "Hands up!" Flick said clearly, jerking the gun to make his point. His blue eyes blazed with fury and Jack's jaw ground, his toothless gums meeting and making a dreadful sucking sound. Jack tried to move his hands together to sign something and

Flick shouted at him, "Don't give me an excuse, old man. Hands u p!"

Jack thought better of it and held his hands halfway between his head and his belt, palms outward.

"Hana, sweetheart, move!" Flick told her and she sobbed and moaned at the same time.

"I can't! I...I...oooh!" The contraction punctuated her sentence as the afterbirth threatened and she gripped her baby son tightly as it rocked her body, dragging at her stomach and tugging on her navel from the inside. Hana had forgotten how agonising it would be. "Bobby help me, please?" Hana's breath hitched in the back of her throat. Flick was conflicted, needing to deal with Jack but desperate to help Hana.

"Hold on, darlin'," his voice wavered. "I just need to deal with the old man." He renewed his efforts with the gun, jerking it towards Jack and Hana's ensuite. "Is there a window in there?" he asked her huskily and Hana nodded. Flick swore. "It will have to do for now. Get in there!" He jerked the gun towards Jack again and advanced. The old man backed up to the bedpost and remained there, his hands dropping slowly downwards. "No you don't," Flick was over to him in a second, spinning him and shoving his face into the post. He lifted the gun barrel and pointed it at the bottom of Jack's neck, holding it one-handed. He pushed his work boot against Jack's heel, stopping him from moving backwards. The stockman swiftly disarmed the old man, throwing a dull black pistol onto the floor behind him and kicking it backwards towards the bedroom door. With another groan from Hana, Flick pushed the stable manager towards the ensuite doorway. Jack shuffled in the direction the gun barrel jabbed him, the elderly persona returned. "You're not foolin' anyone, you cruel..."

"Argh!" Hana's cry made him impatient and he swore at Jack and pushed him headlong into the bathroom.

The internal doors in the house were on rollers, sliding out from the cavity between the wallboards and Flick was momentarily lost. He realised the futility of his action as the old man turned and smirked at him. Jack could lock himself in but Flick couldn't keep him there. He slid the door valiantly closed and then cast around him desperately, running his free hand through his hair and swearing to himself. Another groan of agony from Hana made him panic and he moved his gaze rapidly from her to the door and back again, the gun hanging dangerously from his shaking hand. "I dunno what to do!" he howled in frustration, torn.

Hana's child stopped feeding and his head lolled on his neck, a dribble of milk rolling back towards his left ear. In extreme pain, Hana laid him gently down on the floor next to her in his woolly shroud and collapsed back onto the wooden floor. She moaned out loud as another contraction wracked her body and the afterbirth began to expel itself.

Flick busied himself pulling the huge pine wardrobe across the floor, leaving a deep gouge in the pristine wood. It was full and heavy and he grunted and puffed in his ministrations. "I'm coming, sweetheart," he said to Hana in a break between shoves and a glance in her direction filled him with horror as blood and mess pooled on the ground beneath her. He swore again and put his full weight against the wooden structure. With a clunk it contacted the doorframe, filling its width but not the height of the gap. Flick snatched up Jack's pistol and put it in his pocket, feeling its weight pulling his jacket to one side. He retrieved the gun and lay it on the bed within easy reach, dropping to his knees next to Hana.

"It's gonna be ok, sweetheart, I promise, it's all gonna be fine." He cradled Hana's head in his arms and kissed her sweating, frizzled hair. "I let you down, honey. I'm sorry."

"Rad...i...o," Hana groaned as another contraction bit at her insides.

"What?" Flick failed to understand. Hana flapped her arm at Jack's jacket on the floor where he had dropped it. "I don't get it," Flick panicked, raising his voice in his alarm. "What do you want?"

"Radio," Hana groaned and sank down so that only the back of her head rested against the bed, the rest of her body sprawled inelegantly on the ground. She raised her knees and grunted. "Radio."

Sweat poured in rivulets down the side of Hana's head and dripped onto the stained rug. She groaned loudly and then cried out, calling for Logan as though she wanted to rip his head off. Chastened, Flick snatched the jacket and grappled around in its folds, quickly finding the hard, rectangular body of the walkie-talkie unit. "Sweet!" he squealed in childish glee and lifted the device to his ear. Depressing the call button he heard the beautiful sound of static. "Yesssss!"

The receptionist was aghast to hear the stockman's voice and even more confused when he demanded Logan and the cops. *And an ambulance.* "It's bad," his last sentence was accompanied by a gulp of terror as Flick cast a glance at Hana. "I don't know what to do. Get help. Quick. She's bleeding and it's not stopping!"

"He was going to kill me and the baby," Hana wailed. "He helped me give birth and then he was going to kill him." She started to sit up and Flick helped her reluctantly.

"Stay still, stay where you are," he insisted and she shook her head.

"No, it's done. It's lessening now. I think it's all out. I *hope* it's all out." She heaved herself up and let out a gasp of pain as she tried to sit on her bottom. Hana grabbed at Flick's hand unexpectedly. "The cord, Bobby. He cut the cord, Jack must have a knife!"

The stockman's eyes wandered to the wardrobe blocking the bathroom door. It no longer sat squarely but looked twisted in the aperture. "No, no, no!" he yelled. "Oh, crap, no!" Flick stood up and spun a full circle. "Where is he? Geez Hana, he's gone!" He ran to the empty bathroom and risked poking his head in. "Not good, not good!" he muttered and strutted back over to Hana. "Up! Get up!" he ordered. He gathered the newborn boy roughly into his arms and hauled Hana to her feet.

She wobbled unsteadily and leaned heavily on him. "I need to get you in the bathroom and you'll have to lock yourself in," he said firmly.

"No way!" Hana protested. "Wait, wait!" She bent double for a moment, clutching her stomach. Awful stuff leaked down her legs and dripped onto the wooden floor underneath her.

"Oh, Hana, sweetheart, I'm so sorry." Flick cradled the sleeping boy in one arm and supported Hana with the other. The sleeve of her cardigan dragged on the floor, failing miserably as a baby blanket. Originally cream it was stained beyond recovery. Flick kissed the top of Hana's head. "I need to get you safe and then grab the shotgun, Hana. He can't be far and if he gets a weapon, I won't be able to stop him."

"Give me the baby," Hana insisted, "and you get the gun."

After a moment's hesitation, the man gently handed the infant into Hana's shaking arms and dived back to the bed for the shotgun. He was back in seconds with it in his arms, the pistol clanking in his pocket against his keys. "Come on, quickly." Once in the bathroom, Flick shoved the toilet seat down and helped Hana to sit on the lid.

"Lock the door," Hana begged. "Please don't leave me."

Reluctantly he shot the catch on the ensuite and went back to Hana. He folded her head into his arms and breathed in her scent. Her breathing sounded rasping and shallow. "He killed Sylvia," Hana sniffed. "I just don't understand why he did that. She was leaving."

"He couldn't be sure of that," Flick whispered. "He just saw that she was hell bent on wrecking things for Logan and he dealt with her."

"Why though? What did it have to do with him, Bobby?" Hana pressed her head from his grip and wiped the baby's mouth with her forefinger. Hana stared up at her rescuer with wide green eyes. Flick squatted down next to her, his blue eyes boring into hers.

"He's Logan's grandfather, sweetheart. He was Reuben Du Rose's father."

Hana shook her head instantly. "No, that's not right." Her face dropped its expression of denial as she recalled the strange comment Phoenix Du Rose had made in her diary. She had recounted Reuben arguing with his father, long after Henri Du Rose's death. "Jack?" she asked. "How do *you* know?"

"I took the diaries, love," Flick said softly. "I broke in and took them. You were real upset about something in them and I thought if I got rid of the damn things, it would make you happy. I came to say goodbye and overheard you and Will talking. I watched you reading them heaps of times and they made you sad." He bit his lip. "I shouldn't have read them but I did. Geez Hana. This family's a mess. Jack was Phoenix Du Rose's older brother. His full name is Jacob Darcy Du Rose and he was sent to live with the French side of the family as a small boy. An uncle came for him. Nobody ever heard from him again. Then he came back when he was in his early twenties. Phoenix knew who he was but nobody else. He could read and write French and English and learned sign language in France. He had gotten himself a good education and he taught her everything he knew."

"I don't get how Jack was Reuben's father if he and Phoenix were...brother and sister. You must have read it wrong."

"I didn't, I promise, Hana. I read it over and over again. It only happened the once and they were both devastated."

"No, no," Hana shook her head. "It's not true."

"It is, you'll see. They didn't grow up together, they were like two strangers with lots in common. They were gutted, especially when the old lady found she was pregnant with Reuben. Look Hana, I went to Jack's house. On the walls he's got photos of him with a baby and a wee boy. Black and white photos..."

"His grandchildren!" Hana groaned and Flick shook his head decisively.

"No, Hana. The photos are him and Reuben. He brought Reuben up after Henri Du Rose died and he had a massive influence on Logan. There's copies of the same photos between the pages of one of the diaries. Phoenix wrote on the back that it was Reuben and JD. Jacob Darcy Du Rose."

"But I thought he had a wife and children and...grandchildren," Hana sobbed, rocking herself back and forwards disturbing the little boy in her arms.

"He's got nobody, Hana. He never did have. I promise you, the photos are him and Reuben as a baby and toddler. They obviously didn't risk it as the kid got older and more recognisable."

"What a mess," Hana groaned. "What a damn big mess. But how come the people of the township didn't recognise him when he came back? It doesn't make sense. This town knows everything about everyone. Nobody has ever mentioned him. Someone would have said."

"Look, love," Flick stroked his finger gently across Hana's cheek, removing a tear streak she hadn't known was there. "Having a handicapped kid back then wouldn't have been much fun. It was a harder life, unimaginable. Those kids didn't stand much chance, they were seen as a burden and you know how Leslie goes mad now whenever she thinks that something's *tapu* or cursed." Hana nodded. "Well, maybe they sent him away for his own good."

Hana's son let out a strangled cry that made both adults jump and she almost dropped him.

"Hana, I need to go and find Jack," Flick said softly. "He's only got to come back here with a decent shotgun and he could blow us all into orbit."

"That's what he wants," she wailed. "Both of us and this baby dead, would only achieve what he wanted."

"Well he's gonna be disappointed then." Flick smiled at Hana and she sniffed disgustingly. He laughed softly at her.

"Do you think he killed the blond drover who had an affair with Reuben's wife then? Caroline's father."

Flick nodded his head. "Fairly certain he did. I wonder if he buried him near where they found the woman recently."

"Sylvia," Hana said sadly. "I think so. When the cops showed up, I really thought that was who they'd found, but then it turned out to be her."

"He thought we were having an affair. He's been watching this house at night, trying to catch us out. I've been tracking him for the last few weeks."

Hana's eyes were wide and disbelieving. "Did he give you the black eye? I thought it was Logan."

"Yeah he crept up on me. For a deaf guy he's pretty silent. I didn't know what it was for at first, but after the other guys started calling me 'the blond drover' and I got the diaries, I knew. He would have killed me and dumped my body and just made sure everyone knew I left of my own accord."

"How come he still owns part of the property at the bottom of the mountain?" Hana asked and Flick shrugged.

"That I don't know, but I figure it should all have been his as the eldest son. Nobody knew he was still alive so the chief named Phoenix. Maybe there was provision in his will for a portion to stay his, or maybe Phoenix gave it to him. We might never know, Hana. But I definitely need to go."

"No, please," Hana panicked as she grappled with the child in the woolly cardigan. She lifted the baby over her shoulder, patting his back gently and he fretted less.

"Where are Logan's guns?" Flick checked the pistol quickly and pushed it into his jacket pocket. He spoke as he worked, cracking the shotgun, peering at the cartridges and snapping it closed again.

"In the gun cupboard in the garage," Hana sniffed, her voice sounding tiny and insignificant against the clicking of metal. "He keeps the key on him."

"Sweetheart, think. Could Jack have the spare?"

"No, yes, no...I don't know." Hana closed her eyes and tipped her head back in desperation. "No. I'm sure no. I had to ask him for it when I wanted to practice. I always dreaded him turning up and telling me that I was doing it wrong."

"Hana, I'm gonna sort this and then I need to leave."

"Leave? But you're coming back?"

"No, sweetheart, I can't come back."

"Why? Why not? I don't understand!" Her voice rose and the baby's face puckered again. Flick squatted down next to her and rested his forearms on her thigh.

"I love you, Hana. I love you like Reuben loved Miriam and like Jack so obviously loved Phoenix. And I can't spend the rest of my life watching you with your husband and children and knowing that I get to have no part of that. Jack hitting me and then reading those diaries…it's made me see what I've got to look forward to. I don't want a messed up life where I spend my days wishing I could wake up next to you or engineer ways to see you. When I drove you to the hospital, I imagined what it would be like to be your husband and this wee boy to be mine and I hated Logan for turning up like that. I asked you that night in your kitchen to come with me and I saw it in your face, you don't feel that way about me."

Hana's face was screwed up in agony and fat tears rolled down her pale skin. Even dark eyed and in distress she was beautiful and Flick ran his thumb down her cheek wistfully. "I've watched you for most of the last month, sweetheart. I've seen you up late reading and playing with your wee girl. And I've seen you with him. You love him and I know that you can't love that way twice. It's all or nothing with you and it makes me hurt…in here." Flick placed an unsteady hand on his chest. "I need to go, Hana. I need to leave before you end up hating me or Logan puts a bullet in my head."

"I won't hate you, Bobby," Hana sobbed. Flick laughed sadly. "I notice you didn't deny that your husband might shoot me though. And he'd be right. Because if I stay here, darlin', I will dedicate my life to wrecking your marriage until I get what I want, or destroy both of us in the process. And you don't deserve that." Flick stood up and looked down on Hana for the last time. "I'm leavin' you the shotgun. If you hear someone moving that cupboard, put the baby in the bath and cover him with the towels. It'll stop his ears being damaged, because when this thing goes off, sweetheart, it will deafen both of you. Don't hesitate, shoot. I know you can." Flick leaned the gun up against the wall next to Hana. "You're a pretty crack shot, lady." His eyes crinkled at the edges as he smiled fondly at her. "You've got heaps better in the last few months. I watched you on and off. It was hard not to walk over and give you pointers, but you're doin' just fine."

"You've been coming up that long?" Hana's eyes were wide and he nodded.

"*Jack's* been coming up that long, ever since you got back from Europe. So yes. I have."

"Did you leave the cigarette ends?" Hana asked him unexpectedly, wiping her nose on her arm. "The cows trampled them but I definitely saw them there."

Flick shook his head. "No sweetheart. That was Jack's secret vice. He grows it at his place. He got Alfred into it. Jack rolled his own and smoked a couple up here each night. He came up on the quad bike and left it on the other side of the paddock down in the bush. I camped not far from here in the dense part about quarter of a kilometre away. I'd get into position earlier than him. You heard him arrive once. I saw you stop and look confused. You heard the bike because the wind was in the wrong direction."

"How could an old man just stand there all night?" Hana sighed and Flick shook his head.

"He's a maniac, sweetheart. But you're just trying to delay me. I'd never have let him touch you. I'm going, Hana. Remember what I said, if you hear anyone on the other side of the door, just pull the trigger. But I'll find him first, so don't worry."

Flick's ash blond head dipped in reverence to her and Hana saw tears in his vivid blue eyes as he fixed his top teeth firmly over his lower lip. He held his hand out to her. "Lock the door after me, can you stand up?"

Hana nodded and reached for his strong fingers, hauling herself up and managing to balance the baby one-handed. "You don't have to go, Bobby. You said the receptionist was sending help."

Flick smiled and kept her fingers held tightly in his. "She is, but it won't be quick. And if Jack means to take you and that wee one out, he'll be making his move soon. Guys like him always have a Plan B. Hana, let me go."

Hana's face crumpled and she tried to mouth the words, "Thank you," failing miserably as they came out garbled and messy. Robert Dressler, also known as 'Flick' for his legendary skill with a knife, wrapped his arms around Hana and gave her a squeeze of solidarity and love. Then he leaned down and kissed her gently on her wet cheek, his bristles scratching her soft skin.

"Be happy," he whispered, his voice husky and laden with sadness. He unlocked the bathroom door and slid it back into the wall slowly, taking the gun from his pocket and poking his head cautiously around the wardrobe. His body slid through the gap and without looking at Hana again, he closed the aperture gently and with a start, Hana stepped forward and shot the catch upwards with trembling fingers. The baby over her shoulder snuffled and complained as she took his weight one handed.

"Just us now," Hana said, hearing how pitiful she sounded as though observing herself through another's eyes. She felt the blood running down her legs and stepped carefully so that she didn't slip. The light tiles looked like they had entertained a massacre. Hana settled herself on the toilet lid again and exposed her other breast for the baby. He opened his mouth and made distressed noises, smelling the milk and latching on easily. It caused the stomach cramps to increase again and Hana persuaded herself that it was natural and good. "Come on little piggy," she groaned. "Feed quickly and then mama needs to put you in the bath for a little while. There's something I have to do." With her free hand, Hana stroked the baby's tuft of auburn hair. It stuck up on his head exactly like his daddy's and apart from his un-Du-Rose-like colour, he was pure Logan. His skin was soft and porcelain and he fed greedily.

Hana felt the wetness percolate through the cardigan and soak her dress, mingling with the other awful stuff in the material. It felt uncomfortable. "Well, at least we know everything's working," she told her son optimistically. He snuffed into her breast and Hana heard the satisfying *sloop, sloop* of him drinking deeply. She smiled to herself at her baby's strength, already apparent at less than an hour old. "Be a survivor, baby," she willed him.

The boy was done quickly, efficiently feeding himself to sleep. Hana winded him for a little while, hearing a small burp pop out of his tiny mouth. She wrapped the cardigan tighter, swaddling up his arms and legs and balling the wet part away from his body as she laid him in the dry bath. Hana laid a towel under his body to stop the chill from the cold metal and covered him with another one from the heated towel rail, momentarily comforted by the artificial warmth and the scent of Logan that drifted up from it. "Sorry, boy," she whispered as she balled up tiny pieces of cotton wool from the vanity drawer and slipped it into his ears. "Not meant to do this but I don't want to deafen you."

Hana used Phoenix's plastic tray across the bath to make a bridge over the baby's sleeping head. She draped the last two bath towels over it, making a tent that might absorb a little of the sound of the shotgun discharging.

Hana picked up the heavy gun and balanced it against her shoulder, just as Logan had taught her. It was far weightier than the gun she sometimes used but the principle was the same. She lined up the tiny sight with the centre of the door, squeezing her left eye closed and sighting with her right. Her finger on the trigger was light and Hana felt surprised at how natural it seemed after her hours of practice. Flick evidently saw her outside with her small pistol, shooting cans off the rail at the side of the house while Phoenix slept. It was a curiously violating sensation. "That's embarrassing," she groaned quietly to herself. He would have seen all the tantrums she had when she missed and probably laughed at the swearing she used to vent her frustration. "Surprised he managed to resist putting me straight," she said out loud and heard her son move his limbs in the bath. "Please don't cry, baby," she begged him. "I don't think I can make that tent twice if I have to pick you up."

Hana settled herself gingerly on the toilet seat, wincing at the pain between her legs. She daren't look at the blood stained floor anymore. She kept the gun trained on the door, but its weight cramped her arms after a short time. Her mind strayed to everything Flick had told her. She couldn't seem to process it all properly, her brain fogged and incapable. "Oh, God, please help me!" she prayed, her voice a low wail. "I've messed up everything!"

A low rumble came through the floor to Hana's bare feet as the wardrobe moved and she held her breath in trepidation. "Please God, help me defend my son," she begged, her face stiff and tight from her dried tears. Unable to stand, she stayed on the toilet seat and supported the weapon, taking aim at the spot where the intruder's heart would likely be as soon as he stepped through the door. *Breathe in, breathe out, fire, breathe in, breathe out, fire*, she told herself, stilling her body. Someone pulled at the door, trying to slide it sideways but prevented by the lock. Hana's breathing made the sight move up and down on the point she concentrated on and she worked hard to bring it under control, feeling the pounding of her heart rendering an accurate shot impossible. "Please be Bobby," she begged in a hushed whisper, knowing that it wasn't. The blond drover would have shouted that it was safe and told her to unlock the d oor. *Unless he was already dead.*

Jack had killed him and come back for her, expunging any trace of anyone who could hurt his twisted legacy. The denied Du Rose son intended to kill her and what? Subject Logan to starting again? He wouldn't, Hana knew it deep down in her soul. Her husband had nothing left to give and nobody to give it to. "*I'm not going to die, I'm not going to die,*" she chanted, silencing herself when the tiny movement of her lips made the ridged sights move wildly up and down on the target.

Hana heard the sound of metal on metal. The lock had a screw type thing on the outside and whenever she locked herself in the bathroom in a strop, Logan always appeared with a coin in his hand looking smug. "Jack would have taught him," Hana whispered out loud, her voice a husky squawk, "Jack taught him everything." *It was Jack.* She knew it in her heart of hearts. Hana heard a dull thwack come from outside, reverberating around the bush and echoing off the mountains and she recognised it as a gunshot. It triggered something in her brain and she took careful aim at the door. Nobody would help her in time and Jack clattered against the door as the lock slowly turned.

Hana trained the tiny pronged sight on the centre of the door, willing her vision to settle on the space between the markers. She depressed the trigger slowly, feeling the tension against her index finger. Her stomach ached, her heart pounded in her breast, bringing problems of its own and her maternalism dictated that her child's welfare was infinitely more important than hers. The door creaked as it started to slide open and Hana's finger closed the final millimetres required by the trigger. The heavy gun kicked back against her shoulder, harder than she expected and her shot went too high and wide. The cartridge shattered the doorframe to the left of the opening, ripping the wood wide open and sending shards in every direction. Hana put her hands over her head and dropped the gun which kicked again, accidentally blowing a hole in the wall to the left of the door and narrowly missing the glass shower cubicle. Shocked grey eyes in a wizened face peered around the remainder of the door frame after a few moments of deafening silence, as the air molecules resettled themselves. It was over and Hana had failed.

Chapter 57

The bath towels over Hana's son were decorated in wood shards and chunks of plasterboard. But the tent held its shape and he was safe. He gave a frightened wail which galvanised his mother and she set her body rigidly and turned to greet her killer.

Alfred's terrified eyes glinted at her from his position in the doorway, with only his head poking through. He hadn't come empty handed and the gun in his hand matched Hana's like a twin. They stared at each other for a long moment and then Alfred knitted his brow and handed the gun behind him. "Hana?" he said cautiously, venturing further into the room. His boots stuck to the blood on the tiled surface, making the sound of a child pulling off wrongly stuck stickers and reattaching them. *Stick, rip, stick.* He leaned down and picked up the gun, pulling it towards him using the centre of the barrel. Cracking it open he looked inside and then back at Hana, before handing that backwards too. A hand appeared in the doorway and took it and Hana heard it being laid down on the floorboards in the bedroom. Alfred approached his daughter-in-law extremely carefully, eyeing her hands and body for other weapons. When he turned his head she saw cuts on the side of his face from the shattered doorframe, one of them bleeding in a steady, relentless flow.

She closed her eyes and raised her hands to her face. *I just nearly shot my father-in-law.* Hana breathed in and her green eyes widened in fear as the inhale kept on coming, locked on a one way system that threatened to explode her chest. She made dreadful noises and saw her own hands streaked with the baby's mess and her own.

"Shush, shush, it's over now *kōtiro*," Alfred whispered and sat on the side of the bath next to Hana. He leaned over and put his long arms around her shaking frame. "It's just shock, honey. It'll pass." He said something in *Māori* to the person in the bedroom and Hana clung to the gentle lilt of his voice and the comforting language.

"Bobby," she cried, hearing the hysteria in her voice. "Jack's killed Bobby."

"Who's she talking about?" Alfred shot his question towards the doorway and Toby's face appeared. The head stockman swore and looked guilty.

"Flick. Jack said he'd moved on. We thought it was weird at the time." He said a swear word that was infinitely unrepeatable. "I should have checked it out. Sorry. He must still be around here."

"He gave me the gun," Hana rambled into Alfred's shoulder. "He told me to shoot whoever came through that door. I didn't know it was you, I'm so sorry."

"So youse didn't mean to nearly take my bloody head off then?" Hana heard the smirk in Alfred's voice. "Well, that's a relief. When did Flick give youse the gun?"

"Now! Just now!" Hana wailed. "Then he went after Jack to stop him coming back for me and..."

"Flick's still here?" Toby looked rapidly alert. "That must have been the shot we heard." He jerked his head towards Alfred who nodded and turned back to Hana.

"Ella on reception said she was sure it was Flick who called in. Geez I thought she made a mistake. We came up here to check it out. It sounded like some half-baked story...go help him Toby. Be careful."

"Help Flick, not Jack!" Hana screamed. "Jack wants me dead! He killed Sylvia and the blond drover. He wants me *dead!*"

Toby stopped in the doorway looking ashen. "No! I came up here to deal with Flick. You're not making any sense."

"Bobby...Flick helped me. He hid me in here with the gun and told me to shoot Jack when he came after me. Please. I think he's shot Bobby outside. Please find him."

"Jack did *this?*" Toby indicated the blood soaked floor and the shattered room. Hana halted in confusion and then nodded the lie. *No, Jack hadn't spread afterbirth all over two rooms or shot the crap out of her ensuite. She had.* But it seemed too hard to explain and Hana felt a wave of guilt as Toby disappeared from the bathroom and Hana heard him gabbling into the radio. Then she felt the vibration of his heavy footsteps disappearing at a run down the hallway and the sound of the gun barrel cracking closed.

Alfred's arms around Hana felt heavy and claustrophobic and she wriggled free. "I want Logan," she demanded and he nodded.

"Ok." He ran his hand through his hair and then looked hard at Hana. "Jack tried to kill you? Our Jack?"

Hana nodded, relieved to feel her heart rate subsiding and the hazy lightness of her vision slowly returning to normal. "He thought I was having an affair with Flick because he took me to the hospital. Then when he saw the baby, he decided it was true. He's been watching me..."

"Wait up, saw what baby?"

"*My* baby!" Hana's eyes widened in fear as she contemplated the towel-tent in the bath. Panic raced her heart again as she listened to the silence. She pushed Alfred roughly out of the way and peeled the top layer of towel away, dropping it with its builders' rubble at the plug end. The next layer was clean and when she moved the plastic tray, the pink cheeked child peered out at her, his brow knitted and his eyes flicking around at the abrupt invasion of light. Hana lifted him like china and put him over her shoulder, pulling the cotton wool from his tiny ears. Without meaning to, Hana had recreated her womb for him, the darkness of the expensive, heavy towels and the cotton wool in his ears amplifying his heartbeat and giving him comfort. He didn't behave like anything hurt and shattered eardrums would have yielded an instant response. He lay over her shoulder and sucked on his fist, hungry again.

Alfred stared at the child in amazement, instantly understanding the blood-stained floor and state of Hana's clothing. "Sit down," he ordered her. "Before you fall down. I'll get yer man up 'ere quick."

Logan didn't respond to Alfred's radio call as he galloped Sacha the fast route through the bush, arriving a few minutes afterwards. He flung himself from the mare and ran into the house, leaving her to find grass and water for herself. He had free ridden up, bareback with only a halter rope around her neck. Sacha sensed the spite and tension in the laden air and her body stiffened.

Hana saw her husband's grey eyes, dark and conflicted as he appeared in the ensuite doorway, having passed by the ruined, bloodied rug and seen the holes in the walls and doorframe. For once, her stunning husband was speechless.

Without permission, Hana's soul instantly plugged into his and drew safety from his presence, releasing her to resume her role as the frightened woman. She sniffed and tears ran like she had flicked a switch and Alfred stepped back to allow Logan to clear up the mess that was his wife. "I'm not sure which will take longer," the old man remarked to Toby, "the bathroom or the woman."

Hana heard their muffled conversation but couldn't let go of Logan. Squashed between them, their redheaded son fed happily, the constriction familiar and safe and the added bonus of real sustenance pleasing.

Alfred walked back into the room. "The emergency services are here," he announced in hushed tones. "Loge, I need to talk to you."

A paramedic pushed past him, closely followed by a uniformed policeman. Both took in the blood spattered floor and the state of Hana. As Logan stood up, the cop noticed Hana feeding the baby and respectfully looked away but the paramedic blundered straight on in, kneeling in the mess and pressing her with a series of questions. Logan went to the doorway in response to Alfred's look and they had a whispered conversation with Toby over by the bedroom window. Their faces were grave.

"He tried to kill me," Hana told the paramedic in a strangled voice, the tears dripping into the baby's silky red hair. "He helped to deliver my son and when he saw him...he had a pistol."

The policeman's interest was piqued and he listened carefully to Hana's ramblings. "Touch nothing!" he said to the men in the bedroom. "In fact, I want you out of here, now."

"Not without my wife!" Logan said with a glare. The local cop bit his lip at the tone in Logan's voice and contemplated making him leave. But not for long. "I go when she goes," Logan reiterated and the cop backed down, forcing Alfred and Toby to leave the room while he used the radio on his vest. Responding to a hazy, crackled sound from the device, the cop appealed to Logan in a different tone, putting his head around the doorway and averting his eyes. "Mr Du Rose, there's a problem. I need your help."

Logan lifted his backside from the side of the bath and walked towards the door. "What?"

The cop lowered his voice and looked at Hana sideways as the paramedic withdrew his stethoscope from inside her shirt. "There's a massive white horse blocking the gate. It won't let anyone else in. My colleague just radioed to say that it's kicked the side of the squad car in."

The baby fell asleep on his mother's chest, his arms splayed out to the sides and his soft cheek pressing into her neck. Logan sat on the bench seat opposite, swaying with the movement of the ambulance as it surged towards Auckland General Hospital. He watched Hana intently but his mind was conflicted. Hana saw that he felt split. He wanted to be with her and their son, but he needed to be elsewhere. "Did Toby find Bobby?" Hana whispered as the paramedic moved away with the packaging from the cannula in his fingers.

Logan shook his head. "No, don't worry about him. I know him. He'll be ok."

"What about...*him*..." Hana began and Logan reached across and laid his hand over hers, their son's body underneath the pile of fingers. He tried not to bang the cannula, aware of the cop to his left listening and watching everything. "It's all fine," his eyes promised.

"Bobby was a hero," Hana said and Logan's eyes flashed as his head moved imperceptibly side to side. Hana shut up.

"Trust me," he whispered and leaned in far enough to kiss her on the forehead. The vehicle lurched and Logan braced his arm against the window ledge above Hana so that his body shielded her from view. "He's beautiful," he said, staring down at his son. "He looks exactly like Phoe, but just more...orange."

"Jack thought he wasn't yours," Hana choked, "he was going to kill us."

"Geez," Logan sighed. "How the hell did he think you managed that in Europe with me less than a metre away from you for four months? Stupid old man!"

"He thought I had an affair with Bobby," Hana whispered, alarmed to see the cop appear next to the stretcher. "But I didn't, I promise." Her eyes darted back to Logan, wide and afraid.

Logan shook his head. "I've been a dick lately and I wouldn't have been able to blame you if you had. But I know you didn't, it's fine. He looks like one of us, just...orange."

"Stop saying that!" Hana hissed, her offence rising.

Logan smirked. "What you gonna do, woman? Shoot more of the house to sh..." Hana put her free hand over her husband's mouth.

"It was an accident."

"Er, Ma'am, you need to wait until I've taken your statement before you start explaining things to your husband."

"Sod off," Logan said bridling. "I'm talking to my wife." His face set hard and his jaw ground furiously under his bristly cheek.

"Sir!" the policeman exercised his authority and Logan's eyes flicked to Hana's face. She rolled her eyes and looked exhausted. Logan kissed her on the lips just to make his point and then sat back on his seat, giving the cop sideways looks of pure malice. The paramedic pushed his body into the small space and shielded Hana from further testosterone laden muscle flexing and by the time they reached the emergency department, Logan felt sorely ashamed of himself.

The police officer stood outside the curtain while an obstetrician examined Hana and Logan stayed with her. They were transferred quickly to the maternity ward and the cop accompanied them. "This is embarrassing," Hana groaned to the uniformed man as everyone stared at the little group entering the ward. "Don't you have some mufti clothes to change into and then at least I can pretend you're my brother or something?" Her eyes widened as she stared at her husband in horror. "Oh, no! My brother. Please could you ring Mark? And the children, what about Bo and Izzie?"

"Hana," Logan's irritation was almost at surface level. "I will deal with it. Please just let them check you out properly and when I know that you're ok and my son is ok, I will tell the whole bloody world!"

"What about Phoe?"

"Phoe doesn't know anything. She's having a great time with Leslie and Wiri at the hotel. She wants a sister, Hana. She won't care."

"No, I mean, is she ok?"

"She's fine, babe. She'd rather you gave birth to a puppy, but she'll be fine. Let's just stop worrying about things we can't change."

Hana looked at her husband through narrowed eyes. He wasn't talking about *her* worrying at all, but about himself. She settled down and allowed the midwife to peel the sleeping baby off her chest and take him away to be measured, weighed and properly looked at. When Hana could no longer see the fluffy red topknot she panicked. "Logan go with him, please. Don't leave him."

Logan felt torn. He hovered next to the bed, unsure which direction to go in and then left the room, jogging quickly after the midwife. They were back within a few minutes and Logan held a cleaner version of his son in his arms, wrapped in a hospital blanket. A tiny nappy with blue edging peeked out of the fold, wrinkling one fat little thigh. Hana relaxed when she saw her baby again and mouthed a silent, "*Thank you,*" at her husband. He winked at her and that reassured her further.

The female obstetrician finished poking Hana's stomach and pulled her dress down over her exposed thighs. She stood up and washed her hands at the sink next to the bed. "Well, that's not bad at all," she smiled back at Hana. "A little tearing but everything seems to be going back to where it should. I'd rather not stitch anything that will heal by itself. There's no way of knowing if the placenta is complete, obviously what the paramedics collected wasn't all of it."

"Yeah, sorry about that," Hana pulled a face and shoved her feet underneath the blanket, feeling the cold. She had noticed a strange tremor happening underneath the bed. It was irritating. "I think the afterbirth is pretty much spread across the bedroom rug and there's quite a bit in the bathroom." She looked at Logan. "I'm so sorry, you built me a beautiful house and I've shot it up and spread stuff everywhere." Hana shivered. "Are we having an earthquake, I can't keep still."

The obstetrician and Hana's husband exchanged a concerned look. "Er...no," Logan began but the doctor smiled in complete control and studied the monitors attached to Hana's body. Pulse, temperature and blood pressure listed in front of her at the push of a button.

"Your body temperature is low, possibly from shock." She smiled again, a white-toothed woman in her late twenties, "And you're not wearing very much."

Hana looked down at her shabby maternity dress and bare knees. She bit her lip, feeling embarrassed. "What do I do?" she asked.

"Well, you can try not worrying for a start," the doctor patted her on the shoulder. "Let's get you mobile and then you need to go for a nice hot shower, get cleaned up and we'll find you a gown."

"I don't want my clothes anymore," Hana told her husband. "I never want to see them again."

The policeman's face appeared through a chink in the curtains. "I'll be taking those thanks."

Logan gritted his teeth and his grey eyes flashed. The cop's head disappeared and the gap closed.

"Why does he want my clothes?" Hana panicked. "Is it because I fired the gun? I don't have a licence to fire the big ones. What's going to happen?"

Logan gritted his teeth and the doctor disappeared outside. Hana heard hushed voices arguing outside the cubicle.

"I'm in trouble, aren't I? What's going to happen to me?"

"Nothing, Hana! Nothing's going to happen to you, babe. Just ignore that dick, he doesn't know what he's talking about. Jack wanted to hurt you so they need your clothes as evidence. That's all."

Hana watched as Logan became momentarily distracted by the tiny boy in his arms. All she saw was white blanket and fat, waving arms. She saw her husband smile and look entranced. *His son*. She calmed down. *It would be ok.*

The hot shower was glorious and Hana washed herself several times. The midwives allowed Logan to sit in with her, balancing his backside on the rounded toilet seat still cradling his son. She washed her hair twice, silently pondering the mess in her bathroom at home. "I'm never going to get it clean," she sighed, her breath fogging up the wall tiles as she watched the soapy water disappear through the drain hole under her feet.

"You'll be fine, babe. You must be clean now," Logan answered.

"Yeah, I think I am," Hana said, turning off the water. "I meant the house. I don't think I'll ever get it clean."

"Least of our problems at the moment," Logan gave his wife a wooden smile. Hana's brow furrowed as she slid the curtain aside and reached for the towel on a heated rail nearby.

"What do you mean?"

"Nothing, I'm just worried about you right now. I don't care about the house."

"About Flick," Hana started, seeing how Logan's eyes flashed dangerously. "I need to talk to you about him."

"Why?" Logan's answer was sharp.

"Jack beat him up and threatened to kill him...because of how he felt about me..."

Logan stood up. "You said there was nothing between you."

"There wasn't on my side, but Bobby did love me. He hung around because he saw Jack watching the house. The cigarette ends were Jack's. Bobby went after Jack because he said he wouldn't let it drop. Logan, I heard a gunshot from the bathroom. I need to know where they both are." Hana struggled with the hospital's paper underwear and the enormous sanitary towel. She sighed with relief. It felt good to achieve some level of normality. Her green eyes fixed on her husband's face.

He took a deep breath and answered her, "Jack's dead and Flick's gone."

Chapter 58

Logan looked at his wife with suspicion as she clutched at the sink unit. "What do you mean, *Flick's gone?*"

"Well, not dead gone," he said crassly and his eyes narrowed at her. "I don't want you to be concerned about him, Hana. He's not your business."

"He saved my life, Logan. And that baby in your arms and don't you forget it!"

Logan looked down at his sleeping son and exhaled in a snort of irritation, shaking his head in annoyance.

"Did he kill Jack?" Hana asked. "Where did it happen?"

"Jack's body was...mashed, Hana. Totally mashed. He had a bullet wound in his leg to incapacitate him, but the pistol was clean and thrown just out of his reach. Whoever shot him wanted the cops to find him, but they can't work out what happened after that. Toby reckons it's a blood bath. The body's in the bush away down the mountain. The cops were looking at him when we left. Alfred's sorting it all out."

Hana dropped the towel and put her arms through the pale blue hospital gown. She reached behind her and struggled to do up the tie behind her neck. "This is going to be fun to breastfeed in," she commented. Logan's eyes never moved from his wife's face and his jaw worked slowly over a piece of chewing gum. "Stop staring at me like that," she told him.

"Can look if I want to," he said insolently. "Got a marriage licence says I can."

"Not if I poke your eyes out," Hana replied and Logan snorted.

"I'll poke..."

Hana held her hand up, "Don't be vulgar in front of the children. And for the record, I can't sit down, let alone think about anything else."

Logan observed his wife in his unsettling way while she wrestled with a tie above the waistband of the knickers. "I just told you a man got smashed to bits on our property and you're surprisingly calm," Logan said, his eyes flashing their smoke grey warning. "Don't you care that your mate Flick might have executed him on your behalf?"

Hana turned to face her husband. "I should care, shouldn't I? It's not very Christian to feel relieved that Jack's dead. But I am. He won't be coming after me or our son and that awful eerie feeling I've had for months now, is gone. I can go back to leaving the curtains open at night and not sense that I'm being watched." She shrugged. "God forgive me but I'm relieved. I'm sorry for you because he was family." Hana studied Logan with a practiced eye. "But then you already knew that, didn't you?"

Logan twitched his lips, offering Hana his tell-tale confession without saying anything. Hana held onto the sink and watched her silent husband. "Who told you?" she asked softly.

"He did. When Kane and Barry split me open with the machete when I was eleven. He told me in the barn when nobody had time to take me back to the hospital to get the stitches out. He took them out for me and helped me get rid of the infection with plants from the bush. I wasn't allowed to tell anyone else, not even Alfred or Mum; it was between us. After that, he taught me everything he knew about horses and cattle and to some extent, people."

"But I don't understand. You thought Alfred was your father up until the day after the fire. Otherwise why did you get so upset when you found out Reuben was?"

Logan sighed and ran a hand over his face. "Jack told me he was *my* grandfather. I just assumed it meant Alfred was his. It never occurred to me Reuben was actually his son and he never elaborated. He either didn't want to spell it out or he figured I'd work it out. We never discussed it again, not even after Reuben died and the truth came out. But Reuben's death definitely affected him real deep. Now we know why."

"Did you know his real name?" Hana asked and Logan nodded. "Did you know he killed Caroline's birth father?" Logan's face dropped and he shook his head.

"No, I didn't know that. Why?"

"Her father was the blond drover who had an affair with Reuben's wife. Antoinette went up north to have the baby and left her there. But she couldn't cope and sent for her when she was almost two. Reuben knew, but allowed Antoinette to keep her daughter. You would never have been allowed to marry Caroline, Logan. You were both played by your family. Phoenix wrote in her diary that Caroline could never bear the Du Rose name and I'm certain that Jack would have fulfilled her wishes somehow. Maybe he scared her off on the day, or got Reuben to do it. We'll never know and I'm not going to ask her."

Logan tipped his son upright, his large hand behind the sleeping baby's head and laid him against his shoulder. "It's all academic now," he said with a wistful smile. "Because she's married Kane anyway, so she's a Du Rose..." his lips dropped open and his face looked aghast. "Oh that's sick."

Hana nodded. "But you know what? Antoinette was already a Du Rose, which makes Caroline half family anyway. She was just like Tama; she could have changed her name at any point. Instead, she grew up not really understanding who her parents were and striving to belong to something she already had a right to be part of. I think her father is buried on the property somewhere, possibly near Nev's new house. I think that's why

Jack lured Sylvia there before killing her. It was like a repeat of the first time."

Logan sighed and kissed the baby's downy crown. He swore softly and stared at a mark on the mirror with a faraway look in his eyes. "What a bloody mess."

"It is but I think we can sort this out. Logan, I need two things from you now," Hana said softly. "I need you to help me get Flick out of the country and I also need you to tell me how to smooth all of this out with the cops; without being untruthful. I don't want to have to lie to Bodie about any of this."

To her surprise, Logan nodded. "Ok."

Chapter 59

"So, you believe that..." Odering looked at his notebook, "this Jack person, killed Sylvia Clark? I thought he was in his nineties. How would he have managed that?"

"He worked with horses. He was strong as an ox," Logan replied. "He wasn't quite the doddery old man he appeared."

Hana remained silent, nursing her son underneath the large cardigan that one of the midwives had lent her. She felt scruffy and hopelessly exhausted. Part of her silence was because she had asked Logan for help and the other dominating factor - she didn't want any attention while she fed her baby and looked such a mess.

"So all the damage at the property recently, bricks through windows, cows let out, wire fences cut, you think that was all his doing? That a ninety year old man wandered the mountains doing damage and killing people? You expect me to believe that, do you? And how come this elderly man had no health service code, no documents, no income tax number, no driving licence, no bank account, no gun licence, nothing?"

"No idea," Logan answered, maintaining his usual calm, calculating exterior.

"But you're his employer," Odering pushed. "You can't just employ people without documentation and pay them cash their whole lives. The tax office isn't going to be happy with you." Odering looked particularly smug about that fact, imagining the Du Rose empire crumbling like a washout against the might of the New Zealand Inland Revenue Department. To his dismay, Logan shrugged, infuriating the detective with his practiced nonchalance.

"I never employed him. He was here when I was born. I never paid him a single day's wages. My grandmother gifted him the house behind the bunkhouse and the land it's on and he owned land at the front of the property up near the main road. He had nobody else and nowhere to go. His whole life was bound up in my family and his life's work was on that mountain. He ate the hotel food and he got people to fetch him stuff from town when he needed it. He was part of the furniture. You can turn my accounts inside out and you won't find anything to nail me or my predecessors."

Logan stood up finally. His height and stance were imposing. "Now, my wife's given you a statement of what happened to her, you have her clothing and presumably everything else you need is at the house. You've got nothing to keep you here, so it's time you left."

Odering lifted his hand in the air in defiance. "So the gun literally went off by accident?" He directed his question at Hana. She nodded, comfortable with her own honesty.

"Yes, I dropped it and it went off and damaged the room."

"Twice, how convenient," Odering replied, the smarminess in his voice making Logan grind his teeth. Hana neither confirmed, nor denied his statement. He shifted in his seat. "The deceased was on his knees, digging a hole in your garden. Any idea what that was about?"

Logan snorted. "If there's buried treasure, it's mine."

Odering glared at him. "I'm beginning to lose patience."

"How could he be digging?" Hana asked, fondling the tufty red hair on her son's head. He woke up and sucked greedily again, as though he'd forgotten what he was meant to be doing. "You said he was shot dead."

"His hands were covered in loose soil and there was a hole next to his...what remained of his head. The forensic guys found traces of fibre in the soil, some kind of hessian wrapping."

"What was in it?" Dread snaked its fingers around Hana's heart. "What did he find?"

"No idea," Odering said, slamming his notebook closed in temper. "The hole was empty."

Hana looked at her husband and shrugged, met by his confused grey eyes. It didn't take a genius to see they had no clue.

"And the man who was with you and has now disappeared, his name was..."

"Robert Hohaia," Logan responded confidently. "And he *is* on the books because he's worked for me for ages."

"Well I definitely need to speak to him," Odering said, shutting his notebook with a snap.

"You'll be lucky!" Logan snorted. "He only went to see Hana to say goodbye. He had a flight to catch."

"Not funny, Du Rose. I'll need to see him."

Logan shrugged and squared his broad, muscular shoulders. "She's given you what you've asked, now it's time for you to go," Logan took a step towards Odering and Bodie.

"Get lost, Du Rose," Bodie reacted. "This is my mother and you don't get to throw me out of here!"

"So come and see her out of uniform," Logan smiled, but the expression didn't reach his eyes. "Then you'll be welcome. My wife's been through hell today and needs to relax and get used to her new son. So *goodbye*." Logan put his body between the policemen and Hana, opening his long arm span to usher them towards the door.

"I want to say goodbye to my mother," Bodie stated, drawing himself up to his full height, which still didn't match Logan's six feet and four inches. Logan heard Hana sigh behind him and relented, smirking as Bodie brushed roughly past him.

The dark-skinned policeman leaned in and kissed his mother but there was no love in the action. It was done out of pure bloody-mindedness and Hana's face dropped in dismay.

Logan followed the cops out into the wide corridor. He let Odering walk on a short way and stepped close in behind Bodie. The younger man felt his presence and whirled around. Logan pushed his face into his stepson's and hissed, "One day, you little dick, you're going to take that uniform off for good. And that day, I'm gonna drop you harder than you ever thought possible." Logan stepped back, gave the man a nasty smirk and placed himself outside Hana's door like a sentry, leaving Bodie balling his fists, still stationary in the corridor.

Odering turned and found his subordinate missing. He looked confused at first until his eyes fixed on the senior sergeant working himself up into a frenzy about ten metres away from Logan Du Rose. "Johal," he hissed. "Just let it go."

Bodie clenched his jaw in fury and glared at the detective inspector through bottomless dark eyes. He stormed after him in a temper and Odering clapped him casually on the back. "You'll never win against him so don't even bother. I worked that one out a long time ago."

"How long ago?" Bodie asked sulkily, expecting the answer to be a matter of months. To his surprise, his superior put his head back and laughed, the sound hollow and filled with regret.

"Before you were born, my friend."

Hana watched the whole thing from the bedroom doorway, her son balanced over her shoulder. Logan spun on his heel and the smirk died on his face at the sight of her. He pursed his lips and looked like a naughty child. "Happy now?" she asked him, her face stony as she patted her little boy gently on his back. The gown hung limply around her legs and the long cardigan barely reached her thighs, only just hiding her modesty at the back. Logan screwed his face up. *Yeah you should look guilty,* Hana's green eyes told him.

Logan pressed past his wife and slipped into the ward. She kicked him on the ankle with her bare toes as he passed and his eyelashes fluttered with mirth. "Get in there!" she told him crossly, feeling irritated that she had somehow acquired not one, but two extra sons. "You're worse than he is," Hana complained. "I don't know which one is the bigger baby, but this little man has more maturity than either of you."

Logan sat in the seat next to Hana's bed and gazed intently at something out of the window. He stretched his long frame out on the chair and worked to control the blossoming grin on his face. When he turned back to Hana, his eyes crinkled at the edges and he looked like a whipped puppy. "You've got nice legs, woman," he smiled and Hana shook her head.

"No dice, cowboy," she said sarcastically. "Take your son while I nip to the bathroom."

Logan stood up and took the sleeping child from his wife. He leaned in and planted his lips over hers, his smouldering grey eyes glinting with promise. "I love you, Hana Du Rose," he whispered and she rolled her eyes. "I do," he protested, sounding hurt. "I said I'd deal with the cops and I did."

"I didn't mean you to pick a fight with my son!" Hana's irritation lurked dangerously near the surface. "I meant you to get them off Bobby's back and help me with the whole...not having the right gun licence thing.'"

Logan let out a laugh and the baby's arms shot out sideways in a fear reaction. His daddy pulled the blanket tighter round his son and swaddled him close into his strong chest. "I don't know about not having the *right* gun licence, babe. You don't have *any* gun licence!"

"That's completely academic," Hana waved her arm as though it was no big deal. "It's sorted now. Can you boys manage to behave for five minutes?" She eyeballed her husband and he shook his head in exasperation.

"Go woman, we'll be fine." Logan kissed his baby son's soft forehead and sighed, whispering to the sleeping redhead. "Something tells me you're gonna have her sparkling personality."

Chapter 60

Hana sat in the family dining room at the hotel with her son sleeping in Phoenix's old pram. Her daughter played happily on the rug by the sideboard, putting shapes into a box with matching holes. "You ok, baby?" Hana asked her and Phoenix screwed up her face.

"No, Mama. I not baby now. I big girl." She smiled beatifically at her mother and Hana felt sadness creep across her heart.

"You'll always be mine," she said softly. "Wanna cuddle?"

"In a minute," Phoenix replied, pushing the shapes into the holes with dexterous fingers. She fitted the final cube into its square hole and sat back on her heels with a look of satisfaction on her pretty face. "Ok nen, Mama," she said, standing up and tottering over to Hana in a new pair of pink gumboots that her baby brother had allegedly chosen for her. She held her hands up for Hana to lift her and Hana cuddled her beautiful daughter into her breast.

"You'll have to take your boots off to go to bed," she crooned into her hair and kissed her forehead.

"Na, fanks," Phoenix replied softly and pushed her thumb into her mouth.

"Funny girl," Hana breathed. "I love you."

"Luff you, Mama," the little girl whispered and closed her eyes. Hana cradled her daughter and rocked her son with her foot on the wheel of the pram. "What baby's name?" Phoenix asked as she snuggled harder into Hana's body.

"I dunno," Hana whispered. "Daddy's sorting it out. At the moment we're just calling him Baby but he should probably have a name soon. I want to call him Mac because he came from Ireland and my family name on my mother's side was McGillivray. Dad's not sure, he's up to something…" Hana looked down at Phoenix's closed eyes and sighed. "You're not listening are you?"

Hana lay back in her seat and enjoyed the sense of peace her sleeping children brought and prayed that her God would continue to protect them, even when she could not. Her mind reached out to Izzie and Bodie, stretching the fragile cord of maternal love and wishing them well. She started in fright as the heavy fire door shot open and Logan struggled through, carrying something heavy under his arm. "Ssshh," Hana told her husband, indicating the sleeping babies.

"Ok," Logan lowered his voice and leaned the heavy rectangular object against the wall and spun a chair around. He sat astride it, resting his arms along the back. His face was alight with excitement and Hana rolled her eyes. *What now?*

"Will's been helping me," he began. "You remember that really old photo from my grandma's boxes, you know, the one with the guy in all the frilly clothes?" Hana nodded helpfully, the image tugging gently on her memory. "Well, Will and I thought there was something odd about the grey colouring of his portrait so I've been into the attic and done some serious searching over the last few days -whenever you've been asleep at the house. I've uncovered heaps of stuff in those other wings. And I found this!" Logan stood up and spun the object around so Hana could see it.

A faded oil painting of a Frenchman took up most of the canvas, a reasonable likeness of the man in the sepia photograph. Hana bit her lip with surprise at the artist's impression of a curly swathe of bright red hair which coiled around the handsome face. A bushy red beard completed the image of a man with crinkles around his laughing eyes. His face was dour and serious for the era of the painting, but the twinkle remained, betraying a man of standing and wealth with a wicked sense of humour.

"Who is he?" Hana asked, looking at the tatty frame and painting, badly in need of restoration.

Logan's smile broadened. "He's the father of the first Du Rose who came to New Zealand. He put the money up for the family to come over. There's heaps of information about him in the attic. He sounds like an awesome guy. He was an entrepreneur in his time and made his own fortune. Real inspirational stuff."

"You want to name our son after him, don't you?" Hana's heart sank. She had already begun calling the little boy, *Mac*, in her head and it seemed to fit him somehow. "What was his name then?" She tried to make her question sound upbeat, as though the answer didn't have the power to make her miserable.

"That's the thing," Logan leaned the picture face outwards against the wall and sat down on his chair again. "I *would* like to name our son after him, but I need to be sure you're happy with it. I feel like I want to go back to something from before the Du Roses came over here and screwed everything up and I believe he's the last bastion of good sense before it all went wrong." Logan reached for Hana's hand and caressed her fingers in his. "What if we had McGillivray as his middle name after your mum's family and his calling name was Mac? Then have this name as his first name and when he gets older, let him decide?"

"What's the name then?" Hana asked. "Just tell me."

"Well, it's a Scottish name apparently and this particular Du Rose had a Scottish mother from Auchinleck in Ayreshire and it's Gaelic for hollow."

"Wow, that's weird."

"Oh, you think so?" Logan's nerve wavered and he looked nervous and awkward.

"Yes, because that's where my father's from," Hana smiled. "It's very odd. I always assumed your name was French. So what was the man's name? I can't agree to it if I don't know it, can I?"

"His name was Logan," her husband said with the same twinkle in his eye as the man in the painting. "His father took a wife from Scotland - no idea why yet. But the male line remained French and the Scots side went unrecognised - until now anyway." The unmistakeable grey eyes glittered out at Hana through the artist's brush strokes, alive and vital. She laughed and rolled her eyes.

"Are you serious?"

"Deadly," her husband smiled. "What do you think?"

Hana stared at the skirting board, noticing a chip out of the paintwork. She looked up at her husband with a concerned look in her eyes. "Do you ever worry that we called Phoe after your grandmother and...well, she didn't exactly make such a good job of things?"

Logan shook his head with certainty. "No, this wee girlie will do exactly what she wants. I remember my *Karani* Phoenix being a strong woman with a good heart and a headful of incredible knowledge. She had *mana* and greatness and people deferred to her. That's who I see when I look at our daughter, none of the other stuff. She can choose not to carry that forward. We all get that choice, don't we?"

"True," Hana said softly, feeling the warmth of her daughter's body through their combined clothing. "Yeah, actually, I like it. Heaps. Let's do it."

Logan Du Rose drew his wife's body into his, holding her like finest china and breathing in her clean scent. "Thank you," he whispered into her neck and Hana rubbed her free hand over his strong back.

"For what?"

"For being part of this with me. Helping to build this legacy. It's all gonna be ok, you know?"

Hana smiled and nodded, glad her son finally had a proper name. She snuggled into her husband's chest and felt the jade encrusted brooch dig into her thigh through the pocket of her jeans, its prick a timely accusation of her dilemma. The elderly jewellery condemned Hana, removed from Logan's grandfather's grave clothes and lost for two generations, it rested in the new matriarch's pocket. It was as lethally sharp as the day it was created, it's jade and paua decorations intricate and fine. Its preservation under such circumstances was a mystery. Nobody had told her where Jack died but Hana knew. His blood still stained the bottom of the old kauri tree, which bore all the family names except his. Logan's grandmother stole the brooch herself, unleashing the legend of the Du Rose curse more than sixty years before Hana Du Rose ever set foot on the mountain. The linen bag which kept it safe through all those seasons, had disintegrated as Hana picked it up out of the envelope. Will would be incensed if he knew she handled it without gloves. He would quit if he ever found out her intentions.

Logan's happiness seemed so complete, Hana didn't want to be the one to ruin it. She bore the pressing of the sharp needle-like object in her flesh and said nothing. A purely accidental find, the epitome of the Du Rose curse and its very existence weighed heavily on her heart. *Not today*, she told herself. *I'll let him be happy today.*

At home later, Hana stood on the deck in the dying sunshine and let Logan put their children to bed. Bobby's letter, mailed to her from England nestled in her hand, wrapped around the brooch. Hana had read it, reread it and then read it again and it looked creased and tattered around the folds. She wouldn't examine its contents again; she could remember them by heart.

'I found this in the old bastard's hand, Hana. I guess it was his property -now we know who he was, but I feel it belongs to you. I know what it is; I read the diaries, all of them. Thanks for making Logan help me. I know that was your doing. He has the diaries now, cursed things. I gave them to him at the airport, just so you know. I don't think he'll give them back to you; I wouldn't if I was him. I don't know why I kept that brooch. I guess it was so I had an

excuse to write to you and imagine your face one last time. I won't come back, but then you know that, don't you? I love you, Hana Du Rose and I always will. See you on the other side - then again, maybe not. I'm sure you won't end up where I'm going - Hell, not England. Although maybe they will prove to be the same place.

Forever yours,

Your blond drover, Bobby.

PS. I never killed Jack.'

Hana brushed the stray tear away. She was done crying. The object was heavy in her hand, the letter wrapped around the brooch and a heavy stone, barely fitting between her gripped fingers. A small *kete* lay on the ground, its tightly woven flax walls forming a bag of fifteen centimetres high and the same wide. It was adorned with a tiny piece of paua shell at the front in honour of the treasure it would bear. Hana pushed the package inside and slipped the string fastener around the decorative bone button.

"Why do you want a *kete*, girl?" Leslie's voice echoed in Hana's memory. "I haven't made one for years!"

"Just make it for her," Alfred interjected, his voice sounding harsh. His uncanny Du Rose perception made Hana's skin tingle and she nodded her gratitude to him.

Hana stood at the rail before the deadly drop beyond, the cliff falling away at her feet, rampant with native bush and hazardous climbs. The Tasman Sea sparkled in the distance, still turquoise despite the orange sunset blazing overhead. *Last chance*, Hana told herself. She could keep the brooch safe for Phoenix, gift it to her on behalf of her namesake. She could keep the letter too as part of her history. The matriarch's diaries called to Hana from Logan's hiding place, destructive and dangerous; another woman's history. *I don't want that for my daughter.* Bobby's letter and the brooch needed to rot and never be found by human hands, especially not Du Rose hands. Hana had contemplated every possible way of successfully disposing of the items. This was her best plan, unwittingly suggested by Will who once told her that Logan would tow the diaries up the mountain still in the safe and hurl it off. "He said best place for 'em," Will had laughed. Then his face dropped. "I'd kill 'im with me bare hands!"

Still Hana debated with herself. If the curator ever found out, he would leave in a hail of wheelchair wheels and dust.

"Hey gorgeous, what ya doin' out here." Logan's voice made Hana jump in guilt and she fought a flash of irritation.

"Just thinking," she replied, clutching the bag in her hand.

"Mac's a good kid, aye?" Logan reached his long arm around Hana's shoulders and cuddled her close. "He went into the cot like an angel."

Hana smiled, her face serene, belying the agony and dilemma in her chest. Logan looked down at the *kete* and then at Hana, his grey eyes questioning. Hana gulped. "Logan?" Her husband smiled in response. Hana held the bag up towards him and he took it, automatically weighing it in his strong palm. "Would you throw this for me, please? Out there." Hana pointed out towards Port Waikato and the sea in the far distance.

Logan looked down at the intricate *Māori* weaving for a moment and then back at his wife, her teeth gnawing at her bottom lip in a betrayal of her fear. A memory came to him of himself, hurling clods of earth from this place in frustration; throwing his dreams back in *Atua's* smiling face. The day he did that was the day he found Hana.

Logan bounced the bundle in a palm dotted with scars and cuts, exacerbated by his haemophilia. Then he drew his long arm backwards, the muscles rippling on his chest and arms as he released the object with force. It flew upwards, maintaining a decent trajectory as it arced and then coasted down into the canopy with the grace of a falcon. It landed too far away for Hana to hear the sound it made as it cascaded through branches and leaves to the impassable slopes below, but the highest Nikau palms shuddered to admit its cursed entrance. Hana sighed with relief and let her body slump against her husband's, burying her face in his chest.

Further down the mountain, Jacob Darcy Du Rose's killer grazed in peace, her sharp teeth nipping at the tasty summer shoots with contentment, the occasional snort her only speech. Her white ears flicked as something clicked in the universe and she shook the flies away from her face and exhaled a loud, snuffled gratification; her debt finally paid in full.

Du Rose Family Ties

SAMPLE CHAPTER

"Something's wrong!" The redhead lifted the reins in her left hand and the white horse halted under her, drawing a cloud of dust from the baked earth. "Did you hear that?"

"Yeah." Her companion stopped to listen, his Appaloosa shifting with impatience and dragging his hooves on the track.

"Three shots mean there's a hunter in distress." She turned in the saddle, her green eyes intense on his face. "Don't they?"

He groaned and ran his dusty hand through curly, blond hair. "No, please let's not do this, Mrs Du Rose? Your husband warned me you were the biggest distraction on this mountain."

Her inhalation sounded sharp as she widened her eyes and feigned shock. "That's mean! I don't even need you. I know this mountain as well as you do, David Allen!"

"Yeah, well I don't know it that well so get a move on, we need to get the cattle to the bottom before dark." David peered around Hana at the little band of calves who hung around on the track ahead of them. They spread out nervously, tugging at green shoots in the undergrowth, the native ferns unappetising.

Their tufty cream and patchy black bodies made them look more like giant teddy bears than the younger members of a lucrative beef herd. "Do a head count. Have we still got twelve?"

"Er, yeah, I think so. They won't keep still."

David sighed with exaggerated drama, pushing his dusty cowboy hat back on his head. His horse snorted with impatience and pawed the ground again. A crackly sound broke into the calm of the bush as the radio on David's saddle projected Logan Du Rose's voice into the air. David winced. He unhooked the walkie talkie and pushed it towards his companion. "You answer it. He's your husband."

"He's your boss!" Hana smiled smugly and tried to count the cattle, growling her exasperation as two kicked up their heels and fled down the track. The rest surged after them.

"Come in, Hana!" Logan's voice held an edge of impatience, blended with an undertone of fear.

"I hear ya." David's voice was low and deep, feigning calm as he spoke into the handset. "What's up?"

"You're late. There are only thirteen calves. It shouldn't take all day!"

David's mouth dropped open in horror. "Twelve. There were twelve up there. That's what Toby said and that's what we're droving."

"We've been back for hours now. Toby's ridden up the road twice. Where the hell are you?"

"Er..." David bit his lip and watched Hana's shapely form as she weaved the large marc around the calves on the track, herding them back into a tight knot. Her red hair flowed out behind her, the hair clip shucked an hour ago in the mud up near the Du Rose house at the top of the mountain. Dust and bush debris covered the back of her shirt and David gulped. "We took the scenic route and Mrs Du Rose fell off."

A string of expletives split the air with such vehemence, David fumbled the radio. Then, "Is she okay?"

"Logan, she's fine. She got straight back on. She's just..." David bit back the word and saw Hana shake her head and smirk.

"Don't say it to *him!*" she called up the track. "He won't be so understanding."

"Whatever! You are unmanageable. You're a complete bloody nightmare!"

"Are you talking to my wife?" Logan's voice crackled through the radio as David released the call button and his eyes bugged. He stared accusingly at his finger and tried not to cringe. Hana let out a peel of laughter. "Just get back here. Stop mucking around!" Logan's voice crackled again and David sighed as he fixed the radio back over its clip.

"Great, thanks for that. Now I'm offside with him!"

"No, you're not. He worries about me and I'm fine. You shouldn't have told him I fell off though." Hana reached forward and caressed the soft, furry neck beneath her fingers. "It was an accident. It wasn't your fault, was it Sacha?"

The horse's ears flicked back and forth as the mare nodded her head, snuffling softly and crunching on the metal bit in her mouth. David shook his head and edged his horse towards Hana and the surging knot of calves. "You're covered in muck and you've got crap in your hair. He'd have noticed and then yelled at me."

"Coward!" Hana reached behind her and yanked a fern from her long red hair. It resisted, breaking into pieces and she combed it out with slender fingers. "There's a way to tell my husband bad news and that wasn't it. You'll learn." She winked at David and sensed his unease, relenting and nudging Sacha into a tight turn. "It's fine, David. It was my own silly fault. He won't blame you."

"Yeah, he will." The man sounded fed up. "All those years as a British airman and I never had a sergeant like him. He's ruthless."

"He has to be," Hana replied, her voice wistful. "It's a harsh world and there aren't many breaks for people like us.

Loyalty's hard won on this mountain and not everyone we like is trustworthy."

"I know." David pushed his gelding into a lazy trot and rounded up a stray calf pulling at a supplejack vine. "Get on with ya!" He tapped the furry flank with the thong of his bull-whip and the small animal surged forward, nosing into the bunch.

"The gate's round the next bend," Hana said, jerking her head backwards. "Logan wants them in the first paddock so we're done. I'll corral them here if you ride ahead and open the gate, then I'll drive them forward."

David grunted. "Then I'll spend the next six months hearing all the reasons why we should have brought them down by road."

Hana rolled her eyes and tossed her head. The remains of the fern let go of her auburn curls and fluttered into the bush. "Nev told me *not* to take them by road!" Hana protested. "And I'll tell my husband that! Nev said the washout on the cliff would freak them out and make it unsafe."

"Well, get your story straight then!" David bit, urging his horse into a fast trot. He skirted the knot of jittery calves and made for the next bend as Hana's horse ducked and weaved to keep the beasts where she wanted them. She held her bull-whip at arm's length but didn't crack it, not wanting to start a small stampede.

Logan Du Rose owned the mountain, running a hotel, motel units, holiday park and a successful beef and horse stud business. His half-brother, Neville was the farm manager, but their communication skills were sadly lacking sometimes.

"Well, furry babies," Hana spoke to the calves, seeing twelve pairs of brown eyes turn towards her. "Now you've finished eating my front garden, you get promoted to the big paddocks. It's been nice having you stay, but I wish you'd learned to poo in one place."

The sparkiest of the bunch jerked his front feet as though to make a run for it and Hana moved her bull-whip as the group surged in a circle, pinned by her whip and Sacha's exacting hooves. "I actually won't miss *you!*" She directed her comment at the sparky steer with the glint in his eye as he circled and looked for an escape route. "Come on guys, I bottle fed you all and played mummy to you and this is how you repay me? Ingratitude is one of the ugliest sins, ya know?"

Knotty tails flicked against the midges swirling around in the humid bush landscape and the world was silent, except for the occasional snort or stamp. Sacha's body tensed, waiting for one of them to break so she could give chase. Hana felt powerful muscles shift under her thighs. "Yeah, give me warning next time, Sacha. It's great you know what you're doing, but half the time I don't. I'm not Logan; not even a poor substitute." Hana turned her head a fraction, feeling the tension in the herd increase with the prolonged wait. Something caught her eye on the ear of the smallest calf. "Is that a pink ribbon?" she asked, incredulous. She bit back a smile at her daughter's ingenuity. Her tiny children loved bottle feeding the calves. Two-and-a-half-year-old Phoenix and Hana's son, ten-month old Mac, treated them like huge, furry pets, which was probably the reason Logan decided to move them.

"It's open." David cantered up the track on his leggy gelding and the small herd jerked in alarm. Hana lifted Sacha's reins in an upward direction and lowered the whip. The white mare backed up into the bush until her fetlocks encountered the winding supplejack vine and then she halted, crunching on her bit and watching the cattle through experienced eyes.

"Get on!" Hana clicked her tongue and tapped the furry bottoms gently with her whip. They bunched together, their eyes rolling and frightened, staying close to her as their substitute parent. "Come on babies!" she protested and David snorted. Hana sighed. "Right guys, Mama's gonna play dirty if you don't move!"

Frustrated by David's obvious disdain, Hana released the thong on her bull-whip and moved it out to the side. She nudged Sacha, so she was side on to the cattle and saw the mare's skilled ears flick as her body tensed. Hana raised her arm, keeping the whip moving behind her, waiting until she heard the tail make a familiar swish as it straightened. Then she whipped forward, keeping her arm solid as she'd practiced many times. There was a terrific crack and the cattle surged, running and bucking along the track in a furry, cream rush. The biggest calf made a detour into the rugged undergrowth but changed his mind as the others left him. They hurtled down the narrow track as a bunch, spreading out as they turned the corner and spied the lush green grass ahead.

Hana turned with a look of smug satisfaction. It was wasted. David's strong torso bent over his gelding's neck as he cantered after the calves, his hooves kicking up dust and bush debris behind him. The Appaloosa's tail lifted high in the air as he enjoyed the run, dispelling his pent up energy. David managed his reins in his left hand, his right arm straight with the coiled whip. "Well done, Hana!" she called after him, seeking his approval. He raised his arm in response and over the bull-whip, she spied the fingers making a rude gesture. "Telling Logan!" she shouted into the bouncing air molecules. The tui overhead cackled as David disappeared round the corner.

"Good girl, Sacha. I can tell you're impressed." Hana ran her hand down the glossy neck of Logan's favourite mare, rewarded by a toss of the magnificent head. "Come on then, best get down and face the music. Logan and Nev need to start communicating!" Hana clicked her tongue and the mare danced into action, keen to follow the dappled gelding to the fresh grass.

Rounding the corner, Hana found David on the ground waiting. He held his horse's reins and tapped the coiled bull-whip against the fabric of his jeans. "Nice of you to join us!" He kept the gate closed against the calves bunching around him and Hana tutted.

"Stop worrying, David! Nev told me to use the bush track, so we did. Logan will be fine and I won't involve you."

The stockman ran the back of his hand across his sweating forehead. "Just get in the bloody gate!"

Sacha took a step towards the gate and snorted at the gathered crowd behind it, threatening them with her blue wall eye, rolling in its sinister white rim. The calves moved backwards with slow hooves, not yet feeling their freedom in the acreage which rolled out behind them in a healthy green arc. David tapped the whip, growing more impatient by the second. Sweaty blond curls poked from under his hat and his biceps flexed, communicating his irritation.

It came again. The echo of three shots fired together in quick succession. *Hunter in distress.*

Hana's head whipped back towards the mountain and she saw the flutter of native birds as they rose from the trees in a sudden flurry, moving away from the alarm. "That's the ridge above the forty-eighth," she said, turning her eyes back to David's worried face. "Someone's in trouble." With a flick of Hana's reins the white mare whirled on her back feet and took off along the track, galloping uphill at a terrific pace.

"Get back here!" David yelled after Hana, coughing in the dust cloud she kicked up behind her.

"Radio it in!" she shouted over her shoulder as she disappeared back into the dense New Zealand bush.

Dear Reader,

I would love it if you could leave a review at your usual retailer.

I find the opinions of readers helpful and constructive. Reviews are the Holy Grail to an author as they cause our work to sink or swim. It is the bench mark for other readers and can determine whether our work will be successful and reach many or none. It doesn't have to be an essay or a literary criticism. A few words about what you liked would be most appreciated. The shortest review I ever received for my work was, 'Great,' accompanied by five stars and the longest was a whole video from a gorgeous woman in the USA. My favourite to date has to be the lady who said, '*I read until my eyes fell out.*' I keep looking at that one because it makes me laugh.

You can review on my website, ktbowes.com.

Go to the book's buy page where you can follow through to your own retailer and leave a review for me.

And hey, let me know when you've done it. I'd love to hear from you.

About the Author

K T Bowes is a bestselling teen and women's author.

Her novel, *A Trail of Lies*, was the winner of the genre award for Author's Cave in 2014.

Phoenix Du Rose was considered for the prestigious Ngaio Marsh awards for 2021 and *Her Quiet Legacy* in 2022.

K T Bowes is an Englishwoman in exile in New Zealand, swapping rugged cosmopolitan for mountain ranges and terrifying rivers. She loves Māori culture and has learned to weave flax using traditional methods. Her other passion is Rongoa Māori, which involves creating medicines from native plants. She is a student of Te Reo Māori.

You can find her hanging out on social media in the following places.

Check in and say hello. Maybe suggest she gets back to writing and stops watching cat videos.

FACEBOOK

https://www.facebook.com/NZauthorKTBowes/

TWITTER

https://twitter.com/ktboweswrites

INSTAGRAM

https://www.instagram.com/k_t_bowes

Also by this Author

The Hana Du Rose Mysteries Series:
Logan Du Rose
About Hana
Hana Du Rose
Du Rose Legacy
The New Du Rose Matriarch
One Heartbeat
The Du Rose Prophecy
Du Rose Sons
Du Rose Family Ties
Du Rose Vendetta
Phoenix Du Rose
Wiremu Du Rose

The Calculated Risk Series:
The Actuary
The Actuary's Wife
The Actuary in Trouble
The Heart of The Actuary

Troubled series for teens:
Free from the Tracks
Sophia's Dilemma
A Trail of Lies
Gone Phishing

Escaping the Back Country NZ Series:
Pirongia's Secret
Deleilah

Standalone novels:
Artifact
Demons on Her Shoulder
All Saints
Her Quiet Legacy

Humorous Cozy Mystery Series from New Zealand
Dead Straight
Bad Hair Day
Side Parting